HEART LIKE MINE

**ALSO BY
MAGGIE McGINNIS**

Forever This Time

Snowflake Wishes (novella)

HEART LIKE MINE

Maggie McGinnis

St. Martin's Paperbacks

This is a work of fiction. All of the characters, organizations, and events portrayed in this novel are either products of the author's imagination or are used fictitiously.

HEART LIKE MINE

Copyright © 2016 by Maggie McGinnis.

All rights reserved.

For information address St. Martin's Press, 175 Fifth Avenue, New York, NY 10010.

ISBN: 978-1-250-06908-5

Our books may be purchased in bulk for promotional, educational, or business use. Please contact your local bookseller or the Macmillan Corporate and Premium Sales Department at 1-800-221-7945, ext. 5442, or by e-mail at MacmillanSpecialMarkets@macmillan.com.

Printed in the United States of America

St. Martin's Paperbacks edition / April 2016

St. Martin's Paperbacks are published by St. Martin's Press, 175 Fifth Avenue, New York, NY 10010.

10 9 8 7 6 5 4 3 2 1

For my daughters . . .

May they someday find their own imperfect heroes

Acknowledgments

Heart Like Mine marks the third book in the Echo Lake series, and I'm thrilled beyond words that I've had the chance to "live" in this magical little town for the past couple of years. I'm immensely grateful to the following people for their help in making this dream a reality:

To Courtney Miller-Callihan, my sweet, fabulous agent—2016 marks our 5th anniversary, and I couldn't be more thankful that a little under-the-bed book brought us together.

To Holly Ingraham, my fantastic, wonderful editor—Thank you so much for helping me bring the Echo Lake series to life! I'm so honored to be on your team!

To Lizzie Poteet, extra-special pinch-hitting editor—Huge thanks for stepping in when Home-team Holly became an instant foursome. It was such a pleasure to work with you!

To Jennifer Brodie, my critique partner and friend—There are no words big enough to thank you for all you do! Someday, we'll do that white-sand beach . . . and stay for a month.

To the real Millie, Therese, and Kenderly—Super-sweet, generous members of my street team. I hope you love the characters you get to be in this book. And to the rest of my street team—Thank you for your energy and support! I'm a lucky gal to have you!

To the Bartlett Bunnies—Plotters first . . . friends forever.

And of course, to my family. My love for you is endless and indescribable.

Chapter 1

The CFO's office smelled of sweat, burnt coffee, and tears. That's all Delaney Blair could think as she sat in the guest chair, awaiting her doom.

Six people had sat in this same chair over the past week, and every single one of them had left with an HR escort and the ironic farewell gift of a Mercy Hospital mug and tote bag. On the outside, she was a successful financial analyst dressed in a charcoal power suit, a pasted-on smile, and her favorite Jimmy Choos. On the inside, she harbored a pod of baby grasshoppers.

As Gregory fidgeted with his pen, she tried to calculate how long her savings account would pay the mortgage on her brand-new condo.

Not very long.

"Am I being laid off, Gregory? Please just tell me."

"No." He sighed, shaking his head. "But when you hear what I have to say, you're probably going to wish you were."

He rubbed both hands over his face in frustration, a move that sent Delaney's grasshoppers scrambling for cover. She'd never seen Gregory be anything but composed and professional.

"I've got an assignment for you, but . . . you're not going to like it. The board met yesterday, and what came out of the meeting was a fairly dire directive." He sighed, sitting back in his chair. "We need to make serious, across-the-board cuts, or the hospital isn't going to be able to meet its obligations this year."

"*How* across the board?"

"Every department. Every budget."

Delaney sank into her own chair, closing her eyes. She and Gregory both knew there were departments already operating on shoestrings. Such was the fate of small-town hospitals everywhere, but in rural Vermont, it was even more pronounced. With Boston—and its corral of high-powered hospitals—sitting mere hours away, wealthier, well-insured patients could choose to drive the extra hours for care. That left smaller hospitals like Mercy picking up emergencies and fighting for dollars from a rural population that struggled to make ends meet.

Delaney pulled out her yellow-lined pad and uncapped her pen, trying to let relief that she still had a job overpower the distinct *Mission: Impossible* theme song creeping into her brain.

"Okay, what kind of timeline are we on?"

"The board wants proposals in thirty days."

Delaney's jaw dropped. "One month? They're giving us a *month*?"

"I know." He sighed. "I have a feeling the people we've already had to let go are just the beginning."

"So I assume you've assigned me a list of departments?" She gripped the pen to stop her fingers from shaking. How was she going to squeeze blood from granite?

"I'm giving you just one, to start with. The board agreed to a focused list for this first round of cuts, and then we'll target the next tier the following month."

"Okay. Who pulled the first-round short straw?"

Gregory paused, taking a deep breath. "Pediatrics."

"Pedi—what?" Delaney's pen hit the carpet. "You're assigning me to cut *pediatric* funding?"

Gregory stood up and paced to the window, then back toward her, leaning on the corner of his desk. He pointed to his face. "Do you see these bags under my eyes? This is from staying up for the past three nights trying to figure this all out. I didn't want to give you this department."

"So why did you?"

"Because I *more* didn't want to give it to somebody else. It's your baby, Delaney."

"I know! So why would I possibly want to cut anything?"

"You won't. But if I don't give this assignment to you, I'll have to give it to Kevin. Would you want *him* to take a knife to that budget?"

Delaney shook her head quickly, picturing the blond buffoon in the office next to hers. "God, no."

"Rock and a hard place, Delaney. That's where we're at here. I know it'll kill you to cut these numbers, but I figured it would kill you far more to watch somebody *else* do it. I know I can depend on you to take a measured, objective approach. I'm not sure I can say the same for—others."

Delaney leaned down to pick up her pen, emotions whirling. *Dammit!* The pediatric budget was singularly *the* most unpopular place to start playing slice and dice, and here she was, assigned to do just that.

"Is the board aware that we risk losing vital programming? Or personnel?"

He nodded, jaw tight. "Yes, but we're out of options. We just need to figure out how to have the least patient impact possible while we're making budget adjustments."

"Is that what we're supposed to call them?" Delaney shook her head. "Are we supposed to be transparent about this process? Do department heads know where the numbers are at here?"

Gregory sighed. "If they don't, then they've been burying their heads in the proverbial sand. We should be able to expect cooperation, but you know as well as I do that no department head in this hospital is going to volunteer to cut his or her own programs. We're up against a whole maze of walls here, Delaney."

She nodded slowly, her brain whirling. "Do I have a target dollar figure? A percentage? What am I working with here?"

Gregory paused before walking back around to the other side of the desk to grab a clipped pile of paper. He handed it to her, his face grim as he pointed to a figure on the bottom of the top page.

"That's your target figure."

Delaney stared at the numbers until they swam in front of her eyes. There was no way—*no possible freaking way*—to cut that much money out of the pediatric budget. *Any* budget.

"Gregory—"

"I know." He patted her twice on the shoulder before he headed for his door and opened it. "I'd suggest shifting whatever work you can to Megan for the next few weeks, to give you some space to work on this."

She stood up, clearly dismissed. "Thank you. For not firing me."

He smiled, his eyes tired. "Glad I could make *somebody* happy today."

"I'm not sure *happy*—"

"I know." He pointed to the papers, his tone returning to dead serious. "We've got to make this work, Delaney. If we don't, I'm afraid we might both get a mug and an HR escort by the end of the month."

* * *

Ten hours later, Delaney took a long sip of her frozen margarita, longing for the tequila to dull the day into oblivion. She and Megan had scored an outside table at Mexicali, the newest restaurant in town, and five minutes later, had scored drinks designed to dull the pain of *any* day.

Situated in a converted mill building in downtown Echo Lake, Mexicali's high wooden beams, warm brick walls, and killer location overlooking the Abenaki River had already made it one of the most popular restaurants in town. In Delaney's opinion, though, the location fell second to the warm, homemade tortilla chips and margaritas that came with a two-per-night limit.

She lifted her hair off her neck, trying to catch the slight breeze. The only reason they'd actually *gotten* an outside table was because it was actually too hot to be out here baking on the deck, but she could never resist the lure of the river.

Megan fished in her hobo bag, coming up with a rubber band. She twisted her own long, blond curls into a convoluted bun, then wrapped the band around it. Delaney envied her assistant's long peasant skirt and loose blouse tonight. It sure looked cooler than the business suit Delaney still hadn't had time to change out of.

Megan perused the menu. "Are we doing the nachos?"

"Do fish swim?"

"Most do. At least the ones that aren't left with *you* for a long weekend." Megan arched an eyebrow, and Delaney cringed.

"I've apologized, like, a million times. I had no idea Mrs. Riley's cat knew how to sneak onto my porch. Or that she had a penchant for goldfish."

"I won't be having you babysit my someday-children, in case you're wondering."

Delaney shivered dramatically. "Excellent decision."

She looked over the railing at the river, which was still flowing at a pretty good clip for July in Vermont. As she watched the water, a memory flashed into her head—big inner tubes, a hot summer day, lots of splashing and laughing . . . an ambulance.

She shook her head quickly, blinking her eyes hard.

Megan stirred her drink idly, chin in her hands as she peered at Delaney. "You know, this assignment isn't *all* bad."

"*How* is it not all bad?"

"With Dr. Kendrick on sabbatical, you'll be working with the interim head of pediatrics, Josh Mackenzie."

"Okay?" Delaney shrugged, eyebrows up. She'd never met the man, but she'd definitely met the type—overworked, over-meetinged, and definitely overly *un*fond of financial officers.

"Have you ever *met* Josh Mackenzie?"

"No. He's managed to skip every meeting he's been invited to since I took over the pediatrics budget." To Delaney, the name was nothing more than a signature on paperwork.

"You know, I've said this, like, a thousand times before, but it'd be good to step out of the executive suite once in a while and meet the actual humans who work at Mercy Hospital."

"I—meet plenty of them." Delaney felt her eyebrows pull together. She didn't have time to hang out in the hospital cafeteria or at the proverbial water cooler.

"I know. You're shy. You're busy. You don't have time for silly socializing."

"Well, I sure don't now. I showed you Gregory's numbers. We are doomed."

Megan sipped her margarita, which was melting quickly, sending beads of water down the stem of her glass. Delaney was so tired she caught herself watching one of them slither down, down, down until it hit Megan's napkin.

Megan snapped her fingers in front of Delaney's face. "So . . . any ideas for how you're going to approach this project? Because I'm pretty sure people might have to be involved. Possibly many of them."

"Very funny." Delaney tried to spear a piece of ice with her straw. "I started a list of target areas to look at. I have a plan. There has to be something we can cut without risking patient safety, right?"

Delaney's brain had been whirling since her meeting with Gregory. She'd made lists upon lists all afternoon, and her eyes were glazed over from examining five years of budget sheets.

"Okay, lay it on me. What's the plan?"

"I'm going to start by scheduling a meeting with Dr. Mackenzie. Tomorrow morning."

Megan nodded, eyebrows drawn together. "What are you going to say? What's the approach?"

Delaney squared her shoulders, a move she seemed to have done more in the past eight hours than in the past month. "I'm going to introduce myself, tell him I'm doing a periodic review of department budgets, and ask if he has any initial ideas for areas where we could trim."

"Well, that should go well."

Delaney frowned. "I know."

"Might be better to just be straight with him, don't you think?"

"Not if I want a second meeting."

"Good point." Megan tipped her head thoughtfully. "I have an idea."

"I'm all ears."

Megan pointed her straw at Delaney's chest. "Maybe just undo a button or two? For the meeting?"

"*What?* This is you being helpful?"

"I'm just saying. You're on the losing team here before you start. He is *not* going to be happy to see you. And he is *not* going to be cooperative. Guaranteed."

"You are ridiculous." Delaney's hand flew to her blouse. "I will *not* use my—"

"Come on." Megan winked. "Age-old techniques work for a reason, you know. He's young, he's single . . ."

"Seriously, Meg."

"Fine. Want some *real* advice from someone who deals with normal humans all day, instead of numbers?"

"Trying not to be offended here. If it matters."

Megan laughed. "You have to get on his good side—get his trust. Do that before you get to the part about slicing his budget all to shreds."

"Of course. Obviously." Delaney cleared her throat. "Um, any ideas for how I would . . . do that? The trust part?"

Megan put a chip in her mouth, smiling. "Undo a damn button."

Chapter 2

"Ha, doc. Found you."

Josh jumped, blinking as he checked his phone. *Shit*. Last time he'd looked at it, it had been Monday. Now it was seven o'clock on Tuesday morning, he'd been rocking little Kaya for half the night, and his back was screaming from sitting in this wooden rocking chair for so long.

And now Millie, the pediatric head nurse, had arrived for the day. He sighed. She was old enough to be his mother, and anybody who thought anyone *but* her ran this floor was delusional. He might have the interim title, but Millie Swan was most definitely head boss around here.

He ran a tired hand over his face, which was desperate for a razor. "I wasn't hiding."

"How is she?" Millie nodded at four-year-old Kaya.

"Rough night."

Millie's eyebrows arched. "Have you been sitting up with this child all night?"

"Not—*all* night." He winced as he lied, but she'd have a fit if she knew he hadn't actually slept more than in fits and starts since—Sunday, was it?

"Josh, your candle's only got two ends, and you're burning up both of them."

He looked down, cradling Kaya's head as she moaned in her sleep. He lowered his voice to a whisper.

"What was I supposed to do, Millie? Leave her alone? You and I both know we don't have enough nurses to cover on the best of nights. And last night was definitely *not* the best of nights. I'm sure you've heard that by now."

"I know." Millie's voice softened as she brushed blond wisps of hair from Kaya's face. "I just wish her parents could be here with her. Poor thing spends way too much time alone."

He nodded toward the hallway.

"How are things shaping up out there?"

"Well, we've still got a full floor, and today's bonus feature is four new residents who just graduated at the bottoms of their classes."

Josh laughed quietly. "Not nice."

"Well, they're standing around looking useless. How am I supposed to tell?"

"Millie, it's their first week on the floor. They *are* useless. Happens every July."

"Well, I liked the old ones. We don't have time to train fresh meat this week. The floor is full to busting."

"Then they'll get maximum exposure, right from day one. It's a resident's dream."

She blew out a frustrated breath. "It's a head nurse's nightmare. My nurses are about to stick them all in the utility closet."

Josh shook his head, smiling. Millie'd seen new residents come through every July for thirty-plus years. She knew damn well how the system worked, and by the end of their tenure, Mercy's pediatric residents were always the best in the business. She was grumbly about them for the first week, until they learned who was boss.

Which was her.

"We'll figure it out, Millie. We always do."

"Okay." She looked somewhat appeased, but he knew

from experience that it was likely to last all of three-point-five seconds. "Oh—Therese just delivered a hot coffee to your desk. Just saying."

"You're just trying to lure me back down the hallway."

"It's possible, but in my defense, you know I'd let you hide in the on-call room if I could spare you for a few hours."

"I know." He yawned inadvertently.

"Here." Millie leaned down, reaching for Kaya. "Give me this child, and you go drink that coffee. *Then* maybe I'll let you near the patients. No zombie docs walking the halls on my watch."

He handed Kaya gently to her, trying not to jostle the little girl awake, then leaned back in the chair to stretch.

"Oh. One more thing." Millie turned back from the doorway. "Therese just took an interesting call for you. Somebody from finance."

Josh felt his eyes widen. Calls from finance were never good news. "What about?"

"No idea." She shrugged. "You know Therese. She'll want to tell you herself."

As Millie headed down the hallway, Josh smiled, despite a sudden edginess. Oh, he knew Therese, all right. She was the ward secretary, which meant she had her pulse on every phone call and document that passed through the floor. She maintained the schedules, she decided which patients got which rooms, and she decided which staff members got to eat lunch—and when. Her level of control over pediatrics was monumental, but Josh had learned quickly that though she was as tough as nails on the outside, she had a heart of gold.

That's why she had fresh flowers on her desk every Monday morning, courtesy of an autodelivery he'd set up his first month at Mercy. He had her birthday on his calendar, and he made sure his friend Josie helped him pick out just the right present for any occasion that required gift giving.

And *that* is why he generally got to eat lunch . . . sometimes.

He took a deep breath, pushing out of the rocking chair. He paused in the doorway, sighing as he looked toward the nurses' station. The hallway was an absolute anthill of ordered yet frenzied activity, and he wasn't at all sure he was ready to deal with the day.

But he had to. They were already short on doctors, short on nurses . . . short on everything.

Yes, it looked like Tuesday was shaping up to be a no-lunch day.

The finance office would have to wait.

Six hours later, Josh was walking by the nurses' station on his way to a patient room when Therese leaned over the counter and waved him down. "Dr. Mackenzie, when you have a second, I need to go over some things with you."

He looked at his watch as he stopped and turned back. *Christ*—how had it turned into afternoon already? His stomach growled, and he realized he hadn't eaten since inhaling a bowl of microwaved oatmeal in the break room at seven thirty this morning.

"I'll make a deal with you, Therese. If you can score me a sandwich, I'll be your slave."

She laughed, rolling her eyes. "Already got me a slave at home. I just need some signatures right now."

She handed a signature pad across the counter, turning her computer screen so he could see what he was signing off on. As he clicked through orders for therapies and meds, she shuffled some message slips. All hospital messaging was computerized these days, but since Josh never had time to actually sit down in his office, they'd resorted to the old-fashioned pink-slip method as a backup.

"Want the rundown?" She held the stack up, fanning them out like playing cards.

"Lay 'em on me."

"Dr. Peterson needs a callback on Ian. Radiology results are in on the little guy in Room 4, and Sasha's got a spinal tap scheduled tomorrow."

Josh cringed. "She's not going to be happy about that. Can you make sure one of the child life specialists is on hand for her?"

"Already put her on the schedule."

"Thank you." He handed the signature pad back to her. "So, no on the sandwich?"

"Sorry. You're on your own. Already got you coffee today."

He smiled, turning toward his office. Before he hit another patient room, he needed something in his stomach. Maybe he had a package of peanut butter crackers stowed in a desk drawer or something.

However, before he'd taken three steps, Therese's voice stopped him. "Oh, one more message. Delaney Blair from finance wants a meeting."

Josh felt his eyebrows furrow. He knew the name, but couldn't place the face. This must be the call Millie had told him about this morning.

"What does she want?"

"She wouldn't say."

He took the pink slip with Delaney's office extension on it. "I'll give her a ring later."

"She's called twice already today. Sounds like it might be important."

He sighed as he headed back to his office and closed the door. He looked at the chair behind his desk, tempted to try to snatch a five-minute catnap. Then he glanced through the window out to the hallway, and discarded the thought.

They had kids on chemo, kids with isolation infections, and kids whose home-care regimens weren't up to snuff anymore. There were kids with mito disorders, digestive disorders, and anorexia . . . kids with surgery tomorrow, surgery yesterday, surgery this morning.

Nurses buzzed around, doing their level best to keep the chaos under control, but as he watched through the window, he knew he had to find a way to get more staff on board.

Maybe that's what this Delaney Blair wanted to talk about—giving him more staff.

Right.

He looked at the slip in his hand, then wrinkled it up and tossed it toward the wastebasket. He didn't have time to go up to the executive floor and hear some song and dance about doing more with less, or new directions, or supporting the hospital's mission.

Yes, if someone from the hallowed halls of finance wanted to talk, it couldn't be good. He sighed as he looked out at the busy hallway, then back at a desk piled with paperwork he'd never get to.

If Delaney Blair wanted a meeting, then she could come find *him*.

"You're just going to have to go down there, Delaney." Megan propped a hip on Delaney's desk two days later. Delaney envied her assistant's long skirt, gypsy earrings, and long, loose cotton blouse. In college, she'd have topped it off with a head scarf and combat boots, but for the workplace, she'd gone with her standard-issue leather sandals.

Delaney looked down at her own outfit and wondered when she'd turned into a toned-down version of her country club mother. Her neatly ironed blouse was set off by a perfectly matched skirt and jacket, and as she fingered the pearls at her throat, she sighed. Then she let her eyes coast down her calves, down to the Jimmy Choos she'd bought just last month. It was her splurge, her bow to girliness and inappropriate spending, and damn, she loved these shoes.

She really did need to ditch the pearls, though.

"I can't just go down there, Megan." Delaney felt a tingle at the base of her neck, just thinking of walking onto the pediatric floor. No, she definitely couldn't go down there.

"Well, he's obviously not coming to *you*."

"How can he just ignore my messages like this? It's downright rude."

"Or he's downright busy. Have you seen the bed count on pediatrics this week?"

"No." Delaney cringed. It wasn't the kind of thing she kept track of on a daily basis.

"There is always the possibility that he's not intentionally ignoring you. Just saying."

"I'll check." Delaney clicked into the system that listed current inpatient numbers. When she got to the pediatric floor, her eyes widened. "Holy—"

"Exactly." Megan raised her eyebrows.

"We don't even *have* that many pediatric beds."

"I know. They had to move a couple of the teenagers up to adult floors to make space."

Delaney clicked back through the past month, and the patient counts went up and down a little bit, but not much.

"I'm just saying—this could be why Dr. Mackenzie hasn't called back." Megan leaned close to Delaney and plucked open her top button. "Which means you, third floor, this afternoon. He's clearly isn't coming to you."

Delaney felt the chills creep down her spine. She had never actually been on Mercy's pediatric floor—had never been on *any* pediatric floor—not since Parker had died.

"Delaney? You okay?" Megan's brow creased as she studied Delaney's face. "You are six shades of white, girl. Does talking to non-executive-suite people make you *this* scared?"

"No." Delaney's voice came out in a whisper.

"Oh." Megan's hand flew to her mouth. "Oh, God. I'm sorry." She squeezed her eyes shut. "I'm so sorry. I wasn't thinking."

Delaney nodded slowly. "It's okay. It's been—a long time since he died. Not like you would think of it."

"But I should have. I'm really sorry." Megan tried to look into her eyes, but Delaney's felt all shifty. "Do you want me to go with you?"

"No, Meg. I don't want to go at all."

"But—"

"I know. He's not coming to me." She took a deep breath, blowing it out slowly. Maybe it wouldn't be horrible. Maybe she wouldn't melt into a panic-puddle at the elevator doors. Maybe she wouldn't see Parker everywhere she looked.

Maybe pigs flew.

She looked left, looked right, picked up a pile of papers on her desk, put them back down three inches from their original spot when she noticed her hands were shaking.

Dammit.

She had a job to do, and in order to do that job, she needed Dr. Mackenzie's cooperation. And in order to *get* his cooperation, apparently she was going to have to hunt the man down on his own turf.

She took a deep breath. She had to just—go. Get in that elevator, punch the three, and brace herself.

"I'll be okay. I will." She stood up.

"You're going *now*?"

"I have to." Delaney put a hand on her stomach, trying to hold in the grasshoppers she pictured trying to body-slam their way out. "I've got a deadline. Dr. Mackenzie's not really giving me a choice."

"You sure you don't want me to come?"

Delaney smiled at her, but it was forced, and she knew Megan could see right through her. "The executive suite already takes enough crap for being disconnected from the realities of everyday life at Mercy. I probably shouldn't risk people thinking I need an escort to find my way to the third floor."

"I'm your assistant, though. It would look completely normal for me to come with you—to take notes, or whatever."

"I appreciate it. Really. But I need to go by myself. I should have done it long ago. I'll be fine."

Megan didn't comment—just sent her eyebrows upward.

"Okay, I won't be fine. I'll survive. Better?"

"More honest, at least. Yes." Megan pulled Delaney's notebook from her desk. "Do you have your list of target cuts?"

"I thought we decided I would play nice for the first meeting."

"That was our strategy three days ago, honey. We're running out of time for *nice*. You're going to have to go for broke, I'm afraid."

Ten minutes later, Delaney held her breath as the elevator descended to the third floor. As it sank by the fourth floor, she rebuttoned her top button, which kept popping open. No way was she resorting to Megan's tactics, at least not this early in the process.

When the door opened, she paused, her breaths

suddenly coming too fast. The tingly feeling seeped up her spine again, and she was sorely tempted to press the Close Door button and try again later.

Every day when she came to work, she parked in the employee lot, walked a quarter mile across visitor lots, strolled through the lobby, and pressed the top-floor button inside the elevator. Never in five years had she done anything but coast by the third floor on her way up or down.

Unfortunately, she had no idea whether she could do it today.

Finally, she made herself step out, but jumped nervously when the elevator doors swished closed behind her. She took three steps, locking her hands together to prevent herself from turning around to press the Up button. The wall ahead of her was painted with colorful jungle animals, and red, green, and yellow stripes ran along the floors.

She had a sudden vision of Parker on a tricycle, madly pedaling along a green stripe like this one, then falling off when he ran out of breath.

Delaney swallowed, looking left and right, trying to push Parker to the back of her mind. Which way was Dr. Mackenzie's office?

As far as she could tell, a group of offices and conference rooms occupied the center of the wing, with patient rooms running down the left and right hallways. The floors were polished to a high sheen, and as she stood there, she was struck by the ceaseless motion everywhere.

Nurses in colorful scrubs practically flew in and out of patient rooms, and Delaney spotted a small herd of med students looking like they were trying to appear official-ish. Their brand-new white coats were a dead giveaway, though.

Her dad had told her so many stories over the years

about his surgical residents that she knew she'd *never* trust one with her own health. Every July, she did her best *not* to hurt herself or get sick, knowing every hospital in the United States was full of brand-new residents with lots of book knowledge but absolutely *no* patient smarts.

These guys looked no different. As she walked down the hallway, an officious-looking nurse put a hand on each of their arms and pointed them toward a conference room. "If you're going to look useless, do it somewhere where we can't see you."

Delaney winced even as she felt a small smile creep up. Apparently her father wasn't the only one who hated July.

Then the nurse turned and spotted her, and Delaney could swear her lips tightened. She was a dead ringer for Betty White—without the sweet smile. "Help you?" she asked, but her posture said she might . . . or might not.

"Yes, thanks." Delaney tried to employ just the right amount of confidence and warmth in her tone. "I'm Delaney Blair. I'm looking for Dr. Mackenzie."

The nurse narrowed her eyes, and Delaney hitched her shaky chin up a notch. "You from the finance office?"

"Yes." She put out her hand, and the nurse shook it firmly.

"Millie Swan. I think he's in his office." She pointed down the hallway. "Third door on the left."

"Thank you."

Delaney started walking toward the office, but stopped when the nurse continued. "We've got a floor full of really sick kids today. Appreciate it if you'd keep it short."

Delaney nodded slowly, put firmly in her place before she'd even started. "I'll—do my best."

When she got to Dr. Mackenzie's door, it was partially open, but he was bent over a pile of paperwork on his desk, so he didn't immediately see her.

Good thing, since her lower jaw had just opened of its own accord.

At Megan's urging, she'd checked out his hospital profile this morning, but his official ID pic had *nothing* on the real-life man. His dark, dark hair was neatly trimmed, but a perfect stubble colored his cheeks. When he sent a frustrated hand through his hair, she swallowed involuntarily. With a just-right sprinkling of dark hair and strong, sinewy forearm muscles, she could imagine those hands doing—*God*—any number of things.

Looking at him in a smoky-blue Oxford that she'd be willing to bet matched his eyes, she was suddenly convinced that the Fates hated her. She'd dealt with a gazillion doddery, old, crotchety doctors during her tenure here at Mercy, but the first time she got paired with one she could imagine—*gulp*—in bed, she had to tell him she was about to make his life a living hell.

Chapter 3

Josh heard heels clicking down the hallway, and his gut clenched. The nurses on this floor favored shoes that made soft, shuffling sounds as they cruised through the hallways. These, on the other hand, sounded like the kind of heels more suited to the carpeted executive suite. Had Delaney Blair finally given up on waiting for him? Was she here to read him the riot act for tossing her messages?

He was in no mood to talk about finances today. Check that—he was in no mood to talk about them *any* day, especially with somebody who sat up in a windowed office and crunched numbers while the real work got done on the other five floors of the hospital. The only reason anybody from finance ever showed up on a patient floor was to tell you what you were doing wrong . . . or to tell you they were taking something away.

Or both.

The heels slowed outside his door, but he didn't look up. Passive-aggressive parry number one. Maybe he hadn't been at this game for long, but he already had *some* moves. He was busy, dammit. She could wait.

And then she knocked, but it wasn't the authoritative, I'm-from-finance-so-show-some-respect sound he expected. Rather, it was almost tentative. And then a soft voice followed.

"Dr. Mackenzie?"

He looked up. Framed in the doorway was a woman in her late twenties or early thirties—he couldn't quite tell. She had wavy brown hair that fell just past her shoulders, and her body was trapped in a suit-type thing that marked her as a sixth-floor tenant even more than the sound of her shoes.

Before he'd heard those heels—which, now that he checked, were black, high, and sexy as hell—he'd expected Delaney Blair to be some old biddy with geriatric shoes and a pantsuit that was too tight in all the wrong places.

Sometimes it was good to be dead wrong.

He stood up and put out his hand. "You must be Ms. Blair."

She shook his hand, and he noted the just-right, just-long-enough grip. He also noted that there was nothing sparkling on her left hand, then shook his head internally, cursing himself for looking.

She smiled. "I'm sorry to bother you. I've left a couple of messages, but I wasn't sure whether you'd gotten them."

He raised his eyebrows. "You've left six messages, and yes, I got them."

"Oh. But you decided—not to answer them?"

He pointed at the piles on his desk. "Just haven't had time. Sorry."

"May I sit? Do you have a moment?"

He nodded, then watched as she folded herself grace-fully into his guest chair. She tucked her hair behind one tiny ear, but a stubborn strand quickly escaped, and he found himself almost reaching out to fix it. As she ad-justed herself and pulled a small pile of folders out of her bag, he took a deep breath, pulling a notepad out from under one of the many piles on his desk. Delaney Blair looked like she meant business, and he'd better pretend he wasn't too tired to do the same.

He sat back. "So what brings you down from the hallowed halls of finance?"

Oops. Tone.

She uncrossed her legs, then crossed them again, looking inordinately uncomfortable. And pale. Was she nervous? Finally, she took a deep breath and looked him in the eye.

"I'm here to talk about your budget." He closed his eyes. *Shocker.* "I have an assignment."

She paused, and he could tell she was trying to formulate just the right words. He almost felt sympathetic. Almost.

"Does your assignment include making cuts to my budget?"

"Yes."

Well. Points for directness.

"How *many* cuts?"

"As many as possible." She raised her eyebrows. "And I have thirty days to do it. Actually, twenty-eight. I had thirty when I left you the first message."

Touché.

Josh fought the urge to stand up and swear. Instead, he shifted his weight forward, leaning his elbows on the desk, feigning nonchalance.

She continued, her voice shaking a little bit. "I need to examine your budget and look for overruns, areas where we could trim, you know. Just general fluff cutting."

"We have no fluff down here."

"Every—everybody has fluff."

"Not here, we don't." Josh shook his head. "Where's this coming from?"

She shrugged uncomfortably. "Look, I know this is

never fun to hear, but believe me, it's not fun to deliver, either." Her left eye twitched, and he took a tiny bit of pleasure in knowing she was uncomfortable.

"Ms. Blair—"

"It's Delaney. Please."

"Delaney, this department is the tightest ship in the entire hospital, and I can't imagine you don't already know that, being that you have your fingers on the pulse of the place all day long."

She uncrossed her legs, crossed them again . . . and his eyes locked on her damn shoes. Was she trying to torture him?

"I understand your confusion, but whether you believe—or I believe—that there's nothing to cut, the fact remains that I need to find a way to make a substantive revision in your expenditures."

"Or what?"

"What do you mean—or what?"

"You make these—revisions—or what happens?"

She tipped her head. "It would be in your best interest to cooperate."

"She says, in a dire, made-for-TV voice."

She looked down at her left foot, and Joshua found himself trying to remember an old body-language article he'd read. Was a perp lying if they looked down and left? Up and right? He couldn't remember.

She took an audible breath, returning her gaze to his face. "It's hospital-wide, if that helps. Your department isn't being individually targeted."

"I imagine you'll forgive me for saying that doesn't help at all. And any targeting *is* individual."

"Again, I apologize. It's—just the reality of budgeting." She put her hands out in front of her like two sides of a scale. "The inflow has to be higher than the outflow, and right now, it's . . . not."

"Are those technical financial terms, I assume?"

She shrugged. "This will be easier if you're not—"

"Difficult? Suspicious?" He raised his eyebrows.

"*Combative* was the word that came to mind, actually." She squared her shoulders and looked him directly in the eyes, her eyebrows raised in challenge.

He stared back for a long moment, then shook his head and blew out a loud breath. *Shit.* "Have you already made a list of proposed cuts?"

Her posture relaxed almost imperceptibly, making him feel guilty again. Then she tapped the pile of folders on her lap.

"I've come up with some initial ideas, yes."

He sighed, leaning back but not breaking eye contact. "May I see them?"

She opened a folder and took out a sheet of paper, sliding it across the desk toward him. "I've only had time for a brief analysis, so this is just the thirty-thousand-foot view right now. But it'll give you an idea of where I'm looking."

Josh took the piece of paper and scanned her list. It was all as neat as a pin, with columns for item numbers, current costs, official projections, and cost savings. He skipped to the bottom of the page and felt his eyes go wide as he took in her total savings figure.

"You're kidding."

She tipped her head again. "I'm not sure what you mean."

"You really think you just found *this* much fluff in my budget?"

"Projected fluff."

"Right. That's completely different."

"As I said—"

"I know." Josh tried to tamp down his irritation. "You're sorry."

"Actually, I'm not."

He looked up, hearing a steely fire in her voice that surprised him. Maybe she *wasn't* the demure, sweet woman her outer appearance projected?

"Nothing is final, and I'm asking for your input. Whether you give it to me or not is your decision."

"But if I don't cooperate, you'll hand in this list as your proposal?"

She shrugged. "I'm not sure I'd have another choice."

"Really." He set down the paper, feeling anger rise in his gut. Who was she to come waltzing in here with her tight skirt and barely-there blouse and tell him how she envisioned tightening up his department's budget? How much experience did she even *have*, anyway?

She leaned down to put her folder back in her bag, then straightened up. "I've been given a directive. It's not one I chose. I'd appreciate your cooperation. That's all. If you could look my proposal over and get back to me as soon as possible, I'd be grateful."

Her voice was back to its soft tone, but it still had a don't-mess-with-me undertone he couldn't help but appreciate.

He sighed. Usually, finance people came in with a well-practiced spiel about hospital health and growth and values and yadda yadda that made his head spin. But the fancy words were just a cover for the fact that they were taking money from a place that really needed it, and putting it somewhere that—at least in his mind—really didn't.

This wasn't any different just because the message was being delivered by someone he might actually consider asking out, were she not trying to pare his department down to below bare bones.

He pushed the piece of paper back toward her. "This list may seem logical from where you sit on the sixth floor . . . but it's not reality, Ms. Blair. If you cut these items from the budget, this floor will be a disaster."

He saw her tighten her jaw, but she didn't speak.

"You need to find another department for your fluff exercise."

"I'm not doing a fluff exer—" She took a breath, and he could tell she was trying to keep her voice level. "Maybe we could just go through the list, item by item, and you can tell me why my ideas will cause a—quote—'disaster.'"

"Gladly." He picked up the paper. "Item number one— staffing. You have to be kidding me."

"Your clinician-to-patient ratio is sky high. You must know that."

He dropped the paper down to look over it at her. "You do know this is a floor that serves children, right?"

"Of course I do."

"Then you also know that those ratios *have* to be higher?"

"I know that, too, but our numbers are higher than the national average, so theoretically, there's room to trim."

He set the paper back down, fighting the urge to boot her pretty little butt out of his office and tell her never to set foot on the pediatric floor again. Instead, he took a deep breath, trying to corral his racing thoughts. If she cut his nursing staff, they truly *would* have a serious problem on their hands.

"Let me ask you this. Do those national averages take into account the demographics of an area? The incidence of chronic illness? The education level of residents? The foster-child population within a fifty-mile radius?"

Delaney paused before she answered, shuffling her papers. "I'll look into that."

"You haven't already?"

She scribbled on the back of her copy of the list. "I'll do some checking. This is exactly why I need your input."

"We have a social worker on the floor today. I'm sure she'd be more than happy to point you to this kind of information."

"Great." He saw her scan down her paper, stopping her pen near the bottom. "How many hours does she work?"

He narrowed his eyes. "Oh, no, you don't. You will not *touch* social services."

"I'm just information gathering. And no offense, Dr. Mackenzie, but you don't actually have the authority to tell me what I can and cannot . . . touch."

He opened his mouth to retort, then thought better of it. Nothing good would come of him spouting the words circling inside his head right now.

She leaned forward, propping an elbow on her knee, and was it his imagination, or had her top button just come undone? "Shall we move on to item number two?"

He sat back, eyeing her. "Let me ask you this—what happens if you *don't* recommend budget cuts? What if, after thirty days, you conclude that my department is already running on fumes?"

"Twenty-eight, and I don't honestly know at this point." She tapped on the list. "But I don't want to find out, either. We need to at least try."

"Let me ask this another way, then. If you *don't* find a way to make—quote—'substantive' revisions to my budget, what happens to *you*?"

He raised his eyebrows as he watched emotions fly over her face again. Then she deliberately closed her notebook, jaw tight.

"I may lose my job, Dr. Mackenzie. *That's* what happens."

Chapter 4

"You told him you needed to make the cuts or you'd lose your job?" Megan's eyes went golf-ball wide as she cut a croissant and put half of it on Delaney's desk on Friday morning.

Delaney buried her face in her hands. "I know! He was just looking at me with that combination of pissed off and *really* pissed off and I knew he was never going to co-operate and I just—oh, God. I don't know. It was totally unprofessional. I completely lost my composure."

"Wow. Way to play the sympathy ace at the first meeting."

"Can I repeat the oh-God part?"

Megan shook her head, biting into her croissant. "So what are you going to do now? Did you give him a deadline to respond to your proposal?"

"No."

"Why not?"

"Because!" Delaney pressed her fingertips to her eyes. "Between his hands and his chest and his eyes—*God*! Have you seen his eyes?—I got all discombobulated. He is half doctor, half Calvin Klein underwear model! How did I never know this?"

Megan bounced her eyebrows. "Told ya you need to get out of the executive suite once in a while."

"That man"—she shook her head—"that man took me from professional analyst to mushy teenager with a hottie crush in about four seconds flat. How am I supposed to recover from that? He could probably see me blushing right down to my toes."

"Men aren't usually that observant."

"But those eyes." Delaney swallowed and put her head back, picturing them again. "Pretty sure he observes *everything*."

Megan laughed. "Wow. I think I'm going to have to insist on coming to take notes at the next meeting. I've never seen a man make you this crazy in one hour flat."

"I have to go back down there today."

"Oh, do you, now?" Megan's smile was amused.

"I do. As you pointed out, I didn't give him a deadline."

"And you couldn't, say, do that via e-mail? A quick phone call? A message through his floor secretary?"

Delaney shook her head. "He pays attention to none of those things. And he'll *especially* not pay attention to them from me. I'm the chick with the budget scissors, remember?"

"Right." Megan nodded. "You definitely had better get right down there, then."

"Stop smirking. This isn't funny." Delaney tipped her head, eyebrows up. "We're *this* close to getting our own Mercy mugs."

"I know. I get it. It's dead serious. I'm just trying to find the bright side. And Dr. Hottie McHotterson is most *definitely* a bright side."

Exactly three minutes after Megan headed out to her desk, Kevin McConnell poked his head into Delaney's office. The two of them had been hired five years ago, within months of each other, but their personalities couldn't be more different. Where Delaney was determined to someday sit in the CFO's office due to her diligence and aptitude, Kevin was determined to sail in there on his fraternity-boy connections and killer smile.

So far, she wasn't entirely sure which one of them was pulling ahead in the race.

"Morning, Delaney."

She didn't look up. "Kevin. You're here early." *Like, remotely on time.*

"Pool was closed this morning for cleaning. Figured I'd come in a little early so I can sneak out at four for my workout instead."

"You're not *actually* early." She looked up. "You're just on time—which is early—for you."

He grinned, his had-to-be-capped teeth giving off an air of untouchability. She'd be willing to bet that long before he could afford the caps, he'd been practicing that smile.

"Now, now. Not nice to be touchy to people who have a life outside of work."

Delaney sent him a look that had scorched lesser men, but the layers of aftershave and gel must have somehow repelled it, because he didn't back off.

"Can I help you with something?" She raised her eyebrows, keeping her pen poised over a pile of spreadsheets on her desk.

"I'm gonna need you to run me through those cost projection sheets again this morning. I think there was something wrong with the files you sent. I still can't make the damn things work."

Oh, no, there wasn't. She'd handed those files off in pristine condition, though she'd been unbelievably tempted to botch them up just to see if he'd even notice.

"The files were working perfectly when I sent them."
She pointed to her laptop screen. "I'm using one of them
right now."

"Maybe you fixed it after you sent it my way?"

"Not to be disrespectful, Kevin, but if you're going to
work in a financial office, at some point you're going
to need to embrace the power of the spreadsheet."

"Maybe I'll borrow Megan for a couple of hours. She
can help me if you won't."

"Sorry, no. You've already borrowed her three times
this week. She's busy."

He put on his best pathetic face—the one that made
him look like a cross between a St. Bernard puppy and
an injured baby seal—but Delaney was thankfully im-
mune.

"Come on, Delaney. Just walk me through one more
time and I promise I will never ask again."

She looked at him, almost feeling sorry for him for a
brief moment. It stunned her that this man-boy who'd yet
to grow out of the fraternity-row style of communicating
would actually be her primary competition for the CFO
position when Gregory retired . . . if any of them were
still employed, that is. Kevin had gotten this far on his
capped smile and country-club connections, but seriously.
The game had to end at some point. He defined incom-
petence, tied up in a pretty Ken-doll package.

"How's your budget analysis going, Kev?" Delaney
knew he'd been called into Gregory's office directly after
her own meeting, but wasn't yet privy to what departments
he'd landed for this massive budget-trimming project.

"Piece of cake. Yours?"

She smiled tightly. Of course he'd say that. "Easy as
pie."

"Excellent." Kevin thumped on her door frame. "Let
me know when you want to go over those sheets."

Delaney's pencil lead snapped as he headed down the hallway, and when she looked down, she realized she'd poked a hole right through the paper she'd been working on. *Dammit.*

She really needed to get Dr. Mackenzie to cooperate with her so she could present a decent proposal to the board. Otherwise, she'd be watching Kevin move into the corner office . . . while she got a special last-day escort to her car.

"You tell that little number cruncher I'll show *her* some scissors." Millie swore in the staff room as she made a new pot of coffee late Friday morning. "What does Miss Fancy Pants think we should cut? Fluids? Because I gotta tell ya, there is nothing here we can do without."

"I know." Josh leaned against the wall, replaying yesterday's meeting in his mind. Despite his best efforts, he hadn't been able to get Delaney out of his head since she'd flounced out of his office, leaving the faint scent of vanilla in her wake.

"Now, you're not going to get all starry-eyed and say yes to her ideas because she's pretty, right?"

"Millie, seriously."

"I'm just saying, it's happened to lesser men."

Oh, he knew *that.* It had happened to *him* not so long ago.

She shrugged. "Could be a new sixth-floor strategy, you know. Send the hot gal down to do the dirty work, and by the time the guys pick their tongues up off the floor, she'll have their budget sliced to shreds and be on her way."

"Wow." Josh laughed. "Do you have some underlying issues we should discuss here?"

"No. I do not. But you"—she pointed at him—"you operate in a state of sleep deprivation six days out of seven, and you haven't had a date in how long?"

"So therefore I'm likely to be too busy looking for my tongue on the floor to notice the woman with the scissors?"

"Just be careful, okay? That's all I'm saying."

He nodded. "Gotcha. I promise not to sign off on anything unless I've had at least two hours of sleep."

She whacked him with a folder. "Don't get smart with me, young man, or I'll start a rumor among my nurses that you're ready to settle down."

"No." He laughed, putting up both hands in defeat.

"You know what? Here's an idea. That woman wants to revise our budget? Maybe she should move her fancy self down *here* for a month—sit here where we actually do the job of taking care of the patients. I'd like to see what she thinks is fluff after *that*."

Josh raised his eyebrows, picturing those black heels and that business suit down here among the scrubs and Crocs. *Fish out of water* didn't even begin to describe it.

On one hand, he loved the idea of sending her a strong message—*You want to cut our budget? Then come down here and see that budget at work.* On the other hand, having that tight little body, long chestnut hair, and sharp-as-a-tack brain that close to him for days on end could be very, very dangerous.

He smiled.

Now *this* was an idea.

For the second time in two days, Delaney stepped off the elevator on the third floor. For the second time, she fought back the panicky feeling that came with the mixed scent of disinfectant and sick children. For the second time, she had to lean on the jungle-painted wall and focus on her breathing before she could make her feet walk down the hallway.

She massaged her temples, trying to quell the images

that flew into her head when she saw the bright lights, the polished floors, the damn stripes.

Ten deep breaths later, she turned toward the nurses' station, trying to make her stride purposeful but casual. She'd find Dr. Mackenzie, she'd make an attempt to get him to talk, and it if didn't work, she'd leave. From now on, they'd meet elsewhere. She couldn't survive another trip down this hallway without a panic attack.

Just as she went by the nurses' station, a blond woman dressed in hot pink scrubs popped up from her computer and waved a hand.

"May I help you?"

Delaney scanned her quickly. This must be one of the legendary ward secretaries Megan was always talking about. Underpaid, overworked, and the holder of mucho power, they were reputedly a force to be reckoned with.

Delaney looked down the hallway toward Dr. Mackenzie's office. His door was open, but from this angle, she couldn't tell whether he was in there.

"I'm just here to see Dr. Mackenzie."

Delaney turned to keep walking, but the woman cleared her throat purposefully. "And you are?"

"Delaney Blair. I need to follow up on a meeting we had yesterday. I'll check his office to see if he's there." Delaney gave a quick smile and took two steps toward the office before she heard the woman clear her throat again.

She turned to see the woman holding out a yellow note-pad. "I'm Therese, and he's busy. If you would be so kind as to leave your name, I'll be happy to pass along the message that you were here."

The words were delivered in a proper, syrupy way, and a tight smile accompanied them, but it definitely didn't reach Therese's eyes as she handed Delaney the pad and a pen.

Delaney looked around, taking in the bustle of the

hallway. The place defined controlled chaos, but she didn't see him anywhere. Whether that was because he was busy or because he was avoiding her, she didn't know.

She matched Therese's fake smile. "Do you know when he might be free?"

"He's never free." Therese shrugged. "And I'm not saying that to be difficult. It's just the truth."

Delaney reluctantly took the pen and pad, writing her name and office extension on it before handing it back over the counter.

"Thank you," Therese said, again with the smile. "Have a good day, now."

Delaney sighed as she turned back down the hallway. She had a niggling suspicion that piece of paper would hit the trash before she got to the elevators. If his staff had gotten wind that she was on the floor talking about budget cuts, she knew the reception would be decidedly chilly.

"Ms. Blair? Back so soon?"

Delaney's head snapped up at the sound of Dr. Mackenzie's voice. He was striding toward her, a grim smile on his face.

"Hi. Hello—hi." Delaney cringed. She sounded like a thirteen-year-old with a nervous crush.

He stopped walking, putting his hand on her bicep to steer her out of the way of a rolling cart headed their way.

She hated how much her bicep liked it.

Today he had on a dark green Oxford shirt and a black tie under his white coat, and the way the color set off the unique mix of dark blue and green in his eyes was downright swoony. If she had to name a crayon after the color, she'd call it *angry ocean*.

Of course, maybe it was *her* that was bringing out the angry part.

Now that he was standing so close, she could report back to Megan that he was the perfect height. A head taller than her, with shoulders that spoke to a football history and a waist that spoke to a five-mile-a-day running habit.

"I assume you're here to see me?" He raised his eyebrows.

"Yes. I am. Yes." She fought to stop scanning his body. It was destroying her ability to actually put words together. His eyes were a mix of wary and amused, and the way they were looking at her made her swallow nervously.

He looked at his watch. "So what can I do for you?"

"I just wanted to—see if we might schedule a follow-up meeting . . . maybe take another shot at my list?"

"So yesterday's meeting wasn't just a bad dream, then?" His eyes were amused as he took her arm again, steering her out of the way of a stretcher this time. She was probably imagining it, but he didn't seem to let go as quickly as he had the first time.

She pushed back her shoulders. "Bad dream for who?"

"Touché." He smiled, and she got all foolishly melty inside. What was wrong with her? She could smell his spicy aftershave—just a hint of it—and hated that she wanted to step a little closer to get a better whiff.

He leaned against the wall, arms crossed. "So what happens after I convince you there's nothing to cut here? Seems to me you've got quite a lot of skin in the game. If your job's on the line, I'm a little mystified as to how you could possibly stay objective."

Did she hear a note of sympathy in his voice? Or was she just wishing she did?

"It's my job to stay objective, and I will make every effort to do so. That's all I can promise."

He sighed, looking over her shoulder and down the hallway. Then his eyes landed on hers. "Okay. Then in the spirit of cooperation, I'll make every effort to give you the information you need, but I have to tell you, I won't be party to making cuts that impact my patients."

"Understood."

It was really the best she could hope for at this juncture, even though she was starting to fear that there was the very real chance that *any* cut would impact his patients.

He pointed down the hallway. "Look around you, Delaney. Do you see anybody standing around? See anyone who doesn't look busy?"

Against her will, she followed his hand with her eyes. She already knew what she would see: nurses in bright scrubs dodging in and out of rooms, therapists dodging nurses, and parents doing their best to dodge *everyone* as they prayed for miracles.

But she'd known this before she'd ever pressed the third-floor button—known it in a way Dr. Mackenzie would never, ever guess.

He raised his eyebrows. "So, should we find a time to discuss your list?"

"I'm ready when you are."

He paused, studying her eyes for an uncomfortably long moment. Then he turned, motioning for her to follow.

"I have an idea. Come with me."

"Where are we going?" Delaney stepped quickly to catch up with him as he headed down the hallway.

He turned back, a half smile on his face and challenge in his eyes.

"To your new office, Ms. Blair."

Chapter 5

"What are you talking about?" Delaney's voice sounded small as Josh led her to the empty office at the end of the hallway.

Office was actually a kind word for the closet-sized space, but it had the necessities: a desk, two chairs, and—well, nothing else, really. He flipped on the light and motioned for her to look inside, trying not to notice the panicky waves practically wafting off her skin.

"Here. Sit." Josh indicated the ancient desk chair, while he grabbed the even more rickety one squeezed into the corner.

She stepped in and looked down at the desk chair, like she wasn't sure it would hold her.

"When's the last time you guys got new furniture down here?"

"I don't know. 1968?"

She sat gingerly, and he tried not to notice how her blouse gave a peekaboo view to a lacy purple camisole as she did so.

"Okay, I'm sitting. And I'm noticing that your furniture is decrepit. Is that the point you're trying to make?"

"Actually, no. Side benefit, I guess." He sat down in his chair, and it made an ominous creak. Her arms were crossed, defensive as hell, and he almost felt guilty for dragging her into this sorry excuse for an office.

Almost.

Yesterday she'd come down here in that prim little suit that had left a lot to the imagination. Today she had on a filmy blouse with the sexy shell thing underneath, a long skirt, and high-heeled boots that probably ended somewhere close to her knees. Her light brown hair was wavy against her face, and her eyes were the same smoky blue as her blouse—the same blue as his bedroom wall, actually.

For an insane moment, he imagined what her porcelain skin would look like after a long, hot kiss, then had to rip his eyes away before she noticed him—noticing.

"Listen, Delaney." He shifted his weight in the chair, trying to corral his wandering thoughts. "I'm going to be really straight with you, because I don't have time to be anything *but* straight."

Her eyebrows went up, but she didn't speak.

He leaned forward. "See, here's the thing. I think it's probably far too easy to get disconnected, sitting up on the sixth floor working on your computer all day long. Not your fault. It's just the reality of it."

"I'm perfectly well connected, doctor."

He paused. "Are you ever going to call me by my first name?"

"Probably not."

Fine. She was maintaining professional distance so it wouldn't feel personal when she slashed his funding to shreds. He could see how the technique probably worked for her.

So why did he want so badly to hear his own name on her lips?

He shook his head. *Focus, Mackenzie.*

"I think, if you really are interested in pediatric programming—if you're truly invested in making the right financial decisions for this department—then you need to *be* part of this department."

"Meaning—what?"

"Meaning . . . I think you should relocate your office."

"Relocate my—are you insane?"

"Only on Thursdays. Which it isn't." He looked at the ceiling. "I don't think."

"You are nuts. You really think I'm going to move my office down here?"

He laughed. He couldn't help it. Her cheeks were reddening by the second, and her body was as tense as a jaguar in a cage. He couldn't tell whether she was afraid, or just royally pissed off, but either way, he was definitely getting to her.

He put out a placating hand. "Temporarily."

"*How* temporarily?"

"Until you get the information you need."

She uncrossed her arms and leaned her elbows on the desk. He swallowed when he caught another glimpse of purple lace under her very proper blouse. Was she purposely trying to distract him?

"Has it occurred to you that maybe I already *have* the information I need? That maybe I'm just being polite by involving you at all?"

"You don't. You aren't." He pushed his eyebrows upward. "You need me."

He paused, the words feeling strangely enticing on his tongue. Her cheeks darkened. She'd heard them, too.

"You're awfully confident, doctor."

He leaned back, creaky chair be damned. "I am. But I'll sweeten the pot. I will promise to answer your questions, give you access to whatever numbers you need, and be fully invested in this exercise."

"If I live down here on your floor."

"For two weeks."

"Two—no."

A flush crept up her neck as she looked out the window into the hallway. He watched her eyes skate back and forth, tracking on the bustling nurses, and when he slid his own eyes down her face, he caught on the pulse flipping madly just below her earlobe.

He saw her swallow hard, then reach down to adjust her boot. When she was upright again, he could swear her eyes were shiny, but she blinked quickly.

Uh-oh. He'd just hit a nerve.

She took a deep breath and turned back to him. "Fine. I will come down here. But I will do it for *one* week."

He toyed with agreeing, but something made him push. "Two."

"One."

He smiled at her fierce pose. *Fine.* Let her win this one.

"One, then." He stood up, opening the door for her. "But I bet you'll be begging for a second week by the time you finish the first."

She brushed past him into the hallway. "We'll see."

As she went by him, he caught her vanilla scent, and he caught himself leaning to catch another whiff before she was gone.

She headed down the hallway, then stopped and turned to face him.

"I hope you don't regret this, doctor."

"He wants you to move into a closet for two weeks? Because he thinks that will somehow convince you not to cut his budget?" Megan sat down in Delaney's guest chair fifteen minutes later, sliding a salad across the desk, then opening her own.

"Something like that."

"I can't believe you agreed to it."

"It didn't feel like there were a lot of other choices, Megan. He's convinced I'm just another clueless sixth-floor exec."

"Which, of course, you are not." Megan raised her eyebrows. "Right?"

"Of course I'm not." Delaney looked out her window, taking in the lake view, and suddenly felt guilty. From her two brief forays downstairs, she now knew that most of the rooms on the pediatric floor looked out on the facades of parallel wings. All day long, her sixth-floor office was flooded with natural sunlight, while down on the third floor, the only view was . . . brick.

While she worked in her quiet office on a quiet, carpeted wing of a quiet, security-code-required floor, the floors below her buzzed like beehives, chronically understaffed and overpopulated with patients.

But did that really make her disconnected? It was her *job* to be up here on the sixth floor. She spent her days poring over budget sheets and projections and expenditures, working her hardest to make decisions that would have the best possible impact on patient care. Did people like Dr. Mackenzie not believe that? Did doctors and nurses really feel like the sixth floor was so isolated from the rest of the hospital that its residents had no idea how the medical facility really ran on a day-to-day basis?

She swallowed.

Could they be . . . right?

Megan propped a foot on Delaney's desk. "Maybe he's looking for an excuse to work more closely with you. Have you considered that?"

Delaney swallowed a snort. The man oozed sex appeal, and from what she'd seen downstairs, he was surrounded by young, perky, blond nurses who would probably love to have his babies. She, on the other hand, was a nerdy sixth-floor accountant.

Fat chance.

"No, Megan. Attraction—mutual or otherwise—is definitely not at play here."

Megan's eyes widened. "You just said *mutual.*"

Delaney rolled her eyes and shrugged. "He's sex on a stick, for God's sake. He's like an underwear model mixed with a linebacker mixed with a television doctor. It's a wonder we don't have moms faking their kids' illnesses just to come in and be treated by him."

"Not funny. That happens, you know."

"I know." She grimaced. "Bad word choice."

Megan leaned forward. "So he's just as hot up close? Better than his online profile?"

"To-die-for hotter."

"Lucky." Megan frowned and went back to eating her salad.

"Ha. Lucky would be me and Dr. Mackenzie getting assigned to some awesome project where we had to spend endless hours deciding how to spend oodles of money. Instead, I get to spend the next few weeks on a floor that gives me hives, slashing the heck out of a budget while pissing off the most gorgeous eligible bachelor in the entire hospital. Go, me."

"Okay, so maybe not ideal."

"You think?" Delaney put down her fork, her appetite dismal. "I don't know, Meg. What if Dr. Mackenzie's right? What if budget cuts really *would* do serious damage to pediatrics at this point?"

"Do you have the option of recommending that the current budget stand?"

"No. Gregory said the cuts have to happen across the board. You and I both know people try to build insulation into their budgets, but we've had three rounds of cuts in the past three years. I'm starting to wonder if there's any insulation left."

"I can't believe he dared to mention firing you."

Delaney shrugged again, exhausted. "Money has to come from somewhere, right? It'd be one less salary to pay. And in his defense, he included himself on the could-be-fired list."

"You really think it could happen?"

"I really do. You've seen the numbers. It's never been this bad. And now the board's compressed us into a thirty-day window, so we don't have time for the normal back and forth. I need Dr. Mackenzie to sit down with me, go over my proposed cuts, and come up with some sort of working compromise. Like, yesterday."

"Okay. Sounds like a plan." Megan put her fork down and pulled out her phone. "When are we doing this?"

Delaney felt her eyebrows rise. "We?"

"Yes, we. Aren't I your humble, trusty assistant?"

"Who just wants an excuse to sit in a meeting with Dr. Joshua Mackenzie? *That* assistant?"

Megan shrugged innocently. "Can I repeat the part about humble and trusty?"

"Right." Delaney laughed. "No. I need to do this on my own. My assignment, my head on the chopping block if I fail. If I were you, I'd keep your distance."

"If you get fired, I'll quit."

"Aw, Meg. That's really sweet of you. Dumb, but sweet."

"It's not about you." Megan shook her head. "If you get fired, Gregory'll assign me to work for Kevin. And I will *not* work for a man who analyzes his trans fats more carefully than this hospital's budget numbers."

She looked at the floor for a long moment, then tapped her fingers on the desk. "Don't hate me for suggesting this, but—have you thought about asking your dad for help? He's been around the block with this stuff a million times. Maybe he could give you the inside scoop? You know—from the doctors' perspective or whatever?"

"No." Delaney shook her head firmly. "Enough people think he's the reason I *got* the job in the first place. Can you imagine how it would look if people thought I'd used him to unfairly keep it? Or—God forbid—to push my way into the CFO's office?"

"So what's your strategy now?" Megan asked.

"Still working on that. I've only just seen my new office."

"Closet." Megan raised her eyebrows. "I'm sure, being the super-intelligent person that you are, that you've already concluded that's why he *gave* you that office, right? He doesn't *want* you to sit in there. He wants you out on the floor."

Delaney smiled tightly, trying to quell the relentless grasshoppers in her stomach. "You might be right. And you know what? I'll be all *over* that floor. I'll ask questions till I'm blue in the face. He'll be so sick of me by the end of one day that he'll send me back up here."

The words came out all confident and brave, but inside, Delaney felt like a bowl of Jell-O with ginger ale added to it. On her way back up in the elevator just now, she'd sworn silently a few times, stomped once, and then closed her eyes, realizing he'd backed her into a corner.

Dr. Mackenzie wasn't going to cooperate unless she met him on his terms, and as much as it irked her, she respected his stance. The guy had probably sat through more budget meetings than he could stand, and here she was, showing up on his floor to ask for more.

As she looked out her door to the carpeted, wallpapered hallway . . . as she spun slowly in a desk chair that had probably cost more than Joshua's entire office of furniture . . . as she looked out at a view only ten people at this hospital really ever got to see, she swallowed hard.

She *was* disconnected. She *did* sit up here in this cushy office all day while the real medical professionals ran themselves ragged taking care of the actual patients.

But her disconnect was purposeful, in some ways— inherited, in others. Her father never knew patients' names when he came into the OR all scrubbed up. He called them by their disease or their problem of the day, and once they'd cleared the recovery room, he usually never saw them again.

It was perfect for him. No attachment, no loss. When he wasn't able to pull someone through surgery, he felt it as a professional failing, but he'd never attended a patient's funeral. He'd never visited a family in the chapel as they prayed for recovery. He'd played golf or he'd swum laps or he'd tinkered with the antique car in the fourth bay of his massive garage.

It sounded cold, and maybe it was—but it was also survival. Delaney knew that better than anyone. He'd only ever grieved one heart patient . . . and that hadn't been his patient.

It had been his son.

"Laney?"

Megan's voice snapped her out of her thoughts.

"You okay?" Megan closed her plastic salad container, but her eyes were locked on Delaney's.

"Fine. Sure. Yes. Why?" Delaney tried to swallow another bite of lettuce, but it got stuck. She took a swig of water, hoping Megan wouldn't notice.

"I asked if you really think you can handle being on pediatrics, given—you know—everything."

Delaney took a deep breath, looking toward the ceiling,

trying her hardest not to picture Parker on his hospital-issue tricycle, careening down the hallway on one of his better days.

She breathed out, clenching her fingers under her desk. "Piece of cake."

Chapter 6

"Wow, buddy. You look like something the cat dragged in." Josh's friend Ethan clapped him on the back as he sat down at the big kitchen table at Avery's House early Saturday morning. The hospital had been all kinds of crazy this week, but when he stepped onto the wide front porch of the old hotel he and Ethan had converted into a pediatric home-away-from-home facility, he felt like *he* was home.

When Ethan had pooled grant money and his meager-at-the-time life savings to buy this place years ago, he'd only done it after Josh had agreed to serve as the staff physician. Together, they'd redesigned the old hotel, creating top-of-the-line rooms for patients and their families so they could stay at Avery's House, enjoy the adjoining Snowflake Village theme park, and relax in an environment that felt like a B and B, rather than the hospitals they'd all spent too much of their young lives in already.

Two years ago, Ethan's high school girlfriend had finally come back to Echo Lake, and with Josie in the picture, Ethan's life had settled into a rhythm Josh tried not to envy, because it went with a lot of damn hard work . . . and past pain that made their current happiness well earned.

In addition to his work at Avery's House, Ethan also

ran Snowflake Village, the theme park Josie's father had built when they were just kids. He'd been second-in-command until Josie's dad's stroke two summers ago, and now he had the proverbial reins of the entire place while Josie did psych counseling at Avery's House and Mercy Hospital.

"You been up all night again?" Ethan motioned to the coffeepot, and Josh nodded gratefully. "A patient? Or a woman?"

Both.

"I'm pleading the Fifth on that one." He took the coffee. "Thank you."

"Then no offense, but you'd better have a better story before Josie gets down here. She'll never let you get away with pleading out if she thinks there's a woman in the picture."

"There's no—" Josh looked at the clock. "What are you still doing here, anyway? Shouldn't you be at the park?"

"Changing the subject?" Ethan laughed. "There *is* a woman. Who is she?"

"Who's who?" Josie, clad in a T-shirt and yoga pants, pushed through the French doors that separated the owners' quarters from the main house. She wound her way to the coffeepot, rubbing her eyes as she felt blindly for a mug. "There's a woman?"

Josh sighed. "There's no woman."

Josie sat down at the table, folding her hands around her giant mug. "Where'd you meet her? What's she like? Where does she live? When can *we* meet her?"

"Seriously, Ethan." Josh pointed at Josie. "Call off your wife."

Josie shrugged. "I'm just mildly curious. Sue me. I just thought maybe you'd had your first date in—how long? Didn't know if we should be celebrating."

"If I say *shut up*, will you take offense?"

"Totally, yes."

"Shut up, Josie."

She laughed, reaching across the table for Ethan's hand. "There's definitely a woman."

"New topic. Anything but me." Josh shook his head, but couldn't help smiling. "Why aren't you at the park, Ethan?"

Ethan looked at the clock over the sink. "That reporter from the *Globe* is coming this morning to interview us. The minions will have to run Snowflake Village for the first hour."

"But you hate interviews."

"Which is why I've put her off for three months. But she promised her editor a feature on unique pediatric care settings, and we're her—quote—'shining example.' The article's due, and I couldn't put her off any longer without looking like a jerk."

Josh nodded. "Gotcha."

"I'm just trying to focus on the donors we could get out of it. The *Globe* has huge reach."

"Think you can shove any of those donors over to Mercy? Pediatrics, in particular?"

Ethan poured coffee into two cups and handed one Josh's way. "Why? You looking at more budget cuts?"

Josh shook his head, frustrated. "Some woman from the finance office has apparently been charged with making 'substantive revisions' to my budget."

"Revisions."

"Exactly."

"Did you suggest that maybe the folks on the top floor at Mercy could take a pay cut? Think of the programs you could save."

"It was tempting." He took a slug of coffee, then put his cup down. "But their new strategy is to send down someone nice . . . and young . . . and—"

"Hot?" Ethan's eyebrows went upward suggestively.

"So this woman? From finance? Is she the woman?" Josie smiled.

"Shut up, Jos."

He shook his head while Ethan and Josie laughed. Some days it didn't pay to be in business with the two people who'd known you the longest.

There was no way they could tell he'd been up half the night thinking about Delaney. No way they could possibly figure out he couldn't get the vision of her pert little mouth and sassy walk out of his head. No way they could suspect her soft voice and delicate fingers had him imagining things he really shouldn't be imagining about a colleague who had the power to cut him off at the knees.

Josie looked at the clock, then touched her sleep-tousled hair. "Oh, my God. When is the reporter coming?"

"Fifteen minutes, Jos."

She jumped up from the table. "Why didn't you tell me? Look at me!"

"You look perfect." Ethan grabbed her around the waist and planted a kiss squarely on her lips. "But you may want to get dressed."

She pinched his cheek, then scurried back through the French doors, Ethan following her every move with his eyes.

Josh tried to tamp down the spark of jealousy that erupted periodically when he watched them together. They'd walked a long, hard road to get where they were today, but where they were was pretty damn perfect, as far as he could tell.

He folded his elbows on the table. "Did you ever think this is what your life would look like, years ago?"

"This is *exactly* what I hoped it would look like." Ethan winked as he got up to grab creamer from the fridge. "Just took Josie a little longer to come around than I expected."

"Like, ten years." Josh smiled.

"Can't rush these things." Ethan sat back down. "Speaking of not rushing things . . . and since we both know Josie's going to tackle me for information as soon as you're gone . . . let's get back to the finance-office hottie. Anybody you might date?"

Josh shook his head. "Nicole cured me of that for a long time to come."

"Not everybody—"

"I know. Not everybody's like Nicole. But I was the dumbass who got practically to the altar before I figured her out."

"You weren't dumb." Ethan rolled his eyes. "She had you snowed."

"Define *dumb*."

"I know you're smart enough to realize you shouldn't let one person turn you off from the whole breed forever."

"So you won't bother to say that?"

"Exactly."

Josh sipped his coffee, remembering the night he'd headed out early from the hospital, picking up flowers and wine, intent on surprising Nicole.

He'd surprised her, all right.

In hindsight, the BMW parked in front of her condo should have been the first clue, but he'd walked right past it, letting himself in the front door, stopping to take off his boots.

That's when his eyes had caught the trail of clothes leading down the hallway and up the stairs.

And then he'd seen the other pair of boots.

He'd left the flowers on the floor, but had polished off the wine by morning, when a tearful Nicole had showed up at the door pleading misunderstanding and loneliness and *What did you expect? You're never home!*

It was later that afternoon, still bleary from lack of sleep and a red-wine hangover, that he'd decided Nicole had a point. He *wasn't* ever home. His hours were ridiculous, and it wasn't fair of him to pretend otherwise. Someday, when he was done with the hospital rat race and had his own practice, *then* maybe there'd be time for more than a no-strings relationship.

Until then, though, he wasn't going to open up his heart just to get it stomped on again.

Ethan's voice broke through his memory. "Don't you have any hot new nurses on staff? X-ray techs? Phlebotomists with a naughty side?"

Josh rolled his eyes. "None of the above."

"Damn. You'd think, in a hospital the size of Mercy, there'd be *one* female willing to date your sorry ass."

"Ha. The only ones I know are either trying to boss me around, or they're trying to take away all of my money."

"So they're no longer fighting to bring you coffee in the morning? Are you losing your touch?"

Josh shook his head. "The free-coffee thing is more out of control than ever. If I could actually function without it, I'd go cold turkey just to stop them from bringing it to me."

"But not one of these women is someone you'd ever date?"

"They're my employees, Ethan."

Ethan nodded. "Okay, I get that. So what about the woman from finance?"

"Awkward, to say the least. I mentioned the part about her trying to trim my budget, right?"

"Married? Engaged?"

"You're kind of missing the point here." Josh rolled his eyes. "No ring."

"So . . ." Ethan sat back, and Josh could tell he was trying to curb his smile. "She's young, hot, and you checked for a ring. *And* she's not your employee."

"All true. But that doesn't mean I should date her."

Ethan shrugged. "Might make her go a little easier on your budget—just saying. A little wining and dining never hurt a tense negotiation, after all."

On Monday morning, Delaney stepped off the elevator and opened the executive suite door, holding it with her foot as she tried to balance her coffee, laptop, and a box of files she'd brought home for the weekend. It was only seven o'clock, so as usual, she was the first one here. She loved the first hour of the day, when no one else was around and she could plow through piles of work before her e-mail started pinging.

She dropped a couple of files on Megan's desk on her way by, then turned toward her office, running smack into a solid, male body. She stifled a squeak as she dropped the file box on her toes, then swore.

Dr. Mackenzie.

She bit back further curses as she bent down to pick up the box, embarrassed that she'd practically thrown the box at him when he'd startled her.

"What are you doing up here?" *On my turf*, she added internally.

"Giving you a Monday-morning heart attack, I'm afraid."

Oh, he was giving her a heart attack, all right. But it wasn't because he'd just scared the wits right out of her. He looked fresh from the shower—hair damp at his collar, a dark brown shirt and khakis shaping his body deliciously, and God, that sweet, spicy aftershave that she already liked way too much.

Her pulse started rat-tat-tatting, and she ran one hand up her neck to hide it.

He took the box from her and opened her office door. "I'm really sorry. I didn't mean to scare you."

"Then why are you lurking on my floor at seven o'clock in the morning? How did you even get in here?"

He grinned. "I gave Marco the secret password. And also, I resent the term *lurking*."

Marco, the night security officer, was legendary for his loose interpretation of access privileges, especially at the end of his shift.

"What was Marco's version of today's secret password?"

"A hot coffee and a donut."

Delaney closed her eyes. Some freaking security system.

She sat down at her desk, mostly to hide her shaky knees. "So what can I do for you?"

He walked to her window. "Wow. You have quite a view up here."

She cringed, remembering how she'd felt about that same view on Friday, but she didn't speak. What could she say, knowing that the view from *his* office was a chaotic hallway full of sick kids and busy nurses?

He turned. "I just wanted to talk about a few things before we get you started on the floor this morning. Thought it'd be easier to do up here in your territory."

"Because?"

"Because the people in *my* territory are not necessarily fans of the finance office, especially given the climate lately. I know they'll be on their best behavior while you're down there, but still—they're nervous. They all know what it means when the finance office starts paying special attention to your floor."

Delaney didn't know what to say. On one hand, she sort of resented the fact that they'd marked her as an enemy before they even knew her. On the other hand, how could she blame them? They all knew someone who'd gotten the same HR escort she'd seen last week. Nobody felt safe right now.

Finally, she sighed. "What can I do to make this easier on everybody?"

"Probably nothing." He shrugged. "Awkward is awkward. It's just the way it is. But I think it would help if I gave you some information about the floor before you come down again."

"Okay." She folded her hands primly on her desk. "Pediatrics Orientation 101. I'm ready."

"The first thing to know is that if you want to eat lunch, you need to be nice to Therese."

Delaney felt her forehead furrow. "I don't follow."

"She makes the lunch schedule. That means she decides who eats when. And if she doesn't like you, she might just forget to put you *on* the schedule."

"No offense, but how am I figuring into her schedule? I'm just observing."

"You want to really know what it's like to work a patient floor, right?"

She sat back. "Um, no. *You* want me to know what it's like to work a patient floor. Apparently. When did we change the part about me just hanging out in the background?"

"Millie—she's the head nurse you met—and I talked earlier this morning. We both think that if you are really invested in making the best decisions for this floor, then you need to muck right in."

"Muck right in? What does that mean, exactly?" Delaney looked at her watch. It was only seven o'clock, and he'd already had a meeting with the head nurse? "What kind of hours do you *work*, anyway?"

"We work a lot of hours, Delaney. I think this is one of the things you're only going to see if you're down there. I've got salaried nurses doing fifty to sixty hours a week right now."

"How is that possible? Isn't the union going nuts?"

"We're paying hellish overtime, that's how. Because—as you kindly pointed out—our staffing ratios are high enough that I haven't been able to make a case for more nurses."

She sighed quietly. "I'm sorry I said that."

She was. The more research she'd done this weekend, the more convinced she'd become that they didn't, in fact, have *enough* nurses on the floor. The first item on her original proposal had been to reduce staffing, but it was already clear how shortsighted that had been, and she hadn't even started her official observations yet.

He looked at her intently, and she tried not to squirm under his gaze. "I appreciate you saying so."

She put up her hands. "Dr. Mackenzie, I will be the first to admit when I'm wrong, okay?"

"But let me guess. It doesn't happen often?"

"No, it doesn't." She pointed to the box she'd dropped. "That box is full of research I did over the weekend, and it's clear to me that the list I showed you last week was perhaps a bit premature, though it was the best I could come up with on short notice, with limited time to do proper analysis."

He pointed his chin at the box. "And now you think you've done that analysis?"

"I've done a lot of it, yes."

"So do you have a *new* list?"

"Only in my head."

And on my laptop. And on three printed pages in this folder under my hands.

"And are you going to show it to me?"

She took a breath, wondering if it was awful that she was enjoying his momentary discomfort as he wondered just what she'd put on the list this time. "I'd like to do some observing first, to see if my ideas hold water. Then we can talk."

He nodded slowly, sipping his coffee. "I guess that's the best I can ask, given the situation."

"Agreed. And in the future, I'd really like to be involved in any conversation about what I will or won't be doing on your floor. I'm not sure me *mucking in* is an approach that will help us meet our goals here."

She hid her hands under the desk as she realized they'd started shaking. What did *mucking in* mean, exactly? She was completely unqualified to do anything medical—they knew that, right? She was okay with interacting with patients—in a quiet, nonmedical, just-observational way—but that was it.

Her goal for the week was to study their staffing models up close, examine their training programs, and conduct as many interviews as possible so she could make her recommendations with as clear a conscience as possible.

She didn't do anything halfway, and she hoped Dr. Mackenzie realized that.

"Trust me. It's the only way you're going to really understand." He sipped the coffee in his hand. "And no offense, but having my staff see somebody care enough to spend a week on the floor will be a refreshing change for them. I'm sure you realize there's a certain level of distrust between patient floors and the executive suite here."

She tried not to bristle at his words. *Distrust? Really?* Did anyone on pediatrics have *any* idea how much money she'd helped bring to that floor over the past five years? Any idea how many grants she'd researched, proposed, and spent countless hours attaining? Any idea how many hours she'd sat in this office-with-a-view trying to figure out how to keep a pediatric department that ran on a razor's-edge budget from going under?

She didn't think so. Even Dr. Mackenzie seemed unaware of just how hard she'd been working behind the scenes. To him, she was a signature on paperwork, and looking at his desk last week, it was pretty clear the man never had a chance to *read* said paperwork.

Delaney took a steadying breath. "Dr. Mackenzie, no offense right back at you, but I think you—and your staff—need to be careful of your assumptions. There are a lot of people in this hospital who care about pediatrics. I can assure you you're not the only one trying to make things work here."

"I know." He put up a defensive hand. "I do."

She raised her eyebrows. "I can't say I've ever agreed to move into anyone *else's* closet, after all."

"Office."

She tipped her chin down and raised her eyebrows. "That is a closet."

"Fine. It's a closet. In my defense, though, it *is* the only empty four-by-four space on the entire floor. And in my further defense, if you're going to be down there anyway, we don't want you hiding in an office."

Delaney sat back in her chair. "What is it, exactly, that you think I *should* do?"

"Glad you asked." He smiled, and her bristly feeling faded quickly. "We discussed a number of possibilities. I think today we'll let you just observe at will. Tomorrow I'll probably assign you to a staff member to shadow."

"You'll assign me? Really?"

"Does that bother you?" He raised his eyebrows. "Not used to being directed, Delaney?"

She felt her eyes narrow. "How about we keep firmly in mind that I agreed to spend a week down there of my own volition?"

He sighed, putting his head back. "Listen, let's just see if we can make this work, okay? It's way too early in the morning to do the verbal-sparring thing."

She felt a smile poking at the corners of her lips. "Haven't had enough coffee deliveries to think straight yet?"

He popped his head back to its normal position. "How do you know—"

Delaney pointed to her file box. "Research, doctor. I do very thorough research."

Chapter 7

Research, his ass. Josh rolled his eyes as he strode past the nurses' station and into his office. Of course, there was a steaming cup of coffee on the desk, dammit.

He pictured Delaney's cute little smirk as she'd pointed to the box on the floor of her office, and he shook his head. She obviously had him pegged as some lothario doctor who loved having his staff swoon at his feet.

It wasn't *his* fault they did nice things for him. He'd never *asked* anyone to get him a coffee—not once in two years. They just—did it, which even after all this time, still stymied him. He looked in the mirror exactly once a day—typically to make sure he'd remembered to shave, but he just looked like . . . Josh. Not Dr. Dreamy, or whatever he'd caught Therese whispering one day.

Seriously. If Therese had known him in seventh grade, with his dorky cowlick and braces and the God-awful pants that his legs always outgrew before his parents could afford to buy new ones, he was pretty sure she wouldn't be trying so hard to be the one who got coffee to him first in the morning.

"Morning, doc." Millie poked her head into his office, pointing at the cup. "I see you're already supplied this morning?"

He sighed. "Looks like."

"Tough life, honey." She smiled. "Are we expecting Miss Fancy Pants this morning? Or has she changed her mind?"

"She's coming, as far as I know. Said she had to do some paperwork before she came down."

"You want me to do the orienting? Or do you want the honors?"

He pictured Delaney pointing at her door with her eyebrows raised after he'd offered to escort her to pediatrics. *I can find my way, thank you*, she'd said, her voice frosty.

He sighed. "Let's just let her decide what she wants to do today."

"Thought you wanted me to make her an observation schedule?"

"Pretty sure Delaney Blair is used to making her own schedule, Millie. We'll give her free rein today—just make sure everybody's on their best behavior, okay?"

Millie shook her head. "Great. Now I've got a full floor of patients, I'm one nurse short, and I've got to tiptoe around a finance office visitor."

"Sorry."

She sighed as she turned to go. "What's our plan here, Joshua? She serious about the budget cuts?"

"Afraid so." He looked at the mounds of paperwork on his desk. Somewhere under there was a folder of grant paperwork he hadn't yet gotten to. Could he find some grant money to plug the holes she was about to dig?

"Can I give you a little advice, then?"

"Depends on what kind of advice it is."

"Kill her with kindness, honey. Use those looks your mama gave you, and wear her down."

"Not funny, Millie."

She sighed. "We're bare bones, Joshua. We cut any more dollars, we're talking patient safety."

"Miss Blair. Come on in." At nine o'clock sharp, Millie motioned for Delaney to come into the break room, where Therese had just delivered her.

Delaney stepped inside, but it was standing-room only, so she stayed by the door. All eyes were on her, and she tried to keep her chin up and a smile pasted on her face. She'd dressed down a little bit today, anxious not to appear like an officious health inspector—or finance analyst—on a mission. Megan had taken one look at her neat little short-sleeved sweater, skirt, and boots, and had shaken her head. Then she'd reached for Delaney's top button.

"So, everyone, this is Delaney Blair from the finance office. As you know, Dr. Mackenzie has invited her to observe on the floor this week, and she has agreed."

Delaney smiled, trying to give off the impression that yes, she was just here on a friendly observation mission. As she scanned the faces all the way around the room, though, she knew her efforts were in vain. That sort of cover story wouldn't fool anyone.

"Today she'll just be doing a little walking around, and probably asking a lot of questions. Please do your best to answer them, and if you can't, you can direct her to me. Starting tomorrow, we'll be having her shadow some of you for a few hours at a time."

Nobody groaned out loud, but Delaney could swear she heard every one of them do it internally.

Millie turned to Delaney with what looked like a manufactured smile, opening the door to usher her out. "Thank you. I just have a few more things to run through here, but we don't need to take up your time. Just wanted to introduce you so everyone here could put a face to the name."

Delaney took a deep breath and walked down the hallway, heading for her closet. She hadn't even bothered to cart her laptop down with her. No way would she get anything useful done, not with the noise and chaos of this floor. And certainly not if she was—*mucking in.* She'd just have to plan on a lot of late nights upstairs.

As she went by Dr. Mackenzie's office, she stutter-stepped when she saw him at his desk. A pang of sympathy hit her hard when he rubbed his forehead, swearing silently at a piece of paper on his desk. She wondered how many hours he worked in any given week.

Did the man sleep?

She knocked softly on his door, not wanting to startle him. As he looked up, she could actually see him trying to wipe the irritation off his face.

"You made it." He smiled, but it was distracted.

"I did. Millie just told the nursing staff that I'd be lurking around interrogating them all day, but to please pretend I'm their best friend so I don't recommend they be laid off."

He sent his eyebrows upward. "She did not say that."

"No." Delaney shook her head, rolling her eyes. "But they all knew what she meant."

"Now, now."

Delaney stepped into the office, pointing to his guest chair. "Okay if I sit for just a second?"

"Sure." He pushed his chair back, those crazy-gorgeous eyes settling on her.

She closed the door behind her, sitting down carefully in the chair. She glanced at the piles of paper on his desk. "Isn't the hospital fully electronic? Why in the world do you have so much—paper—in here?"

"Yes, we're supposedly electronic, but—executives—made the auspicious decision to buy our systems from different vendors, and those systems still won't talk to each other except on Tuesdays with full moons. So . . . I print."

Delaney felt her eyebrows crowd together. "Our systems aren't fully integrated?"

"No." He tipped his head. "This really is news to you?"

"Ye-es. This is definitely news. We just had a presentation from the EMR folks the other day, and they assured us the transition is ninety-five percent complete."

"Were there any medical staff members in the presentation?"

Delaney thought back, realizing too late that no, there had only been executives in the meeting. And those executives all worked on the sixth floor, never touching the electronic medical records of patients—and therefore having no idea the system apparently wasn't working as promised.

"It was just an executive overview. Their sales guys came in to update us. But they did a full demo. It looked . . . great."

Her voice trailed off as she realized how ridiculous she sounded. Of course the sales teams wouldn't want to let on that things weren't going perfectly. And of course their demo would carefully skate around the areas they knew were problematic.

Dr. Mackenzie's eyebrows went upward again. This was getting to be a habit. "And you didn't hear that there were any glitches? Shocker."

Delaney looked at him for a long moment, but his eyebrows stayed locked halfway up his forehead. *Fine.* She pulled out a notepad and pen. No time like the present to start recording observations, she figured. And a problematic, underutilized EMR system that had cost millions could go right to the top of today's list.

She scribbled a note, then pointed to his laptop. "Do you think the vendors are fully aware that things aren't working correctly?"

"Yes, they're aware. And all three of them have their installation consultants on-site, probably costing us dollars we don't have, trying to make three systems that were never intended to work together—work together."

She paused, hearing the tightly controlled frustration in his voice. *Another decision handed down by a disconnected executive team*, it said.

"There *were* physicians on the vendor selection committees, you know." She hated the defensive tone in her voice, but really? Was he accusing her office of saddling doctors with an unusable system? They weren't the only ones who'd been involved in the purchase decisions.

"I know. I was on one of them. But I bet if you went back through meeting minutes, you'd be hard-pressed to find one physician who voted to go with three separate vendors. We've been down that road before, and this is what always happens. That's all I'm saying. In the end, this came down to a finance office decision."

"Only because we were assured that the systems could work together seamlessly."

"By the salespeople, right?"

Delaney sighed. "Yes."

"Well"—he pointed to the piles on his desk—"in the meantime, until they figure it all out, I print."

"Okay." She nodded, then shook her head. Time to steer the conversation back to her original goal in coming into his office in the first place.

She took a deep breath, crossing her legs. His eyes followed her movements closely, landing squarely on her shoes. Seemed like Dr. Mackenzie had a thing for black heels. Megan would encourage Delaney to use that knowledge . . . as she pointed once again to Delaney's buttons.

She poised her pen, ready to take more notes. "So what can you tell me about Millie?"

His eyes skated back up her body, but she couldn't tell whether he'd even noticed they'd gone wandering. She felt suddenly warmer in the tiny office.

"What do you mean?"

"I just mean—I'd like to know more about her. She's obviously a staff leader down here, and if I'm going to be here for a week, I'd love some insight into what makes her tick."

"And how not to tick her off?"

Delaney laughed, and she saw his eyes go to her lips. "That, too."

"Um." He seemed discombobulated, and she got a funny little fluttery feeling in her stomach, kind of enjoying it. "There's only one way to get on Millie's good side."

"And that is?"

He shook his head. "You have to earn your way there. I could vouch for you from here to kingdom come, but it won't hold water until she decides for herself what she thinks of you."

Delaney pictured Millie's tight smile and stiff posture. "I think I already have a pretty good feel for what she thinks of me."

"She doesn't know you yet."

"Do I have a chance of convincing her I might actually be human, even though I work on the sixth floor?"

He smiled. "Slight one. Can't speak for the rest of the nurses, but if you treat Millie with the respect she's earned, you'll get the same back from her."

Delaney nodded. That was a relief. "How long has she worked here?"

"Thirty-five years."

Holy cow. Delaney mentally calculated the salary-plus-benefits equation on that. Over the weekend, she'd come up with a tick list of things she wanted to dig into while she was down here, and one of those items involved the fact that over a third of Joshua's nurses were at or above the standard retirement age. Her new draft proposal contained a line item for early retirement packages, and Millie looked like a perfect candidate.

"Is she thinking about retiring?"

"No." Dr. Mackenzie shook his head. "And if you mention the *R* word to her, I can't do anything to save you. Millie will probably die on this floor, and I suspect that won't be for another forty years or so."

"So—"

"If you string together the words *early retirement package* right now, I *definitely* can't save you."

"Has someone mentioned those words to her?"

"Yes, and I'll tell you out straight, Delaney. There are people in this hospital who'd be glad to take a shiny retirement package and be on their way. I'd be happy to make one available to them, because they're probably not the people we want still working here. Millie's not one of them. She lives and breathes her patients, and I'm not kidding when I say she'll probably die right here on this floor."

He drilled her with his eyes. "Do not touch her. I mean it. You lay *me* off before you dare to touch her."

"Nobody's laying anybody off." She tried to keep her gaze steady so he wouldn't hear the possible lie in her statement, but she could feel her pulse flipping in her neck as he watched her carefully.

"Yet, right?"

She sighed. "I'll do everything possible to try not to let that happen. Is that better?"

"More honest, maybe." He shook his head. "Don't touch her, Delaney."

She put her hands up. "Message received, Dr. Mackenzie."

"When are you going to start calling me by my first name?"

She shook her head. For some reason, calling him by his first name felt *way* too intimate. Using just his title and last name put an invisible wall between them that she really, really needed.

"Jury's out on that one, doctor."

Chapter 8

An hour later, Delaney poked her head into a patient room where a cystic fibrosis patient was in the far bed. As she'd studied the patient demographics of the pediatric floor, she'd seen the expected convergence of government insurance, chronic illnesses, and lengthier hospital stays, and one of her goals this week was to get a close-up look at some of those patients so she could start figuring out ways to reduce those inpatient days. The unfortunate reality was that private insurance still paid more, so freeing up those beds theoretically made room for more income.

On the sixth floor, it had made complete sense. Looking at the tiny, pale girl in the hospital bed, however, put a face to those numbers.

She took a deep breath and knocked. "Hi, Charlotte. I'm Delaney. Okay if I come in?"

"Sure?" The girl eyed her suspiciously. Her chart said she was twelve, but her stature made her look no more than eight or nine. "Are you the new social worker?"

"No. I work here at the hospital—just not usually with patients. I'm trying to get around and meet some people instead of sitting in my office all day."

"Oh." Charlotte's face was cloaked and curious at the same time.

"Okay if I sit?" Delaney pointed to the chair beside her bed. "I love your pajamas."

Charlotte looked down, fingering the soft purple fabric. "Millie got me these."

Really? Millie obviously had a soft side.

"Wow. That was nice of her."

"Yeah." Charlotte smiled. "She says I'm her favorite, but she says that to all of us."

Delaney sat gingerly beside the bed. Before she'd come down to the floor this morning, she'd been *this* close to accepting Megan's proffered Xanax. Her knees were still wobbly as she walked the hallways and took in the sights and sounds she remembered so well. Half of the reason she'd ducked into Charlotte's room was because she needed a break from the chaotic input.

"Millie knows you pretty well, hm?"

"She's known me since I was three, so yeah." Charlotte coughed, and Delaney felt her eyes widen at the sound. It sounded like the poor girl was about to lose a lung.

When she finally stopped, leaning back on her pillows to catch her breath, Delaney froze when she saw a tinge in her face that reminded her of Parker's, long ago. She swallowed hard, trying to block the memories, but they were stubborn.

"Would you mind getting me some water?" Charlotte's voice was gravelly and shallow at the same time.

"Sure. Of course." Grateful for something to do, Delaney reached for the plastic pitcher on the bedside table, but it was empty.

"Everybody's busy." Charlotte shrugged. "They haven't had time to get me any, but it's okay. Usually I get my own. Just not today." She took a ragged breath. "The respiratory therapists keep beating me up. Now I can't stop coughing."

"Is that supposed to be a good thing?" Delaney cringed as she stood up to take the pitcher into the hallway and search for water.

"Yeah." Charlotte sounded defeated. "They're not really beating me up. I just say that to bug them. I don't get good chest PT at home, so all the stuff gets locked in, and then I get infected. Then I end up here."

She waved her hand around the room. Unlike the anorexia patient's room Delaney had just come from, this one had no pictures, no stuffed animals, no flowers. It was lonely and depressing as hell. She made a mental note to bring the girl something cheerful tomorrow.

Five minutes later, she'd completed a circuit of the west end of the wing, finally landing in a tiny little cubby that had a water dispenser. She'd filled Charlotte's pitcher, wondering how long it might have been before someone else had time to do it for her, and she shook her head. How in the world had she ever thought there were too many nurses on this floor?

When she came back into Charlotte's room, the poor girl had laid her head back on her pillow in exhaustion. Delaney tiptoed over to the bed and poured water in her glass so she'd have it when she woke up, but as she started to tiptoe back out the door, Charlotte's tiny voice stopped her.

"You don't have to go. I'm not really asleep."

Delaney turned around. "Are you sure?"

"Yeah."

Charlotte looked so lonely that it broke Delaney's heart. Here she sat, in a hospital room that looked out on more hospital rooms, on a floor where the nurses were too busy to even fill her water pitcher, with no parents in sight.

Delaney had a gazillion things still left on her list just for this morning, but she couldn't go. She sat back down in the chair beside Charlotte.

"So what grade are you going to be in this fall?"

"Seventh."

"What school do you go to?"

Charlotte frowned. "Probably not one you'd know. I'm from New York."

"Really?"

"Yeah. But I have to come here because there's no CF center any closer."

Wow. It was at least an hour and a half to anywhere in New York from here. The girl really *was* alone.

"Must be hard for your family to visit you."

"Yeah." Charlotte shrugged. "They can't, really."

She said it in a tone that made it clear this was just the way it was. No drama, no tears. But Delaney couldn't imagine being twelve years old, in a hospital hours away, with no friends or family to visit you.

"How long do you think you'll be here?"

Charlotte shrugged again. "Usually two weeks. It's okay. I'm used to it." Then she coughed again, and it was all Delaney could do not to hold the poor girl's shoulders and hug her tightly as her body was wracked with the coughing.

When Charlotte finished the spasm, Delaney felt helpless. Then she noticed Charlotte's long, stringy hair and had a brainstorm. Surely there had to be a sink they could use. And shampoo. It wouldn't cure the cough, but it might make the poor girl feel marginally better.

"Hey, Charlotte. If I can get hold of some shampoo, what would you say to a mini spa appointment?"

"What do you mean?" Her eyes narrowed, and her non-IV hand went to her head. "I don't need a haircut."

"No, of course not." The girl *desperately* needed a haircut. "How about I give you a deluxe shampoo, and then we can fix your hair into a fishtail braid?"

"You know how to do those?"

"I do, and you have the perfect hair for it."

"Really?" Charlotte fingered the split ends doubtfully.

"Really. Let's find your inner gorgeousness before the therapists come back, okay?"

Charlotte's smile as Delaney ducked out of the room gave her a much-needed boost of confidence. As she hunted down a nurse who could point her to some shampoo, she felt her anxiety crank down a couple of notches. She's survived two patient rooms without a panic attack, and she'd even made somebody smile.

Maybe mucking in wouldn't be so bad after all.

An hour later, Josh took a deep breath, reviewing Charlotte's chart before entering her room. Yesterday, he'd ordered a psych eval, concerned that despite their best efforts, the preteen was slipping further into depression. She'd been here for a week now, but even the child life specialist hadn't been able to pull her usual tricks and cheer her up.

Of course, working with a patient who'd just heard the word *transplant* for the first time made Kenderly's job a hell of a lot harder.

As he scanned down her vitals and nursing notes, he heard a giggle come from inside her room, and it made him pause. Then he heard another one, and he peeked in, relieved that at least maybe she'd found a television show that made her laugh.

But it wasn't a TV show at all. It was Delaney, who was sitting on Charlotte's bed with her, stroking glittery purple eye shadow onto Charlotte's eyelids. Instead of looking like the stringy mop he'd seen yesterday, her hair was done up in a convoluted braid of some sort, and under the soft makeup, her face looked fresh and clean.

And happy.

As he stood in the doorway, Delaney dashed some lip gloss onto her lips, then put up a hand mirror so Charlotte could see herself.

"What do you think?"

Delaney's back was to him, so she had no idea he was looking, and Charlotte seemed not to have noticed him yet.

"I think—wow!" Charlotte smiled widely. "I look—"

"Gorgeous?"

"No."

"Yes."

Charlotte appraised herself in the mirror, tipping her head left and right. "I like it." Then she reached out and put tentative arms around Delaney.

"Thanks, Delaney."

Delaney stood up and clicked a little case closed. "You're welcome. You can keep this."

"Really?"

"Yup. That makeup looks way better on you than it would on me. Purple makes me look like an alien."

Josh smiled as Charlotte laughed again.

"Can I come visit you again tomorrow?" Delaney's voice was, once again, far more tentative than Josh would have expected. Didn't she realize Charlotte was dying for company? There was no way the girl was going to say no.

"That would be great. Can you maybe do a French braid tomorrow?" Charlotte lay back in her bed, and Josh could tell she was more spent than she wanted to let on to Delaney.

He must have made a move, because both of them turned toward him at the same second, and he raised a hand.

"Ladies? Am I interrupting spa day?"

Delaney smiled softly as she stepped back to let him get closer to Charlotte's bed. "Twelve-year-olds require regular spa appointments. Could you please make a note of that in her chart?"

Charlotte giggled as he scribbled with his pen. "Absolutely. Anything else?"

"She prefers the coconut shampoo and the spearmint conditioner. Pearl essence for the lips, and purple glitter for her eyes."

Delaney said it all with a straight face, but her eyes sparkled with amusement as he pretended to write down her orders.

"Oh, and we made a deal. If she'll eat her entire lunch, I promised I'd take her down to the cafeteria for a sundae, if you say it's okay."

Josh raised his eyebrows. They'd been having issues all week getting Charlotte to eat enough calories.

He looked at Charlotte. "You agreed to this deal?"

Charlotte shrugged, but then she smiled sassily. "No one else promised me a sundae."

He turned to Delaney, but she put up a hand before he could remind her not to make promises without first running things by him. She wasn't a medical person, after all. Next thing he knew, she'd be promising candy to a diabetic.

She raised her eyebrows in challenge. "I checked with Millie before I offered."

"Oh." He cleared his throat. "Oh."

Delaney tipped her head and waved at Charlotte. "I'll be back after lunch, beautiful. Start thinking about what toppings you want."

After she'd left the room, Josh took a look at Charlotte's records, then sat down in the chair beside her bed.

"How are you feeling today?"

"Pretty okay. Just can't stop coughing. I hate chest PT."

"I know. But it's more important than ever to keep those lungs as clear as we can."

She looked down at her blanket, picking at a thread. "So I can have a transplant, you mean?"

"Well . . . that, yes. But also so you can feel better. I imagine you've got friends waiting for you at home, and we want you swimming and hanging out with them, not staying here."

"I know." She still didn't look up, and Josh cocked his head to try to look at her eyes.

"Keep getting all dolled up like this, and I'm going to have to make sure any guys who come onto the floor get the rooms on the *way* other side."

Charlotte let her eyes flit up to meet his as a tiny giggle escaped her mouth.

"Delaney's nice."

Josh felt his eyebrows hike upward at her words. He'd attached a lot of adjectives to Delaney Blair in the past few days—smart, sexy, ballsy, and shy at the same time—but *nice* might work, if he could convince her not to leave him beached without funding.

Looking at Charlotte, who was smiling for the first time in days, he realized maybe there was a lot more to Delaney Blair than met the eye.

At eight o'clock that night, Delaney pushed back from her desk and rubbed her neck, spinning her chair to look out at the sun setting over Echo Lake in the distance. She'd stayed on the pediatric floor until four, and since then had been back up on the sixth floor trying to peck away at her own job's normal to-do list. Despite Gregory's promise to move some things to Megan's plate, she wasn't even half-done with what she needed to finish before she could leave tonight.

It was going to be a long week.

A knock on the door startled her, and she whipped her chair around, embarrassed to be caught with her shoes off, staring out the window like a zombie.

"I took a chance that you'd still be here." Joshua smiled as he held up two salads from the downstairs cafeteria. "I also took a chance that you hadn't stopped to eat dinner yet, so I brought you something. Hopefully you like chicken Caesar salad."

In answer, her stomach growled, making him laugh.

"Thank you." She reached out for the salad as he handed it to her, along with a plastic fork. "I thought you were probably annoyed with me for bribing your patient with ice cream. I didn't expect—dinner."

"Well, you'll be happy to know outright bribery worked. She ate her lunch like a champ."

"That's good, right?"

He sat down and opened his salad. Apparently he was staying for dinner. "Depends on your ice-cream-sundae budget, I guess. It worked this time, but we can't let her make a habit of it."

"I know. I'm sorry. I should have thought further ahead. I just thought maybe—it would help. That was probably a total first-year-resident move, wasn't it?"

He laughed. "I'm not correcting you. It worked for today, and bonus points for the hair."

"What's the story with her, anyway? She said her family lives over in New York?"

Joshua nodded as he swallowed a bite of chicken. "They do. Dad has an auto body garage, and Mom's a waitress. They can't get down here to visit when she's admitted because neither of them can afford to take a day off."

Delaney nodded slowly, a sad feeling gnawing in her gut.

"So she's down here for two weeks, and nobody comes?"

"Right." He shook his head. "That's why Millie has kind of taken her under her wing. She and Kenderly, actually—the child life specialist."

Delaney took a bite of her salad, anxious to switch gears and get some questions answered, since he was here. "So have Charlotte's parents ever been adequately trained for home care?"

"Depends on how you define *adequately*. They've been trained, but they've got full-time jobs and four other kids. It's easy to let stuff go when somebody doesn't seem all that sick."

"But by letting that stuff go, doesn't that make her sicker?"

"Yes. But it's also a progressive disease, so depending on the family, sometimes it's hard to convince them that their efforts will have any worthwhile effect."

"Oh, God. That's terrible."

"Charlotte's also really good at hiding her symptoms until she's really sick, and she doesn't always do a great job with her own self-care, so it's kind of an endless circle of neglect that ends up landing her in here more and more."

"That's so sad."

He nodded. "But while she's here, we hit her with all barrels. She gets good medicine, good therapy, good nutrition, and every single time, we teach her all of the stuff we taught her the previous time. One of these admissions, it'll finally stick."

"Is this common? Patients not really taking care of themselves? Or—parents not doing the care their kids need?"

Dr. Mackenzie looked at the floor, silent for a long moment. "It's not really that simple. There's a lot none of us know about what goes on in these families once we release the kids back home."

"Is that why your stay rates are higher than the average? Do you try to keep some of them longer than—maybe you need to?"

He raised his eyebrows, pausing his fork on the way to his mouth. "I try to keep them as long as they need to be here. Sometimes that's longer than—the national average."

Delaney's shoulders fell as she heard his sigh. She really hadn't meant to make him feel like he was on trial, but she knew that's exactly how her question had come out.

"I'm sorry. I wasn't making a judgment about whether our stay rates are acceptable. I'm just trying to understand why the numbers sit where they do. One of my goals is to look at reducing inpatient days for chronic patients like her."

"I know. And again, I'd urge you to take into account a wide variety of demographic factors before you determine whether those national averages hold water with our particular patient population."

"I'm trying. Promise. Charlotte was somebody I wanted to meet because, on paper, she's exactly the kind of kid who should garner a seven-day stay, not two weeks."

"By *exactly the kind of kid*, are you referring to the fact that she's covered by Medicaid?"

She bristled at his question, but obviously he'd ask. After all, how many meetings went on where the number of Medicaid beds was discussed? How many times were the words *lost revenue* mentioned in connection with those beds? And in all honesty, wasn't it the primary reason she'd poked her head into Charlotte's room in the first place?

She wasn't ready to admit that to Dr. Mackenzie. "I was

actually referring to her age and her general level of health, not her insurance status."

He looked down, closing his eyes. "I'm sorry. That was out of line."

"Listen." She paused. "I know you don't know me, and I know I'm from the evil sixth floor, but here's the thing—my personal goal here is to get the best care to every child who needs it. I'm not looking at ways to cut services to vulnerable kids. I'm not looking to slash staffing on a floor that can't afford to lose nurses. I'm not looking to boot patients back home, if they should really be here."

"That's all fine and good, but none of that will help you make budget cuts, and if I understand correctly, that part's nonnegotiable, right?"

She sighed, letting her eyes skate over his broad shoulders, over those hands she'd been trying not to fantasize about since they'd met. For about the hundredth time this week, she wished they were working on an uncontentious project together, rather than this unwelcome, unfair exercise in prioritizing a set of items that could all arguably vie for the number one position.

She closed her salad. "If there's any way to make your floor run leaner, we need to figure that out. It's late, and I'll be blunt—I imagine more than *my* job will be on the line if we don't."

"I get it." He put up his hands. "If we really dig deep, we might be able to save a few hundred here or there, but not the kind of money you're talking about. It just isn't there, and I'm not being evasive. I'm telling you straight out that there's just nothing you're going to find that'll have the effect you're looking for—unless you want to start playing God and deciding who gets care and who doesn't."

"Of course not."

"So what do we do?"

Delaney looked up at the ceiling. "We've got a budget number to land on. If we can't get there by cutting expenses, then we need to find a way to increase revenue. I think the first step is for the two of us to sit down with my revised proposal so I can understand the impact of every line item on there. *Then* we can move to alternative avenues. But I've got to be able to show due diligence on this, Dr. Mackenzie. I cannot go before that board and propose level funding because you said so. It'll never fly."

"Understood. Why don't you come down tomorrow and spend another day observing, and then we'll meet when you're ready?"

"I think . . . that sounds fine."

He looked out the window again, then back at the hallway through her open door, shaking his head.

"I can't believe how quiet it is up here."

"Well, it's late. Everybody's gone home."

He nodded, looking in no hurry to leave. "Do you work this late often? Or is this because you spent the day downstairs?"

"Little of both." She shrugged slowly. "It's a nice time of day to get stuff done. No interruptions."

"Ah." He straightened up and gathered his salad container. "Except for rogue docs trying to convince you not to cut their funding?"

"It's a problem. But you brought dinner, so you're excused." She pointed to her salad. "Thank you again, by the way."

He shrugged, smiling. "I figured inviting you out for a lobster dinner would be completely transparent. The other department heads would talk."

She let out a surprised laugh, but felt it falter as she

looked at his face, which had grown suddenly serious. In the soft light of her desk lamp, it was easy to imagine the two of them having a quiet little dinner in her office, followed by—dessert. She felt her cheeks flush as she pictured closing the door, sliding into his arms, clearing her desk as he kissed her silly in the moonlight.

"Right." Her voice was embarrassingly shaky. "Not a big lobster fan, unfortunately."

He pushed the chair back toward her desk, not at all hurried. But then he took two steps toward the door, and she stood up to follow, intending to close it behind him. Clearly, he didn't hear her, because before he reached it, he turned around, and she almost ran into him.

He chuckled as he put out a hand to steady her, and this time, he didn't let go. She looked up, and his eyes scanned her face, landing for a long beat on her lips. Then he blinked hard and let his hand slide from her arm while he reached for the door.

"Good night, Delaney."

Chapter 9

Early the next afternoon, Delaney was walking by a patient room when she heard a commotion and then a scared scream.

"Oh, no! Help! *Help!*"

Delaney looked left, then right, but the hallway was empty for the first time all day. She was the only hospital employee in sight, and somebody needed help. Oh, God. She wasn't trained to help with emergencies down here.

She wasn't trained to help with emergencies *anywhere*.

She ran into the room, then stopped short as she saw a mom with her little boy on the bed. And the blood. So much blood.

"Help! Please help me! He's bleeding!"

The woman grabbed a towel and pushed it down onto the boy's leg, but it quickly turned red. Delaney's stomach lurched when she caught sight of the boy's eyes, which were open wide and terrified.

She ran closer, but couldn't see his call button anywhere on his bed. *God!* Where was it? Where was everybody?

She spotted a pile of white washcloths on a little shelf near the foot of the bed, so she grabbed the whole pile and pressed down on the boy's thigh, keeping her eyes on his face so she didn't faint.

"It's okay, buddy." She tried to keep her voice even and calm. "We'll fix you right up. The doctor's coming."

Please, God, let the damn doctor be coming.

His eyes rolled back as the washcloths soaked through, and Delaney panicked.

"What happened? Where's his call button?"

"I don't know!" The mother looked terrified as she let go of the cloths and pawed through his blankets.

"Go get help!" Delaney motioned with her chin. Somebody had to hold pressure, or this poor kid was going to bleed out. "Go get somebody!"

The woman fled the room, and ten seconds later, Delaney could hear feet running down the hallway. A lot of feet. She'd pulled the end of the boy's sheet loose and was trying to add that to the pile of washcloths, but the bleeding wasn't stopping. Oh, God. Why wasn't the bleeding stopping?

Two hands grabbed her shoulders and pulled her back. "Out of the way, Delaney." She tripped backward but caught her balance as Millie took her place at the bedside. Nurses started hammering out words like *blood* and *platelets* and *stat* and *OR* and Delaney suddenly felt woozy as she watched a crowd of freakishly happy scrubs efficiently surround the little boy.

The scene dissolved into one from her past, and she reached for the wall so she didn't tip over.

She couldn't see what the nurses were doing, and the pace was an absolute frenzy. As she stood in the corner of the room, terrified, Joshua came striding in. She watched as he calmly took charge of the situation, and ten minutes later, the boy was off to the operating room, a pressure bandage of some sort on his thigh. His mother followed, twisting her hands as she practically ran down the hallway behind them.

Once the room cleared, Delaney let out her first audible breath, leaning on the empty bed so she didn't collapse. Then she noticed the blood. It was all over her hands, her arms, her skirt, her shoes. She swallowed hard.

"You okay?" Joshua's voice startled her from the doorway.

She raised her eyes, knowing she must look like she'd just come out a loser in the zombie apocalypse. Words failed her, though. She just held up her hands, looking at them like they belonged to someone else.

"I—think I need to clean up."

He raised his eyebrows, walking quickly toward her. "I think you need to sit down."

"No, I'm fine. I'm—fine. I'm sure I'm fine."

"Delaney, you are deathly white right now. Sit."

He pushed her gently into a chair, then put a warm hand on the back of her neck, urging her head forward.

"Head between your knees."

"I'm not going to keel over."

She was totally going to keel over.

"Yeah, you are. Please just do what I say. I'm a doctor, remember?"

"Okay, okay." Delaney could feel the smile in his words. She let his hand push her head downward, but was surprised when it didn't leave her neck once she was safely in a don't-keel position. Instead, his fingers kneaded slowly, soothingly.

"Take a couple of deep, slow breaths."

His voice was low, soft, calm, like one he'd use with a patient on the edge, and suddenly she felt ridiculous. Here he was in charge of an entire patient floor with thirty patients and ten nurses, and instead of taking care of any of them, he was stuck dealing with an interloper from finance who couldn't handle the sight of blood.

She pushed upward, and he slid his hand away from her neck.

"Easy does it. Take it slow."

"I'm so sorry. You have way more important people to be taking care of right now."

He laughed softly. "Is that what you think?"

"How can I not?" She pointed at the space where the bed had been, then out at the hallway. "Your nurses are scary efficient, by the way."

"Yep. They are." He nodded. "Best in the business. Just not enough of them."

Her eyes skittered around the room, trying not to land again on the empty spot where the little boy's bed had been.

"Delaney." His voice commanded her to look at him, and she couldn't—*not*.

She took a shaky breath. "Is he going to be okay?"

"They're taking good care of him."

She swallowed, wincing. She'd heard those words before, in another lifetime.

Her voice was quiet when she spoke. "Is that what you're trained to say? You know, so you don't have to answer yes or no?"

"It's the truth."

"But is he?"

Joshua blew out a breath. "I don't know. Is that better? Is that what you want to hear?"

She put her head down, picturing the fear in the little boy's eyes. "No."

"That's why I say the other."

"Okay." Her voice was barely a whisper. "Okay."

He stepped back. "I need to get to the nurses' station and check on things. I'll send Millie down here. She'll show you where you can shower and put on some clean scrubs."

"Thank you."

"You did great, Delaney."

"Right." She swallowed. "I'm not—I didn't—oh, God." She felt tears prickling behind her eyes, and she did everything she could not to let them seep out.

"Hey." He stepped back toward her, putting his hand on her shoulder. "You did your best. That's all any of us can do." His eyes searched hers. "Are you okay? Really?"

"Yes." She nodded. "I'm . . . fine. Just need a moment."

He squeezed her, then let go, but paused before he turned. "I'll send Millie down."

As he left the room, Delaney felt her knees start shaking, then her thighs. All of the adrenaline that had fueled her through the past twenty minutes was still cruising around her system with no outlet, and as her fingers tingled, she wondered what it felt like to faint.

She took a deep breath, remembering Joshua's hand on her neck, his quiet words in her ear.

Dammit, this is why she sat on the sixth floor. And this is why med school had only been a pipe dream. She wasn't wired to handle this stuff. Wasn't equipped in the least.

Because creating a pseudo-spa with Charlotte yesterday wasn't pediatric-floor reality.

This was reality.

Twenty minutes later, Delaney turned the water up hotter, nearly scorching her skin. She'd been in the pediatric floor's shower cubicle for ten minutes already, but still couldn't get the feel of the blood off her skin. Couldn't get the smell out of her nose. Couldn't get the sight of the poor little boy's frightened eyes out of her head.

She was still embarrassed at how close she'd been to fainting when Dr. Mackenzie had walked in. The sight of that blood . . . on her own hands . . . had brought her back to med school, back to the horrifying day she'd finally realized that though she'd graduated at the top of her undergrad class and was on a full scholarship, she just—didn't belong there.

She'd spent her entire childhood hearing hospital stories from her dad. He reveled in talking about new procedures, or tough cases he'd had, and through it all, she'd nodded and listened and tried to quell her gag reflex.

When it had come time to pick a college, his alma mater had come calling with a scholarship, and she'd accepted, thinking everything was falling into place just perfectly. Then she'd sailed through four years, got into her top-choice med school, and was pretty sure she was on her way to a stellar medical career.

But then came reality.

She'd run out of the dissection lab on a sunny April afternoon and showered until the water ran cold in her apartment. Then she'd waited an hour for the water heater to warm up the tank, and she'd done it again. She'd been dreading dissection since day one, but had somehow managed to power through . . . until the day they were supposed to work on hands.

As she'd stared down at the table, she hadn't been able to begin. While other body parts were just—parts, this wasn't. All she'd been able to think about was all of the projects these particular hands had done, the little heads they had comforted, the other hands they'd held.

And she just—hadn't been able to continue.

It had taken her a full week to tell her father she was dropping out, and she wasn't sure if he'd recovered even yet. Even though she was in the medical field like him, she wasn't a doctor, and to him, it just wasn't the same.

Getting her MBA hadn't quite impressed him, either, though she'd earned top scores and numerous academic awards. Dad just thought the degree was a waste of a good brain—one he'd been cultivating since she was born, in his mind. He'd never actually spoken those words, but she could just tell.

Because with her failure, his dreams of a Dr. Blair Junior had died not once, but twice.

"You going home tonight, doc?" Millie poked her head into Joshua's office later that afternoon.

Josh pinched the bridge of his nose as he looked at the clock. *Shit*. It wasn't afternoon anymore. "Just waiting for Ian to get back from surgery."

"It's seven o'clock."

"I know. It's been—a day. And you're still here, too, so no harassing me about my hours."

"He'll be okay, Josh."

"I know." He sighed. "Something doesn't sit right on this one, Millie. I want good eyes on that room tonight."

"Already handled. I've got Steph on him tonight. Ten-minute checks."

Josh nodded. Steph was the best nurse on the evening shift.

"You need to go home, Josh. I can have her update you later, if that'll let you feel easier about leaving."

"Ian's only part of my worries right now."

She sat down heavily. "Delaney?"

"Yeah."

"Heck of an introduction to the floor."

Josh pictured Delaney earlier, looking like she was ready to collapse, but not wanting to admit it. Seeing her pale face and trembling fingers had triggered his protective instincts like nothing ever had before, and he still hadn't quite figured out why. Yes, his medical training had compelled him to get her head between her knees before she went down like a lead brick, but that wasn't what had kept his hand on her smooth neck—or kept his fingers stroking her silky hair.

As she'd sat there quivering, he'd been struck with guilt. It had been his idea to have her observe on the floor—his deal, in reality. And then she'd found herself in the middle of a big fat emergency, and it was his fault. She'd done her best—and he was pretty impressed that she'd held her shit together as well as she had—but it was clear to everyone that she was way out of her league down here.

He'd been completely out of line to guilt her into it.

Millie raised her eyebrows. "You think she'll be back?"

"I don't know." He shook his head. "Wouldn't blame her if she decided today was enough."

"Well, if she does come back, we need to get that girl some basic training. If she's going to be here, she needs to know what to do if something like this happens again."

"She was doing her best, Millie."

"I know, and we're lucky she's got a level head on her shoulders. But you and I both saw her face afterward. Next time, we might not be so lucky."

"Agreed."

"First thing I'm going to teach her is how to call for help."

He sighed, exhausted by . . . everything. "I'm sure she didn't even have time to think. She just—acted."

Millie looked at him for a long moment, not speaking. "Huh."

"Don't *huh* me. I know that tone."

A small smile appeared on her face before she had time to erase it and turn the other way. "Either way, if she shows up in the morning, I own her for the first hour. If she's going to hang out on this floor, where things *do* happen, I want her to know what to do about them."

"Promise you won't scare her?"

Millie appraised him again. "I may be wrong, but I don't think *scared* is the primary emotion Miss Fancy Pants is feeling right now, honey."

Chapter 10

"You okay?" Megan stopped short as she walked into Delaney's office with a pile of paperwork an hour later. "Why are you still here? It's eight o'clock. And why are you in *scrubs*?"

Delaney looked up. "You don't want to know. Why are *you* still here?"

"I asked you first." Megan sat down, flopping the papers onto Delaney's desk. "But I'll give you my standard answer. I work for a slave driver."

"Poor girl."

"I know. But wait till you see what I got done today. You might actually be able to leave before midnight."

"You're totally getting a raise."

"Don't say that around Dr. Mackenzie. If he finds out you're funneling pediatric funds to your assistant, it will never fly."

"I'm not—shut up. I'm too tired to tell whether you're kidding."

Megan eyed her carefully. "No offense, Laney, but you look like hell. Tough day at the office?"

"Something like that."

"Did today convince you that you don't want to be a nurse when you grow up?"

"Today certainly didn't make me change my mind."

Delaney shivered, remembering the way the nurses had surrounded Ian's bed—remembering how he'd disappeared from her view, just like Parker had.

Megan sat back. "So what's it really like down there?"

"Busy. It's just—busy. I don't think I ever realized how many ways kids can be so sick."

"Sounds depressing."

"It is." Delaney thought about the kids she'd met over the past two days, and the parents. The fear on the floor was practically palpable. So many tests, so many treatments, so much damn waiting.

"Are you still planning to stay down there all week?"

"As much as I really, really don't want to at this point, I honestly can't believe how much I've learned just by being on the floor for two days. If Dr. Mackenzie will still have me, I really need to stick out the week."

"Because it's going to help you make better decisions about your budget proposal? Or because you get to spend more time with Dr. Hottie?"

"The first, obviously." She looked down at her scrubs. "But I think I need a different wardrobe. The head nurse suggested I not show up in civilian clothes again."

Megan raised her eyebrows. "Does this mean you need to go scrubs shopping?"

"No. We have plenty of them right here at the hospital. Closets full, actually. I had no idea."

"You know you look like a surgeon in those, right?"

"What's wrong with that?"

Megan appraised her like she wasn't sure whether Delaney was kidding. Then she put up one finger.

"Reason number one: surgeons are scary."

"Hey, my dad's a surgeon."

Megan didn't answer—just raised an eyebrow.

"Fine." Delaney rolled her eyes. "Surgeons are scary."

"Especially to little kids, and little kids' parents. You go walking around that floor in surgeon garb, you're going to give heart attacks left and right when you walk in those rooms."

Delaney took a deep breath. Megan was probably right. She tried to imagine what it would be like to sit in one of the depressing little rooms hoping for good news, and instead, see a surgeon walk through the door.

Yeah, it would be terrifying.

"Okay, I will lose the surgeon scrubs before I go back down there. Got it."

Megan shook her head. "Don't you want to hear reason number two before you agree with me?"

"But I already capitulated."

"Reason number two: Dr. Mackenzie."

Delaney felt her eyebrows pull together. "I don't follow."

Megan smiled. "Because you have only three days left to make an impression on the man, and I'm sorry, but those scrubs are *not* going to make the most of your assets. Are you *sure* you have to wear them?"

"Have you *met* Millie Swan? This is not a woman you argue with. She told me I need scrubs, and if she says *scrubs*, you say *yes, ma'am*. Plus, I don't have time to be concerned about my—assets. I'm pretty sure he's not paying attention, anyway."

Except for the way his eyes kept catching on her lips . . . and the way his hand had seemed to linger on her shoulder earlier.

"Well, then, let's make sure he does." Megan laughed. "Come on. I know where we can find some cute scrubs, but they close at nine."

"I still have hours of work to do. I can't go shopping right now."

Megan reached over the top of Delaney's monitor and

clicked it off. "This will all be here in the morning. You're too fried to get anything done right now, anyway."

Delaney started to argue, but Megan put up a hand and fixed her with a look she must have learned from her police officer mother.

"We're still in kill-him-with-kindness mode, right? Then let's be kind and give the man something to look at besides surgical scrubs." Megan winked. "Maybe they have those dominatrix ones we saw at the costume shop that time."

"Good morning."

Delaney jumped as Dr. Mackenzie stepped out of the cafeteria Wednesday morning, looking just-showered delicious. She'd been replaying last night's dream sequence in her head—this one featuring the sexy doctor, some definitely-not-appropriate-for-pediatrics scrubs, and a hospital storage room—as she'd walked into the hospital, and now she shook her head, trying to clear the memory as he fell into step beside her. It was only six o'clock in the morning, and she'd come in early, hoping to put in a few hours of work before she headed to the third floor. Apparently he was one step ahead of her.

"I like the outfit." His eyes scanned down her body as he met her pace. "Does this mean you've decided to join us again today?"

"Actually, it's scrubs day in the executive suite. We do it once a month."

He laughed. "Well, if you're in baby sheep, I'd love to see what Gregory shows up in."

They reached the elevator bank, and she pushed the Up button with her elbow. "I'm sworn to secrecy on that one."

"My lips are sealed." He held out a coffee, and for the

first time, she realized he had two. "I guessed cream, no sugar. Am I right?"

"You are, actually." She reached out tentatively for the cup, wishing she didn't hope their fingers would brush when she did so. "How'd you guess?"

"Research."

She narrowed her eyes. "Have you been quizzing my assistant?"

Just then the elevator doors opened, and he motioned for her to step in before him. "I would never resort to underhanded tactics like that."

As the doors swished closed, she studied him. She knew he'd probably worked later than she had last night, but here it was, six o'clock in the morning, and he looked as chipper and ready for the day as if he'd had a full twelve hours of sleep.

"How'd you know I'd be here this early?"

"I didn't, actually. I was headed up to bribe Marco into leaving this on your desk as a peace offering."

"Peace offering? For what?"

Josh cringed. "For insisting that we throw you right in yesterday. Obviously, I had no idea that was going to happen with Ian."

"I know."

"I feel awful about it. When I wanted you to get a real feel for the floor, that wasn't exactly what I meant."

Delaney watched the elevator numbers slide by the third floor without stopping, trying to block out the images of yesterday's scene. What had happened with Ian hadn't been Dr. Mackenzie's fault, and though she was sure emergencies brought things to a screaming halt all the time, he'd certainly had no way to predict one would occur while *she* was there.

"You don't need to apologize. Emergencies—happen." She shrugged, trying to look casual, even though she was anything but. It had taken her almost an hour to convince herself into the scrubs this morning. "If it matters, I was impressed with how your team handled it. I couldn't believe how quickly they stabilized him and had him off to—wherever he went."

He nodded. "Best of the best. Millie doesn't tolerate anything less."

The elevator doors opened, and Delaney paused before she stepped out. "How will she feel about me being on the floor again today? After what happened yesterday?"

"Pretty sure she's planning to give you the Pediatrics Orientation 102 we should have done two days ago. Apparently my version didn't cover things like patients trying to bleed out on your watch."

"No. It really didn't. Orientation's probably a good idea."

He held the elevator door open as she brushed past him into the carpeted hallway of the executive suite, and she half wished he would follow her, but he stayed inside the elevator.

"Listen, Delaney." His eyes met hers, and she wished again that they weren't colleagues on opposing sides of a funding crevasse. "I know yesterday was a really freaky scene, and I know you're putting a brave face on it. If you don't want to come back down there today, it's okay. I can try to find some time to meet with you later tonight, or maybe in the morning."

"I appreciate that." She took a deep breath. "And believe me, I considered putting a suit and heels on this morning and parking my butt in my own cushy office for the day. But as much as that whole situation did—freak me out a little, I think it's also good that I saw it. You wanted me to get a feel for life on the floor, and, well, that's life on the floor, right?"

He nodded. "Unfortunately."

"I may keep my distance from blood going forward, though. Just saying."

"I think that's a good idea." He smiled. "Ian's doing all right this morning. I'm sure he'd love to see you."

Delaney swallowed. She wasn't sure she'd be able to step into his room without yesterday's events assaulting her.

"Up to you, of course. I thought I'd have you shadow Kenderly today. I have a feeling you'll like what she does."

"No blood?"

"No blood." He winked, finally letting the elevator doors close. "See you in a few hours, Delaney. If we survive the day intact, let's see if we can tackle your list later."

At nine o'clock sharp, Delaney took a deep breath and stepped out of the elevator again, this time on the third floor. She saw Millie standing at the nurses' station, her back to the elevators, so she pasted on her best confident smile and pushed her shoulders back, eager to appear like yesterday had been just a small blip in her existence, rather than a traumatic, memory-inducing panic attack in the making.

Therese saw her first, and Delaney knew she wasn't imagining the surprise in the tiny woman's eyes.

"Good morning, Delaney. You're back."

Millie turned and lifted her eyebrows. "You go shopping?"

"Nurse's orders, right?"

"Good." Millie nodded briskly. "Shame to throw away perfectly good clothes. Sorry you got a quick lesson in why nurses wear scrubs."

"Thank you. It's okay. I'm—good."

Millie motioned her toward the break room. "Come with me. I own you for the first hour—doctor's orders."

An hour later, Delaney'd had the fire-hose version of

pediatric emergency training. Millie had gone over what to do in the event of a bleed, a sugar crash, and a choking situation, as well as how to perform CPR. Despite the training, Delaney actually felt more scared now than she'd been when she'd walked onto the floor. Good Lord, look at all that could go wrong! Millie'd only skated over the surface of possible emergencies, and had ended every single lesson with *Remember, you only do this if you've called for help and they're not there yet.*

"Okay, quiz time." Millie pulled out a piece of paper and handed it to Delaney.

She took it gingerly. "What if I don't pass?"

"You take it again. And if you don't pass it that time, you take it *again*. We can do it all day."

Did she hear a smile behind Millie's steely voice?

Delaney fished a pen out of her pocket. She had to hand it to scrubs designers—the pockets were like magical, endless caverns. She could probably fit her lunch in one if she tried.

"Okay, I'm ready." She poised her pen above the paper.

"Number one. What's the first thing you do for a sugar crash?"

Delaney knew that one. She scribbled quickly, then put a number two on her paper.

"Next question—what's the first step in CPR?"

Delaney looked at the ceiling, trying to think. It had changed since she'd originally been trained. She wrote down her answer, then looked up at Millie.

Millie leaned over to scan her paper, then shook her head.

"It's gonna be a long day here."

Delaney looked down, mystified. She knew the answers were correct. She'd paid damn good attention to every word that had come out of Millie's mouth for the past hour. No way did she ever want to get caught like yesterday, having no clue what to do for a poor kid who was having a serious emergency.

"What do you mean? These aren't correct?"

Millie shook her head again. "No. They're not." Then she braced her arms on the table, looking right into Delaney's eyes. "What is *the* first step in *any* emergency down here when you are not a medically trained professional?"

"Oh. God." Delaney felt her cheeks go red. "Call for help."

"Yes."

"I'm so sorry. I thought that part was understood." She pointed vaguely at her paper. "These are the first steps that come *after* the—first step."

"Mm hm. Flip your paper over. Let's start again."

Delaney blew out a breath. It *was* going to be a long day.

Late that morning, Delaney sat in Kenderly's tiny office, getting a thirty-thousand-foot overview of what a child life specialist did all day. The more Kenderly talked about how her job was to support the patients and families, ease fear, and come up with creative ways to teach patients and their parents about their own conditions, the more intrigued Delaney became.

She cringed internally, picturing the two child life positions sitting squarely on her targeted layoff list. In all the research she'd done so far, she'd certainly seen the value of the role. It was just that, compared to the other medical professionals on staff, she'd had an easier time calling these positions "nice to have," rather than "need to have."

"No matter what—and no matter who asks you to do otherwise—you *never* take part in anything that could cause pain. You never hold anybody down, never help a nurse or doctor do something scary, never be part of pain. You are the safe person—the one that kids know *isn't* going to ever hurt them."

"That sounds fantastic, to be honest."

"It is. It's a great career for people who want to be involved with medicine—but don't *really* want to be involved with medicine, if you know what I mean."

Delaney sighed quietly. "Believe me, I do."

Maybe it was a career *she* should have explored after she'd finished fleeing medical school.

She pulled out her notepad, flipping to the page where she'd jotted down her questions for Kenderly. She needed to tread carefully with her queries so she didn't give away the fact that in her mind, she'd practically already decided this job was ancillary and optional.

She leaned forward. "So what's a typical day like for you?"

Kenderly looked at her, a half smile on her face. "There's no such thing." She shuffled a couple of pieces of paper on her desk. "Looks like we've got a spinal tap this afternoon, some CF education with Charlotte, and some diabetes training with Milo's parents. That's my Top Three list. The rest of the hours will fill in as needs arise, but today there'll be two of us, so there's a chance we can meet maybe one-quarter of the needs."

"Really? You feel like we're understaffed in this area?"

Kenderly's eyebrows went up. "We have a thirty-bed floor. We have one child life specialist on days and one on evenings. None at night. That's it. We are *bleakly* understaffed, though I know that's not what you're hoping to hear."

"I'm only after the truth. It's not always going to be pretty, I know."

Delaney knew damn well these positions would be on the chopping block in no time flat, whether she recommended it or not. *Somebody* would find them ancillary, she could almost guarantee.

But in only two days, she'd seen Kenderly work her magic all over the floor, and after sitting here talking with her about everything she did all day, Delaney kept wondering how much better Parker's hospitalizations might have been if there had been someone like her to help keep him sane amid the chaos. To these kids, and definitely to their parents, this position was anything *but* ancillary.

Then she had an idea. She took a moment to gather her thoughts, then flipped to a fresh piece of paper. She crossed her legs and sat back like they had hours to sit here and chat, hoping she could get Kenderly to drop her please-don't-fire-me armor if she backed off in her own intensity.

"Okay, another question for you. Let's pretend we're making a case to get *more* child life positions. I've seen how what you're doing impacts the kids. If you had to play the dollars, cents, and time game, how is your work helping the nurses and doctors on the floor get *their* work done more efficiently?"

Kenderly sat back, eyeing Delaney with a glimmer of respect, rather than distrust. Then she nodded slowly. "Now *this* is a conversation I'm happy to have."

Chapter 11

"You're slouching, dear." Delaney's mother raised a sculpted eyebrow as she sipped zinfandel from a crystal goblet.

Delaney sighed, adjusting her shoulders. It was Wednesday night, she was seated in her customary position at her parents' dining room table, and though she'd only been there for fifteen minutes, she was already stealing glances at the grandfather clock in the corner. She'd left the hospital so she could be here at six o'clock sharp, as expected, but she still had hours of work on her desk, so after dinner, she'd be heading back to Mercy.

She wondered if maybe Dr. Mackenzie would still be there, too.

Her father sat in his seat, scrolling on his phone with one hand while he shoveled in steak and potatoes with the other. He'd spoken perhaps ten words to her, which was par for the course. Mom sliced her steak into tiny pieces, pushing them around her plate more than eating them, so as usual, the burden of conversation fell on Delaney.

It was her fault, really. She was the one who'd insisted long ago that they set aside one night a week to eat together, in some vain attempt to preserve the illusion that they were a connected, happy-ish family.

But every time they sat at the table, Mom's eyes would

dart to Parker's spot, even these many years later. And every Wednesday night, Mom would make brownies for dessert, because it was family night and they'd been Parker's favorite.

Delaney had never had the heart to remind her that she, too, had a favorite dessert. It wasn't brownies.

"So . . . how's everyone's week been?" Delaney took a bite of her steak, which was to-die-for delicious. Before Parker had died, Mom had been the queen of the dinner party. If there was a surgery department celebration, their home had been the de facto location, and Mom had gladly served as the de facto chef. Her home had sparkled, her kids had sparkled, and—Delaney glanced at her—even *she* had sparkled, way back then.

"Oh, the usual," Mom replied, a tight smile on her face. "This and that. You know."

Delaney nodded. She had no idea.

"Dad? How about you? Any fascinating cases this week?" She braced herself. "Remembering, of course, that we're at a table, eating food?"

Dad put down his phone and actually looked at her. As he cut his meat, he shook his head. "I imagine you have a pretty good idea how my week's going."

Though they worked in the same hospital, Delaney rarely saw him, so his response stymied her.

"I'm not sure what you mean."

"The budget cuts?" He paused his fork halfway to his mouth. "Imagine you've heard?"

"Oh." She nodded. Must be his department had made the short list, too. "Of course. Sorry."

"Not your fault. Frigging economy's in the toilet, nobody can pay a living wage, and now we're supposed to make cuts where there isn't any room to do so. I offered to stop stitching my patients back up after surgery to save on thread, but Gregory wasn't amused."

Delaney smiled. "They told us to be creative, right?"

"So where do you fall on this? Whose budget did they assign you to butcher?"

"Ouch." She winced. "*Butcher*'s kind of a strong word, don't you think?"

He leaned his elbows on the table, pushing away his plate. "Tell me this—you know of any budget at Mercy that isn't already running on empty?"

"I—don't have my hands on all of them. I really don't know."

"You're a smart girl. I'm sure you have a pretty good idea. You tell me why they're going after surgery. Radiology just bought *another* MRI machine. Where'd *that* money come from?"

"Those things pay themselves off much faster than a lot of—other things." Delaney shrugged apologetically, knowing it sounded lame. "They have an easier time making a case for it."

"Meanwhile, I'm going to have to put my patients just half under so we can save on anesthetics. That oughtta be fun."

"What?"

He matched her shrug. "It's the only thing I can see to cut. What's a surgical department to do?"

"Dad, seriously. Gregory gave me pediatrics, so believe me, I'm in hell as well."

"How much do you have to cut?"

Delaney rattled off the figure, and to her surprise, Dad sat back in his chair, shaking his head in disgust.

"I guess we'd better hope the fund-raising dinner goes well next week, then. Think we should tell the donors that if they don't give generously, their next surgery might be anesthesia-free?"

Delaney froze, her glass halfway to her mouth. How had she forgotten about the dinner? She'd been going to it every year since her dad had started at Mercy, but for the past five years, Delaney had skated a tightrope between representing the finance office and playing the dutiful daughter to one of Mercy's preeminent surgeons. It wasn't necessarily hard to smile for the publicity cameras and make small talk with donors . . . or it wouldn't be, if she didn't still practically break out in hives at the thought of talking with strangers who knew she was only talking with them about their grandchildren and pets because she really, *really* just hoped they'd open up their pockets and give generously.

She *hated* the annual hospital fund-raiser.

She always practiced her spiels in front of the mirror before she left, had them written on index cards in her purse, and drank a glass of wine as soon as she got there to help calm her nerves, but it was never, ever comfortable. While Kevin worked the room like a used-car salesman, stunning people into donor submission with his sparkling smile and gelled hair, she had to call up every ounce of courage to approach even one person she'd targeted ahead of time.

But this year, of all years, her pet programs were at stake, and after just three days on pediatrics, she knew without a doubt that their only hope for balancing the budget was to find additional funding. Unfortunately, grants took forever—and were hardly guaranteed—and they'd finessed the insurance-payment process to the highest efficiency possible already.

That meant she had a date with her event dress, her event shoes, and her event smile. She, Delaney Blair, poster child of the clinically shy, needed to find the pediatric floor a big, fat donor pocket. And she needed to find one who was ready to sign on the proverbial dotted line in the next three weeks.

One glass of wine was never going to be enough.

* * *

Two days later, Delaney was heading past Ian's room when something made her back up. She could see his mother fiddling with his IV tubes, which wasn't necessarily odd. The darn tubes got tangled on arms and pillows and bed rails constantly, so she'd seen moms do this all over the floor this week. Something pinged Delaney's radar, though, and without really knowing *why*, she felt like she should stop.

Then Ian's monitors started beeping in a wild cacophony, and his mom looked panicked. Before Delaney could take a breath—*or* call for help, because she knew Millie would have her head if she didn't—three nurses emerged from other rooms and strode purposefully into Ian's.

The beeps stopped as someone punched buttons on the monitors, and his mom stepped back as the nurses took over, untangling tubes and talking quietly to one another. Before long, Ian was settled and quiet, and the nurses filed out one by one, leaving his mom wringing her hands beside his bed.

Delaney stepped into the room. "You okay?"

Ian's mom jumped, like she hadn't heard Delaney come in.

"I'm Delaney." She put out her hand, and the woman shook it with her own icy, trembling hand.

"Fiona." She pointed to Ian. "That's Ian."

"How's he doing?" Delaney kept her voice quiet, trying not to startle Ian.

"Not good. Not good at all." Tears escaped the corners of Fiona's eyes as she looked at him, and something twisted inside Delaney. "They just can't figure out what's wrong with him."

"Really?"

"This is our third admission this year. He just keeps getting sicker."

"I'm really sorry, Fiona. I'm sure they're doing everything they can to figure it out."

"Oh, yes." She nodded. "Everyone here's so wonderful. They treat us so nicely. I just wish"—she patted his little foot under the covers—"I wish they could figure him out so he could go back to being a little boy."

Delaney watched him for a moment, seeing the blanket over his chest rise and fall evenly. What must it be like to sit here day after day and watch your own child suffer? The pain in her stomach tightened again, remembering another little boy, another little blanket rising and falling in a rhythm too slow.

"Do you want to—play cards or something?" Delaney grasped at anything she could think of. Fiona looked so lonely, her scared eyes so much like Delaney's own mother's that Delaney had to look away so she didn't get sucked in.

Parker had always hated the hospital. The doctors had scared him, the nurses had scared him—even the lights had scared him. He'd hated the noise, hated the stretchers that brought him to scary places, and hated sleeping, always fearing that someone would come in and do something to him if he wasn't vigilant.

Delaney wondered again what it would have been like for him if he'd had just one safe person he could rely on—someone like Kenderly to play Go Fish with him or rock him to sleep or make him laugh before a procedure instead of cry. Her mother had done her level best, but even little Parker could feel the waves of fear and hopelessness wafting from her.

Delaney had always wanted to serve his memory by becoming the kind of doctor who *could* have saved him, and had spent eons feeling like a failure because she hadn't made it through med school.

And now? She'd studied her ass off to get her MBA.

She'd worked herself into a hospital position because she'd thought she could make a difference for kids like Parker. She sighed. Instead, she was now in the unenviable position of cutting the very services that could help children like Ian and her little brother survive their stays with*out* long-term psychological scars.

She really should have found a way to stick with med school.

Four hours later, she sat in Dr. Mackenzie's office, hoping she could speak to him before he left for the night. The faint scent of his aftershave was in the air, like he'd been here not long ago, and she took a deep breath. Then she shook her head, feeling heat creep up her cheeks. She was here to *talk* to the man, not lust after his cologne—or him.

As she waited, she looked around, trying to get a better feel for him. On the wall behind his desk, there was a collection of framed pictures, all of Dr. Mackenzie with a variety of kids. She stood up to look at them, and as her eyes traveled from frame to frame, she felt her fingers slide up to her mouth. The photos were so—poignant. Some of them looked like they'd been taken here at the hospital, but a slew of others had Avery's House in the background.

She stepped back, eyes wide. She'd known about Avery's House for years—the getaway home for kids with life-threatening illnesses was local legend, really. Ethan and Josie Miller ran it, in addition to Snowflake Village, the adjoining theme park, and their venture had been covered by the *Boston Globe*, NPR, and probably every news outlet in New England.

Was Dr. Mackenzie involved, too? She stepped closer to the pictures again, noting the wide front porch of the converted old hotel in the background of many of them.

Her eyes noticed the kids, of course, but they seemed a lot more intent on checking out the doctor in the shots.

All week long, she'd felt like a teenager with a crush, and had had to stop herself more than once from asking the nurses if he was dating anyone. The sound of his voice coming from a patient room had her leaning against the wall just to listen. The sight of him coming down the hallway toward her had her practically tripping over her own shoes.

The way he touched her arm as he spoke, or winked at her over a patient's head, or smiled like they had a secret kept her knees going to Jell-O, and she hated to admit that she'd gone to sleep with him in her head every night since she'd met him.

Hardly professional.

She shook her head, focusing on the wall. In the pictures, he didn't have on a white coat, or a tie, or scrubs. He usually had jeans on, maybe a polo shirt, maybe a dress shirt. He looked omigod-hot in every single one, and she fought not to steal one right off the wall.

"Hey there."

She turned quickly at the sound of his voice, knocking over a picture on his desk, then banging into a shelf while she scrambled to put it right.

He laughed as he touched her elbow, and she felt it low and deep. "Remind me not to trust you with fragile equipment, would you?"

She steadied everything with her hands, then moved slowly out from behind his desk, making room for him to slide by.

"I'm so sorry. I was just looking at your pictures."

He glanced at the wall as he set his laptop on the desk. "They're great, aren't they?"

She nodded. They really were. She mentally calculated how long it would take to grab one off the wall, run down to the copy shop, and get it back before he noticed.

"So." He sat down in his chair, looking at her with his eyebrows raised. "Want to sit?"

"Thanks." She took a deep breath. "I wanted to catch you before you left for the weekend."

He looked at his watch. "It's seven o'clock. How long have you been waiting?"

"Long enough to know that your favorite color shirt—at least for pictures—is green, you have way too much paperwork on your desk, and we really need to get the facilities crew to paint your walls."

He laughed again, looking at the pictures. "Apparently all true." Then he looked at her for a long moment. "So you survived the week."

"Yes." She nodded. "Much to everyone's surprise, I imagine."

"How'd you like working with Kenderly?"

"Honestly? I think I want her job when I grow up."

"She predicted as much." He raised his eyebrows. "So is now the part where we finally get to look at your list together . . . before you go back to the sixth floor and do your calculator magic?"

Delaney took a deep breath, trying to corral the thoughts that had been circling in her head while she'd waited for him. "Actually, I have an idea."

"Okay." He sat back, linking his hands behind his head, and it was all Delaney could do not to get up and run her hands over the pecs that were straining at the front of his shirt. No wonder the nurses fought to buy him coffee in the morning. Good God, any catalog in the country would sign him immediately.

"Okay, what?" Delaney shook her head, feeling heat

creep up her cheeks. What had she been saying before she'd started picturing him with fewer clothes on?

"You were about to tell me your idea."

"Right. I . . . was wondering . . . what would you think of me maybe spending one more week down here?"

He lowered his hands and leaned forward, but she couldn't read the expression on his face. "Why?"

She took a deep breath. "Because I was wrong. Wrong about every line item I was ready to propose. Wrong about every service I thought was ancillary."

"Oh." He shook his head. "Wow."

"We need a new approach, and I have some ideas."

"Excellent. Lay them on me." He leaned forward, but his eyes were tired, and she felt guilty for making him stay even longer tonight.

Just then, her stomach let out an impressive, hollow rumble, and she clutched her midsection in embarrassment.

He smiled. "Hungry?"

"Sorry. I think I forgot to eat lunch."

He laughed, but it was tight. "*Now* you're getting a feel for pediatrics." He stood up and closed his laptop. "Tell you what. I can't think on an empty stomach, and clearly you need to eat as well. How about I take you to dinner—somewhere that *isn't* this hospital?"

"You want to—take me to dinner?"

"I'll try not to be insulted by your shocked tone."

"I'm sorry. It's just—unexpected." *And sort of date-ish sounding.*

"Do you like Bellinis?"

"Does anyone *not* like Bellinis?" Delaney smiled. Bellinis was the best restaurant *in* Echo Lake, but not because of its fancy menu or elegant service. It was an Italian place that looked more like an Irish pub, but the food Mama

Bellini served could rival anything from Boston's North End.

He shook his head. "Not that I've found." He pointed at her. "You'll have to change, though. Mama B has a no-scrubs-in-my-pub rule."

"Really?"

"Something about not wanting to think about what people in scrubs do all day." He shrugged. "I really don't know."

"Should we meet there?"

"Sounds good. Eight o'clock give you enough time?"

She pulled her purse from the back of the chair. By the time she made her way out of the hospital and back to her condo, she'd have a full two point five minutes to change before she'd need to leave again to meet him.

Eek. "Perfect."

As she rode down the elevator two minutes later, she caught her reflection in the metal slats beside the door, and she brought her hands to her face. With her flushed cheeks and smile that wouldn't quit, she looked like a woman who'd just been kissed silly.

Or maybe one who *wanted* to be.

Chapter 12

Forty-five minutes later, Josh scored the back booth in Bellinis and settled in. He pinched the bridge of his nose, blinking his eyes shut to try to clear the cobwebs sneaking in. Good God, it'd been a long week. The last thing he wanted to do right now was spend another hour discussing dollars and cents, but when he'd looked at Delaney sitting in that chair, asking for another week on his floor, he'd been torn.

On one hand, he couldn't get enough of the woman. Every time he'd left a patient room all week, he'd caught himself scanning the halls for a glimpse of her. Every time he'd heard her laughter coming from the playroom, he'd made an excuse to stop in to talk to whoever else was with her. Every morning, when he'd stepped into the elevator, he'd toyed with whether to stop on the third floor . . . or head up to the sixth.

On the *other* hand, he was ready for his staff to get back to business without looking over their shoulders to see if she was watching. He was ready to stop calculating the ROI of every procedure and meeting and bandage.

He sighed. He was ready to stop wishing maybe she was more than a colleague.

"You want coffee?" Molly appeared at his elbow. "No offense, but you look like hell."

"Thanks, Mols. I hear that a lot these days."

Molly sat down across from him, probably grateful for a break. The woman defined *Italian spitfire*, but he could tell she'd been run ragged by the dinner crowd. Her parents had owned the restaurant since she was just a glimmer in their eyes, and although she had a business degree and a full-time job at the Snowflake Village offices, she still pulled more waitressing shifts here than she had when they'd been seniors at Echo Lake High.

She twisted her dark hair into a ponytail, fanning her neck with a menu. "Ethan joining you tonight?"

"Nope."

Molly shook her head. "Told you this would happen when they got married. Now they just want to stay home all the time."

"If you lived in the owners' half of Avery's House, would *you* ever want to leave?"

"Nope. But I gave all that up when I let Ethan marry Josie instead of me."

Josh laughed. "Is that how that went?"

"Something like that." She fluttered her fingers. "Or, y'know, they'd been in love since they were in diapers and finally realized it. One or the other."

"Right."

"You eating alone?"

Josh sighed. "No, actually."

"Omigod, do you have a date?" Molly's eyes went wide.

He looked around, sure the entire pub had heard her. "Could you maybe try not to sound like that would be such a miracle?"

"Wouldn't it, though?"

"Shut up, Mols."

She laughed. "Just kidding. Is it a real date, though?"

"No. It's not *any* kind of a date. It's a business dinner."

"Oh." She wrinkled her nose. "Boring."

"I wish."

It definitely wouldn't be boring. Not with Delaney, any-way. The biggest challenge would be keeping his atten-tion on her little notebook full of questions, rather than on her silky neck, or the way her hair fell right to her collar-bone, or the way her lips—

Molly raised her eyebrows. "Well, it's Friday night. Maybe it can turn *into* a date after the business part is done."

He cleared his throat, blocking the visions. "No, it can't. We work together."

"Oh. Right." Molly nodded sagely. "I forgot. Nobody at that hospital ever dates anyone *else* who works there."

"Did I say *shut up* yet?"

"At least once, yes. But I'm used to it because you've been saying it since third grade, and I know you don't really mean it. Plus, you're meeting her here, which must mean you want me to check her out for you and thumbs-up or thumbs-down her potential, right?"

"God, no."

"Oh." Molly tried to look hurt. "But I'm practically a professional at it. Did I not totally call Cherise?"

He grimaced, remembering the traveling nurse who'd come through one spring. She'd been bubbly and fun . . . and completely psychotic in the end.

Molly raised her eyebrows. "Well? Did I?"

"Yes, you totally called Cherise."

"And Melody?"

"Melody, too."

"Ooh, and who was that one—you know—with the crazy hair?" Molly circled a hand over her head.

"Dara."

"Right! Dara." Molly laughed. "Yeah, that was scary. You're lucky I had a fake kitchen fire that night."

He smiled, shaking his head. "I'll give you that one."

Too bad none of them had figured out Nicole before it was too late.

Molly got up, tapping him on the nose and squeezing his shoulder. "Just give me the signal if you need me to pretend the place is on fire again."

He rolled his eyes. "I won't need the signal."

"You don't know that. Coffee with three creamers if you need an extraction. I can go less dramatic than fire." She leaned down and planted a kiss on his head. "Have fun. I'll be back when she gets here. Ten bucks she orders seltzer with lime. And a salad."

She stuck her hand out to seal the bet, and again Josh rolled his eyes, but he shook her hand. "Ten bucks she goes for the special."

As soon as Molly cleared the counter and headed back into the kitchen, Josh looked toward the front door, and had to actually catch his breath as he saw Delaney standing there. She'd changed from her scrubs into a sweet little sundress that he'd swear matched her blue eyes, and she'd pulled her hair into some sort of half-up-half-down configuration that—with the sundress—made her look like she'd just barely left college.

And though he knew she must not have had more than ten minutes at her house to get ready, it even looked like she'd put on makeup. Just a touch—there was a little color in her cheeks, and a sheen to her lips that he hadn't noticed before—but it was enough to make her look like a woman meeting . . . a date.

He took a deep breath and squared his shoulders, then got up to go meet her, wishing for an insane second that it *was*.

When Delaney walked through the front door of Bellinis, she could practically taste the garlic, and her mouth watered. She just hoped her stomach didn't growl again before dinner got to the table.

And then she spotted Dr. Mackenzie sitting in a back booth across from the petite brunette whose parents owned Bellinis. They were laughing like old friends, but then the waitress stood up and kissed him fondly on the head, and Delaney felt her stomach clutch.

Oh.

Maybe the good doctor *wasn't* single, despite Megan's pipeline information that he most assuredly was.

She hated how her stomach fell, felt stupid that she'd taken the extra minute to dash on lip gloss. Felt *really* ridiculous for waking up three times this week with dreams of him fresh in her mind.

But this was good to know, right? Before she harbored any stupid delusions of being more than a colleague?

Yes, it was definitely good to know.

And when had she started harboring delusions, anyway? She shook her head. She needed to focus. So she'd reapplied her mascara and made sure she'd tamed her hair into some semblance of order before she left the condo. So she'd tried on three different dresses and left them flung all over the bedroom when she'd left. So she'd headed out the door, then back inside to spray just a teeny bit of perfume on her wrists.

It was just a business dinner. Nothing more, nothing less, even though her pulse had started racing when he'd invited her. It was pretty pathetic that a business invitation had made her stomach jump and her cheeks flush as she'd raced home and gotten ready.

She took a deep breath, gathering her stupid senses. This was not a date. Not. A. Date.

And then he spotted her, and she saw him take a breath before he pasted on a smile and got up to greet her. *Fabulous.* He looked like he was dreading this dinner just as much as he'd dreaded having her on his floor all week. Heck, he'd probably worked out an extraction signal with his girlfriend while he'd been waiting for Delaney.

She walked toward him, and he showed her to the booth and waited politely while she sat. As he settled into his side, their knees bumped, and though she'd have much rather let them brush idly throughout dinner, she pulled hers back immediately.

"Sorry," she blurted, then felt her cheeks heat. Good Lord, she'd blushed more in the past week than she had in years.

"No, I am." He grimaced. "I always forget how—cozy—these booths are. I should have chosen a table, but I figured it'd be easier to talk back here."

Just then, his girlfriend appeared at the table, smiling widely. "Hey there. I'm Molly. Can I get you a drink?"

Delaney suddenly felt stupid for wasting those precious minutes on mascara and perfume. Molly here was a petite little Italian beauty with gorgeous hair and a killer bod, and Delaney had watched her flirt up customers for years. She and Dr. Mackenzie would make adorable children.

Delaney cleared her throat nervously, kicking herself for doing so. "Could I just have some seltzer? With a lime?"

"Absolutely."

She saw Molly bite her lip in amusement as she turned to Dr. Mackenzie. What was so funny about seltzer with lime? "And for you, doc?"

Doc?

He tipped his head in consternation, rolling his eyes. "The usual, Mols."

"Coming right up." Molly spun and headed back to the kitchen, and Delaney picked up her menu, trying not to look at the man who was clearly already spoken for.

But it was impossible. As he glanced down at his own menu, she took in his dark brown, thick hair and impossibly long eyelashes that she knew hid those gorgeous blue-green eyes. He'd removed his tie, leaving his shirt open at the neck, and an image of her lips on his collarbone made her swallow hard.

He looked up, catching her watching, and she felt heat envelop her cheeks.

Again.

"See anything good?" His eyebrows were up, and she couldn't tell if he meant the double entendre, or if she was just hearing it that way.

"Um, yes." *God, yes.* "Everything looks good . . . here."

She closed her eyes and slid the menu upward to hide her face. She needed to get a grip. It wasn't like she hadn't dated, like, ever. She had proverbial notches on her bedpost. A few, and they were faded, but still.

Sitting here in this booth, in this dimly lit pub, with this drool-worthy man was kicking off all sorts of fantasies she hadn't even known she harbored.

Molly chose that moment to arrive back at the table with their drinks—Delaney's seltzer and some sort of foamy draft beer for him. She flipped open her pad, and after Delaney ordered a salad, she *knew* she saw Molly wink as she turned to get Dr. Mackenzie's order.

"I'll have the special." He slid his beer over. "Delaney? Don't you want something besides rabbit food?"

"You know what? Actually, I do. I'll have the special, too. Thank you."

She saw a triumphant look pass from him to Molly, and now she *knew* they'd been talking about her before she'd come in. She just wished she knew what he'd said.

When Molly headed back to the kitchen, Delaney reached for her notebook. She was getting the strong sense that he was anxious to be free of this dinner—and her—

so she might as well get started putting him out of his misery.

However, when she set the notebook on the table and went fishing for a pen, he picked up the little pad and put it down on the seat beside him.

"Later," he said. "Until I have food, I can't think. And since you've worked at least as many hours as I have today, I imagine you could use an hour of downtime before we tackle this, right?"

"Maybe?" She wasn't sure what to answer. He suddenly didn't sound like a man quite so eager to be free of her.

He picked up his beer and handed her the glass of seltzer. "Shall we toast?"

She laughed uncomfortably. "Depends on whether you still think I'm the enemy." She peered into her drink. "Did you have your girlfriend spike this, by any chance?"

"My—" He looked confused until she pointed at Molly. "Oh. Molly. No, not my girlfriend."

"Oh. Sorry. I thought—"

"Just friends," he said, and was she imagining the firmness in his tone? Was he making really sure she knew? Her stomach commenced its earlier gymnastics at the possibility he really was single.

He sipped his beer. "And no, I am pretty convinced you're not the enemy. Never thought you were. As for the spiking, as far as I know, you haven't given her any reason to take out her Italian temper on you."

"I hear a *yet* at the end of that sentence."

He laughed. "She *is* sort of a mama bear in a tiny package. Better be careful."

"Gotcha. Did you work out some sort of signal before I got here, in case I try to talk about cutting your favorite programs? Like, one blink—add chili pepper to her mostaccioli—two blinks—chili pepper *and* jalapenos?"

"Absolutely." He laughed softly as he set down his beer

and looked at her intently. "So just a request for you. Any chance you could stop calling me Dr. Mackenzie and use my first name? I'm pretty sure you know what it is by now."

Delaney cringed. "I'm not sure I can."

"Because?" He drew his eyebrows together.

"Because the voice of my father—who is very much alive, I should clarify—will haunt me. He beat a lot of things into my head over the years, and one of them was *thou shalt always address doctors with their appropriate title*."

"I'm going to take a wild stab here and guess that he's a doctor?"

"Surgeon, actually." She nodded. "Cardiothoracic."

He raised his eyebrows. "I'm impressed."

"That's a pretty standard reaction." She tried to quell the feeling that always rose when people got unduly impressed with his position, but had never met the man.

"One that's gotten old over the years?"

"Little bit, yeah." She tipped her head, feeling guilty. "But he deserves it. He's worked hard for a long time to get where he is."

"That's quite a pair of shoes to fill." He shrugged. "Unless he's one of those dads who'd be happy with whatever career choice you made, of course."

"He's not. Doctor or bust."

"Ouch. But you're in medicine, at least."

"Not the same, unfortunately. I don't get any fancy initials after *my* name."

Dr. Mackenzie tipped his head. "MBA doesn't count?"

"They're not the *right* initials."

"Ah, I see." He took a sip of his beer. "Finance is a perfectly respectable field. I mean, it's no secret between us that it's my least favorite department at Mercy, but it's—necessary."

She rolled her eyes. "Thank you."

He laughed. "Sorry. So did dear old dad have med-school dreams for you?"

Delaney nodded. "Despite the fact that I fainted on frog dissection day in tenth grade, yes."

"You didn't."

"Oh, I did." She lifted her hair and pointed at her right temple. "I still have the scar from where I hit the lab table on the way down."

He leaned closer, then reached out his index finger to trace the scar. She swallowed hard at his touch.

"Ouch," he said. "You must have gone down hard."

He brushed her hair back down over the scar, and maybe it was her imagination, but he didn't seem to want to pull his hand back.

"Ten stitches. That should have been my first sign that med school would be a disaster."

"Wait. Did you actually *go* to med school?"

"Did."

He drew his eyebrows together. "Did you *want* to go? Or did you have to?"

"A little bit of both, probably, but I really did want to be a doctor."

"Wow." He raised his eyebrows as he drank another swallow of his beer. "What happened?"

She took a deep breath, still feeling the choke of failure every time she pictured herself throwing up in the ladies' room outside the dissection suite. "I dropped out during hands."

He set down his beer, studying her, but instead of making her feel uncomfortable, it made her feel—warm. Then he reached across the table and touched her fingers with his—just a light stroke, not even a squeeze—before he pulled back.

"Hands were the worst for me, too."

"Really?"

"Totally. And I didn't expect it. That was the hardest part."

"Exactly." She sipped her seltzer, grateful for his understanding.

"So that was it for you? You never went back after that?"

Delaney shook her head. "I just—couldn't. Straw, camel's back, you know. Other—stuff—had happened, too." Like two weeks before that, when she'd seen the bulletin board in the oncology suite's break room, full of pictures of children who were no longer here, and had run out of the building in tears.

"And yet after all of that, you still chose to work in a hospital?"

She nodded. "In the executive wing, as you've pointed out on more than one occasion. We deal with numbers up there, not humans."

Molly appeared with their salads, sliding them onto the table and setting down silverware. "Enjoy! Dinners will be out in a few minutes."

Delaney tossed her salad with her fork, dying to dig in, but not wanting to appear half-starved. "Does anyone call you Joshua?"

"Um, my mother used to when I was in trouble. Millie does sometimes when she's perturbed at me. Why?"

"Because I've been thinking of you as Dr. Mackenzie all week, and you just asked me to call you Josh, and . . . I'm sorry. It's just—you seem like more of a Joshua to me."

"Huh. I don't know what to say to that."

"I'm sorry." She waved her fork. "Just struck me. I'll try to call you Josh."

"I answer to either, but if I twitch first, it's because I think I'm in trouble." He winked. "However, I think it'll sound much better coming from you than it does from Millie."

Delaney felt her cheeks heat up at his words. Was he flirting? Sort of? It'd been so long since she'd played the dating game that she couldn't even tell anymore.

Not that this was a date. Of course it wasn't.

But in the garlic-scented air, in a booth small enough that they kept bumping knees, just close enough that she could tell he'd jumped in the shower before coming here to meet her, it was hard not to imagine what it might be like if this *was* a date.

And despite the professional ethics that should have had her running the other way, all she wanted to do was stay.

Chapter 13

Joshua pointed to her salad. "You have to be starving. Eat."

She picked up her fork, grateful for the distraction, and they both dug in like they hadn't eaten all day. Delaney expected the silence to stretch long and uncomfortable between them, but it didn't. The pub was filling up with its second round of diners—those coming out of the early show at the movie theater next door, or getting off a second shift somewhere else in town. Pans clattered in the kitchen, the hum of voices was low and animated, and the smell of garlic was going to stick deliciously to her hair until she washed it in the morning.

"So, what brought you to Echo Lake?" He set his fork down and slid his salad plate to the end of the table.

"My parents, actually. When Dad took the job at Mercy—"

"Wait." Joshua put up a hand. "Your dad is *the* Dr. Blair?"

"Yes." She took a breath. "And he would love the way you emphasized the word *the* in that description."

"Holy—wow. I had no idea."

"Does that give me points in the positive direction? Or negative?"

"Neither. I don't know him personally. He doesn't do

pediatric surgeries, that I know of. I just know him by reputation."

"Which is?" Delaney braced herself. Her dad was one of the most skilled surgeons in his field—consulting at Mass General, Cleveland, and Johns Hopkins—but his abrasive, condescending manner had never enamored him to his staff or colleagues.

Joshua paused. "That's not really fair to ask, since he's your father."

"It's okay. I know him pretty well. And I know his reputation. He's not the easiest person to work with."

"He's a brilliant surgeon."

"That is true."

Joshua smiled. "Should we go with that, then?"

She smiled. "Sure."

"Wow." He sat back. "I can't imagine the pressure of growing up as *that* Dr. Blair's daughter."

"I know. Poor me. I lived in a huge house, went to private school, got a car for my birthday, and had med school fully paid for. It was tough, let me tell you."

He laughed. "Sounds awful."

"Worst part was the housekeeper and nanny. Oh, and the Olympic-sized pool. I mean, who survives these things, right?"

"I'm so sorry. I had no idea." He put his hand on hers in mock sympathy, and before she could stop herself, she squeezed his fingers. He smiled. "Should we talk about something else?"

"Please. Yes. Let's. I can hardly bear it." She rolled her eyes, but didn't pull her hand away. He didn't either—not for a few seconds, when he seemed to realize it was still touching hers.

Molly chose that moment to deliver their dinners—the chicken and mostaccioli special for both of them—and clear their salad plates. Delaney saw her eyes freeze on their entwined fingers, and then go wide.

"Everything good?" she asked.

Joshua looked up, pulling his hand back. "Everything's great."

"You need any coffee?" Her eyebrows went up, and a tiny alarm rang in Delaney's stomach. It was kind of odd to order coffee mid-meal, wasn't it?

"Nope. Don't need coffee yet, thanks."

"You're sure?"

He nodded. "Delaney? Coffee?"

Molly turned to her, and Delaney could tell she was straining to do the waitress-smile thing. "Coffee?"

"I'm all set, thanks. Maybe in a bit."

"Okay. *Mangia taj!*"

Delaney smiled as she picked up her fork. "What does that mean? Do you know?"

"It means shut up and eat, but somehow it doesn't sound so rude in Italian."

"Ah." She unwrapped a pat of butter and spread it on a hot, yeasty roll that had to have just come out of the oven. "God, this smells good."

"Mama B is a genius back there."

They took a few bites, and Delaney sighed when she caught the mix of spices and tender chicken on her tongue. "I think I was meant to be Italian."

"Mama B would be thrilled to hear you say that." He lifted his water glass, but didn't drink. "So I know how your father ended up here—but what about you? Were the two of you a package deal?"

"No." She shivered, hating that so many people thought so. "Definitely not. He worked here for years before I decided to leave Mass General and move up here."

His eyes widened. "Wow. That's quite a change of pace."

"Yeah." She nodded. "I was commuting in from the North Shore every day, and then Dad got this job, and I started coming up to visit Mom once in a while on weekends." She shrugged. "I don't know. I kind of fell in love with Echo Lake—the pace, the trees, the sunsets—and when I saw a posting for the finance office, I sort of applied on a lark."

"I imagine having a famous surgeon as a father here didn't hurt your chances."

Delaney felt her hands clench in her lap at his words. This is what everyone thought, so it shouldn't stab at her to hear him voice what she already knew was the prevailing opinion.

But it did.

She wanted him to believe she'd gotten the job on her own experience and education, wanted him to believe she deserved that position—and the one above it, maybe, if things worked out.

At the moment, that seemed like a really long shot.

"I believe I was hired on my own merits. He didn't even know I'd applied."

She tried to keep the tightness out of her voice, but when he sat back, she realized she'd done a lousy job.

He raised his eyebrows. "Sorry. I didn't mean to imply— sore subject?"

"Little bit, yes." She picked up her fork, waving it carelessly. "It's okay. You're one of many." And he'd be one of many who—if she did manage to capture the CFO position—would believe famous-surgeon daddy paved the way to that, too.

"I'm sure you're very good at your job." His voice was quieter, apologetic, but his supposition still rankled her.

"I am." She took a deep breath. "But enough about me and my questionable path to the golden palace. What brought *you* to Mercy?"

"I grew up here, actually. Went to UVM for med school, and came the whole two hours back down here."

"Did you always know you wanted to be a doctor?"

He averted his eyes for a long moment, and she suspected there was a story there. "Not until high school. Have you ever met Ethan and Josie Miller?"

Delaney shook her head. "I've heard of them, but no. They run Avery's House, right?"

"And Snowflake Village."

"Right." She remembered the pictures on his office wall—remembered wondering whether he was involved as well. "Do you have something to do with Avery's House, too?"

He nodded. "My official title is medical director, but really, I just do rounds there every day and serve as backup if the nurses have questions."

"That sounds like a full-time job."

"Nah. It's really not. Mercy is more than a full-time job. Avery's House is the fun part of the day."

"How'd you get involved?"

"Josie was in one of those Big Sister–Little Sister programs in high school, and she ended up being paired with this awesome little kid named Avery." Joshua sighed. "So we all hung out with Avery a lot—me and Molly, along with Josie and Ethan. She had a pretty hellish life, so we sort of took her under our wings. But then she was diagnosed with a neuroblastoma."

"Oh, God." Delaney put her hand to her mouth.

She'd done just enough first-year med school to know the survival rates of childhood brain tumors, and though it was getting better, it still wasn't great.

"Yeah." He frowned, and Delaney could practically see memories skittering through his brain. "She didn't—make it, and then the whole thing completely blew Ethan and Josie to pieces, and it just . . . was terrible."

"I'm really sorry."

She wished she couldn't relate, but anytime she thought of Parker, the pain was still sharp and ugly, even after all these years.

"So did they start Avery's House? They're so—young."

Delaney envied the sense of purpose they shared. What had *she* done to honor Parker's memory, really? She struggled daily to answer that question, still.

He shrugged. "Sort of. Josie left town right after it happened. She just couldn't take it here—couldn't be where the memories were eating her alive. Ethan stayed, and when the old hotel went up for sale, he did everything in his power to buy it and turn it into what it is today. And then Josie came back two years ago, and the rest is history, I guess. Avery kind of drove all of us into what we're doing today."

"It sounds like an incredible place."

"You'll have to come see it one of these days." He nodded thoughtfully, like the idea had just occurred to him. "I think you'd like it there."

She smiled. It almost sounded like a second-date invitation . . . if this were, in fact, a first date.

A little while later, she noticed both of them had managed to clear their plates. Once they'd steered away from Avery, their conversation had flowed comfortably, interspersed with laughter.

Delaney pointed at the table. "Good thing we weren't hungry."

He laughed. "Want dessert?"

"God, no. I couldn't eat another bite."

"You sure?" He raised his eyebrows. "Have you tasted Mama B's tiramisu?"

Delaney's mouth watered, and she swallowed without meaning to. "I'll have to run six miles tomorrow to work off just this dinner. I'm not sure I'm up for seven."

"No problem. She makes the no-calorie version on Fridays." Joshua signaled for Molly, who appeared immediately, as if she'd been waiting eagerly to be called over.

She looked back and forth at them. "Ready for coffee now?"

"I think we are." He smiled, and Molly got a self-satisfied look on her face. It disappeared when he said, "I think we'll have some tiramisu as well."

"Really?" Confusion clouded her face, and Delaney wished she could read the woman's mind.

"Really. Delaney? Coffee?"

"Please." She nodded, and Molly flashed her that fake smile again.

"So two coffees, two tiramisus?"

Joshua nodded.

"You want cream with your coffee?" Molly's eyebrows went up.

"No. Black's good."

"You're sure."

Delaney almost smiled. Creamers had to be the extraction signal, and he was decidedly not using it.

She was almost embarrassed at how giddy that made her feel.

"All right." Josh slid her notebook toward her. "Now that we have food on board, should we get to the business part of this business dinner?"

The giddy feeling whooshed out.

Chapter 14

Josh looked at Delaney as she fished a pen out of her purse, and for about the hundredth time that hour, he thought about what it might be like to kiss her. As he'd watched her talk about med school and her father, he'd been struck by the emotions flipping over her face, and he couldn't believe he'd actually reached out to touch her. Multiple times, for God's sake.

Who did that at a business dinner?

Someone who needed to get control of himself, that's who.

He sat up straighter and cleared his throat, determined to handle whatever came next in a professional, detached manner. Yeah, she was hot. And yeah, he could imagine taking her out to the lake after dinner, finding a sweet spot to watch the sunset, kissing her, taking her home.

But no. He had to focus on why they were here, and concentrating on the pulse in her throat wasn't getting him anywhere but completely distracted, dammit.

"Okay." He motioned toward the notebook. "Where are we at? I'm assuming you've ditched the original list?"

"Yes, in a sense."

"In *what* sense? I thought we agreed it was—"

"Ill-informed? Presumptuous?"

He shook his head. "Just numbers-informed, rather than—"

"Reality?"

He sighed. "Are you going to interrupt every sentence I try here?"

"Possibly. But I let you get that one out, so maybe not." She winked, and he couldn't help but smile.

"Fine." He sat back. "You speak. I'll listen."

"Excellent plan." She squared her shoulders. "Okay, here's where we're at. I've got a number I have to meet, or there is very real danger that discussion could move toward transferring pediatrics out of this hospital altogether."

"What?"

She slid a piece of paper toward him. "Board minutes from the last meeting. My admin was asked to type them up. She forgot a copy on my desk."

He raised his eyebrows. "Forgot?"

"It happens." She raised hers to match. "Tell me after you read it whether you're glad she's—forgetful."

He picked up the page and scanned it quickly, feeling his eyes widen as he did. This particular meeting had been facilitated by some sort of company the hospital had brought in to help them think creatively about budgeting issues, and it looked like the floor had been open for a good long time so board members could toss ideas on the table, willy-nilly. A lot of the ones Megan had typed up were just plain ridiculous or untenable, but one that had gotten some discussion traction was the idea of shuttering the pediatric department for all but emergency cases, and funding transport to Boston Children's for the rest.

"Why pediatrics?" He set the paper down, feeling his gut sink.

She handed him another piece of paper, a frown taking over her face. "Because of this." As he scanned the figures, she cleared her throat uncomfortably. "It's not a profitable department right now—hasn't been for three years running. And with Boston only two-ish hours away by ambulance, there's a case to be made for turning the floor space into something that'll bring in the dollars."

He peered at her over the paper, tensing for her answer to the question at the top of his mind. "Do you agree?"

"No." She shook her head firmly. "But I also can't find even a dollar to cut from your current budget. So . . . let's talk about the opposite approach. We need to find us a Daddy Warbucks."

"Ah." He slid the papers back toward her. "Well, that shouldn't be hard, sitting here in rural Vermont."

"Am I hearing tone?"

"Sorry. Yes. It's a good idea, but where exactly do you plan to look? We're a little low on millionaires here in Echo Lake."

"The big hospital fund-raiser is next week, right?"

"Ye-es. You're thinking we'll find deep-enough pockets there?" He pointed at the stack of papers. "To get to the number you've got on that list?"

"Maybe. Maybe not." She brought the tip of her pen to her mouth, and he had to blink hard to stop staring at the way her lips teased it as she pondered. "I'm checking the records on previous years to see if there's anyone in particular who might have a soft spot for pediatrics."

"Okay, but if that doesn't work out, do you have a plan B?"

"Sort of." She pointed at him with the pen. "All that paperwork I saw on your desk—any chance any of it is grant proposals you haven't finished?"

"A whole folder of it, yes. But they don't add up to the number you're looking at."

"They could be a start, though, right?"

He shrugged slowly. "Maybe? But those things take

eons to compose, and even longer to go through all of the channels. And even then, there's no guarantee we'll end up getting the money. It's a crapshoot."

"True, but it might buy us a little time. If we can show that we've got *x* number of dollars possibly coming in within *x* number of weeks or months, it might back the board off a little bit. If we work together on the proposals, maybe it wouldn't take so long."

Work together? When, for God's sake? Both of them were already working double shifts, for all intents and purposes. There *wasn't* any time.

He sighed. "I don't know, Delaney. Pretty sure you can think of a lot more interesting things to do than fill out grant paperwork. Not sure it makes sense to invest that much effort into a non-guarantee at this point."

"*Everybody* can think of more interesting things to do than that. But that money's out there. Somebody's going to get it. Why not us?"

He put up his hands. Clearly, she'd already decided they were doing the grant paperwork. "Okay. We'll work on the grants, and we'll go pocket to pocket at the dinner. But let me ask you this—is there a second magic number? If we can't get to the target they gave you, is there another one that, if we hit it, could at least compel the board to back off for a bit? One that shows we're doing everything we can?"

She shook her head. "I have no idea. That's why I have a plan C. But I need you."

He blinked, hearing the words in a different context, dammit. Then he shook his head.

"Need me?"

He saw color wash her cheeks . . . again. If he was a better person, he wouldn't be quite so thrilled that he could make her blush so easily. She reached for her water glass, and he swore he tried to stop, but his damn eyes wouldn't unlock themselves from her lips as she sipped, then swallowed. The cool water left a delicious sheen that made her look so damn kissable he had to close his eyes for a long moment. Jesus. He needed some sleep. Yeah, that had to be it.

She tapped her pen against her lips, obviously having no idea how the repetitive motion was torturing him. Then she tapped on the paper, seeming to come to a decision.

"You and I both know that if the board decides to shut down pediatrics, there will be a public uproar, right? They know it, too, so if they're truly going to look at this option, one of the first things they're going to do is fire up the spin machine. They're going to try to convince people that the department is bare bones and underutilized, and they'll try to make it sound like we're actually *improving* pediatric care by getting kids faster, better access to Boston hospitals."

Josh shook his head. Yes, he could imagine the meetings.

"So," she continued, "I think our best bet is to work the publicity machine ourselves. First side to get the spin *controls* the spin, right?"

He shook his head again, trying to follow her train of thought. "How do you propose to—quote—'work the machine'?"

He saw a sparkle in her eyes. "We make Mercy Hospital's pediatric department the focus of as much positive news as we can, as widely as we can, for the next few weeks."

"How do we do that?"

"I was hoping you'd ask." She smiled and pulled a third piece of paper from her notebook, sliding it toward him. "This is a quick list I drew up this morning—initiatives I see working, unique treatments we could publicize, kids we could profile—all with the end goal of making this entire community see how valuable this pediatric department is to the area."

She paused as he picked up the list. "And with the *end* end goal of making the board too afraid to risk community outrage by closing it down."

"So what did he say?" Megan handed Delaney a Dunkin' Donuts coffee as she blasted through the front door of Delaney's condo the next morning. "And why are we wearing a dress on a Saturday morning?"

Delaney looked down at the peach-colored dress she'd finally settled on after discarding one of her suits as too stiff, and her shorts as too casual.

"I have another—meeting—this morning."

Megan lifted her eyebrows as she settled her butt on one of Delaney's counter stools. "A meeting? With who?"

"Whom. Joshua."

Her eyebrows lifted farther. "We're finally on a first-name basis?"

"He keeps asking me to call him—Josh. At some point, it felt rude not to. But I think Joshua suits him better. He just seems like more of a Joshua to me." Delaney shrugged, taking a sip of the scalding-hot coffee.

Joshua. Delaney rolled the name around in her head, loving the sound of it.

"So I'm assuming dinner went well, if it's leading to breakfast? What'd he think of your ideas?"

Delaney pictured Joshua's face after she'd presented her publicity idea—a mix of disbelief, relief, and fear competing for control.

"It took him a few minutes to process, but in the end, I think he agreed with me."

"That's good, right? Why don't you look happier about it?"

"Because I still don't know if it'll work. This plan is a seriously last-ditch effort."

Megan looked hurt. "Hey, we worked hard on that list. There's a lot of good stuff going on at Mercy, and nobody knows about it. This is a good plan."

"I know. He thinks it's worth a shot." Delaney clasped a gold locket around her neck and checked her reflection in the mirror. "He invited me to Avery's House this morning. Some reporter from the *Boston Globe* is coming to interview Ethan and Josie Miller about the house, and I think I convinced him that maybe we can get her interested in Mercy as well."

"I'll call Felicity Johnson from WFET this morning. She owes me a favor. I bet I can get something on within a week."

Delaney felt her own eyebrows rise this time. "What *kind* of a favor?"

"Can't tell." Megan shook her head. "But trust me. She'll do this. And I've got calls in to the *Free Press* and the *Times Argus* and the *Herald*. We'll *kill* them with coverage. The board will never know what hit them."

"They'll have to be overwhelmed with all of the positive energy." Delaney smiled. "Right?"

"Let's hope so." Megan stood up and made a spinning motion with her hand. "Come on. Let's see you. I need to approve the sexy factor here."

"I'm not going for the sexy factor." Delaney did an obligatory spin, rolling her eyes. It wasn't like she hadn't spent half the night thinking about . . . sexy.

But sometime before dawn, as she'd woken up from a sweet dream that had her all hot and bothered, she'd given herself a firm shake. There was no future with a man like Joshua, who worked from dawn until way past dusk. Sure, he might be a great dinner date—funny and sweet wrapped up in a crazy-hot package—but she already knew what life with a doctor looked like.

She'd lived it, and she'd watched her mother live it, and when tragedy had struck, her parents' marriage had been so tenuous that they'd become just another tick on some statistician's scale—the kind that measured marital survival after a child's death.

Yes, they were still married, but her mother's room was fully on the other end of the house from her father's, and the only dinners they ate together were the ones they faked for Delaney's benefit, or the ones put on by one charitable group or another—the kind where Mom would pick out a new dress, make a salon appointment, and sit through the event with that empty smile she'd perfected after Parker's death.

Delaney had been dragged to enough of those dinners that she could predict the sound track down to the ten-minute mark. First there would be the comments on one another's dresses, which led inevitably to the latest fad in magic vegetables that let them *fit* into said dresses.

Eventually talk would come around to new boats, or next winter's vacations, and through it all ran a thread of quiet, but powerful, competition. Who made the most, who had the biggest whatever, who was traveling the farthest—it was always the undertone.

But the overwhelming feeling she left each event with was a disquieting realization that so many of the wives didn't even know their husbands—not really. How could they? The hours doctors kept were insane. Yes, the bank accounts were nice, and she knew some of those wives were in it exactly *for* those accounts, but really?

She knew figures were available for the divorce rate among physicians, but had anyone ever tried to calculate the empty-marriage rate?

She'd decided a long time ago that she was never going

to be one of those statistics. And as much as it pained her to realize it, entertaining any delusions about a possible future with Joshua was just inviting heartbreak.

"Why such a glum face?" Megan tipped her head as she adjusted a flyaway hair on Delaney's forehead, jarring her out of her memories. "I'd be happy to go in your place."

Delaney smiled, but she knew it looked forced. "I need to find me a nice auto mechanic or hardware store owner or something."

"You can't force yourself to fall for a nine-to-five guy, Laney—not if you're already falling for one who decidedly—isn't."

"Not falling."

"I call bullshit."

Delaney sighed. "Okay, then. How about this? It would be a very bad *idea* to fall for him."

"Agreed."

Delaney frowned. "You're not going to argue?"

"You'd just argue back, and we'd waste all that time. It's kind of pointless, when we both know you're already ten steps into quicksand here."

Delaney sat down hard on the other bar stool. "This isn't how this was supposed to go. It's completely unprofessional to have feelings for this guy. Which I don't. But if I did . . ."

"Can't control these things."

"Remember how I pictured him before you showed me his profile?"

"Middle-aged and sloppy? Yes."

"I'm just saying, I think I'd rather he was that."

"Guess the Fates had a different plan for you, honey."

"Stupid Fates."

Megan laughed, pulling out her phone to check the time. "When are you meeting Mister Not-Sloppy-Not-Old?"

Delaney looked at the clock over her sink. "Oh, God. Now. I have to go."

"I'll expect a full report later."

"Wish me luck." Delaney blew out a breath as she took one more look in the mirror. Her cheeks were pink, like she'd already run her miles this morning.

"I wish you luck *and* sex."

"Megan!"

"What?" Megan shrugged, feigning innocence. "I do!"

Delaney opened the door, waving her through. "I'll work on the luck, if it's all the same to you."

"Fine." Megan ducked through. "Then *I'll* wish for the sex."

Chapter 15

"So, Josh says you two are on a mission." Josie Miller leaned across the table at Avery's House late that afternoon, conspiracy in her tone. Despite her intent to stay for an hour or two at most, Delaney had been at the converted hotel for eight hours now, and she was ready to move in. She'd never seen a more gorgeous place in her entire life.

She shrugged uncomfortably, unsure of how much Josh had told Josie. She was dead sure he wouldn't have mentioned the confidential board minutes, but these were his best friends. What if he had? He and Ethan were currently giving the *Globe* reporter an extended tour of the house, hoping to drum up sympathy, donors, and a couple of feature spots for Mercy in one fell swoop.

Delaney picked her words carefully. "We're just trying to reach out and make sure people know all the good things going on."

That sounded plausible, right?

Josie eyed her curiously, like she could feel the bullshit oozing from Delaney's pores, but she didn't say anything.

Delaney looked out the back window, desperate to change the subject, and a riot of flowers caught her eye.

"Wow. It's gorgeous out there. Did you do the landscape design yourself?"

Josie looked at her for one beat too long, letting her know that she knew exactly what Delaney was doing, but for some reason, she let her get away with it.

"Do you know Molly Bellini?"

"Just met her last night, actually." Delaney nodded. "Is she a designer?"

"No. But she wields a mean shovel after a breakup."

Delaney laughed, then cringed. "Sorry. Not funny, I'm sure."

Josie shrugged. "It's okay. It wasn't meant to be. She's better single, most of the time. For now, anyway."

"So . . ." Delaney struggled to find the words to ask the question that had been burning in her stomach since last night. "Do she and Joshua ever date?"

"Not since middle school. So yes. Josh is single, if you're at all curious."

"What? No," Delaney stammered. "I don't—"

Josie rolled her eyes, but not unkindly. "Honey, I may be married, but I'm not blind. That man is one gorgeous specimen, and he's the nicest guy you'll ever meet, besides Ethan." She smiled fondly. "The two of them are quite a pair."

"I can't believe you've all known each other since high school."

"Friends forever, and all that." Delaney saw a cloud pass over Josie's face, but then her smile returned. "Just so you know, Josh has very definite plans about his future."

"Oh?" Delaney swallowed. She was about to get a talking-to. She could feel it.

"They include not getting serious with anyone until he has his own pediatric practice all established. This is why he doesn't have a girlfriend. He's pretty careful not to."

"Oh." Delaney's stomach fell, and she hated that it did so. "Really?"

"Yup. I mean, not that you care, particularly. Just want you to know that, even though you're not—whatever." She shrugged, but Delaney swore she could see amusement in her eyes. Still, there was a serious undertone she couldn't ignore.

She shifted uncomfortably. "Is this—are you giving me a warning?"

"Nah." Josie raised her eyebrows. "I'm giving you an abject challenge."

"Got any champagne, you guys?" Joshua came back into the kitchen of Avery's House after seeing off the reporter, his smile bigger than Delaney had seen it all week. "I think we just nailed a page one story."

"Really?" Josie leaped up from the table, hugging him hard. "That's fantastic!"

Ethan nodded as he gathered wineglasses from a top shelf and brought them to the table. "She said she got so much good stuff that she's going to split it into two top-fold Sunday features. First half runs this coming Sunday."

"Oh, my God." Josie motioned toward Delaney. "What about a tie-in to Mercy? Did she bite?"

Josh nodded, pulling out the chair next to Delaney. "She *loved* that angle. She's coming back up on Monday to do some spots on the floor. I need to talk to somebody about getting parental permission for her to talk to a couple of the kids. Delaney? Do you know who we should talk to?"

She nodded, already making a mental list. "I'm sure we can find out. Think we can get Charlotte's parents to okay it?"

"She'd be perfect. Let's try."

Just then, Molly Bellini blasted through the side door, then raised her eyebrows when she saw them sitting at the table. She raised her eyebrows even farther when she noticed Delaney, but shook her head quickly and refocused on Ethan.

"What are we celebrating, peeps?" She set down her purse and pulled out a chair, bouncing into it like she might pop right back out. "And yes, I'll have whatever we're having."

Ethan laughed. "It might be sparkling grape juice, at this rate. Not sure we have anything more serious here."

"Sounds good. Don't want to get too inebriated too early. I hate when people show up trashed to their own surprise parties."

The table went silent, and Delaney felt suddenly like the one person in the room who wasn't in on the joke.

"What are you talking about, Mols?" Joshua tipped his head and did a really good mystified look, if indeed they were trying to cover for a surprise party.

"Oh, come on." She looked around at all of them. "I'm so onto you. My birthday's in three days, it's Saturday, Mama gave me a rare night off, and Josie just happened to invite me up here for drinks?" She wrinkled her nose. "Which—okay, a little weird—turn out to be grape juice?"

"Highly suspicious." Ethan nodded as he opened the bottle of juice and poured the carbonated beverage into their glasses. "But you're wrong, Mols. No surprise party. This is it."

"Seriously?"

Josie turned to her. "Don't you think we'd find somewhere better to go than a kitchen? You spend half your life in a kitchen."

Molly eyed them all, including Delaney. Then she jumped up and pushed through the swinging doors that led to the living room. One second later, she pushed back through them and sat back down in her seat.

"Huh."

Josie giggled. "Think there was a herd of people out there waiting to yell *'Surprise!'*?"

"No."

"Sure." Josh leaned over and squeezed her shoulder. Delaney kind of wished it was hers.

"Fine. Maybe." Molly picked up her glass. "Okay, enough about me—you know, since nothing apparently *is* about me tonight. What are we toasting?"

Josie lifted her glass. "A successful interview with the *Boston Globe*."

"You nailed it?" Molly's eyes widened as she looked at Ethan and Joshua.

Ethan nodded. "We totally nailed it." Then he looked at his watch. "I'm starving. You guys want to throw some steaks on the grill?"

Josie put her hand to her mouth, looking stricken. "Oh, no. I never went for groceries today. We have lettuce, pickles, and an egg, I think."

He grimaced, looking around the table. "Anybody want to go out?"

Delaney felt suddenly out of place among this crowd who'd known each other since high school. They were so easy with one another—an ease that came only from a shared history . . . and a shared present. They probably hung out together every weekend.

Josie put her hand on Molly's. "Can you stand to go to Bellinis? Might be the only place we can get a table at this hour, if we call Mama B before we leave."

Molly sank down in her chair. "Now I *know* there's no

surprise party, because you people would never make me have it at my own flipping restaurant."

Josie and Ethan stood up, and Molly gathered her purse, eyes landing on Joshua and Delaney. "You two coming?"

Delaney shook her head. "Oh, thanks. I'd love to, but I need to get back to—"

"Come on." Josie grabbed her elbow. "We know you just ate there last night, but really, can you get too much Bellinis? You've barely eaten all day."

Delaney turned to Joshua. How'd they know about last night? And why did she get a secret little thrill knowing he'd maybe told them? "I don't want to crash your dinner. I was just here for the interview."

Joshua stood up, holding out a hand. "The interview ended up lasting all day. You must be starving, too. Come with us."

"Are you—sure?"

This was so awkward—him practically being forced to ask her while his three friends stood waiting.

He smiled, and her knees felt it first. "Can you stand another dinner with me?"

"I'm not at all sure."

Ethan laughed as he opened the door and motioned everyone outside. "Okay, we're settled. Molly? Ride with me and Josie? Josh and Delaney, want to follow?"

They all filed out the door, and when they got outside, Delaney automatically started for her own car as Josie, Ethan, and Molly piled into an SUV at the edge of the driveway.

Before she got to her car, Joshua put a hand on her elbow. "Want to ride down there with me?" He waved as the SUV left the driveway, and then he leaned close. "This totally *is* Molly's surprise party. Parking down there's going to be a nightmare. Ride with me. I promise I'll bring you back whenever you want to leave."

"I don't know, Joshua. I should probably get home. You have plans already. I don't want to crash. Really."

"You wouldn't be crashing. Half of Echo Lake will be there. It's going to be loud and crazy and Italian, in all the best ways. You'll be family by the time you finish your first drink."

She smiled. "Is that how Bellinis parties work?"

"All the ones I've seen." He shrugged. "Come with me, Delaney. I'd really like it if you would."

"Have I mentioned the part about how I break out in hives in crowds?"

"Stranger danger?" He winked.

"Pretty much. Just one of the reasons I work on the sixth floor. Fewer humans up there."

He laughed. "Well, from what I've seen this week, nobody would know you're clinically terrified. You've handled the third-floor strangers pretty well."

"Right." She rolled her eyes. "Those ones are scared not to be nice to me. They're all sure I have their employee ID numbers recorded on my layoff sheet."

"True." He nodded, smiling. Then he put his arm around her shoulders and squeezed gently, steering them toward his truck. "Come on. Let's go to the party. I have a feeling you get out just about as much as I do these days. We could both use a couple of hours away from the hospital, don't you think?"

She bit her lip as he opened the truck door, letting his hand slide down her back. When she turned to answer, she found herself deliciously trapped between his body and the truck, and for a long moment, neither of them spoke. His eyes went to her lips, and she felt her breathing go shallow as her own eyes traced his five o'clock shadow, then the open collar of his shirt, then back up to his eyes, which had cruised silently from friendly and amused to downright hot.

She swallowed. Oh, God. He was going to kiss her.

And oh, *God*, she was dying for him to. If he *didn't* kiss her right now, *she* was going to kiss *him*.

Then he closed his eyes tightly for a brief second, stepping back. "We should—the party."

"Right." She swallowed. "Of course."

He took her hand to help her into the truck, but didn't linger this time. Instead, he closed the door and headed around the truck, leaving Delaney to attempt a two-second recovery before he got into the other side.

He opened his door and slid inside, throwing her a friendly smile, like the previous minute hadn't actually happened. "Ready?"

She took a deep breath. *More ready than either of us wants to know right now.*

"Ready."

"Quick piece of advice, since this is your first Bellini party." He started the engine, then squeezed her knee. "No matter how hard Molly's dad tries, do *not* have more than one of his killer drinks, or I will have to carry you out of there."

Delaney's stomach jumped again, picturing him slinging her over his shoulder and taking her home. She wished the thought wasn't so appealing.

"I might have three, just to see if you can do it."

Oh. God. Had she really just said that?

He looked over, his eyebrows up.

Yep. She'd said that.

He cleared his throat. "I'll keep that in mind."

"So." Ethan sidled up to the bar next to Josh two hours later, lifting a beer as he scanned the crowd.

"So—what?"

"So—Delaney."

Josh's eyes locked on her, sitting in a booth across the

restaurant with Josie. She was laughing at something Josie'd just said, and though he couldn't hear the sound over the noise of the crowd, he'd heard it last night in that same booth, and he could feel it in his gut.

He looked sidelong at Ethan. "Have you been assigned by Josie and Molly to get the scoop?"

"Absolutely."

Josh rolled his eyes, lifting his beer to his lips, trying not to think of her tongue nervously licking her own lips just a couple of hours ago, sending him to a fresh hell as he'd watched.

"Colleague. She's just a colleague."

"You're sure?"

"Let me ask you something." Josh turned toward him. "Why is it that everyone is suddenly so interested in my nonexistent dating life?"

Ethan shrugged, a sly smile on his face. "Maybe because it looks like the nonexistent part might be waning?"

"We're not dating."

"I know. Self-imposed hospital-employee dating ban and all."

"Exactly."

"So tell me this—if you didn't work with her, would you want to date her?"

Josh paused, not willing to answer. His eyes traveled to the far booth again, and he could see Delaney's shoulder where her lacy summer sweater had slipped down. He had an overwhelming urge to push through the crowd, kiss that shoulder, and then slide the fabric back up for her.

He cleared his throat. "I might."

"You're in so much trouble, buddy." Ethan laughed as he clapped him on the shoulder. "Tell you what. I'll cover for you if you want to go offer her a ride home. If you leave now, you might be able to catch the sunset down at Twilight Cove."

"I'm not dragging her out to our old high school make-out spot."

"She didn't grow up here. She won't know. She'll just think you're a sucker for sunsets."

Josh rolled his eyes. "You know, you're starting to sound an awful lot like a sappy old married guy."

"Scary, isn't it?" Ethan put his empty bottle on the bar. "Go get the girl, Josh."

"I don't have time to date somebody. You know that. It'll end just like the rest of them have, and Delaney's too—nice—to do that to."

"Or . . . maybe it *won't* end like the rest of them have. Maybe she's different."

Josh paused, picturing her walking around his pediatric floor all week. "Oh, she's definitely different."

"Well? How can you not want to at least find out if there might be something there? Don't be a dumbass, or you'll end up watching somebody *else* leave with her. How's that gonna feel?" Ethan clapped him on the shoulder again, then turned to head across the room toward Josie and Delaney.

Josh *did* want to find out if there was something. He so did. But who was he kidding? The heat between them at his truck earlier could have seared them both, had he actually leaned in and kissed her. She'd wanted him to—he'd felt it. But really, that's what would do him in eventually. He'd ask her out on a real date, things would maybe go well, and a month down the road, she'd be itching for more time together and he'd be unable to deliver it.

And *kaput*.

That's how his relationships went. Every single time. Even the one that he'd *thought* was different.

Since Nicole, he hadn't actually dated women he could

envision spending more than a month with, anyway, but still. Between the hospital and Avery's House, he was lucky to have five free hours a week. It wasn't fair to make any woman think he had any more to give than that right now.

Maybe someday, when he had his own practice and could make his own schedule, he could finally think about more than casual, once-in-a-great-while dating. But right now, with both of his workplaces operating on shoestring budgets and not enough people, he was much better off keeping to himself.

His parents had sacrificed everything so he could be a doctor, and then they'd died before he'd even graduated. They'd been so tied down with his debt that they hadn't even retired yet, and the guilt of that still ate at him every day. So no way was he going to do his job halfway. Ever. He owed them that.

He looked at Delaney again, but this time, she was looking straight at him, and he felt suddenly guilty for leaving her alone for so long. She didn't know a soul besides Josie and Ethan in this crowd of Bellini family members and restaurant regulars.

Then his view was interrupted as Molly's dad pushed through the crowd with a pitcher of his signature lemonade, headed straight for Josie and Delaney's table. *Ah, hell.* If that man filled up their glasses again, both he and Ethan would be hauling the women out of here in wheelbarrows tonight.

He headed across the bar, determined to get to Delaney before she regretted the entire evening.

Chapter 16

"Delaney, have you tried my lemonade yet?" Papi held up a frosty pitcher, tipping it toward her empty glass. Delaney blinked hard, realizing she was seeing two of him. Either she was way more tired than she thought, or the delicious lemonade she'd just inhaled was spiked.

She pulled her glass toward her. "Just finished one, Mr. Bellini. I think I'm all set."

He raised his eyebrows. "You come to my restaurant for a private party—you call me Papi. That's the way it goes. And you drink my lemonade."

He poured the icy liquid into her glass, then turned to Josie. "Josie? You want some more?"

Josie shook her head. "One's good for me, Papi."

"Okay, then. You girls have fun. You want we should start the music?" He did a funny jig-style dance move, making both of them laugh, then moved back toward the bar, stopping to refill glasses along the way.

Knowing she probably shouldn't, Delaney took a long sip of the lemonade, loving the way it slid down her throat with both a chill and a tiny burn. It was getting hot in the restaurant, and the drink was refreshing and delicious.

"Careful with that." Josie pointed at her glass. "They catch up with you."

"Is this the drink Joshua warned me about?"

Josie tipped her head. "Joshua?" Then she smiled. "Yes, this is exactly the one he warned you about."

Delaney subtly flexed her fingers, blinking her eyes as she looked down at her lap. "Does the fact that I see fifteen fingers and three hands mean I've maybe had enough?"

"Sounds like it." Josie laughed as she pulled Delaney's glass toward her, then looked into her eyes. "You don't drink often, do you?"

"Hardly ever." Delaney shook her head, which suddenly seemed awfully dizzy. This reminded her of that time she'd had two drinks at a Chinese restaurant, having no indication they were even alcoholic until she'd stumbled on her way to the bathroom. When she'd checked the ingredient list later, she'd realized that though the drink tasted just like a sweet summer lemonade, there was absolutely *nothing* nonalcoholic *in* the damn glass.

"Oh, God. What will Joshua think?" She blinked again, trying to bring Josie's two heads back onto her neck. *Holy cow.* She'd flown right past pleasantly buzzed in 0.5 seconds. "What does Papi put *in* this stuff?"

Josie smiled. "Nobody knows. It's a secret recipe from the old country, he says. He loves that everybody always downs at least a glass before it really hits. That way, he can get them to do his bidding before they know they're drunk."

"That's—terrible."

She shrugged. "It's Papi. He just likes everybody to have a good time." Josie glanced over Delaney's shoulder as she slid farther into the booth. "I think the men smell trouble. Here they come to rescue us."

Ethan sat down next to her, then tipped his head as he looked at Delaney. "Uh-oh." He winked. "Has Papi been feeding Delaney his lemonade?"

Delaney closed her eyes, nodding carefully. "I feel a

little bit like I'm being hazed. Give the new gal the mystery punch, you know?"

"Josh didn't warn you to steer clear of it?"

"I did too."

Delaney snapped her head up as she heard Joshua's voice right beside her. He was looking down on her with an expression that was half-amused, half-concerned. She slid over in the booth to make room for him, but did it gingerly. Then she propped her chin on her hand, hoping it would help her head stop swimming.

She smelled the light cinnamon of his aftershave and leaned slightly to the left to catch a better whiff, but her balance was obviously off, because before she knew it, her head was leaning on his shoulder.

She tried to right herself—she swore she did, but her head seemed quite happy exactly where it was, dammit.

Ethan raised his eyebrows. "Did you tell her to avoid the lemonade, in particular?"

"I did." Joshua cringed, looking down at her carefully, sliding his arm around her. "Didn't I?"

"You told me he made killer drinks. I didn't realize you meant—lemonade. Who spikes lemonade?"

"Papi." All three of them laughed.

Joshua squeezed her lightly. "You okay?"

"Yup." Delaney tried to focus as she looked up at him. "But you have an awful lot of noses for a doctor."

Ethan shook his head. "Can't believe you let her drink the lemonade." Then he took Josie's hand. "How about a dance?"

"Um . . ." Josie's worried eyes flitted between Delaney and Joshua, like she wasn't sure whether she should leave them alone.

"Come on." Ethan gave her arm a tug as he slid out of the booth, and Delaney almost laughed at his obvious attempt to leave Joshua alone with her. "We'll see you two later."

As the jukebox cranked out an old country song, Joshua squeezed her hand. "I should have—"

"Been more specific?" She raised her eyebrows.

"Been more attentive."

Her stomach warmed, and it wasn't just because of the lemonade. His thumb was stroking her hand, and maybe it was the alcohol, but it was all she could do to not kiss him.

He adjusted her sweater, and was it her imagination? Or did his fingers linger on her shoulder?

He leaned close to her ear, and this time she definitely wasn't imagining the linger. "Do you want to get out of here?"

Oh, heck yes. She wanted to get out of here, find a secluded spot by the lake, and let him kiss her senseless.

She cleared her throat. "I'm fine. It's Molly's party. Wouldn't be polite to sneak out early on one of your best friends."

He laughed and gave her hand a little tug. "Come on. Let's go get some fresh air. It's a good antidote for Papi's Poison."

Her eyes widened. "Is that what he calls it?"

"No. That's what everyone *else* calls it."

They said their good-byes to Josie and Ethan, and as they wound their way through the tables toward the door, Delaney felt Joshua's hand on her lower back, helping to keep her admittedly tipsy feet from tripping over themselves.

Could she blame Papi's Poison tomorrow morning if she made a monumental mistake tonight?

She shook her head. If she was already clear-minded enough to be making a *plan* to blame the lemonade, it might be hard to make that defense.

When they reached Joshua's truck, he opened the passenger door. He had one hand on the door and one on the side of the truck, and as she turned slowly around, she found herself deliciously trapped. His eyes locked on her lips, but then he shook his head and closed his eyes.

"What's the matter?" Delaney's voice was quiet, tight. Did he *not* want to kiss her?

Instead of answering, he dropped his hand from the door and slid it slowly along her neck and through her hair, pulling her head into his chest.

"You're killing me," he said, and she could hear the pain in his voice.

"Not intentionally," she whispered against his shirt.

He groaned softly. "That's the worst part." He slid his other arm around her and hugged her tightly.

After a moment, she pulled back, looking into his eyes. "We could always go back in. If you down some of Papi's Poison, too, then we can't be responsible for our actions, right?"

Joshua chuckled. "I'm sure we wouldn't be the first to use that excuse." He gently brushed hair back from her face, tracing her earlobe slowly as he tucked the strand behind her ear. "But I have a feeling that once the fog cleared, you would regret it. A lot."

"Pretty sure I wouldn't." Delaney shook her head.

She totally would.

Even through the alcohol fumes, she definitely knew she would. And as much as she hated to admit it, she would probably be thankful tomorrow morning that he'd put the brakes on tonight when she was good and ready to go full throttle.

Maybe.

He kissed her forehead, then pulled away. "Liar." He motioned toward the seat, and helped her inside, then shut the door softly. As he walked around the truck, she pinched the bridge of her nose, trying to recover.

He slid in and put the key in the ignition. "How about I take you home? We can get your car back to you in the morning, if you want. I'm definitely not putting you behind a wheel right now."

The last place she wanted to go right now was back to her condo, where she'd collapse into bed alone and spend the night wishing she wasn't falling so damn hard for exactly the wrong kind of man. But what was the alternative? She was a hospital administrator making budgetary decisions that directly impacted the doctor currently sitting two feet from her. The *only* place she should allow him to take her right now was home.

"I . . . don't want to go home."

Joshua smiled. "Okay? Where do you want to go?"

"Honestly? Somewhere where I can make a monumentally terrible decision I'll regret, but blame on Papi's alcohol."

Oh, God. Still speaking with alcohol-brain.

He laughed. "*How* monumentally terrible?"

"Depends whether you're willing to make a blood oath that when the evening ends, we shall never speak of it again."

"Wow." He nodded like he was considering the offer, then shook his head. "As tempting as that is, I don't make oaths with intoxicated women."

"I'm not *that* intoxicated."

"Delaney, you have enough of Papi's Poison cruising through your system that you're offering blood oaths. Pretty sure you wouldn't think very highly of me if I took advantage of that."

She sighed. "I hate when people make good points that I don't want to hear."

"Tell you what." He turned the key in the ignition.

"Let's go catch the sunset on the lake. I know a perfect spot."

She raised her eyebrows. Of course he did. He'd probably taken half of the pediatric nurses out there at one point or another. And why wouldn't he? He was young, single, and ungodly hot. The thought of it shouldn't make her jealous.

But it did.

As they drove out of the parking lot, he took her hand in his, lifting her fingers up so he could place a soft kiss on her knuckles.

"Thanks for coming with me tonight. I know it's not really your—scene."

She pondered his comment through an admittedly slight haze. "What exactly do you think is my *scene*?"

He shrugged. "I don't know yet, really. You're kind of an enigma."

"Ooh. Woman of mystery and all that?"

"Yes. That." He rolled his eyes. "The first time we met, you were all buttoned up in a very proper suit-ish sort of thing. I figured you for the accountant type, all black and white and bottom line. But then you showed up in baby-sheep scrubs, and I heard you laughing with Charlotte, then saw you leap right in to help Ian. Totally different woman."

"No." Delaney felt her eyebrows furrow. Were the facets of her personality really that different? "Same woman."

"Thus the enigma."

She pondered his words for a long moment. She'd always considered herself pretty much a what-you-see-is-what-you-get type, and she got a definite tingle realizing Joshua found her a little mysterious. Mysterious was good, right?

He looked over, letting his eyes wander from her face down to her feet and back up again. "You've got this sort of—I don't know—country-club vibe on the outside, but I have a feeling there's a little bit of wild child underneath."

"Oh, really." She glanced down, wondering if her hot pink bra was somehow showing through her dress.

"Pretty sure, yes. I have to admit, I was a little scared of you that first couple of days, all in your proper little suit things . . . and those heels. But—I probably shouldn't tell you this—on the second day, your top button kept popping open, and it was distracting as hell."

Delaney put her hand to her chest. "It did not."

"Did." He smiled, keeping his eyes glued to the road. "I kept trying to figure out if you were doing it on purpose to keep me off guard."

"No!"

He laughed, then cocked one eyebrow. "Purple is a really good color for you, by the way."

"*What?*" She crossed her arms. She'd totally had on purple undergarments that day—she remembered because she'd changed her blouse so her bra wouldn't show through.

"I'm sorry. I couldn't help—it wasn't my fault. You were just sitting there and—God, never mind." He shook his head.

Delaney bit her lip, trying not to smile as she saw a blush creep up his cheeks.

"I can't believe you looked."

He braked at an intersection, and he looked over, heat in his eyes. "No offense, Delaney, but no man in his right mind would have—not looked."

They rode in silence for a few long minutes until Joshua turned down a dirt road and Delaney realized she had no idea where they were.

"Where are we going?" Trees were closing in on both sides, darkening the dirt road, which was narrowing rapidly. It occurred to her that this would make a great backdrop for a Stephen King novel.

"To the best sunset spot on Echo Lake."

"Are we going to get there soon? Because I have to be honest—these woods are kind of creeping me out."

As she spoke, Joshua took a sharp left onto what looked like an old cow path, and Delaney's stomach jumped. *This is how innocent women end up dead*, she thought. *They put their trust in someone they barely know, let him drive them out into the boonies, and bam. The end.*

But Joshua was a pediatrician. Serial killers didn't do time as pediatricians, right? She was fine. She was definitely fine.

She felt around in her purse, looking for her pepper spray, just in case.

Two minutes later, at just about the same time Delaney thought she might lose her stomach to the combination of potholes and nerves, Joshua pulled out of the trees into a clearing at the top of a steep bluff overlooking the lake, and Delaney inhaled sharply at the view.

Below them, Echo Lake stretched out in shimmery sunset glory. The sun was low in the western sky, sinking toward the horizon as it sent out ribbons of pink and purple into the clouds and water. Here and there, small sailboats fought to catch the last wisps of wind, and Delaney could hear the calls of gulls as they circled low.

"Wow."

"You said you fell in love with the lake when you used to come up to visit your parents. Thought you might like to see it from this angle." Joshua smiled, squeezing her hand before he let go. "Come on. I know a great spot to watch the sun go down."

He got out of the truck and came around to her side, opening the door for her as she slid out. He pointed toward what looked like a cliff at the edge of the bluff, taking her hand. "Follow me."

"Follow you? Over the cliff? Said the lemming to the lemming?" Delaney pulled back. "I don't think so."

Joshua laughed. "It's not really a cliff. Just looks like it from here. There's a perfect rock just fifty feet down."

"Um . . ." Delaney followed him toward the edge, and when she got there, she realized he was right. It wasn't a cliff at all—just a steep decline interrupted by massive glacial rocks. Still, she was in sandals and a dress, not climbing gear.

He looked back at her, seeming to notice her current clothing just as she did. He stopped, smiling. "I have a different idea. Ever watch the sunset from the hood of a Chevy?"

"Can't say as I ever have."

He winked. "City girl."

He headed back toward the truck, pulling a couple of beach towels from behind the seat. He spread them out on the hood, then looked at her, eyebrows raised.

"Need a boost?"

Delaney eyed the truck. "Depends how slippery your towels are. I'd rather not go home with gravel implanted in my knees."

Before she could argue, Joshua's hands were at her waist, and she was in the air. She barely had time to wonder when he had time to work out before she was seated comfortably on the hood, her back leaning against the windshield. A moment later, he was beside her. They sat in silence for a few seconds before Delaney spoke.

"So . . . sunsets and Chevy hoods. That's a Vermont thing?"

"We're actually getting overrun with Subarus, but yes to the sunsets."

She smiled. "I can't imagine growing up here. It's so—Norman Rockwell–ish."

"Yeah." He shrugged slowly. "I guess it is. Easy to lose sight of that part when it's all you've ever really known."

He leaned back, hands clasped behind his head, and though all she wanted to do was sidle closer so he could put his arm around her, she held back. Papi's alcohol was starting to fade from her system, and with it, her confidence. What was she doing out here? With him? Where had her professional detachment gone?

Then he looked at her, and his eyes warmed her from her throat right to her toes. He smiled, and she was sure he could tell how nervous she was. How could he not?

She cleared her throat. "So is this spot top secret? Or does every guy in town know about it?"

"Every guy. First-date ritual. It's a small-town thing."

He said the words seriously, but she saw his eyes crinkle.

"Fine." She elbowed him. "But we're not on a date. Is it cheating to come out here if you're *not* dating?"

"Totally, yes, but I'll take the risk." He pointed down the lake, where Delaney could see a flotilla of kayakers moving slowly westward. "See those kids paddling? They're from Camp Echo. Lots of city kids getting their first dose of wilderness. Local kids considered it our job to haze them as much as possible."

"Another small-town ritual?"

"Yeah. But generally more fun than most first dates."

Delaney laughed. "Sounds like there's a story there."

"Nope. You first. Do you remember your first date?"

"First date, like, ever?" She pulled her knees up to her chest, fixing her sundress to fall around them. He nodded. She looked out toward the water, remembering a pink dress, a nervous Cory Mohegan, a sobbing mother. Every milestone Delaney hit, after all, was one that Parker never would.

"Junior prom. The theme was Magic Under the Stars—but it was anything but."

Joshua laughed. "Uh-oh."

"My—date—hung with me through dinner, then ditched the prom and got drunk with his buddies in the hotel parking garage."

"Ouch."

She rolled her eyes. "Turns out it's a lot easier to ditch your female date if you've recently realized you don't play on that team."

"Oh. God." He laughed. "Your prom date was gay?"

"Yes. And that would have been completely fine, had I *known* it. But my prom night fantasies went flying out the window pretty quickly when I realized he was bringing somebody *else* home."

His face sobered. "He ditched you? At prom?"

"I guess he was done with the charade. The timing just happened to suck for *me*."

Joshua dropped his arm so that it hugged her shoulders. "He sounds like a first-class jerk."

She shook her head. "He wasn't. Not really. It wasn't like he planned for it to happen. And in all honesty"—she sighed—"my gaydar *was* seriously flawed. I dated two more guys after that who ended up coming out later." Delaney elbowed Joshua as she felt him shaking. "It's not funny."

"It's *kind of* funny."

"You say that, but you've never been a twenty-two-year-old woman trying to figure out why guys date you, then immediately head for the other side of the field."

"You thought you were *turning* them—"

"Well, what did I know? I didn't have any experience. I went to boarding school, for God's sake."

Joshua laughed out loud, and the sound of it tickled her way down low. Then he squeezed her shoulder, letting his fingers linger on her skin.

"If we were, in fact, dating, I might be worried right now. Just saying." He winked. "You'll feel better when you hear about my first date."

"Was *she* gay?"

"No. She was a nympho."

Delaney rolled her eyes. "Oh, poor you. Every teen-aged boy's nightmare."

"It was a summer camp romance, and we had one fumbling, awkward, terrible kiss. But by the next morning, we'd apparently done a whole lot more than that."

"Uh-oh. Did she put your name on the girls' room wall?"

"Under the dock, actually. That's where the tallies were."

Delaney laughed. "That's kind of funny. But at least you got credit for more than you deserved. That couldn't have been all bad."

"Not the kind of credit I wanted."

"Sorry." She shook her head. "I think getting ditched by a gay prom date beats nympho overcrediting."

"They both kind of sucked."

"Agreed."

He raised his eyebrows. "Good thing we're older and wiser and all that. First dates are so much easier now."

"Right. Exactly." Her stomach fluttered as his fingers caressed her shoulder. "Not that we're having one."

"How about first kisses? Think those are easier now?" He kept his eyes on the lake, but her face heated like he was staring straight at her.

"I—don't know." She swallowed. "It's been—a while—since I've tried one."

He looked at her then, his eyes skating over her forehead, her eyes, her lips before his left hand came up to caress her cheek.

"Me, too," he finally said, then tipped up her chin, leaning closer as the pad of his thumb traced her lips. "But I'm game to try one if you are."

"Okay," she whispered, but before the word was fully out of her mouth, his lips touched hers gently—a sweet, promising caress. His hand slid through her hair, bracing her head as he deepened the kiss, and she struggled to remember to breathe. As the twilight darkened around them, all she wanted to do was bury herself in the kiss . . . in *him*.

No, a first kiss had never felt so . . . perfect. Joshua was gentle and demanding at the same time, his fingers skating over her skin like he had all night, but couldn't wait to undress her. He pulled her closer, closer as his lips moved to her neck, her collarbone, her earlobe, and his hand inched achingly up her ribs, then back downward.

A long while later, he pulled back, kissing her gently on the nose, and Delaney struggled to catch her breath. Her heart felt like it might launch its way right out from between her ribs, and she knew he must be able to see her pulse hammering in her neck, even though it was almost dark.

When she looked at his face, though, she was relieved to see that she wasn't the only one affected. There was color in his cheeks, and when he brushed her flyaway hair back from her forehead, his smile was genuine.

"That was *way* better than my *first* first kiss."

She closed her eyes, assaulted by emotions she wasn't ready to process. "Mine, too. By, like, a million times."

He kissed her again, but just as his hand slid tantalizingly up her ribs, she heard the incessant whine of a mosquito, and she hated that it matched the incessant warning tone pinging inside her brain.

Just as she felt another mosquito pierce her shoulder, he pulled away and slapped his neck. "I think we're about to be dinner."

"I think you're right."

He slid down the hood, reaching up to lift her down, then kissing her softly one more time before he handed her up into the truck. After he'd jumped into his side, they sat in silence for a long moment, and Delaney tried to return her heartbeat to a normal pace while she berated herself for letting tonight happen at all.

"Delaney?" Joshua's voice was soft as he looked across the almost-dark cab.

"Mm hm?"

"Think I could talk you into a second date?"

Chapter 17

"No." Delaney's voice came out in a whisper, but she knew it must feel like a slap.

"No?" Joshua cocked his head. "I'm sorry. Were we not just—was that—" He looked out the windshield, his head still tipped in confusion, and Delaney's stomach hurt. "Do you not *want*—"

"We were. It *was*." She took a shaky breath. "I do. But we can't."

"Can't what, exactly?"

"I don't know." Her voice revealed only half the pain she was feeling inside. "*Anything*, really. We can't date, Joshua. We can't do—this."

"Because?"

"Because we're colleagues. Because in less than two weeks, I'm supposed to stand in front of the hospital board and deliver a proposal for how to cut the pediatric budget. And right now, my professional recommendation is to leave that budget intact, at whatever cost to other areas of the hospital. That proposal's chances of flying are hanging at about zero percent already. If somebody suspects I'm involved with the head of pediatrics, do you have any idea what will happen?"

"Your proposal will go down in flames, and we'll all be looking for jobs?"

Delaney nodded sadly. "It's possible."

"I was exaggerating."

"I'm not." She shook her head, an image of Kevin McConnell popping suddenly into her brain. Kevin, who wanted nothing less than to roll his overpriced chair to the CFO's office once Gregory retired. Kevin, who'd do anything in his power to get there, despite the fact that he was dismally unqualified. Delaney was his direct competition for his dream job, and if he saw an opportunity to discredit her in order to pave his own way to the corner of the executive suite, she knew he'd take it.

Her dating Joshua Mackenzie, interim head of pediatrics, was an avenue paved with gold bricks. Even if they were ridiculously careful to stay under the radar, somebody would find out, and that somebody would tell another somebody, and before Delaney or Joshua could control this particular spin, the entire hospital would know. She hadn't been at Mercy long, in small-town-hospital tenure terms, but she'd certainly been here long enough to see the rumor mill in action. It was an impressive machine, to say the least.

As much as she'd love to turn to Joshua right now and ask him to take her home—and stay there till morning— she had to do the exact opposite, and it made her chest actually hurt as she tried to formulate the words.

"I've had a really great time tonight, Joshua."

He closed his eyes, his jaw set in sudden frustration as he turned the key in the ignition. "Okay."

"I'm sorry. You know it's the right thing to do. There's too much at stake—for both of us."

"I get it, Delaney." He backed the truck around, and she held the door handle, praying he knew where the edge of the bluff was now that it was almost pitch dark. But apparently he'd done this move enough times in the dark— *dammit*—because before she'd taken two breaths, they were heading back down the dirt pathway, bouncing through potholes once again.

When they finally got to the paved road, silence stretching uncomfortably between them, he reached for her hand, and she let him take it.

"I had a great time tonight, too. And I don't want to be the reason you compromise your professionalism. We can pretend this never happened, if that's what you want." He made a swiping motion with their entwined hands. "No lake, no sunset, no first kiss—or second, or third, or . . ." He let the words drift off in a whisper that had her almost reaching for the seat belt so she could slide onto his lap and say to hell with her damn professionalism. "We'll forget tonight ever happened. Deal?"

She swallowed, but it wasn't easy, given the golf ball suddenly lodged in her throat. There was no way she'd ever forget the way his lips had heated her up from the outside in, and back again. No way she'd forget the way he'd lifted her onto his truck hood, no way she'd stop thinking about the way his fingers felt on her skin.

Dammit.

She took a deep breath, hating herself for ever going to Bellinis tonight and opening the door to this moment that she was going to relive for a long, long time. Then she pulled her hand slowly, painfully free of his.

"Deal."

An hour later, Josh tossed his keys on the kitchen table of the old Victorian he'd inherited from his parents, then clicked on a light in the living room. Habit made him pull the curtain back and glance up the hill toward Avery's House. Lights twinkled from the expected upstairs rooms, and it looked like the bottom floor had been buttoned up for the night.

He let the curtain fall, then looked around the room. It

was late—he needed to head upstairs to bed, but there was no way he was going to sleep anytime soon, and he knew it. He hadn't been able to get Delaney out of his head since she'd showed up at his office door last week, and now? *Good God.* Now he'd actually touched her, tasted her . . . wanted her.

He'd had to say a proverbial good-bye before they'd hardly said hello.

Sleep was going to be a long time coming.

He pictured her eyes, looking up at him at their table at Bellinis, or as they'd leaned on the windshield earlier tonight. For hours he'd tried to figure out what color they were, but it was like someone had taken the greens and blues from a crayon box and melted them together, then added a tiny piece of gold at the end. When she laughed, the edges of her eyes crinkled in a way that made him just want to keep her amused.

He stood at the sink, looking through the darkness into a backyard that hadn't changed since he was a kid. The old tree fort was still up in the tree, though it was probably rotted by now, and in the moonlight, he could see the old tire swing still hanging from the oak tree.

He'd left everything intact because he'd assumed that someday he'd be the one climbing those limbs and fixing up the boards for his own kids. He'd figured someday a little girl with pigtails would spin herself silly on that tire swing, after he put on a new rope.

But when? His dad had worked sixty hours a week, but had still managed to find time to build Joshua a tree house, had still managed to take him camping and teach him survival skills, had still managed to tell him stories at night and take him to rent his first tuxedo for prom.

Josh shook his head. Why hadn't *he* managed to strike that kind of balance in his own life? Was it because he was balancing two demanding jobs?

Or was he balancing two demanding jobs so he wouldn't have to think too hard about why he was still too damn gun-shy to do anything more than pursue throw-away, casual dates?

Usually, on a night like tonight, he'd have welcomed the end play he'd just gotten slapped with. *It was fun, thank you, good night, and let's never speak of this again.* It was a casual dater's dream, but when Delaney had delivered similar words, it had felt like knives were slicing through his gut.

But why?

Was it because there was nothing casual about the woman? Was it because kissing her felt like holding precious porcelain? Was it because once he had his lips on hers, it was all he could do to keep things from heating up too fast, too far?

He sighed. Or was it because she was the one who'd called it a wrap, rather than him?

Just then, the phone rang, startling him. He automatically looked at his watch, wondering if something was wrong up at Avery's House. He braced himself before he answered, trying to sound less agitated than he felt.

"You owe me ten bucks." Molly's voice came over the line before he even said hello.

He shook his head, smiling. "For what?"

"She ordered salad and sparkling water last night. With lime. I called it perfectly."

"Yes, you did. But she also ordered the special, so actually, I think we're even." There was unusual silence on the other end of the line. "But I imagine that's not why you're calling."

"I don't have any ulterior motives here. Just checking in to see if you had fun at the party. And to thank you for surprising me."

He sighed. Molly was the queen of ulterior motives. "You're welcome. And yes. It was a good party."

"How about the after party?"

"There was an after party?" With his free hand, he rubbed his temple, trying to keep up the charade Delaney had forced upon him. "Why wasn't I invited?"

Molly growled on the other end of the line. "Don't play dense with me, Josh. *You're* the one who headed out for an after party. The rest of us just want to know how it went."

"It was—fine."

"Fine." Her tone was mocking.

"Yes, fine."

"I'm afraid I require more detail than that, mister."

"Molly?"

She sighed. "I know. I *know* it's none of my business, but you're my oldest, best friend besides Josie. And I've never seen you look at anybody the way you were looking at Delaney tonight. And then you give me *fine*? It's desperately unfair."

"I'm sorry." He smiled sadly, wishing right now that things had ended differently with Delaney . . . wishing right now that he could do the sly, I'm-not-telling-you-nuthin' thing that would tell Molly that things had gone perfectly, but he wasn't talking.

But they hadn't.

Well, they *had*. Until the end.

"Be careful, Josh."

Too late, Mols.

Molly sighed, and it was one of those long, drawn-out ones that made him wish he could read the female mind. "It didn't look like you hate each other."

"Well, that's terrifying."

"And she's pretty."

"Yes." *God, yes.* "She's attractive."

"Oh, seriously. She's drag-home-to-bed-and-then-have-Sunday-brunch-*in*-bed pretty."

He sighed, running a hand through hair that was probably already sticking straight up, given the number of times he'd done it since he'd followed Delaney back to her condo, giving a quick, pretend-careless wave as she went inside, then driving back to his huge, empty house on Sugar Maple Drive.

"Nobody's dragging anybody home, Mols."

"Don't sleep with her, Josh. Just promise me you won't sleep with her."

He sighed. Again. It was too late for the third degree. "Mols, I love you like a sister, but I'm pretty sure you don't get to vet who I do or don't bring home."

"Even if I can already tell she'll take you to heaven and hell, maybe in the same week?"

Oh, he already knew that.

"Even if, yes." He took a sip of his beer. "And can I just point out that you're making an awful lot of suppositions based on meeting her exactly twice?"

"I'm a watcher. You know that. And her body language was all *about* getting you in bed."

He got a secret thrill hearing Molly's words, then kicked himself as she spoke again.

"Just one more thing."

He sighed, raking his fingers through his hair. "One more thing."

"Be careful. Her motives might not be as pure as they seem."

"Motives? What?" He shook his head. "I have no idea what you're talking about."

Molly paused. "I'm just saying—if her job's at risk, and doing something momentous with your department might save it . . . then maybe she's got other goals here. Besides getting you into bed, I mean."

No. He couldn't have imagined the way her fingers had heated under his touch. She couldn't have made her own cheeks blush when he'd looked at her for one beat too long. He definitely couldn't have imagined the look of desire in her eyes as they'd kissed.

"Sorry," Molly continued. "Not trying to shoot your evening all to heck, but I just think it's worth—a little caution. Lesser women than her have used their cute laughs and little sundresses to get what they want."

On Monday morning, Delaney was trying to finish up three reports that were due Friday, but her concentration was completely shot. As hard as she tried to focus on the figures on her screen, her mind kept flipping back to Saturday night.

Even before they'd snuck off to the lake—because, if she was being honest, that's exactly what they'd done— she'd felt an unusual sense of peace sitting in that Bellinis booth with Joshua's friends. She'd expected to feel awkward and out of place among a sea of strangers, but everyone had made her feel like she'd actually been on the guest list in the first place.

As she'd sipped that sinfully delicious lemonade and dished on Josie's shared addiction to the reality show that sent contestants all over the world in teams, she'd felt a sense of belonging she really hadn't expected . . . and she'd liked it—a lot. When she'd moved here from the city five years ago, she hadn't expected to blend right into small-town life, but she hadn't expected it to be quite so hard to find a new peer group, either. Sometimes it felt like everyone in Echo Lake had grown up here, and they already had enough friends, thank you very much.

But to be honest, between her hours at the hospital and the fact that she was much more comfortable with a book than a stranger, she hadn't really made a Herculean effort in that department, either.

And then there was the Joshua piece of the equation. As she'd watched him talk with his high school buddies, as she'd scooted over to make room in their booth, as they'd talked and laughed with Ethan and Josie, she'd found herself imagining what it might be like if they truly *were* on a date. He'd been attentive and funny and sweet, and she shivered when she remembered him leaning close and asking if she wanted to head out.

It had sounded so innocent, but so—not.

But all of her daydreams paled in comparison to their first kiss—and all of the ones that followed. Holy hotness—the man definitely knew his way around a kiss.

"Hey. Dreamer-girl." Megan stepped into her office, closing the door behind her. "One kiss, and it's like you've been struck with adult ADD or something."

Delaney blinked hard, trying to clear her head. "This is why women get stupid."

"Hormones'll get you every time." Megan nodded sagely as she sat down in the guest chair. "Just sucks that these particular hormones aren't very well-timed."

"You think?" Delaney blew out a breath, trying to erase the memory of the look on Joshua's face when he'd held her car door for her in the driveway at Avery's House Saturday night.

"Okay. Focus." Megan snapped her fingers in front of Delaney's face. "*Globe* reporter's on her way up. You ready? Or do I need to stall her while you clear Dr. Mackenzie out of your head?"

Ha. Dr. Joshua Mackenzie was *firmly* lodged in her head this morning. There was nothing she was going to be able to do about it.

But Amanda Sleighton was currently in an elevator

heading Delaney's way, and since the reporter was Delaney's best chance to save both Joshua's department and her own job, she really needed to push Saturday night out of her mind and focus on the task at hand.

"Do you have your notes?" Megan pointed to Delaney's desk, which was uncharacteristically messy this morning. "You ready?"

Delaney took a deep breath. "Ready."

Not ready. Not ready at all.

Forty-five minutes later, Amanda was ensconced in her guest chair, notebook open, hammering Delaney with what felt like a hundred questions at a time. The reporter was at the top of her game for a reason, and Delaney was experiencing that reason first-hand. Amanda was as smart as she was pretty, and knew this feature series was going to be just the kind of heartstrings-pulling one that people loved. She was giving it 110 percent, and Delaney could appreciate her drive.

If that drive somehow helped them keep pediatrics thriving at Mercy, all the better.

"So . . ." Amanda leaned forward. "I think I have what I need to get started down on the floor. But I need to know your goals for this feature."

"To be blunt, I would like this feature to scare up enough donors to keep Mercy's pediatric department in the black for years to come."

"So the rumors I'm hearing are true?"

Delaney paused. In a way, she wished she could dish to Amanda, be the source-who-cannot-be-revealed in a startling expose that would prevent the board from decimating pediatrics. Unfortunately, it'd be all too obvious who the source had been. Delaney's hands were tied.

"I'm sorry, Amanda. You know I can't comment on that."

Amanda shrugged. "It was worth a try." Then she smiled. "Okay. So how do you think we should approach this?"

"I was hoping you'd ask."

Chapter 18

Half an hour later, Delaney knocked on Charlotte's door and motioned Amanda through. "And this is Charlotte. She's our twelve-year-old diva-in-training."

Charlotte laughed her gravelly laugh as she rolled her eyes and stood up to greet Amanda Sleighton.

Amanda shook her hand, smiling warmly. "Thanks so much for letting me hang out with you for a few minutes." She pointed to Charlotte's braids, which Delaney had scrambled to do just a few minutes ago. "I love your hair."

Charlotte touched her head gingerly as she sat back down on her bed. "Delaney did it. She's got mad hair skills."

"Oh, really? Think she could do something with *my* mop?"

Delaney and Charlotte laughed together. The reporter had glistening, perfectly salon-sculpted waves, and Delaney imagined she tipped her Boston colorist *very* well for the shades of blond cascading through her hair.

For the next half hour, Amanda made seemingly casual conversation with Charlotte, and Delaney marveled at how the woman was able to get so personal without the girl really even noticing.

"Do you ever go to summer camp?" Amanda asked, after their first conversational lull in a full sixty minutes.

Charlotte shook her head. "No. My parents can't really"—she shrugged—"we're just really busy in the summertime."

Amanda nodded, smiling. "Would you *like* to go to camp someday? If it were possible?"

"Definitely. Horse camp. Sleepover." Charlotte smiled, but a cough wiped away the look on her face. "But camps don't really have anybody who's trained to give me my treatments."

Amanda looked thoughtful, then like she was hatching a plan. "Charlotte, have you ever been on television?"

"Me?" The girl's eyes widened. "No."

"Would you like to be?"

"Um." Charlotte glanced at Delaney, her eyes mystified. "What do you mean?"

"Well, I happen to have a network buddy who's covering another story up here today, and you are a very, very cool twelve-year-old. Plus, you have camera-ready hair." Charlotte laughed nervously. "If I called him to come over here later, do you think you'd be willing to talk to him on-camera? Just kind of like we just did?"

"Maybe? I don't know." Charlotte looked a little scared. "Why?"

"Because a lot of people don't know what goes on inside hospitals when they're not the ones unlucky enough to have to be here. We'd love to show people the kind of kids who stay here, and I think you are the perfect person to do it."

Charlotte stared down at her hands, where Delaney could see her fingernails curving over the ends of her fingers, typical of someone whose tissues got consistently less oxygen than they needed. To her credit, Amanda stayed silent, waiting for her answer.

Then Charlotte looked up, a small smile gaining

traction on her face. "Okay. I'll do it. If Delaney can be here with me."

"It's a deal." Amanda stood up, shaking her hand in mock formality. She looked at her phone, then at Delaney. "I'm going to go talk to some other patients, but I'll be back in about an hour with my friend. His name's Matt, and he's super awesome. You'll like him."

"Okay."

Delaney followed Amanda out of the room, and once they were in the hallway, Amanda's fingers typed madly on her phone while a grin took over her face.

"She's perfect. Absolutely perfect."

Delaney crossed her arms, feeling a strange sense of protectiveness. "Amanda?"

"Isn't this great?" She didn't even look up.

"What are you doing? We didn't talk about TV."

Amanda looked up from the phone. "You want donors, right?"

"Yes, but—"

"But nothing. Charlotte will get you donors. You called that one right on the nose. She's adorable, she's sweet, and her story will break people's hearts." Amanda leaned close. "And crack their wallets. It's brilliant."

"But this isn't what we discussed."

Delaney scrambled for traction. Amanda was taking the bull by the proverbial horns, but Delaney wasn't at all sure where she was dragging the damn bull.

Amanda sighed. "Does the release cover television?"

"Yes. She's legally okay. But she doesn't have parents here, and I don't want to freak her out."

"Did I freak her out just now?"

"No, but—"

"Then I promise not to freak her out in an hour. Matt's a sweetheart. Charlotte will love him. Delaney, this is good. This is better than we were hoping. If we get that girl on television, combined with weekend *Globe* coverage, I think you'll be very, very happy with the results."

As Amanda returned her attention to her phone, tapping out texts like machine-gun fire, Delaney watched color rise in her cheeks. Something about this story was touching more than the usual nerves for Amanda—Delaney could sense it. Before she let the woman have at Charlotte on-camera, she had to ask.

"I can't help but feel like this is more than just an assignment to you, Amanda."

Amanda nodded slowly, pausing her fingers. "It is."

The protective instinct kicked into high gear. Did Amanda smell a story? One that they *wouldn't* want on the air?

"Why? What's your angle here?"

Amanda paused. "My angle is to help you. I'm a huge fan of Ethan and Josie, and by extension, Joshua. I just . . . want to help." Amanda paused, gazing down the hallway. Then she took a deep breath, looking straight at Delaney. "I have a little sister who's alive today because of this hospital. *That* is my angle."

That afternoon, Delaney was crammed into Charlotte's room along with Amanda, Matt, and a cameraman. Once they were all set up and poor Charlotte had adjusted to the bright lights, Amanda started feeding her easy questions to get her comfortable. As she talked with her in that soft, inviting voice that could probably work on the Italian mob, Charlotte visibly relaxed and seemed to forget a camera was rolling, recording her every word and gesture.

After getting a half hour of film, the cameraman turned off his camera and lights, and Amanda leaned forward.

"So Charlotte, when we were talking before, you mentioned that someday you'd love to go to a horse camp."

"That would be awesome." Charlotte smiled sadly. "But it's probably not going to happen."

"Well, I'm not so sure."

"What do you mean?"

Amanda stood up and slid a manila envelope across Charlotte's bed. "Open that up and let me know what's inside."

Charlotte looked at the envelope like it was rigged with explosives, but then finally picked it up and opened the flap. She slid out a small sheaf of papers, and her eyes widened as she fingered a bank check.

"Is this an April Fool's joke?"

Amanda laughed. "No, it's July. I just happen to know an anonymous donor who sent me on a mission to find a deserving kid who could use a reason to smile."

"And you picked—me? Seriously?" Charlotte pointed out the doorway of her room. "There are kids here who are way worse off than me. Why didn't you pick them?"

"Because." Amanda nodded, her jaw set. "You remind me of someone, and everybody here who knows you thinks *you* are a young lady who deserves this."

"I'm going to—camp?" Charlotte tested the word on her tongue, like she was afraid saying it out loud might make it go away.

"Two weeks. Horseback riding every day, a nice cabin at night."

"What about—" She pointed at her chest, and Delaney felt crushed as she watched Charlotte realize maybe this *was* too good to be true.

"This camp employs two full-time nurses, and they're both trained in CF care."

"Really?"

"Really."

Charlotte jumped off the bed, forgetting her IV lines

for a moment. Amanda noticed before she went too far, and leaned in to hug her.

"Thank you!"

"You're very, very welcome." Amanda ruffled her hair where it had poked out of the braids. "You'll have to send us pictures. All of your new fans will want an update, once they see you on television."

As Delaney watched the two of them, she felt eyes on her, and she looked up to see Joshua smiling softly at her. He nodded, and she felt heat travel from her throat right to her toes. She followed him out to the hallway, where he leaned against the wall, crossing his arms.

He raised his eyebrows, and she couldn't tell whether he was amused or mad. "TV cameras?"

"I know. Not exactly what we discussed."

"Not at *all* what we discussed."

"I'm sorry. Amanda suggested it, and then I couldn't find you, and then Matt was here, and then cameras were rolling, and—" Delaney's hands flailed nervously. *Crap.* She'd just stepped way over the line here.

"Delaney." He put his hand gently on her shoulder. "It's okay."

She looked up, not sure whether to trust the words. "It is?"

"Yeah. Amanda's pretty hard to say no to, once she gets rolling."

Delaney smiled in relief. "Pretty much. How much did you hear of the interview?"

"Enough to feel like I want to kiss you right here, right now, in this hallway."

"Joshua!" Delaney whispered, feeling heat flame up her cheeks.

"Sorry." He shrugged. "Can't help it. You fed Amanda exactly the kind of information to make for one hell of a story. And Charlotte was the perfect choice for her to interview. Well done."

"So . . . you're not mad about the cameras?"

"A little surprised, that's all. Didn't exactly expect an entire crew to descend on the floor this afternoon."

"I'm sorry. Again."

"You can stop apologizing." He pushed away from the wall. "It's going to be great."

"Agreed." Delaney couldn't help the grin that took over her face. "Charlotte was awesome. I'm dying to know who Amanda's secret donor is."

"So you can go after the same donor for more than camp fees?"

"Am I really that transparent?"

He smiled. "While I appreciate your drive, I'll save you some trouble. I have a feeling I know exactly who her secret donor is."

"Who?"

"It's her, Delaney."

"Really? You think so?"

"I do. And unfortunately, her pockets probably aren't deep enough to help us out of the hole we're in. But her story might find us someone whose pockets are."

Delaney sighed. "We can only hope."

Chapter 19

"Hey, Delaney." Millie poked her head into Kaya's room on Tuesday afternoon. "I've got a job for you."

"Okay?" Delaney set the little girl back into her bed, straightening out her IV tubes and tucking the blanket around her. Four more days of chemo and hopefully she'd get to go home, the poor little thing.

She pulled the door partially closed, joining Millie in the hallway. "What's up?"

"You remember Ian, right?"

Delaney swallowed. She'd stopped in to see him every day, but still had to take a deep breath and brace herself before she entered his room. He reminded her—way too much—of Parker.

"Yes. Of course. I know him."

"I need some eyes on him this afternoon."

"His mom's not here?"

"Yes, she's here." Millie looked to the left, toward the wall, and Delaney felt her own eyebrows pull together.

"Does she need a break?"

Millie nodded. "We need her to talk . . . to Josh. But she doesn't want to leave Ian alone. She seems to have connected with you, so I thought maybe she'd be okay if you offered to stay with him for a little bit."

"Okay. Sure. I can do that."

As Delaney followed Millie down the hallway, she noticed that most of the patient room doors were closed. Unusual, but it was crazy hot outside. Maybe they did it to keep the rooms cooler? It was also strangely quiet, but again, maybe it was the heat keeping everybody suppressed.

When they got to the nurses' station, Millie reached out an arm to stop Delaney. "You just tell her Dr. Mackenzie needs to speak with her for a minute, and you're happy to sit with Ian while she does, okay?"

Delaney tipped her head, a strange feeling gnawing in her gut. "What's going on, Millie?"

"Nothing." Millie looked at her watch, then down the hallway, like she was expecting someone. Then she pointed toward Ian's room. "Just go sit for a few minutes."

When Delaney knocked on Ian's open door, Fiona looked up from the chair beside his bed, where she was nervously holding his hand.

"Hey, Fiona. How are you doing?"

Fiona shrugged. "I don't know. Not great."

Delaney stepped closer. The woman's hair looked like she'd slept in her chair, and she had the same clothes on as yesterday.

"Can I get you a coffee or anything?"

"No. Thank you, though. I don't need anything right now."

"I think Dr. Mackenzie is hoping to have a minute to talk with you. Do you mind if I hang out with Ian while you go speak to him?"

"I don't want to talk to him." Her voice was quiet, but strong, and this time, alarm bells rang in Delaney's stomach.

She tried to keep her voice soft and inviting as she responded. "Why not?"

"Because—because he's going to tell me bad news. I just know it."

"What makes you think that?"

"Because if it was good news, he'd just tell me right here."

Delaney started to argue, but instead, she bit her lip. Fiona had a point. Delaney wondered what Joshua needed to talk to her about that he couldn't do right here with Ian present. She shivered, thinking Fiona was right. It probably *was* bad news, but Joshua didn't want to scare the poor boy by sharing it in front of him.

She put her hand tentatively on Fiona's shoulder, and to her surprise, Fiona reached up with her free hand and gripped it hard.

"I just want him better, you know? He has to get better. He was never supposed to get this sick."

Delaney nodded slowly, while running the woman's words around her head. What did she mean, he was never supposed to get this sick? Was she one of the millions who Googled symptoms and latched on to the one positive piece of news they could find? Had she convinced herself that Ian was going to beat something that he—wasn't?

She took a deep breath, trying not to draw parallels with Parker as she looked at the tiny freckles dotting Ian's nose. He slept quietly, and if you didn't know better, you'd think he was just peacefully snoozing off his morning antics.

"Listen"—she squeezed Fiona's hand—"I promise I'll sit right here in your chair while you're gone. I'll even hold his hand. I won't go anywhere."

Fiona shook her head. "I wish Dan was here. He's better at bad news than I am."

"Maybe it's not bad news. I see Dr. Mackenzie having conferences with people all the time to tell them good

news, too." Did she? Was a white lie permissible in this
sort of situation? Or just unduly cruel? "Maybe he has
some information on a new medicine or something. You
never know."

Fiona looked up at her, eyes watery. "Do you think so?"

"I don't know. But I think you should go find out."

Fiona looked at Ian, wiping her eyes quickly. She stood
up slowly, but didn't take her eyes from the sleeping boy.

"You promise you won't leave him alone?"

"Promise." Delaney sat down in the chair she'd just va-
cated, sliding her hand over Parker's tiny one. "I will be
sitting right here when you get done with your meeting."

Delaney could see Millie waiting outside the door, and
as Fiona looked back one last time, Millie gently took her
arm and steered her toward the other hallway, where Joshua's office was.

"Hey, buddy. It's Delaney." She kept her voice soft as
she held Ian's little hand and looked at the monitors over
his head. "I'm just going to sit here with you until your
mom comes back."

She thought she saw his eyelids flutter, but he didn't
further acknowledge her. She just kept talking quietly as
he breathed in, out, in, out—more to keep her own self
sane than because she thought he needed inane conversation to keep him company.

As she watched him, his little body reminded her so
much of Parker's that she had to blink back tears. He had
the same reddish-brown hair, the same tiny freckles, the
same sort of dump-truck pajamas Parker had always worn
in the hospital. He had the same little ears, too, and she'd
be willing to bet they heard just as much as Parker's had.

She remembered one night, she'd crept to the top of the
stairs because her parents were arguing, and knowing full
well that she shouldn't be listening, she did anyway. That
was the night she'd learned her brother was never going

to grow up, and she'd fled back to her bed, sobbing into her pillow until she felt a little hand rubbing her back.

What's matter, Laney? Parker had had one thumb in his mouth while his other hand had rubbed her back. *Why you sad?*

Delaney grabbed a ragged breath as her tears threatened to escape her eyes. *Dammit.* This was exactly why she hadn't been able to continue with med school. She could have gotten over the physical aspects—she knew she could have. But this? This sitting with a little boy who *also* wasn't going to grow up? This trying not to compare him to Parker?

This is why she couldn't do medicine. Ever.

There would always be something—tiny toes, a crooked smile, a left-cheek dimple, a giggle—that would send Parker right to the forefront of her brain, and send her memories spiraling through her head.

How did Joshua do this every day? How could he handle the fact that some kids never left the hospital? Or only left it to spend their last days at home? How did he let himself get attached, knowing his heart would get broken?

Because she knew it would. She hadn't known him long, but the man treated every single one of these kids like they were his own. It had to kill him every time things didn't go well. It had to kill him every time he had to have a hard conversation with a parent, especially a mom like Fiona.

Delaney squeezed Ian's hand gently. She knew that's what was happening in Joshua's office right now. Knew it so much that it made her own stomach hurt. She didn't know if she'd ever find out what he was telling Fiona— didn't know if she *wanted* to know. Parker and Ian were already going to be in her mixed-up dreams tonight, and knowing Ian's fate would only make that exponentially worse.

Just then, Millie and two other nurses came hurrying through the door, along with two orderlies, making Delaney jump in surprise.

"Okay, Delaney. Thank you. You can go now."

Millie motioned toward the door, but Delaney didn't move. "I said I'd stay. I promised her I'd—stay." She watched as the other nurses quickly positioned the bed and IV poles for transport, stepping between her and Ian, making her let go of his hand. "What are you doing? Where are you taking him?"

She hated the tinge of panic she heard in her own voice, hated the way the nurses paused to look at her, then at Millie, before they refocused on tucking the blankets around him and gently lowering the head of the bed.

She grabbed the metal bar on the side of his bed as a memory assaulted her—another little bed, another little boy, another transport team taking him away from her again.

"Let go, Delaney." Millie's voice was firm, but curious.

"I—can't. Fiona will freak out if she comes back and he's not here. Can't you wait till she gets back? Where are you *taking* him?"

Her voice kept getting higher, and the nurses were eyeing her curiously.

Millie bent down, leveling her face with Delaney's. "We need to move him right now. *Now.* I will explain later, but I need you to let go. Now."

Something in the tone of her voice shocked Delaney into loosening her grip on the bed, and before she knew it, they'd practically shot out of the room with Ian. Delaney was left sitting alone in Fiona's chair, wondering what in the world was going on.

She looked down and noticed that they'd forgotten the tiny giraffe that seemed always to be tucked into the little boy's hand, and she grabbed it and leaped toward the doorway. But the hallway was strangely empty. Wherever they'd taken him, they were already gone. She leaned unsteadily on the wall, looking left and right. Feeling tingly and chilled, she forced herself to walk back into the room and sit down in the chair again, letting her head drop toward her knees before she fainted.

What in the world was going on?

And why in the name of God had she let herself be part of it?

"She was poisoning her own child?" Delaney gripped her stomach with both arms as she rocked slowly in Joshua's guest chair an hour later.

He nodded, blowing out a breath, and his eyes looked more tired than she'd ever seen them. "We think so."

Delaney swallowed, trying not to let the sick feeling overcome her. She could hardly find her voice, but when she did, it came out all hoarse and afraid. "Why?"

He sighed again. "It's called Munchausen by Proxy."

Delaney nodded slowly. Now that he'd said it, she remembered the term from one of her first med school classes, before she'd dropped out. What she didn't understand—and hadn't then—was why anyone would intentionally hurt her own child. Didn't she know how lucky she was to *have* a perfectly healthy child?

"God."

"I know."

"Where is he now?" Her voice was so quiet she could barely hear it.

"He's safe—somewhere else in the hospital."

"Is he—"

"Going to be okay?"

She nodded, looking at his eyes, trying not to let her tears fall. "I know. You can't tell me."

"I think he is, Delaney. I think we got him in time."

She felt relief flood through her body, then fury as she pictured Fiona sitting by his bed day after day, playing the poor-mom-with-mystery-sick-child thing to the hilt.

"Where's Fiona?"

"She's being evaluated."

"By the police?"

He tipped his head, closing his eyes. "I don't know what I'm allowed to tell you. I'm sorry. Just know everything possible is being done, okay?"

Delaney sat back, arms still crossed defensively over her stomach.

"Is this"—she motioned vaguely toward the hallway—"is this the kind of stuff that—happens down here? A lot?"

He sat back in his own chair, matching her pose. "Before Ian, I had only read about this, so no. In this case, it's not the kind of thing that's common."

"How—how do you *do* it? How do you handle so much—awfulness?"

He raised his eyes to hers, and held them for a long moment. Then he looked down, a defeated expression on his face.

"I don't always handle it. Not well, anyway. This job rips my heart out and serves it back on a platter at least once a month."

"Then why? How? How do you make yourself keep doing it?"

"Because." He sat forward, elbows on his desk. "Ian, for all I can tell, is going to be okay. He's going to get medical care that gets him better, and he's going to get social services care that gets him out of the toxic environment that put him here in the first place."

"What about Kaya?"

He shrugged carefully. "You know I don't know. I can't answer that. But we can make that little girl's life as rich as possible while she's here, and we can do our damndest to get her better. This job is not for the weak, Delaney. It takes people out on a daily basis, and I don't blame any one of them one bit. But while I can do it—while I *can* handle it—I will do my best to help as many of these kids as I physically can."

Delaney nodded, silence stretching between them. Then she spoke, almost in a whisper.

"What if—what if there wasn't a pediatric hospital here? What would have happened to Ian if he'd had to go to Boston? What happens to the next Ian, if the board decides to shutter this department?"

Joshua looked down at his desk, exhaustion lining his eyes. "That's a question I can't answer."

Chapter 20

When Delaney pushed through the glass doors of the executive suite Wednesday morning, she felt like she had a hangover. She'd left Joshua's office last night and gone straight home, then out for a long-overdue run. Now her legs hurt, her head hurt, and her chest still felt like someone had tightened a belt around it the moment they'd wheeled Ian out of his room yesterday.

She wondered if Joshua would tell her today where the little boy was. If nothing else, she'd like to bring him his giraffe, but she also felt a strong, strange urge to see him and reassure herself that he was okay.

As she rounded the corner by Megan's cubicle, she backed up quickly, startled by the sight of a man leaning over her desk.

Then the smell hit her—a pungent mix of aftershave and hair gel that could only belong to one person.

"Can I help you with something, Kevin?" She walked by, then balanced her coffee cup against her chest as she unlocked her office. What was he doing here so early?

He spun around like he'd been caught doing something he shouldn't be, and Delaney's radar pinged.

"I'm looking for those damn projection sheets. And don't sneak up on people."

"The sheets? Again?"

"Yes, again. Megan promised she'd help me with them, but you've kept her running around like crazy all week, so she hasn't had time."

"Well, she *is* actually *my* assistant." Delaney set her coffee cup down on the file cabinet just inside her door.

"I'm pretty sure she's *everybody's* assistant up here."

"Um, no. Megan is most decidedly mine."

He shook his head, still shuffling through the messy piles on Megan's desk. Delaney made a mental note to track down another file cabinet. If they threw a lit match at her desk right now, it could heat the entire suite for a week.

"Kevin, you're not going to find it. Just wait till she gets here. It may look like a disaster, but I guarantee she knows where everything is."

"But I need to get some numbers to Gregory by ten o'clock."

"Ah, so that's why you're here at the crack of dawn."

He rolled his eyes. "Some of us have a life outside the office, Delaney. We can't all be here twenty-four-seven."

Delaney thought about how Joshua was always here before the birds, and often still busy with patients until well after dark.

"You might be surprised how many people *are* here practically that much, Kevin."

"Well, they need to get a life." He sighed loudly as he moved to yet another pile on Megan's desk. "How does she *work* like this?"

Delaney leaned against her door frame, trying to appear casual while praying that Megan hadn't left anything incriminating *on* her damn desk yesterday.

"Kevin? Have you ever spent any time on patient floors?"

He looked up, pausing his hands. "What do you mean?"

"I mean—have you ever headed downstairs and taken the time to see how Mercy actually treats patients?"

"That's ridiculous." He shook his head. "We have enough to do up here. The people who work down there don't need us watching over their shoulders."

She nodded thoughtfully, ashamed of how long it had taken *her* to punch that Down button and stop at the third floor.

"If I promise to send Megan to your office with the forms as soon as she walks in, will you please stop rifling through her desk?"

His hands finally stilled as he extracted a spreadsheet from one of the piles, his eyes widening.

"Found it."

"So you're good?"

He smiled, and his shoulders dropped a good inch. "I'm fantastic." He rolled the paper up and tapped her on the head like they actually could stand each other. "Thank you."

An hour later, she heard Megan before she saw her, since even carpet couldn't quite muffle the sound of someone running in clogs.

"Omigod! Did you see it?" Megan came blasting into her office, waving a newspaper with Charlotte's face on the front page.

"Already?" Delaney jumped up. "She got that story in *already*?"

Megan handed her the newspaper, and that's when Delaney saw that she had an entire duffel bag of them slung over her shoulder.

"You look like a newsie, Meg. Are you planning to deliver them all over the hospital?"

"Nope. Just to a selection of people who might or might not have board-level influence. I see it as my public service for today. The timing couldn't be better, with the fundraiser tonight."

Delaney smiled as she leaned her hip on the desk and read the story. Amanda had done a beautiful job of painting Charlotte's tale, interspersing quotes here and there, along with the Mercy-specific statistics and facts Delaney had given her.

Megan waited while she read, practically hopping from toe to toe. When Delaney put down the paper, Megan's eyebrows were sky-high.

"Well?"

Delaney shivered. "It's perfect. Beyond perfect. Exactly what we were hoping. She did an amazing job, on completely short notice."

"I'm going to go give one to Kevin." Megan winked as she picked up the duffel bag and headed back toward the door.

"Oh, that reminds me. He was looking for the projection spreadsheets this morning on your desk."

"The what?" Megan looked mystified.

"Cost projections? The thing he can't seem to grasp even though we've both showed him a hundred times? He said you'd agreed to help him with it. He found whatever he was looking for, though."

"He took something? From my disaster area of a desk?"

"He wouldn't wait. I tried to call him off."

"Delaney, I never promised to help him with anything. I have no idea what he took."

Delaney's radar pinged again. "Was there anything on your desk that he *shouldn't* see?"

"No." Megan's face reddened. "I don't think so. God, I hope not." She turned. "I'll go talk to him. I'm sure it's nothing."

After Megan left, Delaney tried to finish the report she'd been working on since seven o'clock, but she just couldn't focus. Last night, during her painful six-mile loop, she'd done her best to remind herself of all the reasons why falling for Joshua was a horrible, terrible, really bad idea, but five miles in, she hadn't had any success.

She'd tried the colleague argument—the one where she fast-forwarded thirty days and sat in a board meeting where her proposal was dismissed because she'd entered into a personal relationship with one of the affected parties—but still found herself getting all swoony when she thought of how he'd held her as they'd watched the sunset.

Then she'd tried the life-after-the-initial-flirtation argument—that one where she envisioned a future with a hospital pediatrician. And though she knew damn well there would never be enough time together, never be enough outside-the-hospital hours to maintain a relationship, she *still* couldn't get the man out of her head.

For the final mile, she'd increased her pace, a self-punishment technique that had worked wonders in the past. But when she'd collapsed on her porch, regret and fear dripping from every pore, she *still* wished she hadn't had to say no to his offer of a second date.

Because in uttering that one word, she felt like she'd just closed a giant door, and she wasn't at all sure it had been the right decision.

Chapter 21

"You're slouching, dear." Delaney's mother spoke out of the side of her mouth that evening, her lacquered lips barely moving as her eyes roved the hotel ballroom.

"I'm fixing my heel, Mom."

I'm thirty-two, Mom.

Delaney fiddled with the silverware set at their table toward the front of the room. As was his custom, Dad had bought the entire table, hand-selecting colleagues and golf buddies he deemed worthy of sitting with him.

"You're fidgeting, dear."

Delaney took a deep breath and clasped her hands in her lap. In her mother's company, it was exceedingly easy to feel like she was twelve again. She looked around the table, smiling tightly at the wives who'd spent the better part of the afternoon at the salon. Their makeup tried to hide self-perceived flaws, and for the most part, their a-little-too-tight, a-little-too-sparkly dresses would have better suited women twenty years younger.

She was the only grown-up daughter at the table this year, Scarlett O'Brien having married her own orthopedist last summer and moved back a row. Delaney tried not to feel pathetic about being the only single-over-thirty person at the table, but it was a little sobering. Five years ago, she'd thought Echo Lake might be the perfect place to find her forever-someone. She hadn't realized just how few *someones* were available, however.

And now it looked like she'd gone and done the stupidest thing possible—allowed herself to risk both her professionalism and her heart by getting pseudo-intimate with a colleague. Sure, all they'd done was kiss, but still. The CFO's office was just beyond her fingertips, and last weekend, she'd completely compromised her integrity by letting Joshua take her out to the lake.

She sighed. Oh, who was she kidding? If he offered right now to take her there again, she'd have an exceptionally hard time saying no.

And that was the scary part. She'd worked so damn hard to get where she was, and she had so many plans for what she'd do if she ever got to take Mercy's financial reins. She had every intention of being the best CFO in the hospital's history, and she'd been cutting her teeth on spreadsheets, funding formulas, and hospital regulations since she'd walked out of med school.

How could she possibly be willing to even think about risking all of that for a relationship that was doomed from the start?

"I need to use the ladies' room," she murmured to her mother. "Be back in a bit."

She sidled through tables all the way to the back of the room, finally breathing freely when she escaped into the lobby area outside the ballroom. The next hour would be filled with the usual pompous speeches by the usual pompous people, and her tolerance level was at an all-time low tonight.

While donors promised money to fund a serenity garden, a healthier cafeteria, and a whole herd of other pet projects, she'd just spent almost two weeks on a floor that was barely able to deliver basic care. To children, for God's sake. That's where the money *needed* to go.

Her mission tonight was to approach four possible big-pocketed donors she and Megan had targeted, and she'd practiced her five-minute spiel about a hundred times this afternoon, hoping she'd convince at least one of them to hear her out until at least the two-minute mark. However, she couldn't do that while everyone was pretending to listen to the speakers, so it was as good a time as any to hide out in the lobby until the mingling portion of the evening began.

As she'd wound her way through the crowded ballroom, she'd found herself scanning the room for Joshua. She knew he'd been invited to this dinner—all department heads always were—but there had been six new admissions on the floor this afternoon, so his chances of breaking free and showing up here were just about nil.

She wished she didn't care.

Delaney headed toward a pair of French doors that opened onto a long balcony facing the lake. The balcony was lit with hurricane candles flickering in the twilight breeze coming off Echo Lake, and she closed her eyes as she leaned against the railing.

"Let me guess—another fund-raiser escapee?" A gravelly voice startled her, and she whipped her head around to see an elderly man with a shock of white hair smoking a cigar at the edge of the balcony. He smiled conspiratorially. "Don't worry. I won't turn you in."

Delaney smiled. "Thank you. I'm not really—escaping. Just taking a break."

He shrugged. "You're taking a break, I'm escaping. Same-same, I think?" He had a slight accent that she couldn't quite place, but it was the kind that made you want to pull up a chair and listen to its cadences.

"Same-same." She nodded. "So what brings you to the fund-raiser?"

Could you be my Daddy Warbucks, by any chance?

"Coincidence, really. My wife and I are here on holiday. We lived here long ago. When she saw the gala on the hotel placard this morning, she just had to come. I suspect she's hoping to run into her first boyfriend. *He* is a doctor."

Delaney laughed. "And what are you?"

"Pah." He swiped a hand. "An inventor of useless gadgets. I'm lucky she's put up with me for forty years, living in swill, when she could have had a doctor." He ground out his cigar and held out a hand. "I am Oscar. You are?"

"Delaney." She shook his hand. "It's nice to meet you."

"So what brings *you* here? Are *you* a doctor?"

Delaney frowned. "No. But my father is. I'm a financial analyst."

"Ah." He nodded. "So you are the one who decides how much begging needs doing at such an event as this?"

She laughed. "Something like that, yes."

"And are you the one who is supposed to be doing the begging?"

"Yes again."

"But you are terrible at it? This is why you're hiding on the balcony?"

"I'm not hid—yes." She smiled. He knew. It was useless to protest. "I'm worse than terrible."

"You want to practice on a stranger?"

"Thank you for offering, but no. I've practiced a hundred times in my mirror already."

Oscar smiled. "So pretend instead of the five dollars I put into a basket downstairs, I gave you a million. What would you do with it?"

Delaney's shoulders fell. Wouldn't *that* be a dream right now.

"I have a soft spot for pediatrics, Oscar. I'd send every penny of it right there."

"And what would they do with it? Something better

than a new garden, I suppose?" He raised his eyebrows, and she knew she'd found a kindred spirit.

"So many things. So, so many things." Delaney took a deep breath, launching into her experience of the past couple of weeks, talking about the patients, the nurses . . . the doctor who held the seams of the floor together practically with packing tape. She talked about Kenderly, and Millie, and even Therese—talked about Kaya and Charlotte and little Ian. Through it all, she was careful not to use their names, or say enough about them for anyone to identify who she was talking about, but as she talked and Oscar nodded, it felt like a fountain had let loose. She had no idea when she'd started caring so much about all of the little souls on that floor, but as she heard her own voice, she realized she'd fallen in love with more than Joshua.

She'd fallen in love with pediatrics.

After ten minutes, she finally paused, embarrassed that she'd talked the poor man's ear off. "I'm so sorry. I didn't realize—I had so much to say."

He smiled, his blue eyes twinkling at her in the fading sunlight. "I've been married for forty years. I am a very good listener." He pushed away from the railing, his hand outstretched once more as he headed toward the doors. "I enjoyed meeting you, Delaney. And very good luck with your begging tonight."

"Thank you, Oscar." She shook his hand. "I'm sorry to talk your ear off."

He made his *pshaw* motion once again, turning to go. "After so long, I have none left anyway." Then he stopped, turning back to her. "If I could offer a small bit of advice?"

"Of course."

"Do not use the speech you practiced in the mirror. I know you have one. Use the stories you just told me." He put his hand over his chest and tapped softly. "That is speaking from the heart, and that is what makes people stop thinking about gardens and start thinking about . . . people."

He put his hand on her shoulder and squeezed. "You have a good heart, Delaney. The hospital is lucky to have you."

And then he was gone, leaving Delaney alone on the balcony with her swirling thoughts. Before she could even begin to corral them, a breeze gently lifted the hem of her skirt, and though she knew she should go back to the ball-room to see if the mingling portion of the evening had started, she just wanted to stay out here on this quiet bal-cony, watching the sunset while the soft breeze played with her hair.

Then a little gust hit, and a memory crept in—one where she and Parker were walking along the coast in Mystic, Connecticut, looking at the submarines. A gale of wind had come across the water, and they'd grabbed on to an iron railing, convinced they were about to blow away.

She felt tears threaten at the backs of her eyes as she pictured him that day—wispy reddish-brown hair and tiny freckles not quite hiding the bluish tinge of his skin. She'd held onto his hand so tightly, sure he actually *could* blow away if she let go.

The next day Mom and Dad and Parker had headed to Boston Children's while she'd stayed with a friend, but they hadn't come home that night . . . or the one after-ward. When Cara's mom had finally delivered her home three days later, the house was silent, her parents moving around like zombies.

Six months later, after trips to every renowned heart specialist her father could dig up, her dad had packed them up for one last camping trip, way up in northern New Hampshire. *Better than a hospital room*, Delaney had heard him whisper to her agitated mother as they'd packed. *Let's let him live while he can.*

But two days later, in a tiny ER in a tiny hospital, things had gone from bad to worse before a medevac could be arranged, and Parker's heart had finally succumbed.

The nurses had taken all of the tubes and wires off him before they'd let eight-year-old Delaney in to say a final good-bye, but she'd still been able to see their imprints on his tiny face.

She remembered sitting in the chair beside his bed, tears dripping onto his favorite dump-truck pajamas as she tried to smooth the lines out of his tiny cheeks. She remembered climbing into that bed with him and gathering him as close as she could while her mother collapsed on the floor.

She remembered her dad trying to lift her out of the bed, and her holding on to Parker's tiny body, refusing to leave him there.

She remembered the sound of her screams as her father had carried her down the stark hallway.

"You trying to escape the festivities?" Joshua's deep voice startled her.

He *was* here.

She turned away from him, trying to swipe her tears before she answered.

"Hey." Joshua came closer, touching her shoulder. "Are you all right?"

"Yes." She turned back toward him. "Wind blew something into my eye, I think."

He looked down at her, seemingly sizing up her story. He didn't look like he believed her, but he let it lie. He brushed her hair back from her shoulder, letting his fingers dance lazily along her jaw.

"So what are you doing out here? Get sick of the self-important bozos up front already?"

She smiled. "Careful. One of those bozos is my father."

"Right." He cringed. "Sorry."

"It's okay. The title suits, at times."

"So what are you doing out here, really? I thought you had your eyes on some Daddy Warbucks types tonight?"

"That part comes after the speeches . . . and hopefully a couple of wallet-loosening drinks."

Joshua nodded sagely. "Sounds like a job for Papi's Poison."

"Oh, God." Delaney laughed. "We should have thought of that."

"Do you want to sit?" Joshua pointed to the two chaise lounges behind them. "Speeches will probably be going on for a while yet, and it looks like we're about to have another impressive sunset."

Delaney looked out at the lake, which was starting to glow as the sun crept downward. Her entire body heated as she remembered the last—sunset—they'd shared. Somehow she knew he was thinking about it, too, though neither of them spoke.

"Okay. Just for a bit."

He shifted the chairs so they were an appropriate, collegial distance apart, then waited for her to sit before he folded himself onto his chair. She tried not to notice the way his dress shirt hugged his pecs, or the way she could see just the right sprinkling of dark hair on his forearms where he'd rolled up the cuffs.

"So . . ." He folded his arms over his chest. "This is where we make professional small talk, right?"

"Yes." She smiled, rolling her eyes.

"So it's not appropriate for me, at this juncture, to tell you I can't get you out of my damn head?"

"No. Definitely not."

"I can't."

She bit her lip, staring over the balcony, feeling his eyes on her.

It's mutual, buddy.

He sighed. "But since we're not talking about that, and since we're at a hospital function, want to talk about the hospital?"

"Not really."

"Okay, small talk. There's actually something I keep wondering about, watching you with the patients on the floor over the past couple of weeks."

"Oh?" She felt her shoulders relax.

"Ever regret that you left med school?"

Delaney took a deep breath. "Every day."

"Feel like you've let your dad down?"

"No. Because I went in all starry-eyed, wanting to be the kind of doctor who never wanted to say *I'm sorry— there's nothing more we can do.* But at some point in that first year, I realized that doctor doesn't exist. I let *me* down." She shook her head. "I make a really lousy surgeon's daughter."

"No, you don't."

"I know. Sometimes." She looked over at him, realizing suddenly how little she knew about him, outside the hospital. "What about you? What do your parents do?"

She saw a shadow pass over his face before he answered. "Substitute teacher and an electrician."

"But you weren't born with the wiring gene? Had to settle for med school?"

"Something like that."

"Why'd you choose pediatrics? Besides Avery, I mean."

Joshua took a deep breath, shifting his gaze out toward the lake. "I actually started out thinking I'd go into oncology, for all the obvious reasons."

"What changed your mind?"

"Honestly?" He sighed. "Like you, I hated the odds. They've made so much progress, but at the time, I didn't know if I could handle knowing that a high percentage of kids on my watch weren't going to make it. I wasn't nearly as attached to Avery as Josie and Ethan were, and her death still cleaned my clock. I couldn't imagine having a hand in—not being able to save somebody's child."

His simple, quiet statement clenched her gut. Hard.

"Yet you ended up choosing pediatrics."

"I know. It doesn't completely make sense, but I'm glad I did. The stars aligned, or whatever nonsense you want to call it. Someday I'll have that little office with my own hand-picked nurses and dozens of cute kids. Mercy is perfect for now, though."

Delaney had only been on the pediatric floor for a week and a half, but that had been enough to witness the hours the man worked, and that was in addition to his rounds at Avery's House.

"Are you ever concerned about burning out? With the schedule you have?"

"All the time, yeah. But it's the life I chose."

"Must not leave you much time for a social life."

He looked at her, smiling. "Well, I found time to come to this to-die-for event, right?"

"I'm sure there's nowhere you'd rather be."

"Maybe." His eyes held hers for one beat longer than was comfortable . . . or casual. "Maybe not."

"Do you—think the speeches are done yet?" She hated that her voice sounded nervous. Again.

"Why? Are you anxious to get back in there?" Before Delaney could answer, he touched her hand, sending zings up her entire arm. "What were you thinking about when I came out here?"

She closed her eyes. Now was not the time or place to tell him about Parker. "Nothing, really."

"I don't buy the speck-of-dust-in-the-eye thing. Just saying."

She looked at him, and the concern in his eyes just about undid her. Why did he care? He barely knew her, for God's sake. And she definitely didn't know him well enough to start spilling her family history all over a hotel balcony.

"Delaney, I know in a way, we've just barely met, and I'm not delusional enough to think that one night at the lake gives me the right to know anything, but if you need one, I've been told I'm a pretty good listener."

She smiled. "I know."

She did know. She'd seen him pull up chairs in patient rooms like he had all day to sit with a particular kid or parent, even though he had mountains of tasks waiting just outside that room. She'd seen moms visibly relax when he appeared, and she'd watched kids reach out to hug him, when they were dead afraid of everybody else who came into their rooms.

Even Charlotte loved him to death, and Delaney was pretty damn sure the girl had a well-oiled bullshit meter.

They sat in silence for a full minute before Joshua turned to her. "I have a really personal question for you, but don't feel like you have to answer it if it's *too* personal."

"Oh, boy."

He smiled. "I know. That's a terrifying way to open a conversation." He took a breath. "I can't help but feel like you've got a personal stake in this somehow. Like it's more than your job you're worried about. Why is pediatrics so important to you?"

"Because it's the right thing to do, Joshua." She fiddled with her purse strap. "Cutting this budget is going to hurt somebody in the end. Maybe more than one somebody."

"Okay." He nodded, looking back out at the lake, where

a fleet of tiny sailboats was cruising along a triangular course, competing in the weekly race.

They sat in silence again, but before she could stop the words from flying out of her mouth, Delaney said, "I had a little brother."

Joshua looked at her quickly. "Had?"

"Had." She nodded, biting her cheek so she wouldn't cry. "He died when he was five."

"Oh, no. I'm so sorry." He reached out again and took her hand. "What was his name?"

"Parker. He was named after my grandfather."

Joshua stroked the back of her hand with his thumb, his eyes serious, eyebrows pushed together in concern.

"What was Parker like?"

Delaney met his eyes. That was never the first question people asked. *What happened? How'd he die?* was the standard response, and for some reason, she felt inordinately happy that Joshua had skipped those two questions and, instead, had wanted to know who Parker was, rather than how he'd died.

"He was amazing. Supersmart, cute, funny. He used to make up these jokes that were just *terrible*, but he'd laugh so hard he'd tip over. And he loved being outside. *Loved* camping. We used to do that all the time."

Delaney's voice trailed off as she realized how many things they'd done as a family, before he'd died. Their annual two-week camping trip had been one of them, and she remembered it as the one time a year that her father actually disconnected from work and turned his attention fully to his own family.

"What did he look like?"

Delaney described him, and as she estimated his height with her hands and pictured his laughing green eyes, she felt him come alive, in a way. Telling Joshua about him,

doing had to be curtailed so he could either spend the next hour on the phone, or head back to the hospital. By the time she'd been a teen, she'd started to suspect some of those calls had been prearranged to get him out of things he hated doing, but she never dared say so, and he never let the beeper out of his sight long enough for her to peek.

But when Joshua's beeper went off, it meant someone at Mercy needed him, and now she knew who a lot of those someones were. Was Charlotte in trouble? Kaya? Ian? She pictured each one of their faces, and her stomach felt tight.

"Anyone I know?" she asked.

He shook his head. "Avery's House call this time. I'm sorry. I really have to go."

"Of course. I'll see you tomorrow."

As he headed down the hallway, she couldn't help but watch him. She also couldn't help feeling a little bit empty when he rounded the corner.

And that was a scary emotion.

Chapter 22

On Thursday afternoon, Joshua leaned out of his office as Delaney wheeled Kaya by his door.

"Hey—I just had an idea."

"Uh-oh."

"I want to know how things went last night after I left, and you haven't eaten all day, so you're definitely hungry, right? How about you tell me over dinner?"

She stopped, looking around to see if anyone had heard him, but all of the nurses she could see looked far too busy to bother listening. *Say no*, her brain shouted, but her mouth was too fast.

"What did you have in mind?"

"Ethan's picking up Bellinis—bringing it to Avery's House. It's kind of our Thursday-night tradition. I know they'd love to hear how things went at the fund-raiser." He winked. "We can call it a business dinner if it'll make you feel better."

She rolled her eyes. She so wanted to say yes, but she knew if she spent one more outside-the-hospital minute with this man, she was going to lose her freaking head. And yet *no thank you* wasn't what came out of her mouth next.

"One question—do you guys ever eat anything *but* Mama B's cooking?"

"Not often, no."

She laughed, then sobered. "Don't you think your friends might get suspicious that I keep tagging along? Have you considered that?"

"No worries." He waved a hand. "They know you work in the finance office. I already told them I was abjectly bribing you for more funding. They're good with it. That's why they've been on their best behavior."

She shook her head, smiling. Then she frowned, remembering Kevin darting around the executive suite this morning, reeking of aftershave and panic as he tried to corral the budgets he'd been assigned. She had no idea whether he'd stoop so low as to throw her under the financial bus if he got wind of her and Joshua having more than a professional relationship, but it was something she really, really didn't want to find out.

"It's just dinner, Delaney." Joshua's eyebrows were still raised.

"All right." She sighed, hating herself for capitulating so easily. "Just dinner."

At eight o'clock that evening, she was seated in the huge farmhouse-style kitchen in Ethan and Josie's section of Avery's House, her stomach aching from laughing so hard. For an hour now, Ethan and Joshua had been going back and forth about their high school antics, with Josie throwing in quips that painted them in a much-less-generous light than they were going for.

"I still can't believe you tried to sell old Mrs. Quimby's house right out from under her," Josie said, laughing.

Joshua lifted his eyebrows. "Mrs. Quimby deserved it. That woman would be outside raking her leaves on Halloween night, and if anyone dared to walk up her driveway, she'd point that rake and growl, 'Nobody's home.'"

"Still, though. Putting up a real estate sign when the leaf peepers were here was—"

"Inspired?" Ethan blurted. "Brilliant? The best part was when that couple from Manhattan knocked on her door and tried to offer her cash." '

Joshua hit the table with his hand, laughing. "And then she came roaring down to Bellinis, sure that Molly had put that stolen sign on her lawn. I thought Mols was going to shoot us. She got grounded for a week because Mama B wouldn't believe she hadn't been part of it."

"It's okay." Josie scooped more spaghetti onto her plate. "She made you pay eventually."

As one, Joshua and Ethan held their stomachs. Then Joshua turned to Delaney. "Just a quick piece of advice. If you ever piss off a Bellini, do *not* accept a dinner invitation within the next month."

"Oh, no." Delaney's eyes widened. "What happened?"

Ethan shook his head. "Let's just say she fed us chili for dinner and chocolate cake for dessert. I'm sure you can imagine what she added to both of those to make our lives miserable for the next forty-eight hours."

Delaney spread butter on a roll as she laughed. "I have a new respect for Molly."

"See that you maintain it," Joshua advised. "That woman is not someone you want on the *other* side of a battle."

"Good to know." She nodded and took a bite of spaghetti, content to listen to the three of them as they laughed and talked over one another for the next hour. The windows were open to the backyard, and she could hear crickets warming up for nightfall. The deep yellow walls of the kitchen were warmly lit by old-fashioned gas lamps and the setting sun, and as time passed, she sat back in her chair and sipped her wine, letting the conversation flow around her.

Being here helped lessen the sting of her abject failure at the fund-raiser last night. Faced with a room full of possible donors, she'd frozen as she'd walked around. Her well-practiced spiel had caught in her throat, and she hadn't even managed to find three of the five donors she and Megan had targeted. Dismal, absolute failure.

But her mood was improving dramatically, sitting here in the back kitchen at Avery's House. Again, she'd expected to feel a little bit left out among these forever-friends, but to her surprise, once again, she didn't. They easily brought her into the conversation, curious about her life before Echo Lake.

When she recounted the tale of her ill-fated ski vacation at Smugglers' Notch ski resort, where first she'd met the three college guys who'd plucked her out of a snowbank—and then had met the ski patrol who had ferried her and her broken ankle to the lodge, all four of them were laughing.

"This is why I'll never feel like a real Vermonter. You people are on skis before you know how to walk."

Josie patted her arm. "Not all of us."

"Exactly." Ethan nodded. "Some of us are born on snowshoes."

Delaney shivered. "I can't even imagine how much damage I could do in *those*. I think I'll stick to my skates."

"I always wanted to learn how to skate." Josie held up her wineglass. "Maybe you could teach me this winter?"

Delaney smiled. She asked it so easily, like she expected Delaney might still be a part of their little crew next winter. It gave her the proverbial warm-fuzzies, and she found herself lifting her glass to tap Josie's.

"I'd be happy to."

Just then a beeper sounded, and when she realized it was coming from Joshua's waist, the warm feeling evaporated.

He sighed, checking the readout, then frowning apologetically. "Excuse me for a minute. I need to call the hospital."

He pushed through the screen door to the backyard, and Delaney watched him put his phone to his ear, talking and shaking his head. She pulled her eyes away to find Josie looking at her intently while Ethan brought their plates to the huge white farmhouse sink under the window.

"So," Josie finally said, putting her glass to her lips. "I'm sensing that you have more than a passing business interest in our dear Joshua."

"God, Josie." Ethan shook his head as he grabbed the spaghetti bowl.

"Has he by any chance taken you to the lake?"

Ethan rolled his eyes as Delaney gulped. "Josie, seriously. Stop interrogating her."

"I'm just asking! As a friend!"

"You're asking because Molly told you to get the scoop."

"She did not." Josie pouted playfully.

"Josie?" He put his hands on his hips, eyebrows hiked, which made Delaney laugh. She couldn't help it.

"Okay, fine. She totally did." She turned back to Delaney. "So what's the scoop?"

"I—I don't know. No scoop, really?"

Oh, holy awkwardness.

"You remember I'm a therapist, right?" Josie tipped her head, smiling invitingly.

Delaney nodded. "Yes, and that scares me more than a little bit right now."

"Good girl." Ethan laughed. "Don't let her get her tentacles into you. You might never survive it."

"Shut up, Ethan. Even *you* can see there's something going on here."

"Whether I do or don't is none of my business." He leaned down to kiss her on the forehead. "And it's not yours, either. Leave the poor girl alone, or Josh will never dare to bring her here again."

"Okay." She sat back, playfully defeated. "But just one question. *Has* he taken you to the lake?"

Delaney sat back, matching her pose. "One question back at you—why is that question so important?"

Ethan chuckled at the sink, but didn't say anything.

Josie eyed her carefully, then picked up her glass and stood up. "Don't break his heart, okay? That's all."

As she went to the sink, Delaney shook her head. Break his heart? Seriously? Like she had the power to even *do* that?

"I have no intention of breaking anybody's heart, just to be clear."

"Good"—Josie smiled—"because if you did, you'd never be able to step foot inside Bellinis again without Molly doing you in, and I'd be kind of bummed if that happened. I like you."

As Delaney laughed, Joshua came back through the screen door, and she could see from his face that he was going to announce that he had to leave.

"You have to go?" She tried to keep even a slight tone of hurt out of her voice. After all, he didn't owe her anything. This wasn't a date, really. He'd invited her to a casual dinner with friends. She had no claim on his evening. And he didn't have backup at the hospital right now because they were so short-staffed. It wasn't his fault he kept getting pulled away.

But it *was* his life.

And as they pulled out of the Avery's House driveway and headed back to the hospital, where he dropped her off beside her car in the parking lot, she tried to keep that firmly in mind.

If she got in any deeper, this would be *her* life, too—
aborted evenings, broken promises, lonely nights.

"I'm sorry to drag you away from dinner." Millie was
shaking her head as he strode down the hallway toward
the nurses' station. "But she's a mess. Doesn't want to go
home tomorrow, won't do her therapies tonight, won't
even talk to anybody."

Josh stopped to lean on the counter, thinking. Poor
Charlotte. The girl was headed home to a double-wide
trailer where the water got turned off monthly, along with
the electricity. She shared a tiny bedroom with four other
siblings, and he knew that during the school year, the
family's weekend food came mostly by way of charity
backpacks sent home from school.

He didn't fault her parents. They were doing their best.
They both worked more than full-time, both worked more
than one job. But none of those jobs came with benefits,
and all of them came with minimum wage. Raising a
seven-person family on that kind of money just wasn't
possible.

While she was here at Mercy, Charlotte almost always
had her own room, she had good, hot meals, and she got
lots of attention she sorely needed. Once she was home,
she'd fade into the cheap paneling again until she got sick
enough to need hospitalization.

Because she would. She'd be back here in a matter of
months, and every time she came, she was a little bit sicker
than the time before. Every time, it was a little bit harder
to get her back to her previous baseline. One of these
times, they weren't going to be able to at all.

By the time her parents got home late at night, she was
asleep. They left before daybreak, leaving the kids to find
breakfast and get themselves on the school bus. Charlotte
might get a couple of chest PT sessions over the weekend,

but not always, and she desperately needed them at least daily. She had a vest that mimicked the PT, but it only worked when there was actual electricity to fuel it.

He sighed. "Ever wish you could adopt a couple of these kids, Millie?"

"Daily."

"What are we going to do?"

"I did notice her cough has increased over the past twenty-four hours." Millie looked to her left, not meeting his eyes.

"Truly?"

Millie shrugged, not answering. "You and I both know that girl's not going to get a whit of therapy once she leaves here. Maybe a few more days would set her up for a better discharge? I could get Kenderly involved a little more, maybe?"

"Maybe."

"Maybe even Delaney? Charlotte has taken to her like nobody else."

Joshua smiled, picturing Delaney sitting on Charlotte's bed braiding her hair while they discussed—well, whatever they discussed. Then his smile faded as he pictured Delaney's face this evening when his beeper had gone off. Again.

She'd tried to hide it, but he'd seen a defeated expression erase her easygoing smile before she had a chance to tamp it down and pretend his leaving didn't bother her. He knew the look. He'd seen that same expression on other women he'd dated—hell, he'd sure seen it enough on Nicole. Before tonight, it had irritated him. He was a doctor, after all. Carrying a beeper and being called away from casual events happened. It was part of the drill.

But this time, he hadn't felt irritated. Instead, he'd felt bad. Seeing the fleeting disappointment on her face had cut him like never before, and the strangest feeling had come over him.

Because as it turned out, he didn't *want* to disappoint her. He didn't want her to feel like anything was more important than her, in that moment. In any moment, really.

And holy hell, that was a revelation that scared him right down to his size tens.

Chapter 23

"Squee! Did you see it yet?" Megan barged into Delaney's office Friday morning, waving the day's copy of the *Boston Globe*.

Delaney blinked hard, tearing her eyes away from her in-box, which had somehow accumulated one hundred new e-mails since yesterday. Her heart was currently at war with her brain, and she was so distracted that she hadn't managed to knock off any of them.

"Look! It's Amanda's second article!" Megan flopped the paper on top of Delaney's keyboard, opened to the headline. "E-mail can wait!"

Delaney picked up the paper, feeling her smile grow as she read each paragraph. Holy cow. Amanda had gone gangbusters here, somehow managing to squeeze in some information about every single one of the programs Delaney had listed for her.

"Wow," she said, putting the paper down. "We couldn't have paid for better PR."

"Exactly." Megan sat down, handing Delaney half of her croissant. "I think we should send her flowers."

Just then, Kevin poked his head in. "What are you gals so excited about?"

Megan turned toward him, picking up the paper. "Did you see this article?"

"What article?" He stepped in, eyebrows pulling together.

"On pediatrics." Megan shared a wink with Delaney while he took the newspaper. "It's so great! The reporter was here last week, and she put together this great Friday edition profile. It's going to be read by"—she turned to Delaney—"what do you think—thousands of people?"

"Oh, at least. And she has colleagues doing their own local features, so I think this is the first of many." Delaney shrugged carelessly, biting her cheek so she wouldn't smile triumphantly. There was a serious flush gathering on Kevin's neck, creeping toward his ears as he read the article.

Megan gushed again, obviously noticing the effect as well. "Isn't it great? I'm going to make sure all of the board members get a copy."

The flush reached his ears and engulfed his cheeks.

Delaney nodded. "That's a great idea. They work so hard—it'd be good for them to see all of their efforts paying off with this amazing publicity. Right, Kevin?"

"Sure. Right. Yes." He shook his head. "How did this reporter find out about all this stuff? All of these programs and everything?"

Delaney shrugged again. "She asked."

"Who did she interview?"

"Nurses, doctors, patients—the whole gamut, looks like." Delaney worked to keep the triumphant tone out of her voice as she watched him seethe, but try not to show it. She could practically see the wheels turning inside his head, wondering how Delaney had grabbed the department destined to get the best PR. He had no idea how hard she'd worked for that PR, however. Nor would he find out, if it was up to her.

"Wonder why she focused so hard on pediatrics?" He

"I know. Charlotte's under her spell, too."

Millie raised her eyebrows. "We're hardly talking about Charlotte."

Josh shook his head, moving to the coffeepot. He had a feeling he was about to get an earful, and despite the fact that he couldn't get Delaney out of his head for more than five minutes straight, he didn't want to talk about it with his head nurse. Late last night, when he'd finally rolled home from the hospital and realized it was too late to even call her, let alone try to see her, he'd sat alone in his living room, frustrated and more depressed than he'd ever want to admit.

There was no question that he and Delaney had chemistry. No question that the two of them together would be like fireworks. But the fear and defeat he'd seen in her eyes last night had just about killed him. He couldn't play games with her—couldn't make promises he couldn't keep.

But hell, it'd sure be easier to stick to that if he didn't want her so damn badly.

"Don't go playing matchmaker, Millie."

"Are you about to tell me you don't have time for a relationship?"

"I don't. You know my schedule. It wouldn't be fair to pretend I have any extra hours in my life." As he said it, his chest squeezed a little. But it was true, right? "Neither Delaney nor I have time to do any more than hang out casually once in a while."

"Then make time."

He paused, throwing her a sidelong glance. "Millie, how many hours do you work?"

"Too many," she grumbled. "And you work even more than me. That's exactly my point."

He shook his head again. "*What's* exactly your point?"

"My *point* is that if you keep waiting around for timing

to be perfect, you're going to be a lonely old man before you know it."

"Oh." He laughed, but it wasn't convincing. "Is that all?"

"Not funny, doc. I'm serious. Your current life plan—correct me if I'm wrong—is to work yourself to the bone here at Mercy until Doc Sullivan or Doc McIntosh retires, or until there's a sudden influx of children in Echo Lake. And then you'll finally have your own practice, right?"

"Right." He smiled at the thought of regular hours, maybe two employees, lots of adorable families with even more adorable kids.

She sat down. "Have you actually thought about what it'd be *like* to be a single-doc practice?"

"Yes. All the time." He sipped his coffee, wincing as it burned his tongue. "Why?"

"I'm just thinking." She motioned for him to sit down at the creaky table with her. "Let's look at a day in the life, shall we?"

"Okay." He sat down, humoring her. "Let's."

"So it's July. We've got, say, three sports physicals, maybe four or five infant slots, and maybe a swimmer's ear or a sprained wrist, right?"

"Sure."

"Times, say, five, right? Because in order to make an actual living, you'll have to get your time slots down to about five to ten minutes per patient?"

"No. No way."

"Have you *done* this math?"

He rolled his eyes, but didn't answer.

"Okay, now." She raised her eyebrows. "Let's move on to February. Still a few physicals, some infants, some hockey and gymnastics injuries. But dum-dum-*dum*. Then the flu hits."

"I'll have a stellar nurse who will field the calls and give fantastic advice."

Millie nodded, eyebrows still up. "You ever been a mother to a feverish toddler at two o'clock in the morning?"

"I'll also have an answering service."

"Who will call *you* at two o'clock in the morning. And three o'clock. And four. And five. For *weeks* on end."

Josh sighed. "Why are you going all doomsday on me here?"

"Because. I might have mentioned the part about your candle burning at two ends already here. And I hate to be the one to give you the cold shower of reality, but getting out of Mercy and starting your own practice isn't going to give you more hours in the day—not if you go it alone."

Millie put her hand on his. "And keeping your heart all locked up because you think no woman can possibly understand the twenty-four-hour requirement of doctor duty isn't going to hold water forever. No woman *should* have to put up with that—because there's a balance, and you need to find it."

"It's not that simple, Millie."

"I know it isn't. I *also* know you carry a three-hundred-pound weight around your neck every day, trying to make your parents proud." She stopped, forcing his eyes to hers. "Honey, I knew your mom, and the only thing she *ever* wanted was for you to be happy. Doctor, dentist, farmer—she didn't care."

"I *am* happy. I'm doing what I love."

"I know you are, but at some point, you need to let yourself fall in love again—the sweet, messy, amazing kind that sends you to work all distracted and asking for a weekend off. *That's* what you need."

He shook his head. "Can I get the sweet and amazing without the messy?"

"You can try." She hugged him. "Just open your eyes, Joshua . . . and maybe your heart."

"Oh, and another thing." Millie reached into her bag and came out with a moose key chain. "Got a cancellation on our cabin this morning. It's all cleaned and ready for guests—who aren't coming—and I think you should go stay there for the weekend."

"Millie, if I didn't know better, I'd think you're afraid I'm heading for a nervous breakdown or something. First the candle comments, and now you're handing me the keys to your cabin?"

She shook her head. "You're nowhere close to a breakdown. However, I've taken the liberty of getting you coverage for the next two days, and I have a sneaking suspicion there's a woman on this floor who might just say yes to a weekend in a little cabin beside the lake. You could—you know—ask."

He smiled, reaching out to hug her.

"You're impossible."

"I know it. Just part of my charm." She put the keys in his hand. "I don't want to see these until Sunday afternoon. And as of tonight at six o'clock, I don't want to see *you*, either."

Chapter 24

An hour later, Josh stepped out of the elevator after checking on Ian, who was in a solitary room on the fourth floor, under twenty-four-hour surveillance. He was improving already, and Josh couldn't wait to tell Delaney the good news.

He stopped in the middle of the hallway.

When had she become the first person he wanted to share a piece of good news with?

Then he heard her voice, and her unmistakable laugh, coming from the playroom. He headed down the hallway, more anxious to see her than he was willing to admit. When he got there, he paused at the doorway, surveying the scene.

Annabeth, the anorexic who Millie'd reported was starting to make some strides with her therapist, was sitting at the card table with her bony knees pulled up to her chest. He winced at how her collarbone still protruded under her T-shirt, but the disease had had her in its grip for two long years. It was going to take time to get her back to a healthy baseline.

"Gin!" Annabeth laid her cards on the table. "Read 'em and weep."

Josh watched as Delaney laid her cards down as well, grinning. "Oh, there will be no weeping."

Annabeth pointed at Delaney's hand. "You have two aces, two kings, and two queens. You should *definitely* be crying. That's seventy points you just lost."

Delaney gathered the cards to shuffle. "No problem. I can totally come back from this. I'm not sure I like how you score this game, by the way."

Annabeth looked at the notepad beside her elbow, grinning. "Omigod, you're three hundred points down."

"This is why I don't like how you score this game. But you know what? There's still time for me to pull off an epic win."

Annabeth laughed, startling Josh. That was a sound he hadn't heard from Annabeth since she'd been here.

Then she seemed to realize she'd done so, and backed off, crossing her arms as Delaney dealt. "Don't you have somewhere to be? Things to do?"

Delaney looked down at her cards, idly sorting them. "Yep."

"So . . . why are you hanging out with me?"

"Because you're way more fun than the other stuff I'm supposed to be doing. Do you have any idea how long it's been since I've creamed somebody at gin rummy?"

Annabeth uncrossed her arms, smiling. "You're *not* creaming somebody. I'm totally winning."

"For now, girlie. For now." Delaney pointed at the deck of cards. "You're up. Shuffle. And there's no way you're winning this time."

Josh smiled as he backed up and turned toward his office. Ian's news could wait. Delaney was doing important work right now.

She just didn't know it.

"What's funny?" Millie came bustling out of a patient room, rubbing sanitizer between her fingers. "You catch the gin rummy tournament down there?"

"Yup."

"You gonna tell Delaney she missed her calling, one of these days?"

"Nah." He shook his head as he ducked into his office. "I think she's figuring that out for herself right now."

He sat down at his desk, cringing when he saw the piles of paperwork waiting there. Then he took a deep breath. "One inch. Just do one inch."

He plucked the top inch from the closest pile and began to read the lab report. Before he got to the second page, however, his thoughts were wandering to a moonlit dock, a cup of coffee on a misty porch, a rumpled bed, and a fireplace stoked high.

He eyed Millie's keys on the corner of his desk, his brain sorting through what Millie had said earlier. He'd been determined to keep things casual with Delaney. Hell, he hadn't planned to keep them *anything*. But it wasn't working. At all.

He hated to admit that he'd started getting off the elevator in the morning looking for her. He hated that he listened for her voice as he met with patients and their parents. He hated that when he finally fell into bed at night, it felt way lonelier than it had in a long time.

"Hey. You okay?"

As if he'd conjured her with his thoughts, Delaney stood in his doorway, her brow furrowed.

He shook his head, blinking his eyes to clear his thoughts. "Yeah, I'm good."

"Paperwork causing you physical pain?" She pointed to the piles on his desk.

"Yes. Does our workers' comp policy cover this?"

She frowned, shaking her head. "I think a match would be the only thing that would cover this."

"I know, I know. I need to embrace the electronic age. And as soon as I trust it, I will."

"I see." She leaned against the door frame, and he had to physically stop himself from pulling her into the office and kissing her. Today she had on a flowery skirt and prim white blouse, and all he could imagine as he looked at her was undoing that top button . . . then the next . . . then the next.

He cleared his throat, eyeing Millie's keys, then asked the question before he could talk himself out of it.

"So I know it's late notice, but do you have plans this weekend?"

She looked startled. "Some, yes."

"Oh." He felt surprisingly defeated.

"Why? What did you have in mind?"

Ah, hell. Should he bother to ask her? Pulling back from a getaway weekend was a lot harder than cooling things down after just a couple of hot kisses. Was he really ready to put that much skin in the game? Especially after they'd—sort of—agreed not to?

"Camping." The word was out before he could swallow it.

"Camping?"

He chuckled. "I didn't know your eyebrows could go that high. Camping not your thing?"

"Not—anymore, no."

He watched emotions flip across her face before she set her jaw, and in that moment he remembered the story about her little brother.

"Oh, God, Delaney. I'm sorry. I wasn't thinking. I didn't—think."

"It's okay. I just haven't ever been—since Parker. Since that time." Then she looked at him, subtly bracing her shoulders. "What kind of camping were you thinking about?"

He cocked his head. *Really?* She wasn't shutting him down?

He held up the keys. "The kind with floors and windows. Adirondack chairs, stone fireplace, couches."

He was sure they both heard him *not* say bed.

"No sleeping bags and mosquitoes?"

"Only if you prefer it that way."

She nodded slowly. Then she looked down, like she was trying to talk herself into it, or out of it. He didn't know her well enough yet to know which it was.

"Do you have a cottage or something?"

"Millie does. She rents it, but her guests cancelled at the last minute, so she gave me the keys and told me I wasn't allowed to be at the hospital this weekend."

Delaney laughed. "And you say *you're* in charge of the pediatric floor."

"I don't say it to anyone who knows better—which is pretty much everybody." He put on his best pleading face, surprised at how anxious he was for her to say yes. "So what do you say? I know we said we wouldn't. But . . . I can't not ask you. Think you could stand a weekend cooped up with a doctor in a cabin by the lake?"

"I don't know." She cringed, and his stomach fell. "Throw in a freak storm, and it sounds like the makings of a horror film."

"Or a romance novel." He shrugged. "You never know."

Ah, double hell. Had he seriously just said that? With a straight face?

She looked at the floor, seemingly weighing the pros and cons as he waited. Finally, she nodded slowly. "Can we order in Bellinis?"

"A few kisses, and now you're doing an entire weekend with the man? Are you really Delaney Blair?" Megan cleared a space on Delaney's bed so she could sit—no easy feat, since it was currently covered with a pile of clothing two feet high.

"I know. It's crazy." Delaney blew out a breath as she flopped another shirt on the pile. "Com*pletely* crazy. What am I doing?"

"Well, it sounds like you're heading off for a weekend of mind-blowing sex with Dr. Dreamy."

"Megan!"

Megan shrugged. "Just calling it like it is."

"I wasn't going to do this. I distinctly remember us deciding we were going to remain strictly professional. Less than a week ago, for God's sake. And now he's inviting me to a cabin by the lake for the weekend? And I'm saying yes? Do I have absolutely no willpower at all?"

"You have a lot of it, actually. Just not with him." Megan picked up a bathing suit from the pile. "Are you bringing this?"

"I don't know. Either that one or the blue. I can't decide."

"You could go totally bonkers and pack both."

"Stop picking on me." Delaney turned back to the closet. "You know my stats. Three. Ever."

"Aw, sweetie. You've been waiting forever for the right guy to come along and be number four. And look! He did! But you're destined to be nervous about it."

"You think?"

"Just remember—thing A goes into slot B."

Megan laughed as a pair of jeans came flying out of the closet and hit her in the head.

Delaney shook her head, trying to decide which shirts would convey just the right balance of little-bit-sexy and I'm-not-trying-here. Unfortunately, it didn't look like she actually owned any.

"When is he picking you up, Cinderella?"

"Nine o'clock in the morning."

"Then we have time to go shopping." Megan pointed

to the bed. "I mean, since it appears your entire wardrobe has been discarded, and you're back to about 1993 in the closet."

"Shopping is your solution for everything."

"No." Megan shook her head. "But shopping *is* a solution for hot-date weekend with a new guy who makes your toes tingle."

"I *have* done this before, you know."

"Oh, I know. You just haven't done it in—"

"Shut up. We're not counting." Delaney backed out of the closet and pushed more clothes off a chair so she could sit. "What am I *doing*? I was never, *ever* going to fall for a doctor."

"Best laid plans and all? News flash—those fail. Often."

"I know."

"Hey." Megan's eyes widened. "Do you still have your Perfect Husband list?"

"No."

"You do, too." Megan stood up and reached for the top drawer of Delaney's bureau.

Delaney leaped up to stop her. "I do not."

She was too late. Megan opened the drawer and shuffled around, coming up with a piece of loose-leaf paper.

"Ha. I knew it."

Great.

Megan glanced through the list, smiling. "When did you make this, anyway?"

"A long, long time ago." Delaney reached for it. "Come on. Hand it over."

"Why do you still *have* it?"

"Because it keeps me honest. Reminds me not to be stupid."

"Item number one." Megan held the paper out in front of her.

"Meg, seriously."

"My perfect husband will not be a doctor." She shook her head. "Uh-oh, Joshua."

"See? Told you."

"Item number two—my perfect husband will be blond." She wrinkled her nose. "Seriously? You were thinking blond?"

"I had a serious crush on that Disney kid who was in all of those movies at the time, okay?"

"Next item—he'll be taller than me. Phew! Joshua's back in the running."

"Megan, come on." Delaney laughed. "Seriously, give me the list."

"No way. I haven't seen it since college. Not giving it back until I've read the whole thing."

Twenty minutes later, Delaney was holding her stomach, which hurt from laughing so hard at Megan's reading of her list.

"So let's summarize." Megan took a deep breath. "What we're apparently looking for here is a tall, blond accountant who loves dogs, hates cats, and wants to travel, but never across the ocean because there's a statistically higher risk of crashing and never being found."

"Shark bait—that's all I'm saying."

Megan laughed. "I love this list. I think you should *frame* this list. We can read it at your wedding someday."

"Right. Because that's looking oh so imminent these days."

"Hey." Megan shrugged. "You have a hot-date weekend planned here. It's a start, right?"

"If I survive it with my heart intact, yes."

Megan looked at her, tapping her on the head with the list. "Am I a bad friend for kind of hoping you don't?"

Chapter 25

"Just cream, right?" Joshua held up a to-go cup of coffee as Delaney answered the door Saturday morning.

"God, yes." She took the cup gratefully, having not yet found time to make her own. Even though she and Megan had spent an hour cruising the downtown shops before they'd closed last night, she'd still struggled to pack this morning.

"Come on in. I'm pretty much ready." She took a long sip as he stepped through the door.

He laughed at her obvious desperation for caffeine. "Should I have gotten a large?"

"No. We can get another on the way."

"The cabin's only a half hour away, on the other side of the lake."

She shook her head. "Too far. My very low pain tolerance is balanced by a freakishly high caffeine tolerance. I may not survive past Dunkin' Donuts."

He smiled, surveying her condo. "This is a great place."

She looked around, trying to see it objectively. With its huge windows, high ceilings, and exposed brick and beams, she knew it appealed only to a select audience. She didn't know him well enough to determine whether he was part of that audience, she realized, and that realization made her stomach even jumpier than it already was.

"Reminds me a little bit of the original part of Avery's House, where the kitchen is." He took a few steps toward the living room, which she'd decorated with Southwestern-style scatter rugs and Navajo pottery, all focused around the huge couch piled with earth-toned pillows that had been her big splurge when she'd moved in.

"Wow." He parted the gauzy curtains at the huge riverside window. "Incredible view."

"It's what sold me. As long as we never have a major flood, it's perfect. If we do, I'm going to need a snorkel."

He laughed. "How long have you lived here?"

"I just barely moved in, actually. I looked at stuff all over town, but this place—I don't know—it has a story. I can still imagine it as a mill, in a way."

His eyes scanned the open living area, and she was thankful she'd closed the bedroom door before he arrived. She hadn't yet cleaned up the piles of clothing scattered all over the room—had in fact slept on the couch because she couldn't *find* the bed—and at this point, she was tempted to bag up the whole lot and make a trip to Goodwill, rather than put anything away.

Joshua moved along the wall, and Delaney put her hand to her throat as he got to a picture and stopped, staring at it for a long few seconds.

"Is this Parker?"

"Yeah."

He straightened the frame slightly. "He looks just like you." He smiled as he turned back toward her. "So, are you packed?"

"Yeah." Delaney's hand dropped slowly as she felt a peaceful feeling steal in. He was so matter-of-fact about Parker. All her life, people had either whispered quietly, just out of earshot, or they'd asked a hundred probing questions. It was refreshing to have Joshua treat him as if he'd just been—her little brother.

Ten minutes later, Joshua pulled his truck into the Dunkin' Donuts drive-thru in the center of town.

"You were serious about more coffee, right?" He looked across the cab at her.

"Unfortunately, yes."

"Good. Because I need donuts."

She laughed. "You're a doctor. You eat donuts?"

"Only on special occasions."

Delaney smiled. "I'm so honored to be part of one."

"What's your favorite flavor?"

"Jelly," she said, without pausing to consider the mess she'd make eating it. "And old-fashioned."

He turned toward the microphone, smiling. "We'll take two large coffees with cream, and a dozen donuts. Half jelly, half old-fashioned."

"A *dozen*?"

He shrugged. "Breakfast *and* lunch. We're on vacation, and when's the last time you had donuts, anyway?"

"It's been a long time." She laughed. "I'm not sure I packed enough workout gear to get rid of a half dozen donuts, though."

"No worries." He winked as he shifted to pull up to the second window. "We'll go out in Millie's canoe. Two miles of paddling, and you'll be *begging* for a donut."

Three hours later, Delaney set her paddle across the canoe, resting her arms. *Holy cow*. He hadn't been kidding about the paddling workout. She ran twenty miles a week, for God's sake, but right now it felt like she hadn't worked out in ten years.

The lake was calm today, and along the shorelines she could see kids splashing and diving from docks. The sky was a perfect summer blue, and there was just enough of a breeze to keep the sun from scorching them.

"How are your arms?" Joshua's voice came from behind

her. He was still paddling, of course. He must have a home gym where he did midnight workouts—there was no way he ever found time to actually go to one.

"They're good. Fine. Just wanted to pause for a second and listen for the loons."

"Oh, you'll hear them, paddles or not. They're usually out a little later, though."

She pointed at the tiny mountain at the north end of the lake. It was more of a hill, really, but she'd been climbing it ever since she'd moved to Vermont.

"Do you ever go up there?"

"Not since I was a kid. You?"

She nodded. "Yeah. I love it. There's a great spot overlooking the lake. You know"—she picked up the paddle again, dipping it into the water—"I haven't been in a canoe since I was little."

"Did you do it back when you used to camp?"

"Yeah." She nodded, picturing Parker sitting on an inflatable cushion in front of her on the floor of her parents' old canoe. That was one of their favorite parts of vacation every year.

"Unfortunately, Mom had a nasty habit of forgetting how tippy canoes are. Every single year, we'd end up in the lake at some point, swimming back to shore."

"I'm sure your father loved *that*."

"You know, it's funny. I don't remember ever thinking he minded. He was—different—on vacation. Totally—present. It was weird. Good weird, but still—weird."

"So you never camped again. What did you do for vacations?"

She shook her head, smile fading. "We never actually did another vacation together after Parker died."

"Oh." He stopped paddling. "Really? None? Ever?"

"No."

"So life as you knew it—"

"Died with Parker, yeah." She paddled, thankful she was facing away from him. "After years of researching grief, I get it now . . . but at the time, it was hell. There's a whole set of grieving moms who cling so tightly to their remaining children that they almost suffocate them. My mother took the opposite approach. She was so afraid to lose someone else she loved that she just—sort of— stopped loving. I mean, I know she *did* love me, way down deep . . . but after Parker, she put up sky-high walls around her heart, and there wasn't a chance in hell I was going to break through them. And Dad buried himself in work. That's just . . . how it went."

"What happened, Delaney?" She felt her paddle still, then his. "How did he die?"

"He had a heart issue, maybe something that could be fixed these days." Her voice came out quiet. "I don't know. He was on a transplant list, but there wasn't a lot of hope for that to come through. My dad thought we should try one more vacation—you know—because it might be the last one." She took a shaky breath. "Turns out it was."

"Oh, no."

"He was doing great, actually. We'd been having a lot of fun. But then one night, he just kind of fell, and it was obvious something was really wrong, but the closest hos- pital didn't really have a pediatric unit or an ICU. And it was too late to medevac him to Boston."

"I'm really sorry, Delaney. I wish—" He sighed, and in that sigh she heard a sort of ragged pain that reflected how she felt. "I wish there was something I could say. There isn't, though. I know that."

"No. You're right. And believe it or not, I appreciate you realizing that, rather than blathering some inane comfort that isn't. You would not believe the things people said afterward."

"I can't imagine."

She put up her hands. "I mean, I know. I get it. What *do* you say to an eight-year-old who just lost her little brother? They were just trying to be nice."

"I'm pretty sure nobody ever knows what to say—at least to the ones left behind."

"Yeah."

They floated in silence for a long moment, and then Joshua picked up his paddle. "Did Parker like canoeing?"

Delaney smiled. "Loved it. Especially the part about getting dunked."

"How about you?" He raised his eyebrows. "Did you like that part?"

"Only if it was really hot."

"Hot like—today?"

The canoe rocked slightly, and she gripped the sides tightly. "Joshua Mackenzie, don't you dare."

He put down his paddle, moving his hands to the sides as well. When she looked back, he had a boyish grin on his face as he started rocking the canoe slowly.

"Can you swim?" he asked.

"Yes." She cringed. "I mean, no. If I say no, will you stop?"

"Nope. Just need to know if I have to rescue you or not."

Then he gave the canoe a mighty heave and dumped them both into the cool lake. She went under, and for a moment, she was eight again. The cool water enveloped her head, and every nerve ending in her body tingled as she fell through the water. When she surfaced, she couldn't help but laugh.

"You are still a teenager at heart."

"Nah." He laughed, wiping droplets of water from his face. "If I was a teenager, I'd have dumped us much farther out so you'd have to cling to me in pretend terror. At least this way we can swim back to the dock before sunset."

Delaney looked back toward the tiny cottage on the shore. The dock was only about three hundred feet away, but she put her hand to her forehead in her best Scarlett O'Hara swoon.

"I'm not sure I can make it. You might have to carry me."

"Gladly." There was heat in his eyes as he grabbed the canoe and flipped it over. "Or we could just get back in the boat."

"Okay. Option B works."

She grabbed the side and tried her best to look remotely graceful climbing back in while he held it as steady as he could. Once she was in, she tried to lean just right and hold it steady enough for him to do the same. But just as he had three limbs aboard and was heaving himself over the side, she inadvertently lost her balance, and back into the lake he went.

She sat down quickly so she wouldn't join him, since the boat was now rocking like crazy, and was still laughing as he sputtered back to the surface.

She put up her hands. "I swear I didn't do that on purpose."

"Sure." He grabbed the side, but didn't pull himself up this time. "I might believe it if you weren't still *in* the canoe. It takes a certain amount of skill to dump only one person out."

"I promise it's a skill I don't have."

As Delaney looked down at him in the water, she swallowed hard. Braced against the canoe, his T-shirt soaked through, Joshua could have held his own on a modeling shoot. His pecs were outlined perfectly, his shirt clinging like it, too, appreciated the curves and hollows.

And his arms—good God, his arms. They looked like

they could lift her high in the air without even trying hard. Or—she swallowed again—maybe brace his body over hers for a long, long night.

She shivered, but it wasn't because the air was cooling.

"Are you cold?" he asked.

"No. Breeze just hit me."

He smiled. "It's better in the water."

"Don't you dare." She held on to the sides again as he tipped the boat gently.

A memory struck her as she sat on the webbed seat— one of her and Parker diving out of their anchored canoe and playing a swimming game while her parents got lunch ready on the shore.

"Ever play Sharks and Minnows?" She raised her eyebrows.

"I don't think so. How do you play?"

She stood up carefully, then dove quickly off the other side of the boat. Her runner's lungs helped as she swam a long circle underwater, ending up under his dangling feet. She reached up to tickle one, then darted away.

When she surfaced, she couldn't see him anywhere. Then, before she could take a breath, she felt strong hands grip her calves and yank her underwater.

"No dunking!" she sputtered as her head broke the surface.

"You never went over the rules," he said, laughing. "That was my best shark impression. And I'm pretty sure dunking is *always* allowed."

"When you're twelve, yes." She splashed him.

"Okay, then. Enlighten me. What are the rules when you're supposed to be acting like a grown-up?"

She paused, thinking as she treaded water. "You know, I have absolutely no idea."

"Good." He swam closer, almost touching her. "Maybe we can learn them together."

"Maybe." Her voice came out all husky as her feet swished against his underwater.

He came closer still, and she was struck by how erotic it was, both of them using their arms and legs to stay afloat, while their bodies swayed together in a gentle rhythm.

"I'm glad you said yes to coming for the weekend."

"Pretty sure I'm insane, but me, too."

He smiled. "I know we said we wouldn't, and I know you're probably questioning it with every fiber of your being, but I have an idea."

"Okay?"

"Nobody but Millie knows we're here, Delaney. Let's just pretend this is our second date. A top-secret, never-to-be-revealed-to-anybody-else weekend. Let's forget we're colleagues who shouldn't be dating. Let's also forget I'm a doctor, since I'm pretty sure you'd never date one on purpose. Plus, maybe I can get extra credit for leaving my beeper at work."

Delaney couldn't help but smile as she watched him in the water, his skin glistening with droplets of water, his hair making her want to run her hands through it as she pulled him close.

"Very tempting, I have to admit. Even though Millie stole it from your desk before you left."

"Details. Point is, I didn't ask for it back."

She laughed. "A huge step, I'm sure."

"So . . . do we have a deal?"

"Sounds like a fantasy. I'm not me, you're not you, and nobody will ever know?"

His eyes heated at her words, and the sight made her pulse race. "I'll entertain any fantasy you can come up with. Promise."

"Oh. God." Her entire body heated at his words. "Okay, okay. Deal."

"Excellent." Then he reached for the tips of her fingers, linking them with his. Feeling the mixed sensation of cool water and strong, warm hands made her long for the fantasy to begin right here, right now.

He raised his eyebrows, smiling. "Have you ever played Kiss the Mermaid?"

"Sounds like a game made up by teenage boys at summer camp."

He laughed. "Maybe." He turned to point down the shoreline. "Ethan and I spent a lot of bored summer nights paddling over to Camp Echo, hoping for a chance to meet some city girls."

"And that's where Kiss the Mermaid originated?"

"Probably." He shrugged, then winked. "Actually, come to think of it, it was two girls from Boston who taught us the game."

"Sure."

"Well, you know what they say about Boston gals." He slid one hand around her waist as his other kept him gently afloat.

"What *do* they say?"

He pulled her closer, then touched his lips to hers.

"They make the best mermaids," he murmured, then ran his hands down her arms, pulling them onto his shoulders.

"You can't hold us both up." She cringed as he paddled slowly, his arms out to the side. "I've eaten, like, three donuts."

"Oh. That explains—" His last word got lost in a bubble as he let his head sink underwater, and she had to let go of his shoulders or risk going under with him.

When he surfaced, she splashed him. "Not funny."

He smiled, reaching out for her again, and though she rolled her eyes, she couldn't help but let herself float back into his embrace. This time when he kissed her, she

hooked her fingers around his neck and let her body press
against his. This time, she longed for his hands to roam
farther than her waist. This time . . .

"Hey." She pulled back, realizing his lower body had
stilled. "You're not swimming."

"Reef," he replied, pointing down, where his feet were
firmly planted in the sand. "Come here, mermaid."

He pulled her firmly against him, and as their bodies
meshed in the water, she felt like every nerve ending was
strangely, gorgeously aware of the touch of his fingertips,
the gentle lapping of the water, the nibbles of the minnows on their toes.

Where their first kisses had been sweet and hot and
new, these were all that, with a shot of smoldering promise layered on top. Tonight they weren't going to have to
go their separate ways and meet for a polite hello at the
hospital in the morning.

No. Tonight they'd have nothing but each other to keep
them occupied. The cabin had no phone service, no television, no computer. Cell service was spotty enough that
they'd turned off their phones when they'd parked in the
gravel driveway, and Delaney shivered at the implications
of spending the next twenty-four hours alone with Joshua,
with no interruptions.

For once, she was glad Megan had dragged her out
shopping last night. She was especially glad she'd pulled
her into the froofy lingerie shop behind Bob's Bait and
Tackle. Waiting in her overnight bag was a lacy, lilac-
colored set *guaranteed to make any man forget his own
name*, Megan had said.

Delaney tightened her legs around his body, and he slid
his hands downward to cup her bottom. Though they were
in the middle of a lake, where anyone with a good pair of
binoculars could clearly see them, all she wanted to do was
strip off their bathing suits and feel his skin against hers.

He pulled her closer, and she closed her eyes tightly, savoring every inch she could feel of his body.

Finally, he pulled his lips from hers, and she could feel his racing pulse against her fingertips.

"We should—probably get back in the boat before we get run over by a rogue water-skier."

She planted a soft kiss on his lips, desperate not to lose contact with him. "I don't see any boats."

He chuckled. "Then we should probably get back in the boat before I lose my head and strip you right here in the water."

"Oh." She smiled against his lips. "I'm glad one of us is thinking straight."

"Mm." He kissed her again. "Have you ever played Kiss the Mermaid in the water after dark?"

"God, no."

He rocked her gently against him, and she gasped as her entire body responded.

"Want to try it later?"

"God, yes."

Chapter 26

"Does Mama B know about this place?" Delaney looked around three hours later as the maître d' of Luciano's seated them at a private corner table. Even though she would have been perfectly happy to stay put at the cabin and cook mac and cheese for dinner, Joshua had insisted on taking her out—*to prove I sometimes eat somewhere besides Bellinis.*

"Mama B sics the health inspectors on this place at least twice a year, yes."

Delaney laughed, picking up the leather-bound menu. "It smells just like Bellinis."

"Believe it or not, the chef is Mama B's cousin Luciano. They grew up together."

"Seriously? Do they share any family recipes from the old country?"

"No sharing." Joshua shook his head. "I think they wrote some agreement on a napkin long ago that said they'd never open up within ten miles of each other, and he wasn't allowed to make chicken and mostaccioli if she agreed not to make his lobster ravioli."

She flipped open the menu. "They have lobster ravioli here? Be still my Italian heart."

"Just promise me you won't tell Mama B or Molly that we came here."

"What would happen if they found out?"

Joshua grimaced. "Have you ever tasted Mama's hot sauce?"

"No."

"Well, you don't want to. If she found out we'd been here, our next spaghetti dinner would light the table on fire."

Delaney laughed. "My lips are sealed."

After they ordered, Joshua pushed the basket of rolls toward her. "These are to die for, but Mama B claims it's only because Luciano stole her secret recipe."

She plucked one from the basket. "Well, if they're anything like Mama's, I might ask if we can order a basket to go. I've already fallen so far off the wagon with the donuts today that I'm a lost cause."

"It's vacation, remember? Carbs don't count." He put a roll on his own plate and slathered butter on it.

"Speaking of which"—she pointed vaguely toward his chest—"how are you doing without your beeper lifeline?"

He raised his eyebrows mischievously. "Just fine, thanks."

"You're not even twitching. How can you stand it?"

"Apparently I'm distracted enough that I haven't even noticed." His foot found hers under the table, and she felt herself blush.

"That's very flattering. Thank you." She rolled her eyes. "Seriously, though. Is it driving you just a little bit crazy to not check in?"

Joshua looked around the room for a long moment, then met her eyes. "Honestly? I expected it to . . . but it isn't. I haven't had this much fun disconnecting in a long, long time."

"Well." She swallowed, feeling heat build between them. "That's good, then."

"How about you? You do just as much dawn-to-dusk

stuff as I do, at least since I've known you. How does it feel for *you* to get free of the office?"

"When I'm not getting dunked, it feels great. I could totally live in the cabin for a week, I'm afraid."

"You wouldn't miss work?"

Delaney felt her nose wrinkle as she shook her head. "It's funny, and please don't be a big dork and say *I told you so* or something—but after spending the past two weeks on pediatrics, I miss *that* more right now than my own job."

"Well, I imagine the change of pace has been nice, if nothing else."

"Sure"—she set down her roll—"but it's a lot more than that. Even though I feel like a poser, there's a weird sense of—I don't know—connecting. I don't get that upstairs. I feel almost—useful." She shook her head. "Never mind. That sounds silly."

"No, it doesn't."

"I'm plenty useful upstairs. I'm *very* useful. But it's a different feeling. I like it."

"More than you thought you would?"

She nodded. "Oh, definitely."

"Ever think maybe you'd like to change gears and do something besides finance? Someday, maybe?"

"Yes? No?" She took a deep breath. "I've always felt like finance was—I don't know—kind of my cop-out. I know objectively, I'm providing a valuable service, but at the end of the day, I don't really go home and say 'Hey, I actually touched somebody's life today,' you know?"

He paused. "What if you get the CFO position when Gregory retires?"

She looked at him. "What do you mean?"

"I don't know." He shrugged carefully. "I've seen a lot of people come through my floor since I started. Some of them were born to love pediatrics, and a lot of them weren't. I have to say, I'd put you pretty firmly in the first group."

"Well, I have a lot of reasons to love it, obviously."

"Maybe, but losing a little brother a long time ago doesn't necessarily set somebody up to be a natural at it. You are definitely a natural."

She shook her head. "I don't know about that."

"I do. Delaney, how many times did you laugh this week?"

"I don't know." She smiled. "A lot."

"And how many times do you laugh—generally—up in the executive suite?"

"I don't. But why would I, really?"

He reached out and squeezed her hand, but didn't let go. "Which job is more fun?"

"That's obvious, but you can't really choose a job for the fun factor, Joshua."

"Why not?"

She tipped her head. "Be serious. I have goals, a mission—bills to pay. Important work to do."

"But maybe you, too, have a balance issue?"

Just then the waiter arrived with their dinners, saving her from answering for a few minutes. Once they'd both had a few bites, Joshua looked at her while he wound fettuccine around his fork. The table candle made his eyes sparkle, and her own eyes caught on his lips—lips she hoped would be keeping her awake later.

She got a nervous tingle as she thought about actually spending the night together, but the more time she spent with him, the more she couldn't wait to be done with dinner so they could make their way back to the cabin—to the gorgeous brass bed with the pieced quilt laid on top.

Later, as the sun set over the water, Josh lit the citronella candles placed along the cabin's dock, then sat back down in an Adirondack chair next to Delaney. He caught her profile in the golden sunlight and had to pinch himself. He'd spent the entire day in a state of heightened awareness of—everything. The sun was hotter, the water was cooler, the sky was bluer, and even the sound of the crickets warming up in the meadow behind the cabin was—sweeter.

He'd never heard a sound he liked better than Delaney's laughter, and the day had been full of it. Whether he'd been dunking her in the water, or tickling her on the dock, or getting lost twice on dirt roads before they'd found Luciano's, he'd loved every second of being with her.

And now, here she was, eyes closed, head back against the chair, sunlight kissing the tips of her eyelashes as her breaths made her chest rise and fall in a slow, contented rhythm.

He could hardly believe she was here with him. Could hardly believe *he* was here at all. Sure, he'd done a B and B weekend here and there over the years, and they were always romantic and fun. But to willingly unplug from the universe and spend almost twenty-four hours with a woman, making himself unavailable to anything else? He'd *never* done that before, even with Nicole.

He swallowed, letting his eyes trace downward over Delaney's slim body.

Why had he never done it before? Was it just that he'd never been in the right place in his life to make it work? Or was it that he'd never found a woman who made him want to?

Delaney stirred, and he swept his eyes back to her face before she could catch him ogling her body. She tapped her fingers nervously on her chair, then spoke.

"So I hate that I want to ask this, because it doesn't matter. Or—well—it shouldn't matter. But it does. I guess. I think."

Josh shook his head, mystified. "Was I supposed to follow that?"

"No." She laughed. "I'm just sitting here, feeling more relaxed than I've been in years, but also unbelievably—tense—in all the best ways, and I find myself naively hoping maybe you don't—do this—often." She grimaced. "Never mind. Please forget I just said that."

"I don't."

"You—don't?"

He reached for her hand, squeezing it as he leaned to kiss her. "No. I don't. I haven't even played Kiss the Mermaid in, like, *days*."

She whacked him playfully, then leaned back in her chair again, closing her eyes. "I think if I was Millie, I'd never want to leave. It's so perfect here."

"It is right now." He nodded, letting his thumb trace circles in her palm. Then he pointed toward the north sky. "Almost time to make a wish on the first star."

She laughed. "I haven't wished on a star in a very long time."

"Oh. Hey." He reached behind him for an old CD player and speakers that Millie kept in the kitchen. "It occurs to me that I still owe you a dance."

"A dance? From what?"

"From the charity fund-raiser thing. You promised me a dance."

"Right." She nodded. "But you had to leave."

She tipped her head like she was calculating. "I'm pretty sure if you ditch a girl before a promised dance, you owe her *two* songs."

"I see. Even if it was an emergency?"

"Depends. Was it a beeper-style emergency? Because beeper emergencies go triple. Sorry. Doctor-dating rule number thirty-four."

He laughed. "Triple it is, then."

He stood up, looking down at her, loving the sundress that showed off her slightly sunburned shoulders and tiny waist. He reached out his hand, taking hers.

"Will you dance with me, Delaney?"

She smiled. "I will."

"You just played 'Stairway to Heaven' three straight times." Delaney pulled back so she could see into Joshua's eyes a half hour later.

He shrugged, a smile playing at his lips. "It's the longest slow song I know. I figured if I owed you three songs, then they'd better be as long and sappy as possible."

"Good thinking."

"I can put the song on continuous loop if you want to keep dancing." He leaned down to kiss her softly. "Or we could go for a swim."

Delaney shivered as she looked at the dark water.

"I'm not sure I'm a big fan of swimming in water where I can't see the fish. The big ones come out after dark, right?"

"Well, in this lake, the biggest ones wouldn't feed you for more than one meal, so I'm pretty sure you don't have to worry about losing an arm or anything."

"I don't know." She shook her head. "I think my adventurous spirit stops at the end of this dock, once the moon's out."

"Okay. No swimming. How about we just dance in the moonlight, then?"

Delaney laughed softly. "You are quite the romantic, you know."

"Am I?"

"Don't worry. I won't tell a soul."

He rolled his eyes. "Definitely the kind of thing a guy doesn't want getting around. Luckily, your rep is shredded as well."

"Well, don't tell anybody I'm actually human. It would totally mess with the next audit."

"My lips are sealed."

The song started again, and Delaney sighed as he pulled her arms gently up to rest on his shoulders, then gathered her close to his body, his chin resting on her head as they swayed.

"Delaney?"

"Mm?"

"Have you ever made love in a big brass bed . . . in a log cabin . . . in the moonlight?"

She took a shaky breath. "No."

He pulled back to look into her eyes, tipping up her chin as he placed a feather-soft kiss on her lips.

"Would you like to?"

Chapter 27

"I don't want to go home." Delaney pouted as she folded herself into the porch swing overlooking the lake on Sunday morning.

Josh chuckled as he handed her a mug of coffee and sat down beside her, wrapping his arm around her shoulders like they'd been sitting out here together on Sunday mornings for months.

"I don't, either."

"Does real life *have* to take back over already? Can't we just keep our phones turned off and stay here for the week?"

"That sounds idyllic." He squeezed her shoulder, surprised at how perfect that actually sounded. Delaney in his space, in his arms, in his bed—for days on end.

She leaned on him, and he smiled as she pulled up her legs and snuggled closer, sipping her coffee. Her skin was soft against his fingers, and part of him wanted to take her hand and pull her back into the bedroom one last time before they had to leave.

He had no idea how things would play out once they left the cabin, but memories of the night they'd just spent together promised to torture him for a long, long time to come. He'd called Delaney an enigma before, and now that he knew her in bed, knew her at the breaking point, knew her in the afterglow . . . the word hardly did her justice.

She was in turns sweet and sassy, timid and sure . . . and the combinations had kept him guessing all night long. He'd spent hours exploring her body, and she his, and neither of them had even thought about sleeping until the sun crept through the lacy curtains.

When they'd awakened two hours later, he'd found Delaney snuggled into him, and despite the fact that his right arm was asleep, he didn't want to move. Didn't want to wake her. Didn't want the idyllic scene to ever be interrupted.

But she'd sensed him awake, and she'd rolled over sleepily, reaching for him, hungry for him. Afterward, they'd showered until the hot water tank ran cold, then gotten dressed slowly, like neither of them could stand to face the morning.

However, Millie needed them out by ten o'clock because new renters were due in this afternoon, and the cleaning crew needed to do their thing before then. He idly rocked the swing with his toes, wishing with all his might that they didn't have to head back to their respective realities in an hour.

"You look good without a beeper, you know." She looked up at him with hooded eyes. "Actually, you look good without a lot of things."

He laughed. "Ditto. I wish I could say I'm sorry you never got to wear half of what you packed—but I'm not."

"Maybe another time."

"Definitely." He said the word automatically . . . but not. He'd said it before on a Sunday morning, and he'd even meant it some of those times. This time, though? This time he felt a physical *need* to know that there *would* be another time.

In only two weeks, Delaney Blair had gotten under his

skin like no one else ever had, and maybe once he got home, he'd be able to figure out how she'd done it. Right now he was too clouded with memories of a long, hot, beautiful night with her in his arms.

She drained her coffee and straightened up slowly, looking out at the lake. In her profile he could see relaxation, satisfaction, and more than a little exhaustion, which made him smile. He predicted they'd both be sacked out on their respective couches later this afternoon, trying to make up for the hours they *hadn't* spent sleeping last night.

She turned to him. "I guess we should get going, hm?"

"Unfortunately, yeah. I guess we should."

"Maybe if I'm really, really nice to Millie, she'll let me come back someday. Do you think?"

"Depends whether the media blitz worked, I think. If she's looking for a job in a month, she might not be feeling too generous."

Delaney put a hand to her forehead, and he felt guilty for plunging her back into the world they'd left behind.

"I guess we should pick up some papers on our way back through town—see if anybody else gave us any help over the weekend."

He put his arm back around her, pulling her close. "We did our best, Delaney. If it all goes sour now, it's not because we didn't try, right?"

"I guess." She sighed. "But it just—can't."

"I agree." He stood and pulled her up from the swing, kissing her gently when she was standing against him. "Let's not think about it yet, okay?"

She kissed him back. "Did I mention I really, really don't want to go home?"

An hour later, they drove back into the village, and Josh felt his throat constrict. The last thing he wanted to do right now was drop Delaney off at her riverfront condo and go home to his huge, lonely house for the rest of the day.

Sure, he could head over to Avery's House—probably should, really. Or he could check in at Mercy to make sure all was well there. Normally, that's exactly what he'd want to do. But not today. When he glanced across the truck cab at Delaney, who was frowning as she watched the little downtown shops go by, he was struck by an urge to just keep her with him for as long as humanly possible.

"Do you have to get home, really?" He raised his eyebrows and reached across for her hand.

She smiled. "Why? Do you have another secret cabin we can disappear to?"

"I wish. I just wondered—want to come back to my place for a while?" He cringed as he realized he sounded like he was crafting a really lousy booty call. "Just to—whatever. Hang out, maybe have some lunch?"

"If your place has coffee, then yes. If not, can we stop for some first?"

He squeezed her hand, then returned his to the wheel. "You have a serious caffeine problem."

"Noted and agreed."

"I do have coffee."

She smiled. "Then I'd love to see your—place."

He turned up Sugar Maple Drive, wondering suddenly if he'd picked up his breakfast dishes yesterday, or hung up the towel from his shower, or—crap—made his bed, even. The last thing he'd expected to do was invite Delaney back here, after all. He'd totally thought the next person walking through the door would be him, and *alone* was the only way he ever walked through that door.

The strangest sensation came over him as he drove up the street—a feeling of hope, of wanting Delaney to love his house as much as he did.

Nicole had hated it—found it big and drafty and old. It should have been just one of many, many signs, but he'd ignored it, figured she'd come around eventually.

He looked over at Delaney, hoping against hope that she wouldn't hate it, too.

"Oh. *My*." When Joshua pulled into a gravel driveway halfway up the hill, he saw Delaney's mouth fall open at the sight of his dark green Victorian with its wide front porch and rounded towers on each corner. "This is your *house*?"

He shrugged. "Yep. It was my parents' house first, though. I came by it on the cheap. No way I could touch it in this market otherwise."

He stepped out of the truck and came around to open her door. As she got out, she stood in the driveway, just staring at the house in awe. He tended to forget how beautiful the place was, given that he'd lived here his entire life, but the look on her face was a warm reminder.

"Did you grow up here? In this house?"

He nodded. "Want to come inside?"

"Oh, I definitely want to come inside. I bet this place has a back stairway and a dusty attic and everything."

"You sound like a kid in a candy store." He laughed in relief. "Dusty attics aren't actually all that cool."

"They are to me. I always, *always* wanted to live in a house like this. I know it sounds completely ridiculous to complain, but the houses I lived in were all modern, with high ceilings and big rooms and lots of designer furniture."

"Sounds terrible." He unlocked the door and motioned her into the foyer, where a wide staircase headed up to the four bedrooms on the second floor.

"It so was."

"Crooked walls and thin insulation and creaky floors are way more fun." He rolled his eyes. "I have all of those here, by the way."

"They give it character." Her eyes widened as she took in the stone fireplace at the end of the huge living room. "Oh, my God. That fireplace!"

For the next half hour, he led her around the house, floor by floor, until they ended up back downstairs in the kitchen. The whole time, she'd oohed and aahed, and he'd actually loved seeing the house through her eyes. He took for granted the way the morning sunlight crept through the kitchen windows, the way the fireplace opened into the master bedroom, the way his dad had built a window seat in each of the towers. But watching Delaney discover the house sent such an incredible buzz of warmth through his body that it floored him.

As Josh got two bottled waters out of the fridge, Delaney sat down on a bar stool, pointing at the cast-iron rack of pots over the granite island.

"Dr. Mackenzie, I think you've been holding out on me. This looks like the kitchen of a real cook."

He shook his head. "Unfortunately, it's all for show. I can't cook any better than my mother ever could."

"Could? Is she not—alive?"

"No." He paused, taking a deep breath. When was the last time he'd talked about this? Had he gotten any better at it since then? "They died when I was in med school. Car accident."

"Oh, I'm so sorry, Joshua. I can't imagine."

He reached up to pull glasses from a cupboard, not sure how much he wanted to share.

"Is that them?" She pointed at a picture he'd hung on the wall—his favorite one of his parents. In it, Dad had his arm looped over Mom's shoulder, and she was laughing. It was the way he liked to remember them—laughing, happy, embarrassingly infatuated with each other even after almost thirty years together.

He glanced over, smiling. "Yeah. That was actually just a month before the accident. My aunt took the picture out at the lake."

"What were they like?" She took the glass he offered her, then followed him out the back door to a stone patio with chaise lounges.

"Oh, that's such a big question." He sat down, looking out at the backyard.

"I know." Her face fell, and he felt guilty. "Sorry. I just—wonder."

"Don't apologize. My mom was funny. She was goofy and smart and sweet, and she kept my dad and me in stitches all the time. She couldn't cook worth a damn, but she didn't care. I ate so much mac and cheese growing up that it's a wonder my skin doesn't have a yellow tinge."

Delaney laughed. "Better than the kale and spinach smoothies *my* mom foisted on me."

"My dad—he was head over heels for her. They were inseparable, you know? A love story for the ages and all that."

"Sounds amazing." Delaney looked away from him, and he could see clouds shadowing her face. He wondered how her parents' marriage had weathered Parker's death. They were still together, defying depressing odds, but he got the strong sense that together didn't necessarily mean they were happy.

She looked back at him. "Do you have any sisters or brothers?"

"No. They tried. But apparently destiny had other plans."

"And then—wow." She took a deep breath. "You ended up alone."

"With this really huge house, yes. My mom inherited

it from her parents, but she and Dad never really had the money—or time—to keep it up the way they wished they could. I think they always had *someday* as their mantra. Someday they'd do the insulation. Someday they'd go to Aruba. Someday they'd actually retire. But then—their someday got taken away from them."

He took a slug of his water, trying to steer his thoughts elsewhere. Before he could, Delaney took his hand.

"I think they'd be really proud of you—of all you do. I also think they never doubted for a second that all of their sacrifices were worth it."

He smiled sadly, squeezing her hand. "I wish I was so sure."

They were quiet for a few minutes, sipping their water and looking out into the yard. Delaney could hear kids playing somewhere on the street, and then the tinny tune of an ice cream truck broke through the relative peace.

She looked at Joshua, a whole new understanding of the man poking at the edges of her heart. No wonder he was so driven. He'd had parents who were behind him every step of the way, sacrificing all they could to help make his dreams come true. And then their lives had been cut short before they'd even gotten to see him realize those dreams. His guilt must have overwhelmed him at times.

No wonder he worked from dawn to dusk. No wonder he'd poured obvious hours and dollars into this house they'd never had time to update. No wonder he—by all accounts except his own—spent every waking hour thinking about other people, rather than himself.

No wonder . . . no wonder she was falling for him fast and hard.

"Joshua?"

He turned to her, eyebrows raised.

"Think I could have another tour? I'm not sure I remember which bedroom is yours."

He smiled, shaking his head as he set down his glass and took hers. Then he pulled her over to where he was half sitting, half lying on the chaise lounge. As she settled her body gently on top of his, he caressed her hair away from her face, looking into her eyes.

"I have to admit, you are not at all what I expected, Ms. Blair."

She laughed. "Good to know, since I'm pretty sure my ice-queen rep preceded me onto your floor."

He kissed her softly. "You are most definitely not an ice queen."

Their kiss turned hotter, deeper as he buried his hands in her hair, then let them travel down her back.

His fingertips brushed across her chest. "You kill me with these blouses. Every time I look at your buttons, I remember that second time you came to my office. I still swear it was a distraction strategy."

She kissed him. "I'll never tell."

He laughed softly. "It worked, by the way." Then he braced her hips against his. "Did you want to go upstairs?"

"You are being impossibly tight-lipped, missy." Megan glared at Delaney across her desk on Monday morning. "And am I to assume that the fact that you're arriving at nine o'clock means your weekend was extended until this morning?"

"Shh, Meg. Seriously." Delaney clicked on random windows, trying to figure out what she needed to do this morning, but the feel of Joshua's lips on her skin was still way too fresh in her mind to even contemplate focusing.

Megan narrowed her eyes as she leaned back and sipped her coffee. "Was he good?"

"Megan!"

"Well, come on. Give me a *little* here. I go shopping with you for sex clothes, and I don't even get to hear whether you wore them?"

"I didn't."

Delaney smiled, biting her lip. No, there'd been no time to put them on. And she hadn't missed them—or anything else—for the entire afternoon Sunday.

"You are impossible. You spent the entire weekend naked, didn't you?"

"Go." Delaney shooed her. "We have a lot to do today."

"Fine. See if I go shopping with you again. That was a perfectly good negligee. Wasted, I tell you!" Megan shook her head as she opened Delaney's office door, then turned around and came back to the desk, leaning over to hug her.

"What's that for?"

"Just happy for you, that's all." Megan hummed her way out of the room, and Delaney couldn't wipe her own silly smile from her face.

One minute later, her intercom buzzed.

"Delaney Blair speaking." She clicked on a report, determined to get it finished by lunchtime.

"It's Gregory. I need to see you in my office. Immediately."

She stopped clicking, eyes wide. What did *that* mean? And why was his tone so dire?

Chapter 28

"What's the status of your proposal?" Gregory's voice assaulted her before she'd even sat down, and she noticed new lines of exhaustion around his eyes.

"It's going—well," she blatantly lied. Despite a valiant effort, she had no cuts to suggest, no money to add to the equation, and the only thing she'd seemed to accomplish was to get some media coverage that hadn't led to one red cent pouring into the pediatric coffers.

Gregory pulled out a piece of paper and waved it her way. "This is your original proposal. Are we still going with this? Or has your research turned up anything else?"

Delaney felt a tinge of panic. "The original proposal needs to be shredded, Gregory. There's no way we can make those cuts."

"Because?"

"Because the impact is huge. Way huger than I could have predicted."

He put down the paper. "So what's your new proposal include?"

Delaney swallowed. *What, indeed?*

"I'm still poring through some grant paperwork, but there's some potential there to bring in some funding. I reached out at the dinner the other night and made some contacts. . . ." Her voice faded as she realized Gregory wasn't going to buy her bullshit any more than she did.

She sighed. "We're sunk, Gregory. There's not one dollar that department can do without, and I haven't managed to find enough other funding sources to fill the gaps. This isn't a process that can happen in a few weeks' time."

"Well, that time just got shorter. Board is meeting on Wednesday. They want to hear proposals, whether they're finalized or not."

"Wednesday? *This* Wednesday? Two days from now Wednesday?" Delaney gripped the arms of Gregory's guest chair, her knuckles going white.

"Wednesday."

"What—what am I going to say? They're not going to want to hear that my conclusion is *not* to cut this budget."

"No. They're not."

"But I have no other option. I can't in good conscience recommend that they take dollars away from this department."

Gregory picked her list back up. "You could always go in with this. Step back from it later. But this at least makes it look like you've done some due diligence. If you go in with nothing, there's gonna be hell to pay."

"If I go in with that, they'll approve it before I can even make my arguments that it was my preliminary and underresearched proposal, which I've now abandoned. No, I can't even put that thing in front of them." She shook her head. "No."

He sat back, crossing his arms, going for a casual pose, but Delaney'd known him just long enough to see one foot tapping on the floor under his desk.

"There's something else we should probably talk about."

"Oh?" Her stomach zinged in alarm.

"Is there any chance anyone could make an accusation of undue influence here?"

She cocked her head. "What?"

"I had a call from a member of the board. She had received information that you were possibly involved personally with Joshua Mackenzie. She thought it would be prudent for the board to be aware of whether that was indeed true, before they voted on any proposals that might come in front of them this week. Her words."

"What? From who? How? *What?*" Delaney's baby grasshoppers returned with a vengeance, making her hold her stomach.

He sighed, leaning forward and putting his elbows on his desk. "Delaney, I know Joshua. He's a good man. He's an excellent doctor. But if you've let yourself get involved with him, you need to think about the possible ramifications."

"Which are?" She crossed her arms. "Not that I'm saying I have."

"You could lose your job, Delaney. So could he. An internal investigation would most certainly be launched, and either or both of you could end up with any number of consequences, the worst of which being dismissal. I'm not saying it *would* happen. I'm saying it *could* happen."

"I'm not—we're not . . . involved. Personally." Delaney closed her eyes, hating the words as they came out of her mouth, hating that she was abjectly lying to a man she had the utmost respect for.

"I'm not asking you. But they're going to." He shuffled papers and pointed to the door, effectively dismissing her. "I'd recommend practicing your answer, because the one you just gave me isn't going to convince a soul."

Later that night, Delaney picked up her pace as she crested the killer hill three miles into her normal circuit. Any other day, she'd stop right here, put her hands on her knees to try to lower her heart rate, and take a nice long drink of water. Today, though, she ran right by her usual stopping spot, didn't drink a drop, and couldn't care less about her heart rate.

Gregory's words had been knocking around in her brain all day, and combined with the freak-out she'd already worked herself into since leaving Joshua's house last night, she was one short step away from a nervous breakdown.

She'd done the *what were you thinking?* exercise till she was blue in the face this afternoon, but besides coming up with a hundred reasons why *anyone* would have found Joshua hard to resist, she wasn't getting anywhere helpful.

She'd promised herself long ago that she'd never get involved with a man who would never, ever be able to put his job in second place. She'd lived that life, she'd seen her parents' marriage disintegrate, and she'd watched hordes of *other* wives head down the same lonely path. It wasn't going to be her life, dammit. *She* would come first, hell or high water. And if that wasn't going to be the case, then she was outta there.

Right.

Decisions like that were so much easier in the hypothetical. Decisions like that didn't take into account a pair of eyes that could melt you with one glance, or a pair of hands that could fire you up with one touch. They didn't take into account the way a certain man's laughter touched you way down deep, or the way the sight of him made you feel like everything—*everything*—was just . . . better.

And who *wouldn't* fall for Dr. Joshua Mackenzie? It wasn't her fault, dammit. He was sweet, funny, and sexy as hell. To his patients, he was dedicated, selfless, and gentle. The man spent his every waking hour taking care of other people—what flaw could she possibly find in that?

None . . . except when she thought ahead. She knew the end play on this already. The thing she most admired about Joshua was his dedication to his patients. The thing that would kill their relationship in the end—not that she was getting ahead of herself or anything after just two nights with the man—would be his dedication to his patients. Work-life balance was a myth, a workshop they all went to once a year . . . but it wasn't reality. Even if he'd *wanted* to change the balance, he was a doctor in an understaffed little hospital. Balance was a joke.

However, it was the life he'd wanted since high school. Ever since little Avery had come into his friends' lives and changed them all forever, he'd chosen this path in hopes that other kids might have it easier . . . in hopes that he could help others come out on the other side, unlike her. His parents had sacrificed *everything* for him, and every day, he was powered by the memory not only of Avery, but also of his parents putting off their new windows, fresh paint, and retirement so that he could live his dreams.

She knew all this. He'd told her.

But she hadn't realized how much it would hurt to realize that all of those things that made her admire him . . . might stand in the way of her being able to love him like she already feared she could—and would—do.

Because where would she fit in? She wasn't going to be the one blowing out candles on a cold supper table. She wasn't going to be the one reaching out at night to feel nothing but empty sheets. She wasn't going to be the one trying to explain to their someday-children that Daddy was busy again . . . always.

Not that she was getting ahead of herself . . . again.

She reached the footbridge where she usually stopped to watch the beavers in Stillwater Pond, but didn't halt. A pulsating, nervous energy was powering her forward, and even if she'd wanted to, it felt like she couldn't stop.

When Gregory had pulled her into his office this morning, he'd added another whole layer of hell onto the whole thing. Good God, how had she let Saturday happen, knowing it could have professional implications for them both? She *knew* it could, and yet she'd said yes, had gotten into his car . . . had gotten into his bed.

And now she was looking down the barrel of a hospital board that might or might not question her about her professional relationships. In one fell swoop, she'd risked her career, *his* career, and the entire pediatric floor.

She'd analyzed all of the angles all afternoon, and by seven o'clock, when she'd donned her running gear and headed out on a desperately overdue run, none of those angles had been remotely appealing. At best, she'd be disciplined. She'd most certainly have the pediatric budget yanked away, which meant it would land squarely in Kevin's lap. That was the *best*-case scenario, and it sucked.

At worst, she actually could be dismissed. The HR policy was pretty clear on that one. No matter what, if there was concrete suspicion of a personal relationship, an investigation *would* happen. And no matter what came out of it, both of their reputations would suffer long-term consequences. That investigation would stay in their files, and any future career move within the hospital could be influenced by the findings.

In essence, it meant that Delaney would never be CFO of Mercy Hospital. It was the position she'd been working toward for five years now, but her actions over one twenty-four-hour period could now derail all of that work.

The fact that she'd let herself become involved with someone would not only color this pediatric proposal—it would color every proposal she'd done prior to it . . . or any she completed in the future. She'd enjoyed a stellar, beyond-reproach rep until now, but it could all go up in a puff of smoke.

She'd known this on Friday. And yet she'd said yes.

Like she was powerless to say no.

And what did that say about her integrity, really? Could she honestly go before the board on Wednesday and be sure she *wasn't* unduly influenced? People looked to her on a daily basis to be analytical, forthright, and objective—to put together recommendations for the hospital's finances based on impartial, analytical, honest research. If even *she* didn't trust her own integrity, how could she expect anyone else to?

It would be like the reporter who did years of killer reporting, but then fabricated one story. In one fell swoop, persona non grata forever. Everything about the reporter's previous stories would come under the microscope, and trust going forward would be fragmented, if not destroyed completely.

She'd worked so damn hard, and it could come to . . . this.

But God, she wanted him. She did. She couldn't help herself. She'd never felt like this before, like already he owned a piece of her heart . . . and she didn't want it back.

Every single one of her internal alarms clanged as she ran down the final hill before the spot where she always met Meg. She was heading into white-water territory if she let this fledgling relationship get wings, and as zingy and warm and amazing as the weekend with Joshua had been, that weekend wasn't reality. It was a little slice of heaven that would turn into a faded memory before long, as reality intruded.

And if she let herself get any further involved, extracting was just going to be worse. For both of their sakes, she needed to stop things in their tracks. For so many reasons, it was the right thing to do.

She stopped, panting, realizing as her throat caught on a sob that the wetness on her cheeks wasn't sweat. It was tears.

Chapter 29

"Okay, I'm sitting." Joshua tipped his head curiously as Delaney closed her office door on Tuesday night. "Why so serious?"

She walked around to sit at her desk, taking a deep, careful breath as she did so. She'd been avoiding Joshua for two days now, but the board meeting was in twelve hours, and she couldn't wait any longer to have this conversation.

"We need to talk," she finally said.

He froze. "About?"

"About the weekend."

"Okay." He shifted uncomfortably. "Any chance you could ease off the death-knell voice while we do so?"

"Joshua . . ." She took a deep breath, trying not to let her shakiness show. "It was a mistake."

His eyes widened for a brief second, and then she saw his eyebrows furrow. "A mistake."

She nodded. "I think . . . we both know that."

"No." He shook his head firmly. "We don't both know that. What the hell, Delaney?"

She took another deep breath, squaring her shoulders. She needed to make this a quick, clean cut. Otherwise, she was going to melt into a teary puddle before she got the words out that she needed to say.

"I think—we got ahead of ourselves a little, you know? And maybe we should have given it more thought before we went to Millie's."

He sat back, jaw clenched. "What kind of thought, exactly?"

"The kind I've been having *since* the weekend. The kind that tells me—I don't know—that really, there's no way we could make something more than a secret-getaway weekend ever work."

"Because?"

"Because a *lot* of things. But first and foremost, because of who you are . . . and what you do."

He closed his eyes like he'd been stung, and guilt sliced through her.

"Seriously, Joshua, when you're not here at this hospital, you're working at Avery's House. I haven't actually figured out when you sleep, and that . . . that scares me."

"Because you think I couldn't possibly make space for someone special?" His words were soft, but his jaw was anything but.

She shrugged slowly, freezing her shoulders as she spoke. "I think you'd *want* to, and you'd *intend* to . . . but when it comes right down to it, you're at the mercy of . . . Mercy." She cringed, shaking her head. "I just don't think that right now, you'd really have time for a relationship, and I don't want to be the one making you feel guilty about that."

"You know, I find it kind of remarkable that *you've* decided so much about *my* life."

"I'm sorry. It's less about you than it is about me."

He sighed. "I'd have expected a more original breakup line from you, honestly."

"It's not a breakup line. We're not—we haven't—this isn't breaking up. We're not even—"

"Together?" His eyebrows went skyward. "In a relationship?"

She blew out a breath, misery making her chest hurt. "It was just one weekend, Joshua. A wonderful, sweet, fantastic weekend I'll never forget."

"But not one you necessarily want to repeat." He nodded. "I see."

She looked at him, but he refused to meet her eyes. Instead, he sat there, silently nodding, looking like he was trying to compose his words, but failing. If he'd had nails to spit, she imagined he'd start firing any moment now.

She bumbled onward. "It's not you, Joshua. It really isn't. I just—I envision a future where I'm not having to fight for first place. And I . . . I just don't see that with you. I wouldn't want you to be a different doctor or person than you are today, but with me, I'm really afraid you'd think you had to be. I don't want to be the woman who ever makes you feel that way. And I don't want to get in any deeper if I already know where we'd end up." She clenched her hands together under her desk, hating every word that was coming out of her mouth . . . hating the way each landed squarely on target. "I'm so, so sorry."

He finally looked up. "Is this really about the personal end of things here? Or the professional one?"

"What do you mean?"

"I mean, did it somehow become clear to you over the past forty-eight hours that a relationship with me could put your career at risk?"

Delaney paused before answering him. Of course it had. But it was way more about *his* career than hers. She had a feeling that argument wasn't going to hold a drop of water, however.

She sighed. "Both of our careers could be at risk here, Joshua. We both know that. We've been around the block enough to know how internal investigations go. However the final recommendations come out, the black marks are permanent."

Joshua stared across the desk at her for so long that she felt like she might break down and leap into his arms, spewing apologies. The truth was, in this moment, she could give a damn about her stupid career. She'd kiss it good-bye and bag groceries if it meant she could be with Joshua.

But his career was his *life*. And she couldn't be responsible for anything happening to *him*.

"So you've decided." He crossed his arms.

She nodded slowly, knowing she needed to stay strong here, even though she was on the verge of melting into tears. "Be realistic, Joshua. You don't have time for a woman in your life. Not really. This would have happened eventually. We're saving ourselves from heading down the road farther than we already went."

At her words, she saw a flush rise up his neck, and his bewildered expression turned to barely concealed anger. He stared at her for a long, long beat, then pushed himself out of the chair and covered the distance to the door in two long strides. With his hand on the doorknob, he turned back.

"Don't worry. If the board asks, I'll deny we've ever met."

"Delaney? Let's have you start." Margaret Stevens, the board chair, pointed a pen toward Delaney. It was ten o'clock on Wednesday morning, she was seated in an overchilled boardroom with Gregory, Kevin, and the nine members of the hospital board, and she had a strong suspicion she might be at her last day of work at Mercy Hospital.

She'd been sitting in her chair for twenty minutes now while Margaret went through the approvals of the last meeting's minutes, the agenda for today, and the introduction of some sort of new cash-out process in the hospital cafeteria that was supposed to save people thirty-three and a half seconds in line, therefore making them able to return to their posts more quickly.

She'd tried to tune out Margaret's voice, but it was like trying to ignore fingernails on a chalkboard. She felt sort of numb, like she couldn't quite process the last twenty-four hours. Last night, she'd rehashed her conversation with Joshua a million times, it felt like, and still, she had no idea whether she'd done the right thing. That moment when his hurt had turned to anger had made her shiver all night as she'd replayed it in her mind, and it had been all she could do to prepare for this meeting this morning.

But now she was here, in a suit that felt constrictive, heels that were far less comfortable than the Crocs she'd been wearing down on pediatrics, and layers of makeup that were doing a pretty poor job of covering up the circles under her eyes.

She caught Gregory's eye across the table, and he sent her a concerned look. She knew he was dead afraid of what this meeting was going to bring.

He wasn't the only one.

"Delaney?" Margaret's voice snapped at her. "Are you ready to present your proposal?"

Delaney took a deep breath. "Yes."

It was now or never. She'd done her due diligence, and the fact that she'd happened to fall hard for the department head while she was doing so had no bearing on her final recommendations this morning. She was almost sure of it . . . but she also knew that it might be damn near impossible to convince the board of this.

She handed out copies of the proposal she'd printed out at four this morning, after brewing a fresh pot of coffee— her third of the night. She'd labored over the thing all night, and even though it was airtight, she knew it was going to be a tough—if not impossible—sell.

Once everyone had the papers, she launched into her presentation. She talked about her experience on the pediatric floor, talked about the personnel, talked about the patients. She talked about how she'd started two weeks ago with a list of items she thought could possibly be trimmed, and how each of those items had come off her list as she'd spent more time on the floor.

She talked about staffing models at other hospitals, demographics unique to Vermont, and every other thing she could think of to support her recommendations. Twenty minutes later, she put down her paper.

"In my professional opinion, after diligent research, that is my proposal."

Dead silence greeted her words. As she looked around, no one met her eyes, not even Gregory. A full minute ticked by as people shuffled pages awkwardly. Then Margaret cleared her throat and looked over the top of her reading glasses at Delaney.

"Level funding? This is your proposal?"

"Yes." Delaney nodded firmly.

"Despite your very clear direction to bring this budget into alignment with the figures you were given?"

Delaney took a deep breath. "Yes. For all the reasons I just stated."

Margaret sat back, eyeing her. She took off her glasses, spinning them on her finger. It was all Delaney could do not to squirm under her gaze.

She could practically feel the question burning its way up Margaret's throat.

"Delaney, I do have a question for you. Regarding

Dr. Joshua Mackenzie." Delaney saw Gregory's head pop up as Margaret continued. "It has come to my attention—"

"Excuse me, if I may." Kevin's voice broke in, and Delaney whipped her head around to look at him. He paused, giving her a look that very clearly said, *You're welcome. I'm totally about to save you here.*

Margaret put her glasses back on, frowning. Nobody interrupted the board chair when she spoke. Not this board chair, anyway.

"Sorry." Kevin put both hands up, the picture of innocence. "I'm really sorry to interrupt. I just have something that might diffuse the—tension—here. If I may?"

Margaret sighed. "Fine. What?"

Delaney's eyes widened at her snippy tone as Kevin stood up and adjusted his tie. He pulled some neatly stapled papers from a folder and sent them around the table, then gave his best sales smile.

"I finished up with my proposals a little bit early, and I knew Delaney was having some trouble with hers." He sent her a sympathetic glance he must have practiced, and Delaney's blood began to simmer with suspicion. "After all, there's a lot of—emotion—tied up with pediatrics. Not an easy department to take things away from, for sure. So I thought I'd take a stab at it, just to see what I could come up with."

What? He had a proposal? For *her* department?

"Okay?" Margaret sounded suspiciously hopeful. "What did you come up with?"

Kevin smiled. "It's all detailed in the report, but I'll run through the items at a thirty-thousand-foot level. If you could open to page three, that's where the itemized list begins."

As everyone at the long table shuffled to open their packets, Kevin sent Delaney a triumphant glance, and it was all she could do not to get up out of her chair, walk to the other side of the table, and strangle the cap-toothed, gel-haired life right out of him.

How dare he?

Once everyone was ready, he started running through the list, and she looked down at her copy, not even wanting to open it. But as his items began to echo things that she'd put on her own original list, her eyes narrowed. She flipped the pages open and scanned, and by the time she got to the bottom of page five, she knew her face probably resembled a cherry tomato.

The bastard had stolen her original proposal.

Her eyes met Gregory's, and he gave a quick shake of his head. *Don't rock the boat, Delaney*, it said. *You're getting off easy here. Margaret didn't even get a chance to ask her question.*

Kevin continued through four more items on his list, then said, "Item number twelve—the child life specialist role." He listed the salary-plus-benefits figure for Kenderly and the other specialist, then said, "From my research, I've concluded that though this role is hugely beneficial, it's not—in reality—a medically necessary position."

Delaney was on her feet before she knew she was going to move, and all eyes shifted to her as she let her fist land on the table.

"Do you know what a child life specialist does, Kevin?"

He looked at her like she was off her meds, speaking like this in a board meeting, and she knew damn well that most of the board members probably echoed his supposition.

"Of course I know what they do. And I just said that I find their service very beneficial."

"Have you ever met one?" She crossed her arms, her jaw set.

"Delaney," Margaret spoke. "We heard you out. Let's please let Kevin continue."

Delaney ignored her. "Have you ever, *Kevin*, met a child on the pediatric floor? Have you seen how all of the pieces of this pediatric equation work? Do you have *any* idea what goes into a pediatric hospitalization?"

Kevin took a deep breath, and she could see his jaw tighten. Then he visibly relaxed his shoulders and nodded sympathetically. "I'm sorry, Delaney. I know that none of us have the background you have with pediatrics. That's why"—he put up his hands in a well-rehearsed defeated motion—"that's why I thought maybe I could help with this. It's obviously very emotional for you."

"Are you *kidding* me? This has *nothing* to do with my background, emotional or otherwise." Delaney picked up the papers and waved them, letting her eyes scan the faces at the table. "This is *my* proposal. Mine. The one I put together before I spent the past two weeks on pediatrics. Before I had *any* clue how care is actually delivered in this hospital. I abandoned this proposal item by item, but Kevin somehow got a copy of it, and now he's presenting it as his own."

"Delaney, please. This isn't necessary." Kevin widened his eyes at Margaret in a help-me-here-there's-a-crazy-woman-in-the-room motion. "This is my own proposal. Maybe some of the items mirror things you came up with, but that's only natural."

Delaney looked around, and as she took in the faces looking her way, she knew she'd lost them. She'd presented a proposal that asked for money that didn't exist. Kevin had done his magic, and they were firmly in his corner.

She'd never been anything but professional during her tenure at Mercy, and right now . . . she was anything but. She looked at the papers, tried to calm her breathing, and found an item near the bottom that he actually had added on his own. She shook her head, defeated.

"Kevin, do you know why so many teenaged cystic fibrosis kids get single rooms?"

He tipped his head, raising his eyebrows. "Because we've tried to give them privacy. I get it. It's important. But we could have two beds in those rooms. We're losing money."

"It's not about privacy." Her voice sounded as hopeless as she suddenly felt. "It's because the types of infections some of them have are highly contagious to other kids with CF."

"I'm sure we have protocols in place to keep that under control. We're a small hospital. We have more leeway on things like this."

She stared at him. "No. We. Don't. They could die, Kevin. We could speed up their *deaths* by going against standard, industry-wide recommendations. You can't play God here."

"Delaney"—Margaret raised her eyebrows—"do you need to perhaps step out and take a moment?"

Delaney looked down at the table, counting to ten. "This proposal is dangerous, Margaret. The items I already had on it are untenable, and he's added even more. Please don't let this proposal go through, in any shape or form. Kevin hasn't done this research. He'll deny it till kingdom come, but this is my work. And because it was my job to present a well-researched, well-documented proposal, I took the time to examine every one of these items."

She took a deep breath. "Because I did *that*, I know that my original thoughts don't hold water. If we make these cuts, we risk patient safety. That's the bottom line."

"Thank you." Margaret nodded. "And now, I think it would be best if you stepped out for the rest of the meeting. We certainly have heard your thoughts, and we will take them into consideration. However, I think we also need to hear the remainder of—Kevin's—proposal."

Delaney looked at her, then at Gregory. *Seriously?* She was being dismissed? She was being shown the door, and Kevin was going to get the chance to continue this bullshit presentation?

Margaret stood up and opened the door. "Thank you, Delaney."

Chapter 30

"Dr. Mackenzie, thank you for joining me." Kevin McConnell shook his hand, indicating a seat in a tiny conference room on the first floor early Wednesday afternoon. "I know this was short notice. I appreciate you making time in your schedule."

Josh looked around at the empty room as he sat down, suspicion crowding out the anger he'd been carrying since his conversation with Delaney last night.

"With all due respect, it didn't sound like this was an optional meeting."

Kevin sat down at the head of the table, shuffling some papers before he clasped his hands and looked at Josh.

"As I'm sure you're aware, we've been doing some very careful budget analysis over the past few weeks, and your department was examined at length. Unfortunately, we've had to make some hard decisions."

Josh's gut squeezed. *Oh, hell.*

Kevin's face was set in a sympathetic—yet business-like—pose, and Josh wondered how hard he'd had to practice it in order to feel like it was working for him.

It wasn't.

"What kinds of decisions are we talking about?"

Kevin pulled out a sheet of paper and looked down at it for a long moment, then sighed. "The board met this morning to look at proposals, and they've voted in some immediate changes. We've had to make some . . . rather substantial revisions to a number of line items. I'm sorry to be the one to tell you, and believe me, I wish we weren't in a position of having to adjust things quite so substantially." He handed the paper to Josh. "I'll give you a minute to look them over, and then we can go through them line by line if it's helpful."

Josh took the sheet, trying to regulate his breathing, trying not to think about what role Delaney might—or might not—have had in pushing through this proposal, whatever it was. He took a deep breath and started slowly scanning the list, letting his eyes take in each item in turn. As he read, a whole different kind of emotion took over.

He'd seen this list before. Delaney had *handed* him this list. But then she'd spent two weeks on his floor, and the last time he'd checked, she'd claimed to have shredded it. She'd said it was premature, not fully researched, not— safe. So why the *hell* was he seeing it again?

"May I ask who was responsible for coming up with this list?" He fought to keep his voice even.

"It was a group effort, of course, but I have to give my colleague, Delaney Blair, credit for most of the heavy lifting here. I'm sure you've seen her around the floor for the past couple of weeks, doing some observations."

Josh nodded slowly. Oh, he'd seen her, all right. On the pediatric floor, on the dock, in his bed . . .

"This"—Kevin pointed to the paper in Josh's hand— "is the culmination of her efforts. She turned in her recommendations on Friday."

No. This had been the *start* of her efforts, which she'd then discarded.

Hadn't she?

"I'm sorry." Josh leaned forward, placing the sheet on

the table. "I'm really confused here. Surely you've determined the impact these cuts would have on our programs. Delaney wouldn't have recommended these cuts. There's no way."

Kevin nodded gravely. "I'm sorry. Nothing was easy about this. For any of us. She warned us that these findings would be . . . upsetting."

"Upsetting? *Upsetting?* You're kidding, right?" Josh felt like the top of his head was about to blow off. The cuts on this list weren't just taking nice-to-have items away in a budget crisis. These were people—people he needed on that floor in order to keep his patients safe and well cared for. These were *not* optional. They were vital.

"Now, let's take this step by step." Kevin put up a placating hand, and Josh fought the urge to shove it down his throat. For Christ's sake, maybe the guy hadn't even had anything to do with the damn recommendations. "Let's run through the list so we can leave the room with a plan for implementing these changes."

"You know, calling them *changes* or *revisions* doesn't fool me into thinking you're doing anything but slicing my programming to shreds. Could we at least cut the bullshit here?"

Kevin sat back, taking a deep breath. *I'm just the messenger*, his posture said.

"Fine." Josh shook his head. "We'll go down the list, but I have one question—why isn't Delaney here herself to present this?"

Kevin took another breath, rocking his head back and forth like a football player with an old neck injury.

"Delaney doesn't tend to get involved at this level."

"This level? What does that mean?"

"She's the lead investigator on these sorts of things. She likes to really dig in and get down in the mud—so to speak—but when it's time to deliver the recommendations that come out of that research, she prefers to let others handle that piece."

Josh shook his head, swallowing hard. None of this made sense. He couldn't believe the woman he'd just spent the weekend with had anything to do with this. Then again, that woman was nothing at all like the one who'd sat upstairs last night and poured a bucket of cold water over his memories of a hot, sweet weekend.

Maybe he didn't really know her at all.

Did she know Kevin was in here right now, delivering this news? Was she *here* in the building? Had she known last night that this was the plan for the morning? Had she cut Josh loose before the board got wind of their possible relationship, knowing he was just about to get sliced off at the budgetary knees, as well?

He'd certainly give her points for keeping things neat and tidy at the end.

Kevin shifted his stack of papers. "I'm sorry. This is just how she does things."

"She's done this before?" Josh felt his eyes widen.

"Yes." Kevin nodded slowly, like he was dealing with a seventh grader who was late to the punch. "This *is* what Delaney does." Then he cocked his head again. "We build the budgets, and she . . . trims them."

"But I've seen this list already. She showed it to me. She *also* said that it risked destroying the entire department if implemented." Josh shook his head, running his eyes back down the list. "So you'll forgive me if this makes no sense at all right now. I'm having a hard time believing Delaney really supported these recommendations."

"I know." Kevin used his placating voice again. "It's difficult for everyone. She wasn't happy about presenting them, if it makes you feel any better. But her hands were tied."

Josh put his hands up, completely confused. "Have you seen all of the news this week? Our pediatric department has been flooded with good publicity. If we make these cuts, the next news story we get is going to be one we really don't want to picture."

He shook his head. He needed to hear this from Delaney. "Can we get her in here? I need to hear this from her own mouth."

"She's not available. I'm sorry."

"Is that part of her strategy, too?"

Kevin shrugged apologetically. "I'm sorry to be the one to deliver this news to you. I really am. How about if I give you some time to digest the recommendations, and we can meet tomorrow instead? Would that work for you?"

Joshua shook his head, staring at the proposal blindly.

Kevin sighed, then stood up, looking at his watch. "I'm really sorry. Give me a call tomorrow, and we'll schedule a time to meet, all right? We have a little time before these changes need to occur."

Five minutes later, Josh still sat at the table, a cold cup of coffee in front of him . . . and a cold lump of ice in his gut.

He picked up the list, scowling as he scanned the items once again. This time he noticed a column he hadn't seen the first two times. His eyes widened in fury as he realized this wasn't just a proposal anymore. This time, every item on the list had an implementation date.

Apparently he had three months before his department imploded.

That was three months longer than he had before *he* did.

"Have you seen Joshua? Dr. Mackenzie, I mean?" Delaney fought to keep her voice level as she leaned over the nurses' station counter to get Therese's attention Wednesday afternoon. She'd spent two hours stewing at her desk after the board meeting, but when Kevin had walked by her office ten minutes ago with a triumphant expression on his face, she'd panicked.

When he'd stopped short and come back in to tell her the news of the board vote, she'd held her stomach, feeling sick. Then, with an I-won-this-round gleam in his eye, he'd told her that he'd saved her the trouble of delivering the news to Dr. Mackenzie.

She'd whipped off her heels and taken the stairs down from the sixth floor, not wanting to wait for the elevator. When she'd reached the third floor, she'd paused, putting on her shoes and trying to catch her breath before she pushed through the doors. She'd already done the crazy-chick act once today. No need to look like she was about to launch it again.

She had to get to Joshua—had to explain what had happened. Had to tell him this wasn't her doing, even though she was dead sure Kevin had spun it that way.

Therese looked up, frowning, and Delaney saw her set her jaw carefully. "I don't know where he is," she answered, turning immediately back to her computer screen.

"Is he on the floor?"

Therese didn't look up. "Check with Millie. She's with Annabeth."

"Thank you." Delaney tapped on the counter, then spun to head toward Annabeth's room. When she got there, she knocked and ducked her head in.

Millie looked up, but *she* didn't bother to wipe the frown from *her* face. Or the frost from her voice. This didn't bode well at all.

"Yes?"

"I'm just looking for Joshua. Have you seen him?"

"No."

"Any idea where he might be?"

Millie's eyebrows went up in challenge. "No." She stood and walked toward Delaney, seemingly sizing her up. She must have seen the desperation in Delaney's expression, because finally, she pointed toward the playroom.

"Last I saw, he was in there with Kaya and her mom."

"Thank you." Delaney quick-stepped down the hall, halting when she heard Kaya's little voice.

"Tomorrow? I get to go home tomorrow?" Kaya was squeaky and elated.

"You betcha," Joshua answered, and Delaney could imagine him squeezing Kaya's little cheek. "But I'm going to miss you."

"I'll miss you, too. Maybe I can come visit just for visiting. Not for staying."

He laughed, but Delaney heard a note of sadness in it. "Just for visiting."

A few seconds later, Kaya and her mother came down the hallway, each with one hand on Kaya's IV pole. Delaney worked up a smile as they ambled by, and then she headed for the playroom, hoping she could catch Joshua before he got tied up with another patient.

When she got to the glass door, her throat felt like she'd tried to swallow a grapefruit. He was sitting in one of the kid chairs, elbows on his knees, head in his hands. He looked positively exhausted—and devastated.

She knocked tentatively, then pushed open the door. He looked up, pasting a smile on his face, then letting it drop as he realized who she was.

"Why are you here?" His voice was clipped, angry.

"I'm here—to talk to you."

"I'm not sure we really have anything to say to each other right now, Delaney." He stood up. "Please. Don't insult me."

She felt a tiny ice ball growing spikes in her stomach. "Kevin was lying."

He pinched the bridge of his nose. "About which part? Your tendency to lie about what you're planning to present to the board? Or your penchant for letting other people deliver your bad news?"

"Wha—"

A loud popping sound silenced her, and Joshua immediately turned back toward Delaney, grabbing her around the waist and pushing her to the floor.

"Get down!" he hissed, pointing. "Go! Over by the bookcase."

"Was that—" Delaney felt her eyes go wide as she scrambled backward.

He nodded, fumbling his phone out of his pocket and dialing 911 as they heard another pop. In a low voice, he gave his name, then said, "Mercy Hospital, third floor pediatrics. Shots fired."

Delaney heard a scream, then a deep voice yelling, "I want the doc. You tell me where the doc is and nobody else gets hurt."

Nobody *else*? Her mind raced through all of the patients and staff members on the floor. Who had he shot, for God's sake? Who *was* he?

She saw Joshua's face go white. They were in a room with glass walls and a glass door. The bookcase was flimsy protection.

The hospital-wide intercom beeped to life, emitting the lockdown code they'd all drilled on, but had prayed they'd never have to use.

"Oh, doc-tor!" the man called out in a singsong voice.

"Any idea who it is?" Delaney whispered.

He shook his head, then grabbed her hand. "Come on. We need to make a run for the storeroom before he gets any closer."

They ran on tiptoes across the hallway to a tiny room that housed a couple of wheeled carts with equipment on them. Joshua closed the metal door silently, flipping off the lights as he turned the lock.

Delaney's phone beeped with an incoming text from Megan, and she scrambled to shut off the sound before she looked at the message.

Where are you? Please not peds!

She tapped out a message back, then pocketed her phone. She tried to calm her ragged breathing as they heard the guy get closer to their end of the hallway, but the closer he got, the more she was afraid he could hear every breath she was taking. The seconds stretched out like minutes, and every terrified cell in her body wanted to bury itself against Joshua right now, but she couldn't.

Where was security, anyway? How long could it take to get up here?

She closed her eyes in the darkness. It had probably only been fifteen seconds since he'd fired the first shot. Even the express elevator couldn't move that fast.

Another shot made her wince. *Oh, God!* She held her breath as she looked at the bottom of the door and saw a shadow of feet walking slowly by the storage room. Then the feet stopped, like he knew exactly where they were. Delaney was sure he could hear her heart trying to thud itself right through her ribs.

"Next one's gonna be a kid, doc." The man's voice was frighteningly calm. "Payback for taking mine away."

Joshua reached for the door handle, motioning for her to move away from the door and stay hidden.

She shook her head rapidly. If he was going, so was she.

He leaned down, mouth at her ear. "Stay here. Security's not going to get here before he hurts more people."

"I'm coming—"

They heard a shuffle, then a screech from Annabeth's room, and they both reached for the door.

"Don't!" Joshua rushed out, Delaney on his heels.

Then they both stopped cold.

The guy was holding Annabeth in front of him like a shield, and the teenager's eyes were wide with terror as he pointed a gun toward her head.

Chapter 31

"You Dr. Mackenzie?"

Joshua put both hands in the air, taking a small step toward him. "Yes. Please let her go."

The man's grip tightened, making Annabeth squeak in fear. "Don't think I will. You and me have some talking to do first."

Delaney froze in place, trying not to startle the guy by moving. Her eyes sought to meet Annabeth's, to somehow try to reassure her she was going to be all right, but she was dead afraid that the girl would see the fear in her own eyes.

She had no idea if they *were* going to be all right.

As she tried to listen for security personnel, she was struck by how completely silent the floor had gone. Instead of the usual bustle and chaos, there was utter, dreadful silence.

"What would you like to talk about?" Joshua's voice was low, calm.

"Not here." He pointed the gun at a patient room across the hall. "Everybody in there."

Delaney caught Joshua's eye as they backed toward the room with their hands in the air. Dammit—she knew the room had two patients in it.

Joshua slowed, but the man waved the gun at Joshua. "Hurry up. Unlock the door."

Joshua kept one hand in the air while he pulled his badge free to wave it against the security pad, and the door clicked. Delaney heard gasps from inside as it opened, and was horrified to see that not only were there two patients in the room—there were four other adults and a nurse as well.

"Well, isn't this just perfect?" The man looked around, taking in the scene. Then he waved the gun again. Annabeth stumbled, and Delaney saw tears running down her cheeks, but the teenager stayed silent.

"Everybody over there by the beds where I can see you. Hands in front of you at all times. Don't even think about trying anything, or you'll have the same fate as the other three."

Delaney swallowed hard. Three. *Oh, God.*

"Okay," Joshua's voice was open, steady. Delaney had no idea how he was staying so calm. "Let's talk. I know you don't really want to hurt anyone. Let's talk this through."

The man raised his eyebrows. "I'm not stupid, you know. Not crazy either, so don't talk to me like I am."

"Okay." Joshua nodded.

"I want my son back. That's why I'm here, and I'm not leaving till I get him."

Delaney felt her eyebrows furrow. Wanted his son back? Had he—died? Had this man gone over the ledge out of grief?

"Who's your son, sir?"

The man tipped his head like *Joshua* was crazy now. "Ian. The one you stole. You and *Delaney*, whoever that is." He spat out her name like it tasted of gasoline.

Joshua closed his eyes and let his head fall back a

millimeter. *Oh*, she could practically hear him saying inside.

The guy waved his gun again, and as one, the people trapped in the room ducked. "I know he's here somewhere. And if I have to start bumping off people in order to get him, then that's what I'll do."

He pointed the gun directly at Delaney, and she swallowed, but tried to keep her chin up. "This Delaney? Maybe I'll start with her."

"Let's focus on Ian." Joshua took a slight step to the left, shielding Delaney.

Delaney breathed out as the gun dipped a couple of inches and the man's eyes went back to Joshua. Then he looked wildly behind him as they all heard pounding feet in the hallway. He'd closed and locked the door when they'd come in, and now he turned to point the gun toward the door.

"Mr. Dawson, this is Lieutenant Schirling. Are you in there, sir?"

Ian's father shook his head, speaking softly. "Only time I get called *sir* is when I've got hostages. Go figure."

Delaney looked around the room while he was focused on the door. Way too many frightened eyes looked back at her.

"Mr. Dawson? We know you're in there, and we know you're upset. How about you come on out, and we can figure this all out?"

Delaney heard the lieutenant's voice, calm and measured like Joshua's had been, but as she watched Ian's dad's eyes, she knew the police weren't going to be any more successful than Joshua had been so far.

"I just want my son," he called through the door. "You give me my son, and we can all walk out of here without any more bloodshed."

"Your son is safe," Joshua said, quietly. "He's safe now."

"Safe where? Safe how? He was *safe* at home. He was *safe* with my wife. And now she's in jail, some bitch social worker has been to the house three times this week, and everybody's saying Fiona tried to—tried to kill him. You've ruined our lives!"

"Ian was a very, very sick boy when he came in. We did our best to help him get better." Joshua sat down slowly on one of the beds, projecting a calm that no one else in the room felt.

"You took him away. You took her, and then you took him. You had no right."

"I had no choice, and I'm sorry that this happened. I really am. I'm sure you had no idea what was going on when you weren't at home, because if you had, you would have stopped it."

Delaney heard his words—heard how he was removing blame in hopes of getting them all out of here alive—and she marveled at his cool control.

"Damn right I would ha—" Mr. Dawson stopped as he seemed to realize what he'd been about to say. "You had no right. I'm taking my boy home."

Delaney couldn't hear anything out in the hallway now, but had a feeling every word spoken inside this room was somehow being monitored and recorded. Without moving her head, she glanced at the intercom over the first patient bed and saw the red light glimmering. They *were* listening.

"Let's see if we can make that happen." Joshua nodded, like he was considering it. "But I have to tell you, coming in here and doing it like this isn't going to work. They'll never let him leave with you if you come in shooting."

"I didn't have a choice. I couldn't get anybody to listen." His voice broke. "You people don't even know him. You don't know what's right for him."

The man took a ragged breath, but didn't let the gun

drop any farther. Joshua just sat quietly, but Delaney could see his calves flexing under his khakis. Was he planning to do something stupid and make a move on the guy? Try to take him out at the knees?

Get shot?

She took a shaky breath, then said, "I know his favorite color is green."

His dad rolled his eyes.

She barreled on. "And he loves carrots but hates peas. He wants to be a veterinarian someday. He loves fish, but not the zebra-striped ones because they freak him out. He likes the tree house you built him last summer, and he's hoping to have a sleepover in it with you when he gets out of the hospital."

He looked at her, narrowing his eyes, but he didn't speak, so she kept going. "He loves Go Fish, but not Old Maid, and he's figured out enough ways to cheat at checkers that nobody here can beat him. He worries about his older sister worrying about *him*, and he wishes you could be home more, but he understands you have a really hard job. Did you know he wears your extra boots around the house all day long, just waiting for the day when he's big enough to go to work with you?"

Delaney kept her eyes steadily on his, and as she did, she noticed his shoulders dropping—noticed the gun falling downward toward his side. She had to keep talking.

"Mr. Dawson, Ian loves you. He wants to go home with you, and we want that, too. But we have to do it the right way. We have to do it when he's all better."

"Where is he?" His voice was soft, pained, and even through her fear, Delaney felt a stab of sympathy for the man who'd lost his son and wife in one fell swoop.

"I don't know," she answered.

The gun came back up, and she tensed. "Bullshit."

"She doesn't." Joshua spoke quietly from the bed. "And now that you're here, I don't, either, because the first thing they would have done upon seeing you come in like this was move him somewhere secure."

"Where I can't get to him, you mean?"

Joshua took a deep breath. "Would you want him to see you like this? Really?"

He sighed. "No."

"How about you let Annabeth go, and we'll take a walk out of the room—see if maybe you can see him?"

Delaney felt her eyebrows furrow. Surely, the moment he left the room, he'd be in handcuffs. Did Joshua really think the guy didn't know that? He wasn't going to fall for a lie—not when he was this far in.

Not when he had hostages to help him control the situation.

"If I walk out of this room, I'm going to get a free ride to the police station, doc. We both know that."

"Maybe," Joshua allowed. "But it'll go a lot better for you if you let this end right now, before anybody else gets hurt."

"Nobody's hurt." He shook his head sadly, like he couldn't believe his life had come to this moment. He gave Annabeth a little push toward Delaney, who caught her in a tight squeeze, then pushed her behind her own body. "I didn't shoot anybody."

Delaney's eyes widened at his words.

"Even better." Joshua stood up slowly, but she could tell from the tone of his voice that he wasn't sure whether he believed him. "How about if you hand me the gun, and then we'll open the door. That way it won't be in your hands when the officers first see you?"

Delaney held her breath. No way would he capitulate this easily. No way would he give over control of his weapon. It was the instrument of his power right now, and once he *did* give it up, all hell was going to break loose. He had to know that.

She saw a look of abject pain cross the man's face. "I'm going to jail, aren't I? My kids are going to have two parents in jail. Who's going to—oh, God—what have I done?" The gun shook in his hand, and Delaney saw Joshua notice as the man's hand gripped it harder, his finger edging closer to the trigger.

Then, in a flash, Joshua leaped toward him and knocked the gun to the floor with a move Delaney might have expected an ex-Marine to execute. Before Ian's father could reach to pick it up, Joshua had him on the floor, both hands behind his back as Delaney scrambled to get the gun.

And then suddenly, the room was filled with uniformed officers, but contrary to scenes she'd seen on television, there was no yelling, no circle of officers with guns raised. Instead, they were quiet, efficient, and in a matter of seconds, Ian's father had been cuffed and led out into the hallway.

When he was out of sight, the lieutenant returned to the room, where they'd all been told to hold tight. He pointed to Joshua and Delaney, motioning them out into the hallway.

"We're going to need to take some statements," he said. "Dr. Mackenzie, you'll come with me. Ms. Blair, you'll go with Officer Farley."

"What about my patients?" Joshua pointed at the room. "I can't just leave them there after what just happened."

Delaney heard the raw pain in his voice. It echoed her own. There were two very scared little kids in that room. They couldn't abandon them right now, even *if* their parents were there.

"Crisis counselors are waiting at the nurses' station."

He pointed down the hallway. "As soon as we give them the okay, they'll be right in with your patients."

Joshua shook his head. "You can't do statements later? These kids need me right now."

"I know, and I'll promise to make this as quick as possible. But we need to get your statement while the situation is still fresh in your mind."

"No offense, lieutenant, but this *situation* isn't likely to fade—not for a long, long time."

"I understand." The lieutenant put a hand on his shoulder. "Make sure *you* get an hour with one of the counselors before you leave, okay? I know you don't think you need it, but we all do."

Delaney reached for Joshua's hand, but as soon as she touched him, he pulled away like he'd been stung. Her chest squeezed as tears pricked her eyes.

"Joshua—"

He shook his head. Then he looked at her, long and hard, and in the same eyes where she'd seen affection and heat just days ago, all she saw now was a dead, cold fury.

Chapter 32

"Ow. *Shit*." Josh shook his hand, which was smarting from the hammer blow he'd just given it. It was Thursday night, today's papers had been filled with stories of the shooting, and he was hiding out at home after an ill-advised stop at the grocery store on the way home from the hospital. By the time he'd gotten through the produce aisle, he'd already been stopped ten times, and he'd ended up leaving his cart at the end of an aisle and escaping without his food.

"Hands better suited to doctoring than construction?" Ethan raised his eyebrows as he came across Josh's back lawn, carrying a cold brew.

"Better than *de*-construction, anyway." He put down the hammer, taking the beer instead. "Thanks."

Ethan shrugged. "Least I can do for the Echo Lake hero of the hour."

"Not exactly my first choice of ways to get onto the front page."

"I know. Hellish scene. I'm sure the last thing you want to do is relive it." Ethan shook his head as he picked up a crowbar and scanned the old tree fort Josh had started taking apart. "You okay?"

"Yeah."

"You sure?"

But he'd always thought it was her. *She* didn't understand, *she* didn't want to adjust *her* life to be with *him*, *she* was somehow lacking in commitment . . . didn't love him enough.

In the past forty-eight hours, though, those arguments had been fading . . . fast. Because Delaney *wasn't* Nicole—wasn't anything like her, really. And yet . . . she'd ended up making the same decision in the end. It was just that the end had come a lot faster than with Nicole. Delaney had seen the future, and she'd found *him* lacking.

And she'd said good-bye.

"What happened, Josh?" Molly touched his arm. "And do I need to deliver a hot-sauce lasagna to the executive suite?"

"No. Definitely not." He shook his head, sighing. "This time—this one's on me."

In the twilight, with the tree frogs warming up all around them and the lightning bugs floating lazily around the yard, he started talking. An hour later, his second beer was empty, Ethan's eyes were wide, and Molly's hands were in fists. "I knew it. Am I not the one who warned you about her motives?"

Ethan nudged her with his elbow. "Not sure you're helping here."

"I'm just saying. I called it, way back—weeks ago." She paused. "Good God, has it only been weeks?"

Josh sighed. Yeah, it had—which was just a drop in the bucket of time, when you thought about it. And yet, on another plane, it seemed like forever. Four weeks ago, Delaney Blair had been nothing but a signature on paperwork. Then she'd been a thorn in his side, sent down from the executive suite.

But then he'd kissed her.

And then he'd spent the weekend wrapped up in her.

"I think I might need another beer."

Molly raised her eyebrows. "You on-call tonight?"

"Would I be asking for another beer if I was?"

"You know what? No offense, hon, but I'm cutting you off."

He leveled a look her way. "Seriously? Two beers, Mols."

"Two beers plus one stomped heart is quite enough for tonight, I think. You add another beer to the equation, and you're going to be drunk-dialing at midnight. We can't let you go there."

Ethan shrugged. "She has a point."

"I have never drunk-dialed in my life."

"There's always a first time." Molly cringed. "And this is not the woman you want to try it on first."

She stood up, taking his bottle. "I'll go make you some coffee."

After she disappeared back into the house, Ethan looked down at the picnic table, tapping a loose nail idly, but not speaking. He did this for an obnoxiously long time, until Josh finally put his hand on the hammer to stop the incessant noise.

"Just say it."

"Say what?" Ethan looked up innocently.

"Say whatever it is that you're thinking right now so we can get it over with."

"Fine. Were you falling for her? Like, really falling?"

Josh rolled his eyes and looked around the yard, but there was no sense lying to his oldest friend. Ethan would see right through him.

"Yeah." He closed his eyes. "Damn it all, yes. I was."

"Are you completely sure you have the story straight?"

"It's hardly complicated. Yes."

"And have you given her a chance to try to explain?"

Josh shook his head. "I don't want to hear a bullshit story. Not again. It's insulting."

"Don't hate me for saying this, but—is there any possibility you're being snowed by someone besides Delaney here?"

"What do you mean?"

Ethan sat back. "I just don't think it makes sense. The Delaney we know—*you* know—wouldn't have made those recommendations. She couldn't have."

"Well, apparently she did. After she dumped me. *After* she apparently got what she needed from me."

"Has she called?"

Josh shook his head in frustration, thinking of the six voice mails waiting on his phone—six messages he'd refused to listen to. "Why does that matter?"

"Because if she truly was a coldhearted bitch just stepping on your head on her way to a corner office, then she probably wouldn't give a damn about you after she got what she wanted."

"Maybe her one shred of decency feels like I'm owed an apology. I don't know."

Molly returned with a coffee for him and a beer for Ethan. As soon as she turned back toward the kitchen, Ethan switched them around so Josh could have the beer.

"I don't buy it, and I don't think you do, either." He pointed to the beer. "Drink it, but promise me you won't call her until tomorrow."

"No worries." Josh picked up the bottle and took a long draw. "I'm not calling her at all."

"Donuts?" Delaney raised her eyebrows as Megan came through her office door with a pink bakery box and two giant cups of coffee on Friday morning. She set everything down on Delaney's desk and turned to shut the door behind her.

"Yes, donuts."

Delaney swallowed hard, remembering another box of donuts, another morning . . . what felt like another life entirely.

"I'm pretty sure I haven't seen you eat in days, despite my delivering the requisite salads and sandwiches to your desk. So this morning, I went with donuts. I've never known you to be able to resist one."

Delaney smiled sadly. "Thank you."

"What kind do you want?" Megan opened the box and tipped it toward her. "Jelly? Glazed? Honey crunch?"

The last thing Delaney wanted right now was a donut—or *any* food, really. Megan was right—she'd hardly eaten since Tuesday, but try as she might, she didn't care.

When Delaney didn't reach in for a donut, Megan growled in frustration and put the box down on the desk. "I told you breaking up with him was a bad idea."

"I didn't have a choice." Delaney closed her eyes, leaning her head back on her chair. She'd never been so exhausted in her entire life. If this was what a broken heart felt like, she was never, *ever* letting herself fall in love again. "It's not like I wanted things to end up this way."

"So now you've broken his heart, he thinks you've killed off his department, and you're both completely miserable. Awesome."

"Are you trying to be helpful here?" Delaney opened one eye.

"I'm a little out of my league on this one. Sorry. You're a planner, Delaney. You're not the girl who goes blindly into a project and comes out blindly in love. I'm not sure what the protocol is on this, okay?"

Delaney couldn't help but let a tiny laugh escape at the

bewildered tone in Megan's voice. Then she sobered. "Yeah. Well, this is kind of a new one for me, too."

"So what are you going to do?"

"I don't know what I *can* do. I've left him a gazillion messages, I've tried to go down and talk to him, I've tried to meet with Margaret to see if there's *any* way to rescind that vote. Brick walls, Megan. It's all brick walls. I can't fix *any*thing."

She sighed. "You know, three weeks ago, completely against my will, I took that elevator down to the third floor, expecting to come running back up with my tail between my legs."

"But you didn't."

"I didn't." Delaney shook her head. "I always wanted to be a doctor, Meg. Always. And then when it became horribly clear that it was never going to happen, I was so—lost. It's all I'd ever planned to do. It's what I'd planned to be. It's what was finally, *finally* going to make my dad proud, you know?"

Megan nodded, but didn't speak.

"And then it all went down the toilet, and I wandered around for weeks thinking I was a failure, that I was never going to be able to affect lives the way I'd planned to, that I was never going to be able to—I don't know, it sounds stupid—never going to be able to save anybody."

She broke off as her throat tightened. "Dammit, I wanted to save *some*body."

Megan put a hand on her shoulder. "Delaney, you *are* affecting lives. Every day you are."

"I know. But I've been doing it from a distance. I've kept myself insulated in our little carpeted suite with the locking doors and big desks. It's not reality. It's not this hospital's reality. It feels like, all this time, I've been kind of phoning it in, not daring to get down and dirty in the mud."

"Not true."

"Totally true. You know I'm right. I was so afraid to get close to patients—so afraid to care about them as any more than numbers. And what did that get me? A bigger cubicle and the ability to go home at night not knowing anybody's face, or anybody's parents, or anybody's problems beyond their ICD-9 codes on a damn report."

"You're doing important work. You know you are."

"I know, but what I don't know is whether it's the kind of work I *want* to do anymore."

"What—*do* you want to do?"

"I think I want to work with patients, Meg. You're going to think I've lost my mind here, but after spending just two weeks on that floor, I don't even know if I care about a windowed office. I want to do a job that lets me feel like I'm doing something to make these families' lives better on a daily, hourly basis. Something I can see, not something on a spreadsheet."

"Has it occurred to you that if you were no longer in your current position, then you'd actually be free to date Joshua?"

Delaney looked down at her desk, tears poking at her eyes. "Pretty sure that's off the table, Meg."

Just then Delaney's intercom buzzed, and she pressed the button. "Delaney Blair. Can I help you?"

"It's Gregory. Can you come into my office, please?"

Delaney's gaze flew up to meet Megan's. "I'll be right in."

She took her finger off the button, but didn't move.

Megan looked at her, eyebrows up in fear she didn't even bother to hide. "What do you think it's about?"

"I don't know." Delaney's voice was a defeated whisper. "But I have a feeling I might be getting a new Mercy mug."

"Stop it. No. It can't be that." Megan started pacing. "You said they didn't even get a chance to talk about it at the board meeting. No way are you being fired because of Dr. Mackenzie."

"Maybe. Maybe not. Maybe I'm being fired because I did a dismal job on the most important project I've ever been assigned." Delaney shook her head, pushing her feet into her heels. "Or maybe . . . maybe I'm just about to become the latest casualty of the Mercy budget crisis."

Chapter 33

When Delaney walked into Gregory's office, struggling to keep her shoulders back and her chin up, she felt her eyebrows pull together as she saw a man with a shock of white hair sitting at Gregory's desk, his back to her.

Gregory walked toward her, motioning her in and closing the door behind her. "Delaney. Thanks for coming in. I have someone here who wants to see you."

Delaney felt her feet go leaden as she walked across the office. She didn't remember anyone from HR having hair like this, but didn't companies hire people just to come in and do the layoff dirty work? Was this her personal escort?

As she reached Gregory's other guest chair, the man turned toward her, an affectionate smile on his face, and she felt her eyes widen as she recognized him from the fund-raiser.

"Oscar?"

He stuck out his hand, shaking hers warmly. "Hello, Delaney. I was just telling Gregory about our mutual escape to the balcony last week."

"I wasn't escap—"

"It's okay." He winked. "Everybody needs to escape sometimes. Hospital fund-raisers can be deadly."

"Have a seat, Delaney." Gregory pointed to the chair. "We have something to discuss."

She sat down gingerly, wheels turning madly in her brain. Who *was* this Oscar? And why was he sitting here in the CFO's office with the comfort of someone who was headed out for golf with Gregory in ten minutes?

"I couldn't help but see the news," Oscar finally said. "I want to commend you on your efforts with the shooter."

"Thank you." Delaney shook her head. "But it was Joshua—Dr. Mackenzie—who really saved us. It's him you should be thanking, in truth."

Oscar shrugged. "From all reports, it was a team effort, both during and after the event." He raised his eyebrows. "The same team I heard you speak of at the fund-raiser, yes?"

She nodded slowly. The way the nurses had handled things on the floor after the police had left had been nothing short of mind-boggling. Between the crisis counselors and the medical personnel, the kids *and* the parents had been smiling by the end of the day.

"I have a confession to make to you." Oscar pulled out a business card. "I told you I am an inventor of useless things, yes?"

"Yes." She nodded again, tipping her head. "You did."

"You see, *I* think they are useless, but other people? Not so much. I have managed to make enough of a living to support my family." He held up a hand to stop her from replying. "And the rest, I like to give. Today, I am here to give you some of the rest."

She smiled, thinking of the five dollars he'd given his wife at the fund-raiser. "Oscar, that's very generous of you, but truly, you already gave money at the fund-raiser. Please don't feel like you should give more."

He waved a hand dismissively, reaching into the inside

pocket of his threadbare suit jacket. "The check is already written. I wish for you to take the money and decide where it will be of the best use. I have written it to Mercy Hospital Pediatric Department, but Gregory has been left with strict instructions that you are to manage how it is spent."

He handed her an envelope, then pushed himself out of his chair. "I don't know how you fared with the other guests at the dinner, but I have a feeling that if you spoke to them with the same—heart—you showed me, you will not need my paltry check."

He bowed slightly. "You will do good work, Delaney." He pointed to the envelope. "Maybe this will help."

"Thank you, Oscar." She reached out to hug him, and he hugged her back, then patted her lightly on the shoulder.

"All right, then. I must go. My wife and my coffee are probably both getting cold in the cafeteria."

He shuffled out the door, closing it behind him, and Delaney watched him with an affectionate smile. Then she turned around and sat back down, fingering the envelope. The man looked like he could barely spare coffee money. Maybe she could pretend to lose this envelope so that the money would never leave his account.

Gregory nodded toward the envelope, a small smile on his face. "You going to open that?"

"I don't know. I feel terrible. He's such a sweet old man."

"That he is." His smile grew. "Open the envelope, Delaney."

She slid her finger along the flap, opening the envelope and plucking the check out. With Gregory's eyes firmly on her, she unfolded it, then saw her fingers begin to shake before she even felt them. Her jaw dropped as she looked at Gregory, and she felt her eyes go wide.

"A million dollars?"

Gregory grinned, but didn't speak.

She flipped the check over, looking for an indication that it was a joke of some sort—like those fake lottery tickets you could buy. But no. It was just a normal, run-of-the-mill check from a personal bank account in Maine.

"You had no idea who you were talking to that night, did you?" Gregory got up and came around to lean against his desk.

"I *still* don't have any idea who I was talking to, apparently." She looked at the name on the check, for the first time seeing Oscar's last name. "Moriarty. Oscar Moriarty. This isn't—it couldn't be—no way."

"Yes. The same man the Moriarty Wing is named after. Oscar donated the money to build it ten years ago."

"Oh, my God. He never said anything—said he was here on vacation with his wife. He told me he gave her five dollars for the auction baskets, Gregory!"

He laughed. "He prefers to stay under the radar. Didn't want that wing named after him, but his wife insisted. He's given this hospital millions over the years."

"Why?" Delaney felt her forehead crease. "Why us?"

Gregory's face grew serious. "He is acquainted with your father. He knows about your brother." He sighed sadly. "And he had a little boy once . . . one who spent most of his very short life here at Mercy."

Josh sat at his computer later that morning, trying to teach himself how to use the damn online lab system to see his patients' results, all the while knowing he was definitely not in the right frame of mind to be attempting new technology right now.

Movement caught his eye, and he looked up to see a feminine arm holding a large cup of coffee.

"Very funny, Therese. I'll acknowledge my bad mood, but I still don't bite."

The arm lowered, but instead of Therese, a woman he didn't recognize stepped tentatively into his office. She had long blond braids and a skirt right out of the seventies, but somehow the look worked for her.

"I heard this was the way to your heart. Or at least your ears."

She set the coffee on his desk, then headed back out into the hallway while he watched, mystified. One moment later, she backed in, rolling a cart with four huge file boxes on top of it.

"What is this?" He cocked his head suspiciously. "Who are you?"

She ignored his second question. "This"—she gave a mighty yank to get the back wheels over the threshold, almost landing on her butt in the guest chair—"is something I bet you've never seen, but I decided you need to." She reached into the box closest to him and pulled out a folder, holding it out to him. "Exhibit A."

He took the folder, shaking his head.

"I don't want to sound rude here, but are you sure you're in the right place?"

She sat down in his guest chair, crossing her legs like she had all day. "I brought you coffee, didn't I? I figure that buys me fifteen minutes, whether you know me or not."

He shook his head again. "I'll give you five. Ten if you tell me who you are."

She shrugged. "Five should be enough, actually. I just started high on purpose."

"Okay, what am I looking at?" He opened the folder, which was full of neatly aligned papers. The first page was a typical grant summary page he'd seen a hundred times. This one was for the first child life specialist role they'd ever funded, back three years ago.

The woman didn't answer—just handed him another

folder. When he opened it, there was an identical first page, this one for a grant they'd used to purchase diabetes education software last year.

"Here's another one." She handed a third folder across his desk, but he already knew what it would contain. He didn't open it—just leveled a look her way.

"Why are you showing me grant paperwork?"

"Because I think there's something you don't know about most of the grants this floor has received over the past five years."

"And that is?"

"Check out the last page of each of those folders—where the original grant proposals are."

He narrowed his eyes, but dutifully opened the first folder again. On the last page was a neatly typed proposal, listing a collection of reasons Mercy Hospital was seeking funding for the child life position, as well as how the position would improve patient comfort and care. He'd done more than one of these during his tenure—he just didn't have time to do nearly enough of them. It was diligent, detail-drowning, backbreaking work.

"Flip it over," the woman said. "Check out the signature."

He sighed as he turned the page over, eyes freezing when they landed on the loopy signature of none other than Delaney Blair. He closed his eyes, suddenly knowing exactly who this woman must be.

He closed the folder, then opened the other two, already knowing what he'd find. Delaney's signature on those, too. He closed them and handed them back to her, then sat back in his chair, mind whirling.

"You must be Megan."

"I am."

"And—I'm assuming this entire cart of grant paperwork has Delaney's signature on the last page?"

Megan pointed at the cart. "Research and proposals. There's another cartful upstairs, but I was hoping one might be enough to make my point."

"Did she send you down here?"

Megan paused. "If you know her at all, you'd know the answer to that. She would kill me if she knew I was even here."

"Why *are* you here, then?" He pointed at the cart. "Why the dramatic demo?"

"Because." She stared at him for a long moment, looking like she was gathering her words. Then she shook her head and cringed. "Because it's obvious that the two of you fell hard and fast for each other, and you're being a pigheaded idiot not calling her back."

He felt his mouth fall open. *What*?

"I'm sorry to be crass, but I can't help it. Dr. Mackenzie, if you think for one second that Delaney would have, in any capacity, used you or your department like this, to somehow fortify her own career goals, then you don't know her at all." She pointed to the cart. "Her mission, since she arrived here at Mercy, has been to *find* you money, not take it away."

"Then why in the world did she deliver a proposal that sliced out programming she knows is vital? Why did she tell me she was going to recommend level funding this department, then go before the board and push for the opposite?"

"She *did* recommend level funding. She was shut down and asked to leave the meeting once Kevin started delivering what he called *his* proposal, which—by the way—he stole from my desk."

"Please." Josh rolled his eyes.

She raised her eyebrows. "Have you *met* Kevin Mc-Connell?"

Oh, yes. He sure had. "Yes."

"The one thing that man wants is Gregory's job. He's frighteningly unqualified, but the only thing bigger than his hair-gel collection is his ego. He has no qualms throwing somebody under the bus if it helps him pave that path to the corner office. He *had* no qualms doing it to Delaney."

She handed a folder to him. "*This* was her proposal. It looks *nothing* like what Kevin presented, or got voted through."

Josh took the folder, then sat back, blowing out a long breath. After he read through it, he squeezed his eyes shut. Was this really true? Or just another layer of deception?

Megan gathered the folders, placing them back in the file boxes. "If you're wondering, she has barely slept or eaten all week. I couldn't even get her to eat a donut this morning, and I have a feeling even you know how much she loves donuts."

He swallowed, remembering her laughing in the passenger seat of his truck, powdered sugar on her chin.

"I'm just saying. You've ruined donuts for her." Megan shrugged. "This is not a small thing."

She was silent for a long moment, then stood up to go. "She wasn't using you, Dr. Mackenzie. And she wasn't lying to you. That's what I thought you needed to know—what she's been trying to tell you, but you haven't let her."

Josh stood up and paced toward the wall, his head spinning. His eyes caught on a photo he'd added to his little gallery just days ago—one of Delaney and Charlotte grinning in matching goofy braids.

He thought back to the first day Delaney had arrived on the floor, looking more like a scared kitten than a hospital executive, and then he stared at the picture. He thought of the brave face she'd tried to put on after Ian's emergency, the terror Millie had reported had been in her eyes as she'd hung on to Ian's bed, the way she'd melted in his arms at the lake.

He swallowed, turning around. Megan stood quietly, looking at the floor, arms crossed. Then he cleared his throat. "Have I—been an idiot?"

"Yes." She smiled sadly.

"How is she—generally . . . with idiots?"

Megan's face sobered. "She has limited experience."

He ran a hand through his hair in frustration. "Is she here today?"

"No. She decided to take the rest of the day off—get some space."

"Any idea where she might be?"

"I'm not sure." Megan shrugged. "The lake is always a good guess."

"Megan, the lake is twenty miles around."

She raised her eyebrows in challenge. "Then I guess you'd better get going."

Josh glanced into the hallway, where normal chaos had resumed. The floor was crazy-busy. He couldn't just— leave. He had patients—a full floor of them. And yet, for the first time ever, he knew they weren't his first priority.

They couldn't be.

"I need to go find her."

Megan nodded. "Agreed."

Just then Millie poked her head in. "Hey. Dr. Hart's at the nurses' station. She says Therese called her in to cover for you, but Therese says she did no such thing. You know anything about this?"

Josh felt his eyebrows come together, and then he noticed Megan was looking suddenly very interested in her manicure.

He pointed to her. "Do *you* know anything about this?"

"Why would I know anything about this?" She smiled,

rolling her eyes, her impression of Therese's Boston accent dead-on.

Millie turned on her. "Did *you* call Dr. Hart? Why?" Then she seemed to notice the cart full of files. "What in the world is all this stuff?"

Josh sent a look Megan's way. "Paperwork I needed to see."

"Looks like a fire hazard waiting to happen."

"Maybe, but I need to look through it." He fingered the folders. "All of it. Millie, tell Dr. Hart we need her for the rest of the day. I need to—go."

Millie backed into the hallway, her eyebrows high. "Go?"

"Yeah. Go." He grabbed his keys, kissing her on the cheek as he sidled past her. "I don't want to be a lonely old man when I grow up."

Chapter 34

"Has anybody ever told you why they named this Kizilla Mountain?"

Joshua's voice came from behind Delaney, startling her so much that she almost fell off the giant boulder she was sitting on. She hadn't seen another human the entire time she'd hiked up the mountain. What in the world was he doing *here*?

Before she could answer—or even snap her jaw back to its normal position—he'd slid his backpack off and hefted himself up beside her. She eyed him warily while he pulled out his water bottle and took a long swallow as he looked out over the tops of the firs toward Echo Lake down below.

She closed her eyes, trying to tamp down a spark of possibility that had ignited at the sound of his voice. It was three o'clock on a Friday afternoon, he had a full floor of patients, and yet—he was here, on top of a mountain . . . with her.

She took a breath. "Why *do* they call it Kizilla Mountain?"

He smiled. "Comes from the Abenaki. It means *maybe*."

"Maybe Mountain?" She felt her eyebrows furrow. "I don't get it."

"Because it's not *really* big enough to be a mountain, but it's too big to call a hill. So?" He shrugged. "Maybe Mountain."

Delaney smiled. She'd been climbing Kizilla since she'd moved here, but had never known what it meant. Apparently the ancient Abenaki had a sense of humor.

"Nice day for a hike." Joshua nodded, looking her way. "Much better than being at work."

She eyed him suspiciously. "You're never—not at work."

"I know." He was silent for a long moment, and then he turned to her. "Maybe I've never had a good-enough reason not to be."

The spark sputtered into a teeny-tiny flame.

"I owe you an apology, Delaney." He shifted his body so he was looking straight at her, but he didn't move to touch her. "I hope that you'll hear me out, and I *really* hope you won't push me off this giant rock at least till after I have a chance to say what I need to."

She smiled feebly and rolled her eyes. "Pretty sure I have enough to think about without adding murder to the list."

"Thank you." He looked down. "I might have preferred to have this conversation at sea level, though. Just saying."

"How did you find me?"

"I had a little help. Megan pointed me to the lake."

Her eyebrows furrowed. "The lake is kind of big. How'd you find me *here*?"

"I remembered you pointing up here when we were canoeing. Took a chance." He smiled. "Lucked out when I saw your car."

"Does Millie know you're gone?"

"Yes." He took a deep breath. "Can I get to the apologizing part?"

"Carry on." She couldn't help letting a tiny smile erupt.

He looked so gorgeously forlorn sitting there that she was hard-pressed not to just put her arms around him and make her own apologies first.

"What is it you're sorry *for*, Joshua?"

He smiled ruefully. "The list is kind of long."

They sat in silence for a few moments, and Delaney could practically hear the words flying around inside his head, trying to organize themselves into some semblance of order. She had a feeling they resembled the chaos inside her own brain right now.

She'd hiked up the mountain faster than her best-ever time, and the entire way up, she'd known her speed was fueled by fury and disappointment, which had somehow replaced the abject sadness that had attacked her throughout the night.

Since then, she'd been sitting here in the sun, a mountain breeze playing with her hair, her thoughts warring with one another inside her head. She'd expected answers to be clearer up here where there were no distractions, but as hard as she tried, she still couldn't figure out what to do.

For most of her childhood, she'd watched her parents build walls in a vain attempt to protect their hearts from further destruction, and she'd internalized that technique, to an extreme degree. When med school had bombed, she'd been lost. She'd had plans, dammit. Her research was going to cure the kind of heart problem Parker had died from. Or her new surgical technique was going to have families crying in relief, rather than grief. Her mission had been to do something big enough to prevent *other* families from ripping apart at the seams.

And she'd failed.

But then she'd discovered finance, and had realized that it was a different way to effect change—a better way, maybe, at least for her. If she couldn't *do* the work, at least she could help figure out how to fund it.

Two years and a fresh MBA degree later, she'd headed into her first executive office, intent on changing the world. She'd dress in nice clothes, she'd decorate a nice office, and she'd make her difference on a daily basis, without ever touching the pain that went along with working directly with patients. It was perfect.

But now, here she was, after two weeks on a patient floor, wondering if she'd missed the boat this entire time. Here she was, after three weeks of knowing Joshua Mackenzie, wondering if she'd *ever* really known her own heart.

A breeze came up, sending her hair flying over her face, and he reached up to brush it gently back over her ear. She closed her eyes, fighting not to melt into his hand.

"I'm sorry I didn't call you back, Delaney. I'm sorry I didn't have the decency to hear you out. And I'm insanely sorry that I let somebody like Kevin McConnell fill my head with lies I knew couldn't possibly be true."

"I never lied to you, Joshua."

"I know. I knew. I just didn't . . . know . . . that I knew." He ran his fingers through his hair. "That doesn't make sense."

"It does." She took a deep breath. "I'm sorry I hurt you. The qualities I admire in you are the same ones I threw in your face. It was despicable."

"It was honest. You were just being dead honest." He shook his head, looking out over the trees. "And scared, I imagine."

She didn't answer.

"I never wanted you to be scared, Delaney."

"I know," she whispered. "It's not your fault."

"Do you think there's any chance we could rescind Tuesday's conversation and—I don't know—maybe find our footing again?"

She wanted to say yes—wanted it more than anything

in the world right now, but if she did, they'd be right back in the same place. She had no idea what her life might look like a year from now, but she knew that in order for her to make a go of whatever her next step was, she needed to do it for the right reasons . . . not because it worked for somebody else.

"I don't know, Joshua. Part of me—a big part—wants to just fall into your arms, kiss you, and drag you back to Millie's cabin for the weekend. But the smaller part of me says, 'Whoa. Hang on there, Nellie. Let's talk reality here.'" She sighed. "And for all the reasons I gave the other night, I just don't think in the end, we'd . . . work."

She sighed. "I keep trying to fall for a pharmacist, or a teacher—a hardware-store guy, even. I'm looking for the nine-to-five guy, not the five-to-nine one."

A smile played at his lips. "I'm pretty good with a hammer."

She laughed and pointed at his thumb, which was still purple from his ill-fated attempt to dismantle the tree fort.

"Evidence says otherwise, doc."

He raised his hand and slid it along her jaw, and she couldn't help but lean into it, closing her eyes. It just felt so . . . perfect.

"I'm maybe never going to be a nine-to-five guy, Delaney. But I could work toward eight to six, if you'd have me."

She smiled. "You say that—and I appreciate it—but it's not your reality. You're at the hospital at the crack of dawn, and you don't leave till dark, unless you're needed at Avery's House."

"Maybe I've never had a reason to stay in bed in the morning." He raised his eyebrows, and she felt heat travel downward. "Maybe I've never had a good reason to come home at night. Right now, I come home to a big, lonely house that's populated only by memories."

He shrugged slowly. "They're good ones, but they're just—memories. I once thought I could never picture someone sharing that space with me—this life with me. But I was wrong. Dead wrong. Did you know I haven't been able to sleep in my bed all week?"

"Why not?"

"Because it smells like you—your shampoo, your lotion, just . . . you." He caressed his thumb along her jaw. "And thinking I've lost you before I ever really had you is killing me."

"Well, I haven't had any problem sleeping at all," she lied.

"Bullshit." He touched her cheek gently. "Charlotte would take one look at you right now and call for a makeup crew to get rid of those purple circles."

"Oh, Joshua." She leaned into him. "What have we done?"

"Pretty sure I've heard of it before, but I'm not sure I knew what it felt like." He smiled, sliding his arm around her. "I don't know about you, but I've spent the last three nights lying awake, wishing you were with me, and that's something I've never had to deal with before."

"Me neither," she whispered, and the admission made her feel like she was opening a raw wound, hoping he wouldn't pour salt inside.

"I know it's way too soon to say I love you, because seriously? I didn't even know you a month ago. It's not supposed to be possible. It doesn't work like that. Plus, I'm dead afraid you *will* give me a push if I say something so insane."

He took a deep breath. "But I've analyzed it from every angle I can see, and I can't come up with any other explanation. I miss you. I can't *stand* not being with you. I have been wandering around in a daze for two days, trying to figure out what the hell happened to my head . . .

my heart. I feel like I want to change anything about me that doesn't work for you . . . because I am dying here, Delaney."

He took both of her hands in his, and she let him. "Sweetheart, you gave me a taste of heaven, and I never, ever want to settle for anything less. If this isn't love, then I can't imagine what is."

Delaney looked out at the lake, trying to slow her pulse, which could have taken on a jackrabbit . . . and won. "I was never *ever* going to fall in love with a doctor."

"Understandable. Sorry lot, we are." He brought her hand to his lips, kissing her fingers one by one. "Any chance I can convince you I'm different from the rest?"

She tipped her head, trying desperately hard to stay calm in the face of his sweet, gorgeous words. "I don't know."

"Can I at least try?"

She studied his eyes, then drew her hand back and looked out at the trees, making him tip his head in question.

"It's not that easy."

"I—I know. I'm not under any delusion that it is."

"Joshua, I grew up in a big house with a big pool and a big playroom and a ton of toys, but I would have given it all up for a dad who could be home for dinner and read me a story at bedtime." She looked at him. "I won't ever sign my own children up for that sort of life."

"I know that. And you never *should* have to settle for that. I can't stand here and tell you everything will change immediately, because it won't—and because you wouldn't believe me, anyway. But I can promise that you make me *want* to." He kissed her softly. "You make me *have* to, and it's the best feeling I've ever known."

He reached up to brush her hair back from her face,

holding her like a porcelain vase that was *this* close to breaking.

"Will you give me a chance, Delaney? *Can* you give me a chance to prove I can love you like you deserve to be loved?"

She looked at him for a long moment, and every fiber of her brain urged her to say no. Every fiber of her *heart* pushed her to wrap her arms around him and say yes.

"Kizilla," she finally said.

He nodded, a sad smile replacing his hopeful one. "Maybe."

Chapter 35

"What are you doing for dinner tonight?" Joshua popped his head into Delaney's office two days later, looking deliciously hot in a dark green shirt and tie.

For two days, she'd ignored his calls. For two days, she'd left his voice mails sitting in her in-box. For two days, she'd played an avoidance game that—to her delight *and* dismay—had told her exactly what she needed to know.

She was stupidly, accidentally, completely in love with the man.

She just hadn't figured out what to do about it yet.

"I'm working, unfortunately." She pointed at her computer screen, full of files she was using to compile an initial proposal for how pediatrics might be able to best use Oscar's generous bequest.

"Would the word *Bellinis* make you change your mind on that?"

"You play dirty, mister."

He smiled. "I know."

She looked at the clock. "What are you doing leaving already? It's only six o'clock."

"I am practicing my new, improved, priorities-in-the-right-place lifestyle."

She laughed. "I see."

"It's funny." He sat down in her guest chair. "When I said, 'I'm leaving,' no one actually—cared. Millie practically pushed me to the elevator."

"Maybe she's glad to see you try a normal schedule?"

He shrugged. "Or she's just sick of me. Either way, I'd love to take you out to dinner, if you'd let me."

"Is Mama B making chicken and mostaccioli tonight?"

"She will for you."

Four hours later, her stomach deliciously full of Italian yumminess, Delaney took Joshua's hand as he drove up the dirt road that led to the bluff over Echo Lake. It was dark, but this time, she found comfort in the privacy the woods offered as they parked in the clearing. He came around to her side of the truck and lifted her down, pausing to kiss her, then putting one hand over her eyes.

"Close your eyes. I have a surprise."

He pulled her a few steps, then let go. Then she heard a match, and when she opened her eyes, Joshua was fanning a small campfire in the middle of the clearing.

"Did you—come out here earlier?" In the growing firelight, now she could see a tent and cooler behind her. Her stomach took a leap. Was he hoping they'd stay the night out here by the lake?

She was almost surprised to realize she was completely okay with that.

"I did. But just because it's all set up to be the most romantic night ever out here, there's absolutely no pressure to stay."

She smiled at his sincere-yet-joking tone. "Noted."

"There are a couple of folding chairs in the tent if you want to grab them." He looked up from the fire. "And donuts in the cooler."

She laughed out loud. "You brought donuts?"

"Megan accused me of ruining donuts for you. It sounded serious. I know I have some work to do."

She laughed again as she ducked into the tent and pulled the two chairs out, setting them near the fire as he put on some more wood. As she sat down, looking past the gentle flames at the moonlit water below them, she felt a peace steal through her.

"I have some news," he said as he sat down beside her.

"I'm intrigued."

"I've decided to officially cut back my hours at Mercy."

"Really?" She turned, shocked.

"It's time." He poked at the fire. "I need a life."

Inside, Delaney felt a warm happiness glow through her chest. It was followed quickly by a sharp slice of guilt, however. Was he doing this because of her?

"You're not doing this for someone—else, are you? Because . . . if you're not doing it for you, you'll end up resenting the decision—and her."

He shook his head. "I'm doing it for me. It was high time I reexamined my life, and upon careful analysis, it appeared I was going to die a lonely old man."

"What?" She sputtered out a laugh.

"It's true." He shrugged. "I could work a hundred hours a week at that hospital, topped off by fifty at Avery's House, and in the end, I'd retire to a big, empty house . . . with nobody besides me in it. That's not what I want for my life."

"What *do* you want?" Her voice was quiet, hopeful.

"You," he said, his voice equally soft as he took her hand. "I know it's crazy. I've only known you for weeks, but it feels like a lifetime already."

Delaney blinked, tears threatening behind her eyes, but she didn't trust herself to speak.

He entwined his fingers with hers. "What I want is you,

Delaney. I want you in my life, I want you on the third floor doing the work your heart should be doing, and . . . I want you . . . in my bed."

He took a deep breath. "And while we're just putting everything out here, can I just say that although you are probably the best financial analyst Mercy has ever had, I can't stop thinking about you with the kids on my floor . . . and I can't stop wondering if maybe there's somewhere else in that hospital that you should be." He tossed a twig into the fire. "It's not where I'd put you if I were in charge of Mercy staffing, your MBA be damned."

"Where *would* you put me?"

"On pediatrics, because *I* think that's where you truly belong."

"Wow." Her voice was quiet.

"I know you're qualified to be the CFO someday, if that's what you want. But honestly?" He squeezed her hand. "Your heart is wasted up there on the sixth floor, Delaney."

She wrinkled her nose as she shook her head. "I don't know about that. My heart—might be safer up there."

"Maybe," he allowed. "Probably. But is it happy? Do you go home at night thinking about the Charlottes and the Kayas and the Ians of the world?"

"No."

That's why my heart is safer.

He sighed. "It hurts like hell some days. I'm not gonna lie to you. Letting yourself let those kids in? It's an act of courage, because sometimes—sometimes they break your heart." He looked at her steadily. "But they only break your heart because they've made it so much bigger in the meantime."

Delaney pulled in a ragged breath, squeezing her eyes shut. "I . . . have some news, too."

His eyes widened. "Oh?"

"At the risk of having to admit you're right, I decided to sign up for a couple of courses this fall. Nothing bold, no big decisions at this point, but I thought maybe it was time to see if maybe . . . maybe you're right. They're just basic ones, but they'd slot nicely into a child life specialist degree, if I decide at some point that maybe it's a job I might really want to do."

She watched a slow smile take over his face. "Really? *Really?*"

"Yeah. Really." She touched his cheek, letting her fingers rest on the five o'clock shadow she remembered doing delicious things to her body. "And I have you to thank for opening my eyes. I never knew."

He shook his head. "It was inside you all the time. But just so you know, I can't promise psychotic gunmen every day. Sometimes the world of pediatrics is downright dull. Can you handle that?"

She pushed herself out of her chair and slid onto his lap, leaning back on his shoulder as his arms came around to hold her tight.

"I'm pretty sure that life with you could never be dull, Dr. Mackenzie."

He buried his nose in her neck, kissing her softly. He nibbled her earlobe, then whispered, "Does this mean you might someday consider the possibility of life with me?"

"Well, it's still early days." She gasped as his hands moved upward. "But you make a compelling argument."

His lips and fingers moved in concert, heating her up in the light of the fire as he kissed her. Then he paused. "We'd make an excellent team, you know."

"I think we already do, Joshua." She smiled as she stood up and pulled him into the tent.

Chapter 36

Ten weeks later, Delaney found herself sitting in the Bellinis booth where she and Joshua had eaten their first dinner together, but this time, her hands weren't shaking, her hair was in a casual ponytail, and she still had on her scrubs from an afternoon of volunteering on the third floor, Mama B's no-scrubs rule be damned.

Joshua sat across from her, an amused expression on his face as he looked at her.

"What's so funny?" she asked.

"Nothing. I was just thinking how lucky I am."

"Mm hm. Sure."

He raised his eyebrows. "Fine. I was just wondering what you have on under those innocent-looking baby elephant scrubs."

"Well, it's going to be a while till you find out." She looked at her phone, smiling. "Ethan and Josie are late."

"How about a hint?"

"Hot pink lace. But not very much of it."

He groaned, letting his hand wander under the table and up her thigh. "If they're not here in five minutes, I say we take our order to go."

"It's a deal."

Just then, Molly appeared with two plates, setting them carefully on the table. "Josie and Ethan are stuck at the park—something went wonky on one of the rides. They said you should go ahead and eat without them."

"Thanks, Molly. It looks delicious, as always." Delaney unwrapped her silverware. "Do you have time to sit and eat with us?"

"Not tonight." Delaney thought she saw her toss a wink Joshua's way. "You'll have to entertain each other, I guess."

Joshua squeezed Delaney's knee. "We'll do our best."

Half an hour later, Molly came back to clear their plates. "Dessert tonight? Mama made tiramisu."

Delaney groaned. "I couldn't eat another bite."

"Tiramisu, Delaney." Molly raised her eyebrows.

"Okay." She smiled. "But only because I don't want to insult Mama B."

"Joshua?" Molly turned to him. "I'm assuming you want one, too?"

"Absolutely. Gotta keep up with my girl."

"Coffee?"

"Yes." He nodded, looking carefully at Delaney. "Three creamers, please."

"Excellent!" Molly grinned and headed back to the kitchen.

Delaney watched her go, feeling her own eyebrows pull together. "Why is she so happy about creamer?"

"I have absolutely no idea. Maybe she's just glad to get this table freed up for people who tip better."

"Wait a minute." Delaney's memory pinged. Another dinner, another creamer order, but she couldn't connect the dots.

Before she could figure it out, Molly was back at the table, two fresh tiramisu plates in hand. She set them down with uncharacteristic care, then paused before she did a little hop-turn and headed back to the kitchen.

"What is up with her tonight?" Delaney picked up her

fork. "She's bouncier than normal, and that's saying something."

"No idea. Maybe the Italian dating site finally worked out and she has a hot date later." He pointed to her dessert. "Go ahead. Taste it."

Delaney looked down at her tiramisu, which was decorated tonight with fancy chocolate shavings and swirls. In the dim light, the dessert positively sparkled.

Wait.

The dessert *was* sparkling.

She dropped her head to examine it, then felt her eyes go wide as she looked up at Joshua.

"Oh, my God. Joshua, she brought me the wrong dessert! There is an *engagement* ring in here!" She looked around wildly, trying to locate a nervous wannabe groom anxiously watching his girlfriend eat her tiramisu. "Signal Molly!"

Joshua didn't move—just smiled and shook his head slowly.

"Seriously, look!" She turned it around so he could see the ring, which—she had to admit—was dead gorgeous. If she was picking out a ring someday, this would totally be the kind she'd pick.

He reached for the ring, and she slapped his hand lightly. "Don't touch it! Look how carefully Mama B wound it into the chocolate swirls! We can't ruin it." She looked toward the bar, but Molly was nowhere in sight. "Oh, my God, Joshua. Some poor guy is sitting in this restaurant wondering where in the world his ring went. I have to bring this back to the kitchen."

"Delaney." He put a hand on her arm to stop her.

"What?" She looked at him, and suddenly, finally, the reality of the situation dawned on her.

She looked down at the ring, looked back up at him, looked down at the ring.

"No way." She shook her head. "This is not for me."

"Well, that's the part you get to decide. I think that's how these things are supposed to work."

"Joshua?" Delaney felt tears prick at her eyes. Could he really, possibly be proposing? After only three months together?

He took both of her hands, stroking his thumbs over her fingers as he looked into her eyes. "I know this is crazy. Totally nuts. Insane. In some ways, I feel like we barely know each other. In others, I feel like you've been part of me for my entire life. I know for absolutely certain that I am going to marry you someday, but I also know it might be a long time before *you're* that certain. So I'm asking, and you can give me whatever answer you need to."

"Oh, my God," Delaney whispered. His face was getting wavery as tears crowded into her eyes.

"Delaney Blair, now that I know what it feels like to have you in my life, I never, ever want to know what it would feel like to *not* have you with me. I want to live on Sugar Maple Drive with you, in a big old house we can fill with whatever you like. I want to have Sunday brunch in bed, want to cancel plans with friends because we just want to stay in, want to build a new tree fort . . . someday. I want to grow old with you, rock on that big old porch and have coffee and donuts every morning."

He paused, and she blinked rapidly, trying to clear the tears from her eyes before they ran down her cheeks. She was too late.

He ran his thumbs across her cheeks, catching the tears. "I want to marry you, Delaney. Someday, once you're sure I'm worthy, will you maybe marry me?" He smiled, and her throat was suddenly squeezed too tightly to talk.

He waited for a few seconds, then tipped his head. "An

answer of some sort would be pretty great right now. Just saying. You're kind of killing me here."

She took a shaky breath, pointing to the ring. "I really thought it was for someone else."

"I know." He let go of her hands and pulled the ring free, holding it toward her. "It's not. I picked it out myself, I promise."

She smiled. "I would love to marry you, Joshua. Tonight, if we could. But tomorrow's fine, too."

He laughed, that deep, rumbling, gorgeous laugh she loved, and he slid out from the table, pulling her into a huge bear hug, then sliding the ring onto her finger.

"Did she say yes?" Molly appeared in Delaney's peripheral vision as she wiped her eyes. "My God, you two were *killing* me back there!"

Delaney held out the ring, but Molly waved her off, pulling her into a huge hug. "I've seen it. Who do you think helped him pick it out?" Then she turned toward the kitchen. "Josie! Ethan! She said yes!"

All of a sudden, the entire restaurant erupted in cheers, and as she looked around, Delaney realized she recognized almost everyone there. Josie came running from the kitchen, throwing her arms around both Delaney and Joshua when she got to their table, and Ethan was only a step behind. He shook Joshua's hand, thumping him on the back.

He turned to Delaney, pulling her into a warm hug. "Welcome to the family, Delaney."

He turned back to Joshua, and all around her, Delaney felt a swell of happiness and love as what felt like the entire restaurant got up from their seats and came to congratulate them.

A few short months ago, she'd still felt like a stranger in this close-knit town. And now?

Now . . . she had a family.

* * *

An hour later, with one—and only one—glass of Papi's Poison on board, Delaney leaned back against Joshua as he put his arms around her and hugged her close.

"Are you happy?" he whispered in her ear.

She turned to him, taking his face in her hands. "I've never been happier."

"Did you really mean it when you said you'd marry me tomorrow?"

"I did."

"Because I know people." He winked. "It could be arranged."

She laughed. "My mother would have a fit. *And* she would assume I'm pregnant."

"Well"—he ran his fingers enticingly down her arms—"someday, I hope you will be."

"Me, too."

"But if you could just wait till I learn to actually use a hammer, that would be great. That tree fort is *not* safe for children, and we'd need rocking horses and swing sets and a new tire swing—"

Delaney put her finger over his lips to shush him. "It'll happen when it's supposed to, whether we're ready or not."

"Kind of like us?"

"Exactly like us, which—actually—should probably scare you." She slid her hands up to link them behind his neck, then kissed him softly. "But don't worry. I *do* know how to use a hammer."

Epilogue

"Whose idea was it to have a Valentine's Day wedding, anyway?" Delaney paced from window to window, watching the snow pile up on Sugar Maple Drive.

Megan smiled. "Yours."

"Are you sure?"

"Yup."

"Then whose idea was it to schedule a blizzard?"

"That one I can't attribute. Sorry." Megan pointed to Delaney's gown, hanging on the back of the bedroom door. "Are you ready to put on your dress?"

Delaney felt tears threaten as the snowflakes thickened. "No one's going to be able to come."

"Delaney, this is Vermont. Everybody who can possibly get here will do so."

"The roads aren't even plowed. They can't keep up. We're supposed to get thirty inches!"

Megan nodded calmly. "Which is a lot of snow. I'll give you that."

Delaney took a deep breath, then hugged Megan tightly. "I'm glad you stayed overnight, at least. I can't imagine having my wedding without you here."

"I would have skied here if that's what it took." Megan smiled. "And Ethan and Josie are downstairs with Joshua.

It'll just be a small, intimate wedding—perfect for the two of you."

A timid knock came from the hallway door, and Megan crossed the room to open it. Outside stood Delaney's mother, dressed in a pastel mother-of-the-bride dress that would have passed all social inspections, had any guests been able to actually make it to the wedding.

"You made it!" Delaney felt her eyes go wide as she motioned her into the room. "How?"

"Ethan and Josie came to get us, actually." Mom stood timidly, just inside the doorway, and Delaney braced herself as she saw tears crowd into her eyes. Oh, here it came. Another crying jag, another milestone Parker would never have.

Mom took a deep breath, squaring her shoulders and fighting back the tears. "You look beautiful, sweetheart."

Delaney froze at her use of the endearment. She looked sidelong at Megan, who shrugged carefully.

"Thank you."

"I—um—brought you a little something." Mom reached into her purse with shaky fingers, coming out with a tiny jewelry box. She took three tentative steps toward Delaney, holding it out to her.

"Mom?" Delaney's eyes widened. She'd seen this box before—had even had her hand soundly slapped one time when she'd dared open it after Parker died.

"It's your grandmother's ring."

"I know," she whispered as she opened the box. Nestled in the satin was a white-gold ring set with sapphires and diamonds. "But it was always supposed to go to Parker—for his bride someday."

"Well"—Mom took another deep breath and let it out slowly—"that's not going to happen. We think you should have it, Delaney. Your grandmother would be so proud of the woman you've become. She'd want you to have it."

"But, Dad?" It was his mother's ring, after all.

"Your father wanted to give it to you last night at the rehearsal dinner, but he was too afraid he'd blubber like a baby."

Delaney let out a surprised laugh at her words, then sobered as she looked at the ring. "You're sure?"

"We're sure." Mom took the ring out of the box and slid it onto Delaney's right hand. She held it up to the window light and smiled—a real smile, a genuine smile . . . the kind of smile Delaney hadn't seen on her face in forever.

"Now." She put down her pastel purse. "Have you got the whole something-borrowed, something-blue thing covered?"

Delaney nodded, her own tears threatening this time. She took Mom's hand and led her to the table under the window, where Megan had placed their bouquets. Beneath the spray of white roses and holly on the bridal bouquet, Delaney had wrapped the stems in a length of fabric she'd stolen long ago from a drawer in Parker's room.

Mom put her hand to her mouth when she saw it, then reached a tentative finger out to touch the dump-truck fabric as her tears did finally spill over. "It's perfect."

Delaney's throat felt tight as she spoke. "I know it's hard. I'm sorry he won't ever get to have his own wedding. I'm sorry he isn't here for mine."

Just then, Mom opened her arms and pulled Delaney into them, hugging her hard. "You're not the one who should be sorry, sweetheart. You did everything . . . right. And I—I am going to try very hard from now on to be . . . better. Today's a happy occasion, a new beginning for you . . . maybe for all of us. I'm so, so sorry for all the times I was there . . . but I wasn't."

Delaney pulled back, prepared to argue, but Mom put a

finger to her lips, shushing her. "I have managed to blubber through every special occasion you've ever had, and I'm determined not to do it today. This is *your* day. It's going to be beautiful and perfect, and Megan and I are going to make sure of it. Am I right, Megan?"

Megan smiled as she touched Delaney's shoulder. "Absolutely, Mrs. Blair."

Delaney hugged them both, but let go when she heard a strange buzzing sound from outside the window. "What is that?"

She and Megan pulled back the lacy curtains, and then Delaney's hand went to her mouth as she laughed out loud. Looking down Sugar Maple Drive, all she could see was a long stream of snowmobiles creeping upward, one after another. As they crested the hill, Delaney saw Ethan and Josie motioning them into the driveway and onto the lawn. Ten minutes later, the entire lawn was covered with snowmobiles, and Delaney could hear a swarm of people downstairs in the living room.

Megan hugged her around the shoulders. "Surprise!"

"You knew?"

"Did you really think anybody was going to miss this? Now come on. Let's get you into this gorgeous dress! We have a wedding to put on!"

Three hours later, Delaney pushed open the back door, pulling a long coat over her wedding gown. Joshua was out on the deck, which someone had shoveled less than an hour ago, but the snow was already three inches deep again.

He turned when he heard the door shut, and she smiled when she saw his eyes light up at the sight of her. He pulled her close to him, planting a kiss on her nose. "Hello, my sweet wife."

"What are you doing out here?" She looked out into

the yard, which right now resembled a moonscape—just mounds of snow covering any previously recognizable objects.

"Just taking a moment. Thinking about my parents. Wishing they were here, hoping they'd be . . . proud."

Delaney reached up to take his face in her hands. "They would be, Joshua. I'm sure they're up there somewhere, toasting with heavenly champagne, happy that *you're* happy."

"You think?" He smiled. "Mom did love a good snowstorm, you know. Maybe she had a hand in this."

Delaney laughed. "You never know." She turned her face up to the falling snow, letting it land softly on her cheeks. "I think your parents would be so, so happy to know that you've found happiness . . . found love . . . and that someday, this house they loved so much will be full of laughter and chaos and little running feet again."

"I can't wait." He kissed her slowly, longingly, making her wish for a moment that they could sneak upstairs, guests be damned.

She pulled away, just the tiniest bit. "Did you know that the hospital schedules more nurses on the maternity floor nine months after a blizzard like this?"

"Really?"

"Apparently people tend to . . . sleep more when there's a blizzard."

Joshua laughed softly, pulling her head to his chest. "And nine months later, little feet?"

"Exactly."

"So"—he tipped his head thoughtfully—"if they're going to be all staffed up anyway . . ."

She smiled. "It *is* officially a blizzard. The power could go out anytime. What's a newly married couple to do?"

He pulled back, searching her eyes. "Are you really saying what—you're saying?"

She nodded, more sure than she'd ever been of anything. "Really."

Then she pulled his hand to her heart, and the warmth of it radiated throughout her whole body. "I gave you my heart, Joshua. Because you taught me that giving away pieces of it . . . just makes it bigger. I know that if we're lucky enough to have children, their hearts will be a beautiful blend of yours and mine. What could be more magical than that?"

"Nothing." He pulled her close, kissing her as snowflakes fell all around them. "Nothing could possibly be more magical than that."

Coming soon . . .

Don't miss the next Echo Lake novel by *USA Today*
bestselling author

Maggie McGinnis

SHE'S GOT A WAY

Available in September 2016 from
St. Martin's Paperbacks